# THE FEAST OF
# PANTHERS

# THE FEAST OF PANTHERS

## SEAN EADS

## SEAN EADS

Queer Space

New Orleans

Published in the United States of America by

Queer Space

A Rebel Satori Imprint

www.rebelsatoripress.com

Fonts used: Section divider Bonnycastle™ and title text Geographica™
are copyright © Three Islands Press (www.3ip.com)

Paperback ISBN: 978-1-60864-224-3

Ebook ISBN: 978-1-60864-225-0

Library of Congress Control Number: 2022942232

For Josh Viola and Aaron Lovett, with love and friensdhip.

# CONTENTS

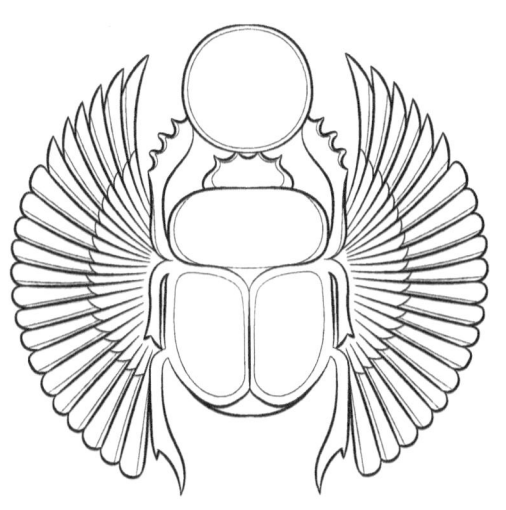

# PROLOGUE

*Wandsworth Prison, July 4, 1895.*

There's an infernal ringing in Oscar Wilde's ears. Hair shorn to the scalp, worked past exhaustion, he sits on the edge of a mattress as hard and vexing as wooden planks. Hunched forward, his large head droops above a space between his spread knees. A water droplet splashes the cold concrete. The delicate sound overmasters the ringing and stirs him. Sweat, he thinks. It must be sweat. Wilde touches his nose, his forehead. *Dry.* All the moisture's in his eyes now and he grits his teeth before making a promise to the gray wall ahead of him.

"I will *not* allow tears."

He obliterates the splotch with his toes before rising and limping to the cell's only window. Less broad than his shoulders, the portal reveals a world barren enough to tempt him with blindness. No roses grow in the prison courtyard, but Wilde's gaze finds cultivations of thorns everywhere.

A dark shape, crouched low, sleek and predatory moves across the grounds, provoking an involuntary cry as Wilde stumbles to the opposite end of the cell. His shoulder strikes the steel prison door and he stands there waiting, watching the window.

The door at his back has two openings, a vertical rectangle large enough to accommodate a man's face and a narrow horizontal slot for food trays. Wilde knows when the rectangle plate slides back it means someone wants to stare at him. Being leered at never offended his sensibilities until he came to prison.

He hears a shriek like a banshee screaming in the night. Other bestial throats join in, creating a hideous noise like a chorus being butchered in the courtyard. Wilde rushes to the bed, rips away the mattress and drags it over to the window intending a barricade. As he reaches it, however, a noise from behind paralyzes him. The larger window in the door rattles. Wilde drops the mattress and turns as the cover plate slides away.

The face in the opening is couched in darkness and unrecognizable. As they stare at each other, Wilde touches his left pinkie where the scarab ring used to be. How he wishes he still had the ring, though he knows the gemstone would be cold and inert, offering no protection.

"Are you friend or foe?"

The face pulls back and a hand juts through, dropping a folded slip of paper to the floor before withdrawing. Wilde waits until the plate closes before moving to retrieve it. The three words he finds there offer more thrill, more hope than he could think possible.

*Qui patitur vincit.*

"He conquers who endures," Wilde says, then looks toward the door in wonder. "*Constance.*"

He turns back to the window, all trace of his prior fatigue vanquished. He rearranges the mattress and sits down to nurse the most unexpected thing of all—renewed spirit.

# CHAPTER ONE

*London, March 24, 1894.*

In the back cranny of a tavern called The Red Tiger, the little barkeep named Chyron reveals the secret Wilde's been craving.

"I do believe fine literature is the door to many things, sir," he says, scanning a bookcase some seven feet tall and lined with volumes of Shakespeare, Ben Johnson and Marlow. "But you seem to have taken a more literal approach."

Chyron laughs. "Aye, a bookcase without books wouldn't be much of an illusion."

Wilde smiles, repeating the phrase. "You've chosen well, Chyron. One look at these titles and your average detective would turn away from quick boredom. But may I say the large reproduction of the King James Bible on the second shelf is suspicious company?"

"You've a keen eye. King Jimmy is the trick book. See here, Mr. Wilde."

Chyron, only a head taller than five feet, stands on his tiptoes and makes a pathetic, inadequate reach. Then he offers a meaningful smile to Wilde and steps aside.

"Of course, let me get that for you," Wilde says, pulling on the book. There's unexpected resistance, like a hidden force tugging back. The book slides out two inches and Wilde hears a delicate click.

The entire bookcase shifts.

"A secret latch," Wilde says, clapping. "*Very* agreeable."

"You'll find something even more agreeable on the other side," Chyron says, pushing the case. It swivels to reveal a dim passage. The air that rushes at Wilde's face has an appealing heat and carries many primal odors. He breathes deep through his nostrils, holds the breath, and shivers.

"You're sure about Stephen?"

"I let him in myself some time ago."

"How long?"

"Pleasure reckons time in its own way, Mr. Wilde. Especially when the breath of the Great Goddess gets involved."

"Breath? You mean opium, don't you?"

Chyron waves the question away. "I know you by reputation. You're not the kind who waits for someone to explain air before you breathe it."

"I still prefer not to partake."

"You may change your mind once you're on the other side. Best be going forward, don't you think?"

Wilde leans into the entrance and cranes his neck. He finds flashes of the bawdy and the profane. His knees weaken. He wants to fall forward but he finds just enough restraint to pull back.

"Describe what you saw, Mr. Wilde. Believe it or not, I've never gone in there. It's not my place."

"Arms and legs sprawling together in a tapestry of youthful flesh."

"Poetry," Chyron says, grinning. "Pure poetry. I take it then you mean to join the skein?"

"Perhaps you're a bit of a poet yourself."

"It's just that I'd hate to take so much money from you just to open the door. I'll almost feel like a robber if you don't see things through.

You came for Stephen. Well, he's right at hand. I hope I didn't take all your money, sir. I suspect you'll be needing some coin, though Stephen's not like anyone else you've met. What he'll want most is your heart."

"It's already beating for him."

Hand over his chest, Wilde steps into the secret room. The bookcase closes shut behind him. He takes two steps forward. On the third, the floor becomes strange and unstable.

He has trodden into a garden of pillows. Wilde bends to touch and test their silky softness. Lounging upon them can only enhance lust. He takes a moment to inspect the lamps on the walls, each covered with some exotic fabric that filters the lights into red and blue, green and yellow. He feels like he's in some submerged world, a sea kingdom with corals of velvet brocade. One would not need the inducement of opium to find the song of mermaids here.

But mermen are the order of the day.

The young men lay in the most enticing tangle of bare arms and legs. Wilde counts nine youths, not all undressed, but none *fully* clothed. They are all so lean and well-shaped. Which one is Stephen?

He will need to make a closer inspection.

Grinning, Wilde removes his frock coat and scarf, both still touched by the cold weather of a world far removed from this place. Tossing them into whatever corner lurks to his right, Wilde bends toward the nest of bodies just as a deep, authoritative voice calls out—

"Not yet."

Wilde turns in the direction of the voice but cannot find the speaker. A moment passes, and then he sees a little flare straight ahead, the burning end of a cigarette.

"Who are you?"

"I keep order," the man says, stepping a little more into the prismatic light. The cascade of colors strip all trace of age from his face, but Wilde guesses he must be at least fifty.

"Am I guilty of causing disorder?"

"Isn't that your hobby?" the man says, and his knowing chuckle makes Wilde flush. Is this a policeman? Has he been led into a trap? Well then, so be it, he thinks. There's an art to getting out of traps, and he's practiced it well the last few years.

"I'm unaware of any true impropriety."

"My friend," the man says, his tone warming, "in this room, the only *impropriety* is to join the lads without first inhaling the breath of the Great Goddess. Come. I will prepare it for you."

Wilde remains in place, gaze fixed on this man. "I came for other pleasures."

"Are you afraid?"

"What would I be afraid of?"

"Your own mind. Does its possibilities scare you?"

"Only when I consider what it might say when I sleep."

He comes closer, navigating the pillows. Now Wilde realizes the man has been standing behind a bar the entire time. The surface has several instruments that look like they belong in a chemist's lab.

"You're intrigued," the man says.

"Curiosity kills the cat."

"Do you have such a low opinion of cats?"

"Not at all. They are the most refined of creatures."

"Then we are in complete agreement," the man says, bending toward his equipment.

"How do you prepare the opium? Is it smoked like tobacco?"

"No, indeed. In fact, you'll find that opium doesn't burn at all."

He puts his hand around the base of a brass lamp with ornamental jewels surrounding the top and base. Or perhaps the jewels are also a trick of light. A hollow tube extends from the middle. Wilde watches the man uncap it.

"Should I expect a genie?"

"Eventually, sir. But first we must put one in."

Wilde's eyes widen and narrow by turns as he observes the process. The lamp is placed into a cradle stand with a bowl of burning coals at the base. The man pours water into the lamp. A few drops spill over the rim, racing down the length of the lamp only to sizzle into steam on the coals.

"Why the fire if the opium doesn't burn?"

"It vaporizes. A transformation I never tire of seeing. Here is the breath of the Great Goddess before flame and water bless it."

Wilde squints at a capsule displayed in the man's palm. Black and smaller than his thumbnail, the opium resembles a caper.

"There is a brazier in the middle of the lamp," the man says. "As the water steams, it swallows the opium into it and becomes a mist."

"Which travels up this pipe?"

"Yes. You will put your mouth on the end of it and suck. Perhaps you'll consider this a . . . foreshadowing."

The man grins, all Cheshire Cat in the shadow and smoke coming off the coals.

"That's quite bold."

"You'll forgive my impudence, sir."

"Forgive?" Wilde says. "I have only admiration for it. Proceed."

The opium is dropped into the lamp and the cap restored.

"Is it ready?"

"No need to be impatient. There are minutes to go yet."

Wilde nods. "It is nervousness rather than impatience. I do not wish to lose my wits. There is no point enjoying that company on the floor if my mind turns them into a nest of vipers."

"Oh, not vipers, sir. Never vipers. Besides, the breath of the Great Goddess only enhances the experience. What's real becomes more real, what's true becomes more true."

"Who is this Great Goddess? Does she have a name?"

The man looks Wilde dead in the eye. "Her name is spoken when she wishes it. But enough with questions. It is time. Ready your lungs, Mr. Wilde. Ready your *soul*."

# CHAPTER TWO

Among the pillows, warmed by the heat of virile bodies, Wilde's head lolls back and forth as his mind battles stupor and exhilaration. One moment he's making love to everyone at once; in the next, he's alone in a darkness that should terrify. But it doesn't. Whoever the Great Goddess may be, her breath gifts fascination rather than fear.

"*Stephen . . .*"

A sly touch along his inner thigh answers the whisper. Wilde smiles, writhes, try to see the lad's face. But when he looks, he finds no one. In the absence of a face, he sees many eyes, noses and mouths. His mind constructs an ideal Stephen based on the scant information he has. The youth is supposed to be nineteen years old and the friend of Wilde's favorite renter, Alfred Wood.

Wood's a dangerous creature, like all renters—eager to squeeze their customers through blackmail. In Wood's case, Wilde finds the potential danger only adds to his charm. He remembers a night two weeks ago when the two of them rested in a hotel bed after hours of passion. He caressed the young man's hair and proclaimed his superiority in words and kisses.

"You only say that because you've not met Stephen."

"And who is Stephen?"

Wood gave a playful squirm and said, "A new mate. There's none like him in all of London. In all the world."

He was damn evasive about other details, and after realizing he'd get no more information from Wood, Wilde has been on a personal quest to find this mysterious Hyacinthus. Most queries were met with blank stares, a few with scorn from men disinterested in anyone not making a direct proposition. But at last Wilde found one boy, too unattractive and dull for his trade, who told him about The Red Tiger.

"What does Stephen look like?"

"All I can remember are his eyes."

"What about them?"

"They make you feel naked before you've got your clothes off."

Wilde paid the lad a handsome price, far more than his physical services would have merited, and set out to follow the lead. After visiting the pub for just a few minutes, however, he began to think he either had the wrong place or was given bad information. Standing there amid so many old drunks slumped here and there, he was about to leave when the dwarfish Chyron rounded the bar and stopped him.

"You're after something besides ale, I think."

Wilde studied the man as he pondered how truthful to be. "I seek—someone with extraordinary eyes."

How long ago did that exchange and the coy negotiations that followed happen? Minutes? Hours? Days? The breath of the Great Goddess has Wilde swimming in vast seas of time, where any concept of *the present* remains an island out of reach. But who cares when the waters are as hot as naked flesh pressing together? All that matters is taking another lungful of breath and diving, diving.

But at some point, the currents and waves do wash him onto shore.

The opium leaves his throat parched and his voice little more than a murmur. He sits up, still surrounded by young men, all beautiful, their eyes closed. Wilde touches the nearest lad and risks thumbing back his eyelids. What he finds makes him gasp and yank back his hand.

He goes quiet, trying to gain control of his senses and shake off what must be a lingering hallucination. What else would explain the boy's slit pupils?

To prove he has a new toehold on sanity, he decides to examine another lad's eyes. As he reaches, however, the youth seizes his wrist and offers a purring, seductive laugh.

"Stephen?"

The man writhes, stretching his body in luxurious ecstasy. The flex of his muscles draws Wilde's gaze down his torso, and he finds his captured hand placed against a flat, hard stomach. Wilde can't imagine ever forgetting the heat and tautness of that flesh.

The opium begins to reassert itself, a heaviness beckoning his head back to the cushions. He slumps back among the bodies even as the sense of his own physicality dissipates. Wilde makes one futile effort to reclaim his mind. He sees a face hovering over him, male, with eyes like he's never seen before, not blue or brown or green, but yellow, glittering like blonde tresses. It reminds him of his lover's hair, the hair of Lord Alfred Douglas, his precious Bosie. The eyes, somehow, give off their own light.

"Stephen? Have I found you at last?"

"I was always with you, as the Goddess is with us."

In that moment, Stephen's assertion seems so real Wilde lifts his arm to embrace its promise. Stephen climbs atop him, a force pressing against his chest yet, somehow, a buoying weightlessness lifting Wilde off the ground.

But where are they drifting? The opium den recedes, one of many shorelines in the greater ocean of the mind. He and Stephen drift on a small boat, its single sail billowing. "The breath of the Great Goddess carries us forward," Stephen says, his back to Wilde. Then he looks over his shoulder to show Wilde those sunlit eyes. But what cold sunlight! Of course, Wilde thinks. Stephen is a renter, not a lover. This is all a game to him, just as it a game to Alfred Wood and all his ilk, and I am the eager mouse bandied back and forth between their opportunistic claws.

Yes, a cat. And these are cat's eyes observing him; the pupils identical to those of the boy whose lids he drew back.

Wilde sits up gasping for air like a man whose lungs burn after a long submersion. Everyone is standing now, stretching and contorting, strange noises pulsating from deep inside their throats. One man tips his head back and unleashes an inhuman yowl. Wilde claws and kicks himself away, scrambling for the closest corner. There he huddles, hands clasped tight to his chest as he stares.

The young men continue their strange pantomime. They sniff, kiss and lick each other. These intimate gestures carry all the eroticism of a handshake. There's something too communal about them, reminding Wilde of the thousands of times he's seen household cats groom each other. Are they in the grip of some shared hallucination? What else explains such behavior?

One man lifts his arms over his head and the bones of his fingers break through the skin at the fingertips and peels down the length of both arms. He claws the skin further back past the elbows like someone rolling up his shirtsleeves. A hairless shape emerges, ashen and dry as chalk. Wilde has no breath to scream as he watches the other men follow suit. Some drop to all fours and adopt postures impossible for human spines, arching high with sharp twists at the shoulders as they shrug off their skins.

"Fancy any of them now, Mr. Wilde?"

He looks to his right and finds the barman there, cleaning his brass lamp as he offers a casual smile and nod.

"Am I . . . seeing what I'm seeing?"

"I don't know. *Are* you?"

Wilde shakes his head, clinging to the notion this vision is just the lingering madness of opium. But reality strikes him with the sharpness of a whip crack. His senses don't *feel* blunted or fringed. Awareness radiates from him like a lighthouse, alerting him to so much jeopardy. The creatures now move in a circle, all of them recognizable as great black cats. The low lighting makes for a handsome sheen on their sleek fur, and the collective purring of their throats provoke a rumble in the floorboards. After a minute more, they break their circle and pad past him, their quiet made even more striking for the sheer power inherent in every step. Wilde stands motionless as they pass, all ignoring him but the last. This one stops to regard him, and its yellow, baleful eyes anticipate a night of much preying.

Then this cat also slinks away.

Wilde waits a hundred more heartbeats—not long, considering the state of his pulse—before breathing again.

"Where did they go?"

"Who knows," the barman says. "No one would begrudge the lads a bit of sport. They've been under wraps a long time, after all."

Wilde stares at him in expectation of more information.

The man leans forward, allowing the light to reveal his eyes. Golden. Bright.

Irresistible.

"You," Wilde says, touching the base of his throat. "*You're* the man I was seeking the entire time. *You're* Stephen."

"And you, Mr. Wilde," the barman says, "are *dreaming*."

# CHAPTER THREE

Wilde wakes, clothed, in a room more familiar to him on every breath. At the window, heavy red velvet drapes rayed with gold trim and tassels deny even the strongest sunlight. The wallpaper has swirling blue crests that always make him think of mating seahorses. He swings his legs out of bed and places his feet on a wooden plank that always creaks and complains about his weight. It does so now.

Somehow, he is at his home on Tite Street.

Remembering Samuel Johnson's test of reality, but having no stone to kick, Wilde touches the mattress and then a bedpost, squeezing both. He prods his body, which has considerable more give. Muscles and joints ache. Good, he thinks. It proves his adventure to The Red Tiger was no hallucination.

He opens the door, leans into the hallway and says, "Constance?"

The silence reaffirms he is in his own home. His wife has gone to the seaside resort at Worthing even though it will be weeks before the weather warms enough to make the excursion pleasant. She took their two young sons with her. That was a week ago. Wilde hopes they are happy. If not happy, then at least content.

Contentment seldom dwells under this roof.

Footsteps on the stairs draw his attention to the end of the hall. Arthur Fenn, a red-haired man in his early twenties, appears and makes tentative eye contact.

"Mr. Wilde, sir? Is there anything I can do for you?"

"Yes, Arthur. You can tell me the time."

"It's ten in the morning, sir."

"So early? I thought I'd overslept."

The young butler has little skill at suppressing emotional responses, especially smiles. Wilde likes that best about him, though his lips are too thin and always look chapped. Yawning, Wilde steps into the hallway and puts his hands into his pockets. "Tell me something. Were you here when I got home?"

"Yes."

"And when was that?"

Arthur's eyebrows knit. "Right around daybreak, I should think."

"Was I alone? I mean, did it seem like someone helped me home? Did you see anyone with me?"

The butler's freckled face hints at nothing embarrassing or suspicious about Wilde's return. His pale blue eyes radiate innocence.

"Is something the matter, Mr. Wilde?"

"No, I suppose not. Except I'm famished."

"I can have breakfast started for you right away."

Wilde smiles. "Good man."

They descend the stairs together but go separate ways on the landing, Arthur heading left toward the kitchen. Wilde turns right and opens the door to his study.

A pile of letters on the table attracts his notice. His mail these days consists of a dreary occurrence of unpaid bills and the occasional unsettling note composed in coded words. Blackmail notices—*unpaid bills* of a more sinister nature. Renters, for all their pretense of rough, unschooled backgrounds, have remarkable handwriting. It makes Wilde wonder if they all employ some underground secretarial service.

He shuffles through several envelopes before encountering an ornate card, sealed with wax. "Here's a pretty invitation," he says, taking it to his armchair before reading the sender's name.

*Edward Maunde Thompson.*

He says the name aloud as Arthur enters with tea and biscuits. Wilde waves the note at him.

"When did this arrive? I don't recall seeing it before."

"You wouldn't, sir. It was delivered yesterday morning."

"But I was here most of the day."

The first trace of uneasiness shows in Arthur's reddening face.

"Begging your pardon, Mr. Wilde, but you weren't."

"What are you saying, Arthur? I left here yesterday around three in the afternoon."

"You did leave at three, sir, but it wasn't yesterday."

Wilde shakes his head. "Then when was it?"

"Two days ago."

Wilde taps the card against the right armrest. "Please tell me what day it is, Arthur."

"It's Monday, sir. And you left here on—"

"Saturday." Wilde settles back, rubbing his chin, gaze fixed on the steam rising from the teacup. For a moment it seems like smoke.

*Breath of the Great Goddess.*

"Are you well, Mr. Wilde? Should I fetch a doctor?"

"No. But take the tea away, Arthur. The biscuits alone will do. It's a funny thing to lose track of time. Perhaps the surest way to live forever is to forget there's a day you must die."

Arthur hurries to remove the tea. A little of it splashes over the side and onto the rug, but Wilde makes no comment. He sinks deeper into his chair and ruminates.

What have I been doing? Where have I been? I cannot believe I spent so much time at The Red Tiger. Hours, I will grant, but not *hours.*

"Stephen," he whispers.

Horrific images enter his mind with the suddenness of a blindfold ripped away. Men stepping out of their skin, men changing into enormous cats. Wilde damages the card as he clutches the armrests.

The fit passes after a moment, leaving his stomach feeling empty to the point of nausea. He eats two of the biscuits. Then he breaks the card's seal.

*Dear Mr. Wilde—*

*Have just had the pleasure of reading your 'Sphynx.' If you'll excuse this informality, I wish to invite you to the Museum for luncheon with me, at my expense, as soon as an agreeable date can be reached. I have much to show you, fascinations and wonders if you'd enjoy a private tour.*

*Yours—*

*EM Thompson*

Arthur returns with bacon, toast and a hard-boiled egg. He places silverware on the table as Wilde mulls the message.

"Who brought this to the house, Arthur? Was it a boy?"

"No, sir. As I recall, the messenger was an older man. Perhaps forty."

"Careful. I will be forty in a few months."

Arthur goes rigid. "I meant not offense, Mr. Wilde."

"No, of course not. Was the messenger well dressed?"

"I should say."

"What did he say?"

"He only inquired if you were at home. He did seem eager to hand the card straight to you. Perhaps he had something else to say. It seemed like he did, if you understand my meaning."

Wilde leans forward to take a slice of bacon. "I'm not sure I do,

Arthur. Please continue."

"I just mean sometimes people come to our door with notes addressed to you, but other things to express that they don't care to put in writing. But it's not my place to—"

"It's your place to do your job, Arthur. No one could execute his duties better."

"I just hate it when people come to our door and act like they're embarrassed to be here."

"Is that how the man seemed? Tense? Nervous, perhaps?"

"Yes, Mr. Wilde." These words come out with the air of a devastating admission. "Begging your pardon, but is it some trouble, sir?"

Wilde smiles. "Just a mundane request for a social call. So yes—a terrible amount of trouble. The man who delivered this card no doubt thought the task beneath him. No doubt he was some underling of the man who extended the invitation."

"Who is that, Mr. Wilde?"

"Edward Thompson."

Arthur makes a show of searching his memory, as if the man's name might be familiar. "A stage manager, Mr. Wilde?"

"A stage manager for the theater of *time*, Arthur. Edward Thompson is the Director of the British Museum. An exceptional scholar by all accounts, even rumored to be on the cusp of knighthood. If he also wrote plays, I should be a jealous man."

"The Director of the British Museum came asking for you?"

Awe saturates Arthur's voice, and he beams at his employer. Smiling like this, with such obvious pride, he looks less like a butler and more like an eager son hoping to see his wayward father find true respectability at long last. Wilde knows others would scorn this level of familiarity, but he finds something endearing about domestic servants being earnest, even if they're being earnest above their station.

When Arthur continues to stand there grinning, Wilde says, "Do I have your permission to see him?"

"Why, you don't need anyone like me telling you what to do, sir! I just think it'd be good having a man like that to take your side if things ever get rough?"

"But Arthur," Wilde said, bringing toast to his mouth, already anticipating the mix of soft butter and hard crunch. "If any man takes my side, I'll have nothing left to call my own."

# CHAPTER FOUR

Approaching the vast exterior of the British Museum, Wilde feels like an emigrant to ancient Athens. Towering Ionic columns frame this extended temple to *What Was*, giving his thoughts a grateful turn from the recent past to things long vanished. How many civilizations have perished from the Earth, their painters and playwrights and sculptors forgotten, their masterpieces made rubble? As an adolescent at Portora Royal School, laboring over the Greek and Latin writers whose work survived any number of collapses and Dark Ages, Wilde often entertained the depressing notion that God or Fate only allowed the poorest of artists to transcend; that these so-called Masters like Aeschylus and Horace were in fact the Dickens' of their day, while the true craftsmen never found an audience popular enough to carry their work through the ashes.

Wasn't there something glorious, something beautiful about being lost to history? To labor in shadow, to be pure and unknown, plying one's art in unvanquished obscurity—the essential tragedy that is work for work's sake?

Wilde stops in amusement at this train of thought, knowing he will have none of it. Let his writing be deemed trash if it means his words will be heard a thousand years later, translated into languages not yet in existence. Let those future youths bend and sweat over his obscure plays while their schoolmasters proclaim the name Oscar Wilde in the same breath as Shakespeare.

Laughing, he passes into the museum's Entrance Hall, where he encounters marble statues of Anne Damer, Joseph Banks, and Shakespeare himself. Speak of the devil, Wilde thinks, stepping up to the bard and placing a hand on the statue's left ear. "Dear William. Still covering my tracks in scandalous adventures, I trust?" He pirouettes and begins an aimless pilgrimage, heading west into the first of several galleries of antiquities. The first should belong to Rome, but he's surprised to find himself standing in Egypt.

He cranes his neck up at massive busts of pharaohs and steles covered in exquisite engravings. Pausing to stare at the hieroglyphics, he notices the image of a woman with a cat's head. She's seated, holding some sort of staff. Is she a queen? A goddess? A male figure approaches her with a platter. How pleasant hieroglyphics are when one has no idea how to interpret them, he thinks. This one, for example, could be profound or it might be nothing more than some tavern advertisement.

Moving on, beginning to forget what brought him here, Wilde notices a collection of small mummies. He steps over to inspect them. There are no explanatory note cards, but these wrapped corpses appear to be cats. He bends nearer and says, "I believe I've had my fill of your kind of late. Let me see if I can find a mummified dog instead."

"Do you need assistance, sir?"

Wilde turns and finds a bespectacled man in a gray suit. Gray everywhere, in fact: hair, bristly moustache, eyes and complexion. He seems powdered with the dust of chalkboards and the charcoal of old tombstone etchings.

"I'm here to see Mr. Thompson."

"The *Director?* I'm afraid that's most impossible. He's a busy man."

Wilde produces the card. "Busy enough to extend me this personal invitation."

The employee takes it with obvious skepticism. Wilde delights in men such as this. Petty people make for pretty victories when they're humbled.

"Mr. Wilde," he says, becoming almost Prussian in his sudden formality. "Forgive me, I didn't know it was you."

"It's often said of London recognizes me on sight, but I must seem quite plain compared to the works of genius you immerse yourself in each day."

"I'll take you to the Director at once. Please follow me."

He leaves on short, officious strides. Wilde strolls after him.

"Have you been with the museum very long?"

"Long enough," the man says, and Wilde believes him. His grayness suggests he might have seen the first Greek column go up. "I am one of the curators of our Assyrian collection, with a specialty in the reign of Shalmaneser III."

"No doubt a fascinating niche. What is your name?"

"Loftus, Mr. Wilde."

They pass through gallery after gallery, all with brass nameplates indicating their theme. *Lyonian Gallery. Elgin Saloons.* Strange, Wilde thinks as they enter the Hellenic Room. His gaze finds no trace of Hellenism anywhere.

They come to a room called *Assyrian Galleries* and the first thing he sees is a broken Egyptian obelisk. Wilde calls for his guide's attention.

"Is the museum under some sort of renovation, Mr. Loftus?"

"What makes you ask?"

"It's impossible for me not to notice the contents of the galleries don't match their themes. We appear to be moving from one Egyptian display to another."

Mr. Loftus nods. "We've had a rather large influx of artifacts from Egypt of late. More, perhaps, than we know what to do with. But each new treasure is so exceptional that we can't refuse them, even if it means positioning some objects where they don't belong. A temporary disarray for a very worthwhile reason, I assure you."

They descend a flight of stairs, reaching the basement where even more galleries and sub-galleries abound in every direction. One room, easily a few thousand square feet in space, is stuffed full of mummies.

"The dead outnumber the living here, Mr. Loftus."

"They do everywhere, Mr. Wilde."

Mr. Loftus turns right down a hallway and opens a door that leads to a much narrower room with three more doors off to the side. Wilde recognizes a business office when he sees one. Theaters are much the same way. Gilt and splendors for the patrons; guilt and ledgers for the clerks.

Mr. Loftus knocks on the center door, which opens a moment later. A tall, bearded man in his fifties appears in the doorway.

"Sir, I have the honor to present—"

"Mr. Wilde!" Edward Thompson says, brushing past the shorter Loftus, right hand extended. "Then you got my invitation?"

"I did," Wilde says, showing the card again. "I thought I'd come at once. I hope it's no inconvenience."

"No inconvenience—only pleasure! Do come into my office. Thank you for showing our guest down, Mr. Loftus."

Before the gray ghost departs, Wilde thanks him and adds, "I do hope there's something left of Assyria after this recent invasion by Egypt."

# CHAPTER FIVE

A sturdy roll-top desks dominates the west end of Edward Thompson's office, leaving scarce room for two leather armchairs and a bookcase with two shelves that only reaches Wilde's hip. If ever there were a hidden door appropriate for Chyron, this would be it, he thinks as he bends to examine the titles. Behind him, Mr. Thompson dictates their lunch requirements to an aide.

Wilde moves his fingers along faded spines of blue, green and brown, humming to himself as the aide leaves.

"I hope you're not too hungry, Mr. Wilde. It will take at least half an hour to bring the food."

"I shall be happy to wait."

He hears a comfortable creak and guesses Mr. Thompson must have settled into one of the chairs.

"Searching for your own works, Mr. Wilde?"

"I am searching," Wilde says, "for a copy of the King James Bible."

"Oh? I admit my limited impression of you did not convey the sense of someone so . . . *devout*."

"Of late I've come to realize bibles can open doors."

Mr. Thompson's grunt proves satisfying. Wilde pivots and sits in the accompanying chair.

"If you wish, Mr. Wilde, I can show you tablets from Babylon that must have inspired the Old Testament writers. I use inspired under the assumption you'll find the word *plagiarized* offensive."

"Plagiarism is never offensive. It simplifies creativity immensely."

"Am I to believe that *you've* plagiarized?"

Wilde smiles. "I fear my Muses are highwaymen. When they offer me a beautiful phrase that feels somewhat familiar, I find it best not to ask questions."

Mr. Thompson laughs, and Wilde finds he likes this gentleman. He reminds Wilde of some schoolmaster who has some adorable trait like forgetfulness. His beard, only just touched with grey, is thickest around his chin and mouth. His hair, pomaded back, curls a little about the ears. No one would doubt the intelligence showing in his bright blue eyes. He pulls a book from the inner pocket of his jacket, and the way he holds it suggests he can rip its knowledge right from the page just as flowers are plucked from a garden.

"Mr. Thompson, either you have very large hands, or that is a very slight book."

"Not slight at all," he says, grinning and holding up the spine.

"My 'Sphinx!'"

Mr. Thompson opens the slim volume of poetry and inclines his gaze to the words—

"*Dawn follows Dawn and Nights grow old and all the while this curious cat*

*Lies crouching on the Chinese mat with eyes of satin rimmed with gold.*"

"My poor verse has never sounded better, sir."

"Few would call it poor, Mr. Wilde. I feel your beguiling words have captured the riddle of the Sphinx itself."

"Which is?"

The director's eyes almost glitter in their excitement, a trait that might enliven Wilde under most circumstances. But other memories of glowing eyes blight his enthusiasm.

"Nothing less than the mystery of existence."

"You'll forgive my frankness, Mr. Thompson, but that answer feels like a cheat. Existence is no mystery to an artist. Like God, we exist to create. To sculpt, to paint, to write—to sing. To bring beauty into the world. The Sphinx is a testament to all art. Intriguing, certainly. But mysterious? It is because it is, just as *I am that I am*. That is answer enough."

Mr. Thompson puts his fingertips together in a steeple, head tipped back in consideration, and Wilde laughs.

"Please don't think too deeply on my creed, Mr. Thompson," he says. "Scrutiny is the devil of every philosopher."

"Regardless, I feel your poem reveals you to have a true affinity for that fabulous land. Perhaps more than an affinity. I've just noticed your remarkable ring, for instance."

Wilde raises his left hand at Mr. Thompson's beckoning. A scarab ring, a green stone in the shape of a beetle, has been on his pinkie finger almost since childhood.

"This was a gift from my mother."

"Very peculiar."

"Well, the Wildes are a peculiar family. My father was a doctor, of course, but passionate about Egyptology."

"Yes, I know."

"He liked telling me of his adventures in Egypt. He once went into a tomb and found the remains of a mummified dwarf. He took its torso back to Ireland with him. I remember how he kept it in his study, the shriveled skin with a luster like pearl shining through frayed, stained strips of linen."

"I take it your mother shared the interest?"

28

"In Egyptian artifacts most certainly. She always claimed this ring was authentic."

"If so, it is quite ancient."

"No doubt the street urchin who sold it to her swore it'd been cut off the finger of Ramses himself."

"What do you believe?"

"I believe the one Egyptian thing that truly interests me at the moment are its cigarettes."

"Oh, be serious, Mr. Wilde!"

Wilde gazes at the ring with the same open admiration he showed when it was first given to him. "I think it is beautiful because it is beautiful. Its age neither adds nor detracts from that fact. Why should it matter if its maker is a retired Dublin jeweler or a craftsman whose bones turned to dust three thousand years ago?"

"Might I get a closer look?"

It takes some twisting to work the ring free, but Wilde surrenders it into Thompson's palm. The director makes his inspection with squinted eyes.

"Well?" Wilde says.

"Authentic, I believe. But my true expertise is in handwriting and ancient manuscripts."

"What might I get for it?"

Wilde delights in seeing Mr. Thompson's eyebrows arch so high, and when he speaks, he sounds like he's fighting off a cough. "You mean you'd consider selling after telling me it was a gift from your mother?"

"Money is also art."

"Mr. Wilde, how can you even think—"

"Be at ease," he says, taking the ring back and slipping it—*working it*—back into place. "I only jest. Considering the abundance of Egyptian relics you've acquired of late, I doubt my ring would even fetch a pound."

"An artifact of that ring's caliber will always be valuable."

"Thank you for the peace of mind, Mr. Thompson."

But his host looks tense, his posture rigid in the chair. Perhaps my flippancy has insulted him, Wilde tells himself. He readies an apology but the director speaks first, each word a little too measured, as if he's forcing politeness.

"It is a bit of a problem, as you've guessed. This sudden deluge of riches. We have a new patron, quite wealthy and generous, and rather insistent. The port of Liverpool is almost overwhelmed with daily shipments from Cairo. Only last week, several thousand mummified cats were unloaded. Can you imagine?"

"Is that what I spotted on my way down the hall?"

"Oh, no. Those are something else. The cats were sold for fertilizer, I'm sorry to say. Of course, we mustn't tell her that."

"*Her?*"

"Lady Gwendoline."

"I don't know the name."

"She prefers discretion and is quite shy, a factor of her youth and gender. I'm pleased to say she'll be present at a very private gala party the museum is hosting."

"When is it?"

"The details aren't complete."

"All parties are surprise parties while still in the planning stage."

"I hope you'll be able to come when the date and time are set. A room full of British lords and politicians won't dispel the notion that academics throw rather drab parties."

"You wish me to be the seasoning in your porridge, is that it?"

"Lady Gwendoline has also read your 'Sphinx' and expressed immense pleasure in it. I think you might enjoy hearing her thoughts on it."

"I should be delighted. But how does she come by so many artifacts as to deluge Liverpool and bring the National Museum to its knees from her generosity?"

"She must be funding at least a hundred archaeological expeditions on our behalf. But it's much more than money, Mr. Wilde. Lady Gwendoline has been on-hand for several imminent discoveries, even directing a digging crew on at least one occasion."

"An adventurer," Wilde says as the door opens and three men step in carrying trays of food.

"Believe me, Mr. Wilde," the director says, rising. "We are exceptionally lucky to have her on our side."

# CHAPTER SIX

The Red Tiger isn't on his way back from the museum, nevertheless Wilde finds himself standing outside it less than an hour after concluding his luncheon with Edward Thompson.

He tries the door and finds it locked. Odd for a tavern to be closed in the early afternoon. Perhaps taverns fronting for opium dens have different hours of operation.

Wilde steps up to one window and swipes at the dust and grime. Darkness within. No sounds. He steps back and moves toward the alleyway between the tavern and the adjacent building, where he discovers the sprawled body of a semi-conscious man. Wilde bends down for a closer inspection. There's no odor of alcohol coming off the man. In fact, he gives off no scent at all despite his shabby, rough appearance. He's not a drunk, then, nor homeless.

"May the breath of the Great Goddess propel your boat to a safe harbor, friend," Wilde says. The man mutters something indistinct as Wilde steps over him and moves down the alleyway, scrutinizing the exterior wall along the way.

It's not long enough.

Wilde touches the brick. His memory works to reconstruct the tavern's layout. Could he be misremembering? The bookcase would be right where the wall ends. There's just no space left to contain a hidden chamber.

It was very dim, he tells himself. And the different convergent lights might have deceived my senses about the size of the space. But the bookcase *has* to be right here!

He darts back to the start of the alleyway, not quite to the drugged man, and begins a more methodical examination. His imagination helps him stare through the wall. That's the entrance, and here, ten strides from the door, is the bar with Chyron behind it. It took two strides to get behind the bar, where I saw the series of crates Chyron walked back and forth along to exaggerate his height.

Wilde stops to tap the brick.

And here is the doorway behind the bar that leads to the hallway that ends in the bookshelf—not more than six strides.

He takes them now and finds himself at the end of the building again.

Wilde leaves before he reaches the end of his sanity as well.

# CHAPTER SEVEN

When Wilde returns to Tite Street, he finds all his household staff absent. Calling their names, moving from room to room, he pauses at the sound of familiar laughter from upstairs.

From his bedroom.

He stands at the landing as the laughter fades, replaced by the soft thud of approaching footsteps. They're too light to involve shoes, and in the brief space of time before Bosie appears, leaning over the banister to smile down at him, Wilde imagines his young lover walking barefoot through the house. How can such a simple thing imply so many inconceivable freedoms? The notion occurs to him that his married life is very much like the brick exterior he just inspected, refusing the existence of hidden spaces that are nonetheless there. What if there could be a different world where Bosie replaced Constance, a world where the brick expanded to show the depths of his secret life? Or would that life no longer be secret? How delicate and elusive true bliss must be if it can be captured by two men walking barefoot together in a house shared and acknowledged before the public eye.

When Bosie appears, he is more than barefoot. Supple, golden, a little bit statue and a little bit flower.

Lord Alfred Douglas, not yet twenty-five years old, stands there as much in the flesh as Wilde can dream.

He moves down a step, and Wilde ascends one in reciprocation.

"How long has Constance been gone now, Oscar?"

"A few days."

"Have you not been lonely?"

"Too much, dear boy."

They each take another step.

"Then where's my invitation? Imagine my hurt when I learned of your situation through *secondary* sources."

"Who informed you?"

Not smiling, Bosie says, "The *other* Alfred in your life."

"Wood," Wilde says. He recalls it now. He sought the lad out not even an hour after Constance and the children left. "It's not what you think."

"No?"

"I was only asking him for information."

"Still chasing Stephen?"

Wilde nods. "Why were *you* with Wood?"

"Oh, I just happened to be in his neighborhood," Bosie says, winking. "I must have arrived to see him soon after you did, Oscar. He smelled so much like you it almost felt like a threesome. You might have stayed to join us rather than going off to chase a shadow."

They now stand a single step removed from each other. Bosie looks perfect on the higher level, a complement to his imperiousness.

"I don't believe your butler wanted me here, but I bought him off. I sent them all away in expectation of your return. I've been here long enough to get drowsy and fall asleep. Where have you been?"

"The museum."

"No need to lie, Oscar."

Wilde laughs. "It's true. I have been wading my way back through the sands of time, and now I find immortal youth under my roof. This is most pleasing."

Bosie descends to Wilde's step and clutches himself against Wilde's far larger frame. Wilde's fingertips caress the young lord's back and both of them slump against the rail, their combined weight daring the strength of the banister.

"Carry me to your bed like a bride."

Wilde has the strength. He manages the stairs, gait stooped but not defeated. His indolence has always hidden more natural physical prowess than a casual glance would credit him, and Bosie presents a burden more emotional than physical.

They enter the bedroom, where Wilde spies more domestic tranquility from an imaginary world: Bosie's clothes spread across the floor. He places his lover upon the mattress, and they lay beside each other, making furtive caresses with their gazes locked.

"I found him," Wilde says.

"In the museum?"

"No, dear boy."

"Then *where?*"

Wilde rolls onto his back. "In perhaps the only place he could exist. My mind."

Bosie's narrowing eyes turn his face into something meaner. The petulance—cruelty, even—the *teeth* on this Venus flytrap that keeps capturing and releasing him, are showing. Wilde holds up a conciliatory hand.

"Are you upset that I found Stephen, or that I found him *first?*"

"Can't I be upset that you were searching for him at all?"

"Quit," Wilde says.

"Quit what?"

"Acting wounded. I know Wood told you about Stephen first, and you never mentioned him to me."

"There was nothing to mention. Wood lies even more than you, and I've better things to occupy my time than seek out a mystery man."

They both lay on their backs and stare at the ceiling, hands at their sides.

"Very well," Bosie says at last. "Tell me about him. Is he everything Wood promised?"

"I'm still not sure."

"What do you mean by that? Did you see the man or didn't you?"

"Let's just say it was not a well-lit room."

"*Where?*"

Wilde tells him about The Red Tiger and the Breath of the Great Goddess without going into the particulars of his hallucinations. The story earns a scornful response.

"You in an opium den? Ridiculous."

"Why is that?"

"I wouldn't credit you with the stomach for such an adventure. Elegant, witty Oscar Wilde willing to lose his mind among a crowd of addicts? Nonsense. It's also disappointing that this Stephen should end up being old like you."

"Bosie—I am not yet forty."

"You'll be 'not yet forty' for the next forty years."

Bosie leaves the bed and starts gathering his clothes, his golden hair mussed and all the more enticing. Wilde frowns nevertheless, though he knows he should be used to Bosie's sudden mood shifts by now.

"Well, come on, Oscar."

"What?"

"Let's go to this opium den. I want to see the secret bookcase. I want to meet Stephen for myself. But what I really want to do is watch you squirm as I prove you to be a liar."

"You don't believe my account?"

"No."

"Why do you always come to me, Bosie, if you hate me so?"

"I suppose everyone has to have a hobby, Oscar. Mine is annoying you. Now lead on!"

# CHAPTER EIGHT

"I thought you said the place was called The Red Tiger."

"I swear it is—or was," Wilde says, frowning at the tavern sign, certain he's made no wrong turns. But here they are, at dusk, standing beneath a placard that says The Black Panther.

"You weren't even trying with this lie," Bosie says, adding a harsh laugh.

Wilde rushes to the alleyway to confirm prior observations. He finds the same brick exterior and the same length. The only difference is the absence of the semi-conscious man on the ground. Defeated and bewildered, he returns to Bosie, who smirks with his arms crossed at the chest.

"How much opium did you have, Oscar?"

"I saw the sign before I took the drug, and it's the name Wood gave me. I cannot explain the discrepancy, although perhaps I approve of it."

"Oh?"

"As our beloved Shakespeare wrote, 'What's in a name?' The answer, I'm afraid, is *everything*."

"Really, Oscar, how am I supposed to believe you? Let's go inside. I want to see what *else* you've fabricated."

Bosie flings the door open and enters. Wilde starts to follow but pauses to regard the sign again. It hangs from a pole high above the window and swings back and forth in the slight breeze. People jostle about him, though the street isn't too crowded just now. One man leaves the tavern just as two men enter. Wilde's peripheral vision notices a flash of the familiar about the departing patron.

"You!"

The man stops.

"Excuse me, but were you not lounging near that alleyway some hours ago?"

"Me, sir? I'm afraid you've got—"

"I have *just* the right man, unless you have a twin. You were there," Wilde says, pointing at the spot.

A slight grin wrinkles the man's mouth. "What was I doing?"

"Adventuring inside your mind."

Now the stranger laughs and bows. "I was sensible of another person stepping over me, only in my head you were a giant, and I was Jack, flat on my back from a tumble down the beanstalk."

"You fell from the beanstalk and dove straight down the white rabbit's hole."

"Aye, sir. Perhaps I did at that."

"What happened when you woke up?"

He points to the tavern. "I went inside. Isn't that obvious?"

"Was this place not called Red Tiger?"

"I'm afraid I don't know that name."

"But it's what the sign said."

The man looks between Wilde and the sign and shrugs his shoulders. "I'm afraid the sign begs to differ."

He heads up the street, forcing Wilde to walk after him. "You were outside in the alleyway because you were in an opium haze."

"I suppose I was."

"Did you get the opium from within?"

"Bless me, sir, I have no memory of where I got it. I only remember walking through cities."

"Cities?"

"Aye. Through London and the cities that overlay it."

"I don't understand."

He laughs. "Me neither, but that's what happened. It was like climbing through layers. Never mind. When I woke, I was thirsty like a man who has been on a voyage, and since I was outside a pub I took advantage. I've always been lucky about passing out near convenient places."

Oscar hears Bosie calling to him and looks back. They've gone half a block from the tavern and Wilde begs the man to wait. Then he rushes back to Bosie.

"Why aren't you coming in?"

"That man was here earlier."

"What man?"

"*Him.*"

But when Wilde looks up the street, he finds nothing but a mangy stray cat scratching its side against the brick and avoiding the careless footfalls of human traffic. The cat turns and runs away as Bosie tugs on his arm.

"Sure you're okay, Oscar?"

"No," Wilde whispers, and surrenders to his lover's pull.

# CHAPTER NINE

"Something unaccountable and strange is at work here," Wilde says to the top of Bosie's head. Bosie slumps toward him across the table after finishing his third pint. One never knows how alcohol will influence the young man's moods. Sometimes drink makes him the most companionable chap in the world; sometimes it opens the door to unexplored degrees of coldness. Right now, he just seems tired. He shows no interest—or even memory—in why they came in the first place. His eyelids droop in the most adorable way.

Few things could tear Wilde's gaze from his lover's charming inebriation, but his determination to investigate the bookcase is one of them. The Black Panther's interior is the same but there's no sign of Chyron. Instead, a lanky, balding man serves drinks and makes small talk with a cluster of customers. Wilde notes the dark doorway behind the bar that should lead to the hallway. He's noticed a few people pass through without returning and the barman has acted oblivious.

He must know them, Wilde thinks. Either that or they all share a secret, subtle form of communication.

Bosie lifts his head and gives him a bleary-eyed stare.

"Are you really still sober, Oscar?"

"Unusual, I know, but I'm too busy observing."

"Oh, you're *such* a spy." Bosie's head lolls to the right in a fit of giggles.

Wilde reaches out to stroke the younger man's blond hair, remembering the first time he ever made the caress. Bosie purrs in response, moving his head back and forth as if to expose his entire scalp to Wilde's fingertips. For a second it feels like every person in the tavern has fallen into a silent stare. A shiver bunches Wilde's shoulders. He starts to pull back. But why should he surrender to fear? What is their judgment to him? Meeting every gaze, he massages Bosie's head with greater force.

And in the blink of an eye, the noise of chatter returns, and no one is looking at them.

"Oscar," Bosie says, his forehead now on the table.

"Easy," Wilde says.

"I just had a dream. I wasn't even asleep, but I had a dream. Everyone was looking at us."

In a cautious tone, he says, "Is that so?"

"You were . . . were . . . brave . . ."

"You're worth being brave for, dear boy."

He glances around the room again. No one seems to regard them, but he feels an immense tension in the air, occupying the edges of the space. A desire to protect Bosie surges through him. Any danger that threatens love makes love more glorious as a result, he thinks. Maybe this is because danger and love are opposites. But is that true? When was love ever *not* the most dangerous emotion in his life, especially when he's found it someone as erratic as Bosie?

"Get me another, Oscar." Bosie's slurred speech renders the request as *Gimme nother scar*. Wilde ponders the phrasing, haunted. Love is the tie that binds, and love is the knife that can cut all ties.

"Perhaps you should wait."

"*Another.*"

There's no point upsetting Bosie's applecart when it's already teetering. A fresh pint has been demanded; a fresh pint will be bestowed. Wilde signals to the barman but finds himself ignored.

I have my opportunity, he tells himself.

"I'll be right back."

He leaves the table and inserts himself at the bar between two men who've drunk themselves into a mutual stupor. Wilde raises a fistful of money and the barman comes to him.

"That looks to be quite a sum, sir. You buying drinks for everyone?"

"Just one."

"We're not that expensive."

Wilde leans over the bar. "I was wondering if you have a bible on the premises."

"If you're looking for a bible, there's a church up the street. Hell, there's a church on every street, usually across from a pub."

"Do those churches worship the Great Goddess?"

"I have no idea what you're talking about."

The barman starts away, but Wilde waves the money again. "May I have a look through that door?"

"Why?"

"Personal interest. I'll be happy to pay."

The barman looks at Wilde's money, shrugs and holds out his hand. The transfer made, he welcomes Wilde around the side, and they go through the doorway together.

They go down the same short hallway, which ends in the bookcase. Wilde's pulse accelerates and he scans the titles. They are all the same as before, and there's the King James bible. Without asking permission, he tugs it—

And the book comes out in his hand.

"Well, what do you know," the barman says. "We did have a bible

44

on the premises. This bookshelf belongs to my wife. She likes to read when the pub's quiet."

"I don't understand."

"I never understand what gentlemen waste their money on. Is your curiosity satisfied, sir? Is there anything else you wish to see?"

Wilde grips the bookcase and tries to shift it. The furniture tilts forward, bringing a shout from the barman as several books fall to the floor. Wilde just manages to get the shelf righted again.

"What the hell are you doing?"

Wilde slaps the side of the case. "There was a *door* here, damn it! This shelf swiveled and there was an opening."

The bartender guffaws at this suggestion and scratches his shiny pate. "You're very strange, but if you want to stay back here, you're welcome to do so. I have customers to see about. If you don't mind reshelving those volumes when you're done, I'll be grateful."

The barman leaves Wilde staring at the bookcase and the wall. There's a clear separation between the two, and no secret door.

He stoops to gather the books, muttering oaths about his sanity along the way. Then there is nothing left for him to do but other than admit defeat. He sulks back to the main room only to find Bosie sitting up straight and sobered by the arrival of a guest at their table. Wilde cheeks burn at the sight of the man, his black hair cropped into short curls.

Who is this dark lamb?

The lads go on talking, steeped in each other's eyes as Wilde stands there, clearing his throat. He feels a keen humiliation at the way they ignore him. When he's stood in a room of men with similar sympathies and desires, he's always noticed how youth clusters toward one side of the room, as if the wallpaper there is reserved for them alone. The older men—and what a maddening, ill-defined notion is *older!*—find themselves isolated, locked away on the other side of an invisible line. Men in their twenties seem to think men near or over forty to be antique.

Wilde puts one hand on Bosie's shoulder, inserting himself into their communion. The stranger turns his gaze to Wilde, who discovers a pair of arresting eyes that capture the depths of the Mediterranean in each iris.

"Oscar," Bosie says, flashing a superior smile as he points at his new companion. "I'd like you to meet Stephen!"

# CHAPTER TEN

Wilde pulls up a third chair. He dabs a napkin at the sweat on his brow, which Bosie seems to find hilarious, perhaps a rare sign of nerves.

"Try not to faint, Oscar."

"It's good to meet you, Mr. Wilde," the stranger says, further surprising Wilde by the courteousness. The typical renter is on a first-name basis before proper introductions are even made.

"You're a friend of Alfred Wood?"

"Friend is overstating matters. I'm sure you can appreciate what I mean."

Wilde nods, offering a faint, uncertain smile. The man's tone sounds educated as well. Wood and all the other renters have Cockney accents, while Stephen sounds like he just came from a lecture at Eton. He even might have been the lecturer.

But if this is the Stephen Wood was talking about, then who was the Stephen who made the opium?

"Yes," Wilde says, unable to push his troubled thoughts aside. "Friendship is the finest of things—but also the most difficult. Wood is a charming lad, but not a friend."

"And the two of you?" Stephen says, gaze shifting back and forth between Wilde and Bosie. "Are you *friends?*"

Even Bosie seems startled by the sudden, leering tone in Stephen's voice. He looks to Wilde as if searching for an answer.

47

"The very best," Wilde says.

Stephen raps his knuckles on the table, grinning. "A round of drinks then. Let's toast *friendship*."

"Oscar, get us beers, would you?"

The lads lean towards each other, youthful conspirers again. Wilde sighs and looks toward the bar. He squints. Something's different, he thinks. The barman is the same, the doorway behind the bar and the bar itself is the same. But those are different drunkards on the stools. I wasn't at the bookcase long enough to let a whole different crowd of people come and go.

He glances back at his table. Stephen is staring with intent into Bosie's eyes, but Wilde senses his actual attention is on Wilde himself. Or is that just a vain hopefulness—or hopeful vanity? He cannot guess, but as Wilde stands there, he feels himself scrutinized through peripheral vision.

"Well, go on, Oscar!" Bosie says, looking up at him. "Get the pints!"

He retrieves his wallet and finds far less money in it than before, as is the rule of thumb anytime he's around Bosie for longer than an hour. He takes what he has left and throws it on the table. "I'm going home. I trust you can find some joy in the evening without me."

Bosie sweeps up the money in one scoop and heads toward the bar.

Wilde leaves, his footsteps both heavier and quicker than his usual tread. Once outside he leans into the walk, finding the night air cold and lonely.

"Mr. Wilde!"

He pivots at the sound of his name. Stephen, somehow even more attractive under the muted mix of moon and streetlight, hurries to him.

"I hope I gave no offense."

"Dear boy—no. It is just—"

Wilde goes quiet and still as Stephen touches his right cheek. The young man's fingertips linger against his skin.

"You've been chasing me for some time."

"Did Wood tell you that?"

"It's disappointing you should flee so soon after finding me."

Stephen presses closer. Wilde's nose detects the strangest scent. It's almost no scent at all. Not sweat, not cologne, not even soap. But *cleanliness*. It's such a balm his nostrils seem to reawaken to the nastier odors he's long grown accustomed to, like the reek of manure from the city's thousands of horse-drawn hansom cabs. He coughs and leans closer to inhale Stephen's cleansing scent again. Then he gazes with open admiration at the man's face, desiring every detail of the chin, the lips, the nose. They make full and direct eye contact. A weakness strikes his knees, and though he stands a head taller than Stephen, he soon finds himself almost propped on the lad's sturdy body for support.

Stephen positions him against the wall.

"Your *friend*—he is Lord Alfred Douglas, yes?"

Wilde nods.

"Brother of Viscount Drumlanrig?"

"Yes."

"And the Viscount is Lord-in-Waiting and *friend* to Rosebery, the new Prime Minister?"

"All true," Wilde says, regaining his strength. "He is also the son of a monstrous man."

Stephen nods. "The Marquess of Queensberry. I know about him, too."

"Beware of him. Should you and Bosie—"

"Should we what?"

"If the two of you develop your own *friendship*, make sure to steer clear of the Marquess. He is dangerous, unsettled and cruel—especially to his sons."

"The Marquess is just another of history's mealy-mouthed fools," Stephen says, seizing Wilde's left hand at the wrist. He brings Wilde's arm up and brings the hand to his mouth. He kisses Wilde's fingertips as Wilde stares in breathless amazement.

"What is *this?*"

Stephen touches Wilde's scarab ring.

"Strange. This gift from my mother has been a particular beacon of praise of late."

"Khepri," he says, nothing but loathing in his tone.

"What's that?"

Stephen ignores the question and pushes Wilde's hand down until the ring is out of sight.

"Perhaps you'd give it to me? You're known to give tokens of your friendship, aren't you? Wood said you gave him a cigarette case."

The urge to say *Yes* sends a nervous thrill through his stomach. He stares into Stephen's blue eyes and at his black, sleek eyebrows, and wonders how he'd ever have the strength to deny this man anything. But he becomes sensible to the fact his left hand is held in both of Stephen's, and that the young man's fingers are even now coaxing the ring up the length of his pinkie.

Wilde closes his hand into a fist. "No."

Stephen frowns. In a way, this gives Wilde a sense of normalcy—and superiority. Renters have asked for the ring before. He's even half-indulged their wishes on drunken nights and let some of them wear the ring, a quick way to win the heart of some pouting youth. He's always remembered to take it back from the unconscious lad in the morning. Stephen's aggressive request for the ring lowers him from his mysterious pedestal. Maybe he's educated, maybe he's at the center of a hundred intrigues with various members of Parliament. But in the end he's just like Wood, a renter pawing at whatever he can get.

Movement at his legs interrupt him. He looks down to find a cat nuzzling his leg. Another one comes. Then another.

Stephen laughs, crouching. "History's oldest beggars," he says, and the cats begin to swarm around his right hand. Even more approach.

Ten, fifteen. Twenty.

Wilde turns and sees hundreds more loping down the street, coming out of every alleyway. The horses in the street stop and whinny in confusion. People gasp and swear.

"It must be every cat in London," a woman says.

A man answers, "Every cat in London? Every cat in *England*, I should think!"

They flow toward Wilde like a river, and some spring at him and land on his chest, driving him away from Stephen and toward the tavern. He winces at the stab of their claws and hears Stephen laughing as he pries them away. For a moment, the onslaught feels impossible to overcome, and Wilde imagines the absurdity of being overwhelmed and killed by hordes of stray cats. But a minute later this feline deluge ends, and the streets are clear. The cab drivers whip their horses and the wheels start turning again. There's no trace of Stephen anywhere. Wilde stands there watching and listening until his ears become sensible to a slight metallic noise that draws his gaze up to the swinging tavern sign.

The Red Tiger.

# CHAPTER ELEVEN

"It's interesting about the cats, Oscar," Robbie says.

Wilde puts down his tea and leans forward in his chair. It is one in the morning, and he's ensconced in the apartment of his most devoted friend, Robbie Ross—the one man who'll always accept anything he has to say.

"The changing tavern sign, the problematic bookcase, the impossible brick wall, the two different men named Stephen—and only the *cats* intrigue you?"

Robbie, on the cusp of twenty-five, always boyish, offers a precocious smile. "It's just that my own cat, Victoria, disappeared around that time, I think. I called for her and she didn't come."

Wilde stiffens. "Are you quite sure, Robbie?"

"I am."

"Where is the cat now?"

Robbie yells the cat's name and soon enough a plump orange tabby makes a cursory appearance in the doorway. She graces them with their presence a moment, then turns and saunters away.

"There, you see? Her majesty is back."

"Could she have escaped through a window?"

Robbie laughs. "Oscar, you're taking my remark with too much seriousness. Victoria was only hiding. She seldom comes when I call for her, and I didn't conduct a search."

"So, she *could* have been gone."

Robbie cocks his head to the right and gives Wilde a rare, critical look. "Maybe a good night's sleep would help."

Wilde grunts and takes up his tea. His right hand has a slight tremor. "I know it all sounds ridiculous. Do you think it could all be from ingesting the opium? I wouldn't think the effects could last so long, but I don't know. Maybe I should see a doctor."

"I think you should consider it. I'm sorry I haven't been of much help."

"Your patient ear has done wonders enough. Maybe if I purge this gibberish series of events out of my head I can get back to life's simpler pleasures."

"*Simpler?*"

They smile at each other.

"I do have one question for you, Oscar. When you saw the sign had changed back, why didn't you go inside? Maybe the bookcase had changed too."

"I can only answer that I was afraid, Robbie."

"What about Bosie? Did you not want to check on him?"

"He had already upset me enough for one evening. At that moment, all I desired was the company of someone I trust, someone who's always in command of his senses."

Robbie's bright smile is a reward with no equal.

"If you want my sensible advice, Oscar, I say go to bed. It doesn't sound like you've had any real sleep in some time. Fatigue may be playing tricks on your mind."

"I'm now certain you're right."

Robbie stands and holds out his hand. "Well then."

*Well then.* Robbie said the same thing the first time he ever seduced

Wilde, and Wilde accepted his offer. Robbie was his first lover. Why did they not become true partners? Why is the obscure *frisson* of romantic love missing in Wilde's heart when it comes to him? Robbie matches or exceeds Bosie in all areas except beauty, but even there the inequality is not lopsided.

He glances at Robbie's hand, but he finds himself thinking of Stephen's engulfing grip and how his fingers tried to work the scarab ring off his pinkie. In his imagination, Stephen succeeded and took the ring. Wilde must look down to affirm it's still there.

"Is that a refusal, Oscar?"

Robbie's hand wavers in front of him, on the verge of retracting. Wilde captures it between his palms.

"A more generous invitation was never proffered, dear boy."

# CHAPTER TWELVE

Wilde wakes in the morning to hushed voices and rising tempers. He keeps still, eyes closed to enhance his hearing.

"I'll only ask one more time, Mr. Ross. *Where* is he?"

"Ask thirty more times. Go to hell and pose your questions to the Devil, Mr. Mathers. In your line of work, I'm sure you've met him."

"He *is* in this house. We already know."

"If you know, then why ask?"

A laugh answers Robbie's question. "Even now you're being judged, Mr. Ross. Judged by forces incomprehensible to you. Loyalty radiates from your soul like rays of sunlight—this is a good thing. But don't confuse loyalty and prideful stubbornness."

"As long as you don't confuse my patience with meekness, Mr. Mathers."

Keeping quiet, Wilde pulls back the bedclothes and swings his feet to the floor. Who is this Mr. Mathers? One of Queensberry's infernal hounds? How confused any private investigator must be if they've followed him around London these last few days.

Robbie orders the man out.

"I'm not leaving without Mr. Wilde."

"Then I'll call the police, Mr. Mathers. This nonsense has gone on long enough."

"He's in that room, isn't he? Behind that door? Wilde! Wilde, come out!"

The sound of a scuffle. Wilde leaves the bed and hurries to the door.

"Leave, damn you!"

"Mr. Wilde! I'm here on urgent business. Your wife has sent me! You are in grave danger."

Wilde pauses with his hand on the knob.

Constance sent this man? His mouth goes dry at a horrific certainty: she's seeking divorce. No wonder she insisted on taking their children when she left. It was part of her brewing plan, and the man outside must be her solicitor.

Robbie says, "What in the bloody hell are you going on about? You must be out of your—"

Wilde opens the door and finds Robbie grappling with a much taller man in his mid-forties, with a wiry build and hawkish eyes that give the impression of swooping down on you from an even greater height.

"I am Mr. Wilde. Unless you happen to be a creditor, in which case Mr. Wilde absconded out the back minutes ago. If you give chase now, you might still capture him."

The man relents and bows. His hair, parted in the middle and swept back, is dark except for a striking patch of gray spreading out from the center of his forehead. Wilde cannot recall paying attention to the different patterns by which men go gray, other to lament the fact it happens at all. But he is sure he's never seen a man with coloration like this. It reminds him of the wings of a phoenix stretching out to shake away the ashes.

"I am Samuel Mathers, Mr. Wilde."

Does he know the name? There does seem to be a recognition, but too distant to be useful. "What may I do for you? What is so urgent?"

"Your wife has sent me to warn you."

"I doubt very much Constance sent you *here*. She is in Worthing. How could she know I'd decided to spend the night with my friend Robbie?"

"She has her ways, Mr. Wilde."

Wilde and Robbie exchange a glance. Robbie, usually so impish, goes pale.

"Constance is employing detectives against me too."

Mr. Mathers laughs. "She has no need for a process so unreliable."

"How did she contact you? By telegram?"

"That, too, would be unreliable and far too crude a way of sending me on such important business."

"Enough of this nonsense! *Tell me.*"

"Why, Mr. Wilde," this strange man says with perfect equanimity. "She told me through a dream."

# CHAPTER THIRTEEN

"The Order of the Golden Dawn?"

"Occultists, Oscar," Robbie says, his tone both amused and sneering. "Grown men and women who believe in—"

"Existences outside of your understanding, young one," Mr. Mathers says, sounding quite bored in the face of Robbie's sarcasm.

"The problem's not with my *understanding*, I assure you."

Wilde puts a gentle hand on Robbie's shoulder as he meets Mr. Mather's gaze.

"I am sorry that our introductions have gotten off to such a difficult start. Perhaps we should look at things we have in common. For example, our beliefs and activities have no doubt brought us both a fair share of public ridicule."

"We have another thing in common, Mr. Wilde: a deep respect for your wife."

"Respect? Yes, no doubt. But if I'm to be truthful, as I feel I must, I will say that you must have the higher portion of her esteem if she is coming to you in dreams. Though I suppose she does haunt mine too, after a fashion. Forgive me: that was a petty and cruel thing for me to say."

"Your marital concerns are not my business. I have only come to fulfill the mission she gave me."

"Which is?"

Mr. Mathers extends a slip of paper. "To make sure you come to this address at once."

Wilde reads the street name and finds it unfamiliar. He shows the paper to Robbie, who likewise shakes his head.

"Why must I go there?"

"For your protection."

"From what?"

"A gathering shadow."

Robbie laughs at this, but Wilde holds up a conciliatory hand.

"Mr. Mathers, let me understand something. You say you belong to the Order of the Golden Dawn. I am not as ignorant of them as my tone suggested. In fact, I am well aware that Constance shares their preoccupation with spiritualism and the like. I recall her efforts to join the club some five or six years ago. She told me the most charming tales of being initiated into its secrets."

Robbie's eyes widen. "You can't be serious, Oscar."

"For a change, I am. She later told me the Golden Dawn expelled her for telling me about its rituals. I suppose this Order of yours believes husbands and wives are not to be trusted with secrets, which may in fact be a very wise policy. Not that I comprehended anything she described."

Samuel Mathers almost pitches out of his chair from laughing so hard, a startling rebuke even for Wilde. The shaking of his head makes the patch of gray look like a bird in flight.

"Mr. Wilde," he says, catching his breath. "What do you think keeps your marriage strong?"

"Strong is not the word I'd use."

"*Active* then."

"Our children, perhaps. Propriety. Social appearance."

"Not love?"

"Love has many forms and definitions. It could be that—"

"*Love*, Mr. Wilde?"

He swallows, contemplates the possibility a moment, and shakes his head. His gaze drops to the floor. Mr. Mathers laughs again, but without a trace of scorn.

"What's so amusing? I often can see the humor in anything, but just now I find myself flailing. A loveless marriage is comedy gold for a farcical play. But it is fodder for tragedy in life."

"Ah, Mr. Wilde. You fancy yourself so adept at living two lives at once. You've lied to your wife."

"Don't speak another word to this man, Oscar," Robbie says.

"I am not a solicitor, Mr. Ross. I am not a detective trying to trick your friend into any kind of confession. I do not even believe in such a thing as sin. Were it within my power, I'd stand in the temple of Christian piety like Samson and knock down all of its obnoxious columns."

"I trust you," Wilde says. "Yes, I've lied to my wife. I also know she's come to see through the lie."

"She always did."

"I doubt that. But no matter. The crisis point has been reached. She's in Worthing with our children. Whether or not I'll ever join her there is an open question."

"She went to Worthing to protect her sons, Mr. Wilde."

"Protect them from what? The scandalous influence of their own father?"

"*No.* From the danger she has foreseen. Do you think you alone operate under appearances? Do you believe your marriage is only a disguise for yourself? Did it not occur to you that Constance might have been seeking a mask of her own, and found a most absurd one as the wife of the Empire's most conspicuous dandy?"

"Should I feel insulted, sir?"

"Should *she?*"

A silence settles upon the room. Mr. Mathers and Wilde trade stares.

"Your wife, Mr. Wilde, is a woman of immense skill. As a believer in the transmigration of souls, I should think hers must have belonged to some great priestess of Atlantis. She alone first detected the danger we all now sense, but even her tremendous knowledge has not helped us determine its nature."

"This is ridiculous," Robbie says, getting up to pace. "You come here demanding to see Oscar, then you make absurd statements about his wife contacting you through *dreams.* Now you claim—what? A conspiracy?"

"We should count ourselves fortunate the sinister influence at work feels it *needs* to be conspiratorial."

Robbie chuckles. "Sinister influence," he says, going to his liquor cabinet. He returns with a bottle of wine. Wilde observes he holds it by the neck like a bat, as if he intends to break it over Mather's head. If so, he hopes Robbie chose a *lesser* vintage.

"I don't know why in the world I opened the door to you in the first place, Mr. Mathers. It must have been madness on my part."

"You call it madness. I call it the machinations of a higher power."

"No one compels me to do anything."

"Enough of this," Wilde says. "Let's say I accept everything you've said as the gospel truth, sir."

"Please do so, though I remind you I'd never put gospel and truth in the same sentence."

"You claim my wife sent a warning to you in a dream. Constance then told you where you could find me. Tell me why she'd have anything to do with you and your Order at all, since I know from her own mouth that she was exiled from it many years ago?"

"Exiled from it, sir?"

Mr. Mathers launches into another uproarious fit of laughter.

"I'm all for mirth," Wilde continues with a quick, sideways glance at Robbie. "But I'd like to be in on the joke so I can appreciate it best. Please explain what is so amusing."

"Oh, forgive me, Mr. Wilde. It's just that far from being exiled from it, your wife is the leader of the Golden Dawn."

# CHAPTER FOURTEEN

"It is good of you to come with me, Robbie," Wilde says as a hansom cab takes them to the address provided by Mr. Mathers. Where their eccentric visitor rushed off to is anyone's guess, though Wilde half-suspects he vanished into thin air, the only proper departure for someone with his *obsessions*.

"I'm not sure we're doing a smart thing, Oscar. These spiritualists are delusional, and that's being charitable."

"You don't believe what he told us about Constance?"

"Do *you*? Oscar, be reasonable. When would she have time to go cavorting off to play dress-up at some temple for hours on end? Who would be watching the children?"

"Not their father, who's too busy cavorting off to theaters to play dress-up for hours on end. Never mind what I'm doing when I'm not at the theater."

The carriage sways. If not for the sound of the horse hooves, Wilde could almost believe himself at sea, sail unfurled. Fate cast to the wind.

To the breath of the Great Goddess.

Robbie squeezes Wilde's forearm. "Cyril and Vyvyan are delightful boys, a treasure in the lives of everyone who knows them. They're none the worse if you're not a traditional father."

Wilde gives a weary smile of thanks and looks out the window, his hands clasped in his lap. After a time, he realizes he's twisting the scarab ring back and forth on his pinkie. Looking down, he tries to recall the day his mother gave it to him and finds a blank place in his memory. He might as well have been born with the ring on his finger.

Twenty minutes later, the coach stops, and the driver announces their arrival. They step onto an unfamiliar street and confront a long row of bland terraced houses.

Robbie surveys the buildings from left to right. "*This* is where the high and mighty order of mystics meet? You'd think the spirits could do better."

"Even fairies and ghosts must appreciate discretion."

The address they want is right in front of them and together they climb the two modest steps the front door, which swings open just before Wilde knocks.

Their greeter looks like an actor interrupted during a dress rehearsal for any random Greek tragedy. Shaggy white hair hides his eyes and an unkempt beard overwhelms his face. Only his large nose gives him a feature and makes him look like a man struggling to poke his head out from a bush. He wears a white tunic with a ruby broach on the right shoulder strap. He says nothing and for once Wilde feels no compunction to speak first.

The man turns and walks away.

"Well," Robbie says.

"I guess we're meant to follow him."

"Are you sure we should?"

"It seems we have no choice. Of course, it's always the people who have a multitude of choices who claim to have none at all."

Robbie steps through first. Wilde follows and closes the door. Their host stays ahead of them, moving further into the house, passing through more rooms than Wilde thinks possible. Each new space has the layout and trappings of a museum, though far sparser—and cleaner—than his recent experience visiting with Edward Thompson. One room has all four walls painted black with an enormous red triangle drawn on the floor. Hieroglyphics and runes decorate another room. Others contain displays of goblets and jewels, gem-encrusted daggers and crystal artifacts.

"Hang on," Robbie says as they enter yet another space. The right wall depicts a wide-open eye with a glittering, golden iris. Turning left, Wilde finds the same eye, but drawn half-shut. He turns again to see the eye rendered fully closed. He makes another turn—half-open—and returns to his starting point.

"If you turn fast enough, the eye seems to blink," Robbie says. He spins to prove his point.

"That's clever."

"But what's this all about, Oscar?"

"No doubt something of mystical significance like everything else."

They hurry to catch up with their guide, locating him in a room with a vast floor labyrinth created by an intricate mosaic of tiles. The sight of it steals Wilde's breath as he contemplates the craft, skill and patience necessary to create it. His gaze follows the path for a few twists and turns before lancing toward the center, where he sees a red circle large enough to accommodate three or four standing men.

"You must both enter."

"Sir," Wilde says, "this labyrinth is a testament to artisanship. But we haven't time for a reflective journey just now."

"Walk."

Wilde shakes his head. "Perhaps there is a misunderstanding about why we're here. Mr. Mathers, whom you must know, sought me out about a warning from my wife. He all but begged me to come here. He

65

was urgent. Time is of the essence, so let us get to the point."

"Time is indeed urgent, Mr. Wilde. But time has many reckonings. Walk the labyrinth. Trust its path."

Wilde glances at Robbie, who shrugs. "Might as well. At worst we're the victims of an elaborate joke."

"Very good. Let us set our feet upon the path to enlightenment."

They move to the labyrinth's starting point. Wilde looks down and takes his first step.

Mist rolls over his shoes.

# CHAPTER FIFTEEN

*"Oscar?"*

"Here, Robbie. Wherever *here* is. Can you see me?"

"No!"

The enveloping mist is magnitudes heavier than any London fog. Wilde extends his right arm and loses sight of his own hand.

"Are you behind me?"

"I don't know," Robbie says.

"Your voice sounds like you are. But I can't tell what direction I'm going. I can't even see my feet."

When he tries to move forward, his body feels like it's making an exaggerated tilt, as if he could fall forward and let the mist hold him aloft. The sensation sends his stomach lurching.

*Take a step.*

The command echoes through his thoughts but not in his own voice. Wilde pivots to the left and right as the fog thickens.

"Robbie? Was that you?"

He receives no answer. Wilde calls again, louder, and finds only silence. The possibility of being alone in this void panics him into action. He makes his feet move. His shoes meet a hard surface yet the feeling of being adrift remains.

*Keep walking.*

"But how can I follow a path I can't see?"

*Surrender to the labyrinth. Let it guide you.*

The voice in his head becomes more familiar on every word. At first it seemed genderless. Now it's become female and confident.

"Constance?"

From *elsewhere*, Robbie's voice answers. "Oscar, are you talking to me? I have no idea where I am."

"Patience, Robbie. Patience and silence. Don't worry about direction. Just—surrender."

He takes his own advice as he talks. His steps become less labored. *You are getting closer, Oscar.*

"I don't feel like I've gone anywhere. When I put my foot down, I feel solid ground. But every time I lift my foot, I lose faith there'll be any floor to support me."

*Qui patitur vincit.*

The Latin provokes Wilde to grin. Constance always had an attractive intellect and wit. So attractive, in fact, he hoped it might outweigh his lack of physical interest in her.

"*He conquers who endures.* Your personal motto. I'll make it mine. God knows you've endured me."

*Keep talking, Oscar. Walk as you speak. Let the steps flow as naturally as speech. Or think of yourself as writing rather than walking. The mist is a white paper eager to capture your sentences.*

"I'm doing it, Constance. Baby steps, perhaps, but better than crawling. I can feel you now. I can—"

He stops.

"There is something in the mist with me. Constance, is it you? Robbie?"

Something brushes past his legs, making a tickle on his ankles. He looks down and swoons, dizzied by the swirling white tendrils of fog.

Wilde reaches out for non-existent support and falls to his knees. The mist rises above him like a wave of cresting water.

*Oscar, get to your feet! Fight your way forward! We see you. We can almost reach you.*

A darkness looms in the mist, moving sly and elusive as a shark circling just below the ocean's surface. Yellow eyes flash through the murk with all the power of a lighthouse beam. He steps toward it.

*No, Oscar. That is the wrong path. Hear my voice. Be drawn to it.*

A roar drowns out Constance's voice and sends him to his knees again, arms over his face, his eyes clenched shut. Breath hot and stamped with a mortuary stench strikes his face. Wilde clutches himself as he shrinks low against the terror he imagines.

"Constance, I can't move. I'm so afraid."

The stalking beast unleashes another roar. He feels its deep thunder in every part of his body, shriveling up him up still further, stealing the marrow from his bones. Something sniffs at him now. He feels the poke of cold, wet flesh like some animal prodding him with its nose.

*Oscar, whatever you're experiencing, just get up and move. Constance can save you just as she saved me.*

"Robbie?"

*I'm in the center of the labyrinth. I can see you, but you're standing in shadow. Step out of it. Constance has her hand out, reaching for you.*

Balling his hands into fists, keeping his eyes shut tight, Wilde finds the courage to stand. The beast in front of him answers with a low, casual rumble, as pure as a sustained peal of thunder.

*You must open your eyes, Oscar.*

He gives a piteous laugh. "You think too much of me."

*Your greatest strength has always been your ability to see and acknowledge things for what they are. Stare at your foe now, Oscar. Stare and refuse to blink.*

Wilde touches his eyes, convinced he'll have to pry the lids open. He lingers there a minute, saturated by the putrid breath of the beast that must be hulking mere feet from his face. His mind conjures a hundred menacing faces.

Trust Constance, he thinks. Open your eyes.

*See.*

He raises his eyelids in agonizing fractions. The dark figure gloats ahead of him in the mist, indistinct at first, but taking definite shape as his vision expands.

He stares at a panther's whose face is twice as large as Wilde's head.

He begins to hyperventilate as the panther's jaws open to reveal teeth as long as his fingers. It could take Wilde's head off his shoulders in one bite.

A blood-red tongue launches at Wilde like an eel shooting out of some underwater cave. It strikes his face, its texture as rough and sharp as a scalding hot towel sewn with gravel. Wilde shrieks convinced his skin's been torn. His knees wobble, sapped, and he falls upon them. The cat's predatory eyes gleam with distinct and gloating pleasure, not unfamiliar with the sight of men groveling.

Now Constance's voice storms through his mind and through the mist itself. A chant dominates the air. The panther springs back, hisses and then unleashes a full-throated retaliatory scream. But Constance's chant rises above it, her voice joined by a chorus of men and women. The chant become more insistent, more powerful. He feels the beat of his heart joining its rhythm.

The panther looks to him one more time, its slit-eyes narrowing, and bounds into the mist, which begins to dissipate. Many strong arms embrace him, and Wilde finds himself standing in the middle of the room, looking back at the labyrinth. Robbie stands amid a group of men and women dressed in robes and cloaks, some clutching amulets, several wearing masks. Mr. Mathers is among them.

"My God, what just happened?" Wilde says, so breathless he can only manage a whisper.

"I'm not sure God had anything to do with it, Oscar."

Robbie points to a figure who steps forward, pulling back a veil of black and red to reveal a smile so at odds with her serious eyes.

"Constance!"

Wilde reaches up and clasps his wife's hands.

"Welcome to the middle of the labyrinth, Oscar," she says.

# CHAPTER SIXTEEN

"How long was the journey?" Wilde says. "Minutes? Hours? Forgive, but of late I've had a devil of a time with . . . time."

"The soul travels in diverse ways, all of them detached from temporal anchors, Oscar."

Wilde blinks. Is this really his *wife* speaking?

"Forgive me, but I feel it necessary to echo Byron's critique of Coleridge's explanation of metaphysics: please explain your explanation."

Constance offers a patient smile and leads them across a broader path that extends from the labyrinth's center to a door. Wilde, Robbie and the rest of her coterie—some fifteen people—enter a cozy room with red carpet, red walls and a mahogany round table large enough to accommodate them all. Constance directs Wilde to a specific chair and then sits next to him.

"Please," he says. "It was a serious question. How long was I in the labyrinth?"

"How long do you think?"

"I have no notion. It could have been days."

"It was closer to twenty minutes."

He grunts. "It felt far longer than that. I wish I could pinpoint why."

"I understand, Oscar," Robbie says. "How can we have spent two days in the water and have it only mean twenty minutes?"

"There was no water, only a mist."

"I saw no mist. We were bobbing in the middle of a dark ocean. You were ahead of me, and you said we must swim stroke by stroke to an island up ahead. I couldn't see it, but I trusted you. Then I couldn't even hear you and I thought I'd drown. Then I saw a shape in the water, coming for me. It was so dark, so sinister I thought I'd die of fright. I could see its mouth opening to eat me. Then a bird came. It was larger than any boat could be, and it swooped down and took me up in its talons."

"But we were on land, Robbie. There was no sea monster. It was a cat—a monstrous panther, larger than anything even Livingstone encountered, with fur as black as char and a tongue that felt capable of scraping a man's flesh off his bones."

Wilde touches his face, his skin tingling from the awful memory.

Constance touches his arm. "No one interprets the journey through the labyrinth in the same way, Oscar, even if they enter it together. It is a subjective experience."

"I'm safe now. That's all the objectivity I need."

He studies the people gathered around the impressive round table, noting the solemnity and determination on the faces he can see. Those wearing veils and masks sit so still he wonders if they're entranced. One particular mask startles him. It shows a painted male face with elongated eyes. An ornate headband of blue silk secures the mask, and the silk is stamped with golden chalices. A bejeweled horn like a rhinoceros rises from the forehead, the tip capped with blue sapphires. The artistry lulls him into a fascinated stare so prolonged it becomes rude.

The wearer begins removing the mask.

"No, please don't take it off," Wilde says. "I apologize if I stared too long. I was fixated by its craftsmanship."

From behind the mask, a familiar male voice answers. "We should see each other for who we are, Oscar."

"I've always felt masks make people more comfortable with the truth."

This remark proves unpersuasive, and Wilde finds a recognizable face when the mask comes off.

"*Yeats!*"

"Mr. Wilde," the poet says with a slight nod.

Though fellow countrymen, they could not be more different in personality and attitude. Wilde has always found the young poet stiff and formal, perhaps fitting for a man whose middle name is Butler. But how could such a reserved man write such dexterous, wonderful verse? Looking at Yeats now, he wonders if his impassive expression is a mask too.

"Very well," a woman's voice said. "If the masks are coming off, then the masks are coming off."

Wilde looks to the person on his immediate right. A slender arm rises to remove a golden mask, revealing another familiar—and very beautiful—face.

"Florence!"

"Oscar," Florence Farr says. The actress and political activist flashes that daring, determined smile he so admires.

Robbie says, "I knew the Golden Dawn was popular, but I assumed it was just a social club for eccentrics."

"And what do you believe now, Mr. Ross?"

"I don't know what to think."

Florence laughs. "Your mind's been turned over like a saltshaker that's been emptied and refilled with pepper. But you'll adjust to the new seasoning. The Order of the Golden Dawn is dedicated to unlocking the deepest secrets of existence. There can be no higher calling."

Wilde raises his eyebrows. "You've always said the independence of Ireland is your one passion."

"Even that is secondary to the mission of the Order. Now more than ever, we're tasked with the independence of humanity."

A murmur of agreement comes from the others as they all discard their masks and veils. Wilde nods to acknowledge them all, the known and unknown.

"Robbie and I were in great peril in the labyrinth. Thank you for saving us."

"It took our combined strength," Constance says.

"Your wife gives us too much credit, Mr. Wilde," says Mr. Mathers. "*She* engaged the enemy in direct combat—and won."

"I cannot say I won."

"You made the thing flee," Florence says. "That's a victory in my book."

"Strategic withdraws and victories are not the same thing, I think. It left the labyrinth out of choice, not necessity."

Wilde stares at his wife. "*Combat?*"

Laughing, Constance says, "Am I so unconvincing a warrior? Perhaps I should be more assertive in our domestic quarrels."

"I respect you in both tooth and claw, Constance. But what I saw in the mist possessed both in sizeable proportions. What was it?"

"We're not sure yet. There's always danger in the world, like foul odors in the air. Some stenches always rise above the others. The Order has been aware of a growing threat for several months."

"But the source remains elusive," Yeats says. "That's all we know."

"That's *not* all we know, William. It's time to be frank."

Another quiet round of agreement goes around the table and Wilde finds everyone looking at him.

"Frank about what?" he says.

Constance places a hand on his forearm and squeezes.

"Whatever this danger is, Oscar, we've come to the unfortunate conclusion that you're at the heart of it."

# CHAPTER SEVENTEEN

They all put their hands flat upon the table, shoulder width apart, fingers spread, pinkies touching. Wilde takes a sideways glance at Robbie. Like everyone but Wilde himself, his eyes are shut, and Wilde begins to feel like a peeking child in church. Frowning, telling himself to surrender to the moment, he too closes his eyes.

"Friends, in our many journeys together we have encountered and overcome a multitude of dangers," Constance says. "We have won forbidden secrets from realms incomprehensible to the minds of ordinary humanity. We call our Order the highest council of mankind's adepts, and not without undue pride or reason. But we now face an entity unlike anything experienced before, a force strong enough to invade and pollute our sacred labyrinth. I need not tell you this means it has power to strike anywhere and at any time. This is no mere demonic threat. We've secured our labyrinth with every protection found in *Liber Imperium*. We've used spells more powerful yet, charms from the decaying scrolls of the Fehmgerichte and spells of our own devising. *Still* our protections were breached."

The steadiness, the heaviness of his wife's voice astounds Wilde. He can't reconcile these words of leadership and warning with the coquettish sprite he thought he married. You were quite right, Mr. Mathers, he thinks. It does seem marriage was a mask for *both* of us.

"Power in the spirit world," Constance continues, "is the most peculiar hunger. It feeds on the corporeal, the physical. It is for this reason alone that demons seek to possess the flesh. This entity, surpassing the demonic as a mountain surpasses an anthill, must desire to feast upon all mankind. That, I believe, is the calling card we must watch for. Let us turn grave attention to the politics of the nation."

"I feel a conspiracy around the Prime Minister," Yeats says.

"I fear it, too. This entity has a greedy ambition; and if I'm not mistaken, it has seen its ambitions fulfilled before. We rest at the heart of the greatest empire ever conceived. What better place to establish its throne among us and decree an everlasting human misery, which is its favorite meat?"

Wilde opens his eyes, consequences be damned. He finds concern and concentration engraved on every expression. Even Robbie seems absorbed, his eyebrows knitted, rapid movement under his lids. Setting his jaw, pulse speeding, Wilde says—

"Rosebery and his personal aide, Viscount Drumlanrig."

Constance seizes his wrist as the circle breaks contact. Everyone opens their eyes to stare at him.

"Lord Drumlanrig's younger brother is a great friend of mine. We were together last night when we met a man I've been seeking for . . . personal reasons. He calls himself Stephen. This man interrogated me about Lord Alfred and asked me to confirm his brother was the Prime Minister's assistant."

Constance laces her fingers together. "Can you describe Stephen?"

Wilde tries his best. "It is difficult. You see, in a prior search, I met another man named Stephen who was much older and not as . . . attractive."

"Where?" Yeats says.

"Both encounters happened at a pub I knew to be called The Red

Tiger. However, last night the pub's name changed to Black Panther—which, of course, is what I encountered in the labyrinth."

Constance motions to Yeats, who rises and leaves with three other members.

"Where are they going?" Wilde says.

"Off to have a drink at this mysterious pub of yours," Florence says.

"But what if it's dangerous?"

"It is dangerous," Constance says. "But we will be cautious in our surveillance of both the pub and the Prime Minister. It might be we were wrong to put you at the center of the disturbance after all, Oscar. The intensity of your friendship with Lord Douglas makes the two of you seem like the same person. Perhaps you even share part of the same soul."

He stares at his wife and finds no trace of judgment in her eyes, but her frankness surprises him with emotion. He finds himself on the verge of tears.

"Could we perhaps speak alone and in confidence?" he says, leaning in to whisper. "There's something I must tell you as a husband. Perhaps you'll already know what I have to say. I can't conceive of any secret I could hide from you."

She offers him her hand. "In my opinion, Oscar, our hearts shouldn't be judged by what we try to hide, but what we choose with great difficulty to reveal."

# CHAPTER EIGHTEEN

They go to a private chamber and Constance closes the door behind them.

"Considering the magnitude of what you're dealing with, I realize this may be an inappropriate time to talk about something so personal," Wilde says.

"I'm still a wife. I'm interested in the life of my husband."

His throat goes dry. Wilde has no doubt that Constance knows everything he's about to say. Maybe she knew about his persuasion before she married him.

"Very well, then. Here's my life."

Constance listens to him list his infidelities with men. She remains expressionless throughout, neither sympathetic nor scolding. Wilde can only marvel at this display of stoicism.

"I've been with Alfred Wood several times. Bosie and I both. And through him, I met many others. Collectively they're called renters because—"

"I understand the economics, Oscar."

"Once a gentleman falls in with them he soon becomes blackmailed for money and favors. They're the most ruthless and hungriest of men. Some might call the danger they present part of their appeal. Being with them is like feasting with panthers."

Constance grunts at this, silencing Wilde a moment. But she tells him to go on.

"One day, Wood told me about a renter named Stephen. He described him as a second Hyacinth, possessed of bewitching eyes. I pressed Wood for more information. What was his last name? Where did he live? How might I find him? Wood taunted me with elusive clues. Rather than panthers, it became a game of fishing. He'd baited the hook and knew I'd bite. But I got tired of his intrigues and began seeking out Stephen for myself. I talked to other renters. They, too, seemed to know who he was. That's how I at last learned about The Red Tiger. I was told Stephen frequented an opium den concealed on the premises."

"Oh, Oscar," she says, with the first and faintest stern edge in her tone. "You've been playing a dark game, haven't you?"

"I've been a stupid fool. I can only apologize to you and hope you'll forgive."

"What's done is done. Tell me what happened?"

"There were many young men inside the den, all sprawled upon the floor. The first Stephen I met was behind a bar. He prepared the opium for me and called it the Breath of the Great Goddess."

"*Indeed?* Was this goddess given a name?"

"No. I took it for poetry."

"It may end up being a line from Dante. Go on."

"I took the drug and lost all sense of time and myself. I lay with the lads on the floor, but if I did anything with them, I'm unaware of it."

"And none of them were the second Stephen?"

"No, but the first Stephen was still there. He told me I was dreaming. What I saw happen made me want to believe that. The men on the floor began to change. They made a terrible transformation. My own bones ache when I recall their contortions."

"What did they become?"

81

"Cats, Constance. Large cats, though their size was nothing compared to the panther I confronted in the labyrinth. And I've had other strange encounters with cats of late. There must be a connection."

"This is invaluable information, Oscar."

Trembling a little, Wilde tells her about the subsequent return to the tavern and the inexplicable name change and the deceptions of the brick.

"Bosie was drunk so I took the opportunity to inspect the bookcase again. It too had changed. The bible was only a book. There was no secret door. That's when I returned to the table and found Bosie with the second Stephen. I became jealous of how close he and Bosie were acting. I stormed out."

"Stephen followed."

"Yes. That's when he asked me about Bosie's brother and his relationship to the Prime Minister. And then there came a sudden deluge of cats. Every cat in existence seemed to flood the streets for a few minutes. Then they vanished, and so did the second Stephen. I looked at the tavern sign and found it changed back to The Red Tiger. That's when I sought comfort with Robbie."

"Sought comfort," she says, sounding distant.

On the cusp of a lie, Wilde stops himself. What would be the point? All has been laid bare and the overdue truth feels like a waterfall blasting away every speck of dirt on his conscience. Why muddy it again so soon?

"Please hold nothing against him, Constance. He is a loyal friend."

"Yes, he is. You share shards of the same soul too, I think."

He smiles. "I never dreamed you'd have such understanding."

Her eyes narrow and his smile fades. Has he misread her? Hurt her? Sensing this, he begins to apologize.

"Don't," she says.

"I only mean to explain—"

"You mean to justify."

*This* is his wife talking. This is a woman who's been wounded.

"Yes," he says, looking away.

She nods, straightening her posture. "Every member of the Golden Dawn must create or adopt a personal motto. You already know mine."

"Qui patitur vincit."

"*Who triumphs who endures.*"

"You should have added it to your wedding vows, considering who you were marrying."

Constance puts her hands over his. "We all have our desires, whatever they are, and only a fraction ever get fulfilled. The rest torment us."

"It's always been worse with me. I have so many thirsts that I only slacken. I take a full-throated drink from the cup of want, and hours later it seems a sip. I am so weak."

"You're stronger than you know."

"Tell me, Constance. Give me hope."

"The things that torment us are also the things that save us. We reach accommodations with ourselves—and each other. We persevere. We didn't marry each other out of romantic love, Oscar."

"Why *did* you marry me?"

"Out of a desire for continuation," she says.

"I don't understand."

"Our sons, Oscar. I could have chosen an ardent lover but that would have been selfish. I wanted children who had the advantages of inherited genius. They'll need such weapons in the world to come. I could have taken a more physical man and given birth to Achilles. But through you I think I've given the world Odysseus twice over. Who could ask for braver or cleverer sons?"

"Where are our boys, Constance?"

"*Safe.*"

Her tone tells him not to question further. He must trust his wife—and he does.

"What course of action will you take now? Approach Bosie's brother? Seek out Rosebery himself?"

"We'll do neither. If this entity feels the need to engage in subterfuge, we must not tip our hand just yet. Besides, if there is a conspiracy, Rosebery and Lord Drumlanrig might be willing players."

"I didn't get that impression from Stephen's questions."

"His questions might have been masking his real intent. The Order will watch for now."

"Can I do anything to help?"

"Yes, Oscar. Go back to living your life and be our inconspicuous eyes and ears."

"I'm not a spy, Constance—and never inconspicuous."

"All *you* have to do is be yourself—and you're quite good at that. Leave the rest to us. But there is one more thing from you I want."

"Name it!"

Constance takes his left hand and places it against her bosom. Wilde watches her remove the scarab ring off his pinkie. She raises it to her eyes, turns it about in the light—and smiles.

# CHAPTER NINETEEN

He enters his home on Tite Street and calls out for anyone. Arthur Fenn's footsteps make a hurrying answer and the butler appears in an unusual huff, his face as red as his hair.

"What's wrong, Arthur?"

"It just feels odd to be a house servant in a house where no one's ever at home. Mrs. Wilde is gone, the children are gone, and then you're out all of the time. Then Lord Douglas comes and tells us all not to come back until the next day. Then we do and *still* there's no one here to look after, and—"

"It is okay, Arthur. Thank you for doing an outstanding job of making our house feel lived in. *Someone* has to do it."

He claps his butler on the shoulder as he moves past him, heading for the stairs. He stops and pivots on the first step.

"Is Lord Douglas here?"

"No, sir."

"Was he here when you arrived?"

"As I said, Mr. Wilde, the house was empty."

"I see. Carry on, then." He climbs up to his bedroom, each step bringing fresh concerns. I shouldn't have left him alone at the tavern, he tells himself. But perhaps Constance will know where he is. After all, Bosie's important to *both* of them now.

Wilde closes the door, takes off his coat and loosens the top two buttons of his shirt. As he does, he notices a splotch like rust on his left sleeve near the bend of his elbow. Then he feels a sudden, sharp wince.

"What the devil," he says, moving to a full-length mirror. There's a rip in the fabric—and his flesh. The surrounding bloodstain isn't fresh but the cut itself isn't deep. He can only imagine this slight wound happened in the labyrinth and he's been too preoccupied to feel the pain.

After a brief knock on the door, Arthur enters with a pot of tea.

"Thank you, but I didn't ask for this," Wilde says.

"I'm sorry, Mr. Wilde. It just seemed you could do with a drink. Tea will calm your nerves."

"Do I seem nervous, Arthur?"

The butler answers by touching Wilde's cut. "That looks like a nasty scratch, sir. Was it a dog?"

"Yes," Wilde says, pulling his arm away. "A most angry one."

Arthur takes up Wilde's coat and examines the tear. "It bit all the way through your sleeve. What manner of dog was it, sir?"

"I couldn't say."

The butler grunts and drapes the coat over one forearm. "Did you get your ring polished, Mr. Wilde?"

"I beg your pardon?"

"Your green ring, sir. Nice as it is, I've never known it to sparkle like that. I was just wondering if you took it to a jeweler."

He looks down and his lips part. The scarab ring's dull green stone glows like an emerald reflecting candlelight.

"Yes," Wilde says after a moment of decision. He slips his left hand into his pocket. "I had it polished. That will be all for now, Arthur. Please take the coat and have the tear sewn shut."

"Should I call a doctor for the bite?"

"I believe I'll be all right."

"Can I at least bring water for you to wash it clean?"

Wilde smiles. "Of course. Thank you for being so diligent, Arthur. You're a jewel as bright as anything on Victoria's crown."

"I'd be content to shine like your ring. Do you know what kind of polish was used? I might want to try it on the silverware."

"I'm afraid I don't."

"Oh," Arthur says, and Wilde now senses him to be loitering.

"What is it?"

"Might I see the ring again, Mr. Wilde? I was so taken by its color."

What harm can there be in that? Wilde thinks. He brings his hand out and finds the light from the gemstone is gone. The ring looks like it always has, though Arthur whistles and makes another comment about the quality of the polish before leaving.

As soon as Wilde's alone again, he holds the scarab ring up to his eyes. He touches the stone and finds it cold and inert.

Constance, he thinks, what have you done?

He knows only that she took the ring away for about twenty minutes before returning to place it back on his pinkie herself.

*"Keep it with you like you always have. It was precious to you before; it is even more so now."*

*"But what did you—"*

*"I cannot and will not explain now. There is a reason to be kept ignorant. Place your trust in me, Oscar."*

*"I've never trusted anyone more."*

Remembering the exchange, he curls his fingers tight into his palm with all the ardor of a priest bringing his hands together in prayer.

PART TWO

# CHAPTER TWENTY

*Wandsworth Prison, July 10, 1895*

Wilde wakes from a shallow sleep and peers through the darkness of his cell until convinced there's no threat. Then he leaves the cot and limps to the window. He casts a stare of longing at the moon's silver purity and dreams of scooping its glow into his palm to cradle close to his chest.

Qui patitur vincit, he thinks, then lowers his head against an involuntary sob. "Constance, how I need you in this hour." He looks back to the moon. "I and the entire world. We endure but do not triumph. How can we have victory without you? Forgive me my despair, Constance. Forgive my failures that sent you to your death."

Tears in his eyes fragment the moonlight. Wilde wipes them away until the moon glows whole and bright again. For a moment, a conviction his wife's face will appear there settles over him and makes his chest full as a billowing sail. When Constance does not appear, however, the sails go dead and all sensation moves into his stomach, where heaviness now sets like an anchor of lead.

Hopelessness is leaden, Wilde tells himself. But lead can be melted down and reshaped and repurposed. The anchor can become a cannon ball. It need only be exposed to flame.

He touches his heart. Here is the furnace.

Gritting his teeth, Wilde whispers a promise to the moon. Though the fate of the Empire—the fate of the world—is at stake, his chest burns for a more personal reason.

Constance must be avenged.

# CHAPTER TWENTY-ONE

*London, April 7, 1894*

At the present, London seems to have little going on to garner a spy's interest.

So perhaps it is best to draw London's interest in the spy.

Just over a week after his encounter with the Golden Dawn, each day filled by the most ordinary events imaginable, Wilde strolls down Fleet Street in a bright blue suit and yellow scarf, a heavy black cane in his right hand. He holds it in a martial position, as if leading a parade, and offers all gawkers an imperious smirk. With the dome of St. Paul's Cathedral in the distance, Wilde walks under the awnings of assorted businesses, chemists and hatters, cobblers and coffin makers. The road to his right bustles with carriages while foot traffic squeezes in and out of their paths. The odor of horse manure stains the air of an otherwise fresh day in early spring. Wilde glances at the sky and then at the Cathedral's dome, blackened with decades of coal dust, and wonders if Paul is also the patron saint of miners.

He halts to look behind him, scanning for conspicuous characters like the young man standing with his hands in his pockets who now turns his face to look in a window. Wilde first noticed this cross-street shadow a few blocks ago, when he did his first sudden stop and turn.

The man revealed his intent by also coming to a reflexive stop amid the teeming crowd before moving on in a loitering way, stopping to look in shop windows like he's doing now.

Under other circumstances this game would arouse Wilde. Who is this man? A renter? A blackmailer? Distance and the general chaos of Fleet Street keep him from getting too clear of a look, but Wilde senses his pursuer is not some drab scoundrel. No, this charming stalker has a mission.

But who assigned it?

He could cross the street and accost the fellow, but the risk seems too great. He might scare the man off. Plus, Fleet Street is a world of eyes and Wilde can only imagine there are other people with separate agendas observing him. It is best to escape all gazes and try to lure the man into some private conference.

Setting off again, tapping his cane on the ground with every step, Wilde makes his way to a pub called Ye Olde Cheshire Cheese. The Rhymer's Club meets here from time to time, a group of poets founded by Yeats. Considering what he now knows about his fellow Irishman's *other* activities, Wilde wonders if the Rhymer's Club, too, has hidden pursuits. But perhaps it is only what it claims to be: a dinner club and a place to share verse. Even occultists must have mundane pursuits from time to time.

Without turning around again, certain the man is watching, he pauses with his right hand on the door and makes a beckoning gesture with the left. Then he enters the crowded pub and works his way forward. There's a single empty table near the back. This pleases him. Such tables work best for clandestine meetings or, failing that, drinking alone.

He takes a seat, anticipation building with each passing minute, only to ebb when the waiting goes one minute too long. Is the man not coming? Did he not see the signal?

Wilde slumps, lowering his head to rub the bridge of his nose. As he does, a barmaid comes over to see if he'd like a pint. Without looking up, he says he would.

"Make that two."

Wilde flinches back at the sound of the other voice. The barmaid steps aside to reveal a man of about 5'7, compact and sturdy. A brawler. He can't be much older than twenty. He's clean-shaven with brown hair parted on the right. His blue eyes show a liveliness, almost distracting Wilde from observing a nose that's been broken more than once. In that instant, Wilde wants to hear the story behind every break. The man's hands have scabs on the knuckles.

"I'd be pleased if you'd join me."

The man sits down.

"I take it you've been following me."

"Not a hard thing to do with the way you dress."

Wilde smiles. "I like to stand out."

"Not always a good trait, sir, if you're in the mood for advice."

"To me not standing out is unthinkable," Wilde says, and then wishes he'd answered with less flippancy. The young man is being serious, and his seriousness complements him like his broken nose.

"May I have your name?"

"It's Charles. But I go by—"

"*Charlie.*"

"How did you reckon that, sir?"

Wilde grins. "You *look* like a Charlie."

The youth flashes an open-mouthed smile, allowing Wilde a glimpse of a missing bicuspid. Again, this *shouldn't* add to his attractiveness but somehow it does.

"My mates in the ring all call me Charlie Knock Down."

"The ring?"

"The boxing ring, sir. But I guess you wouldn't know much about that."

The barmaid returns with their drinks. Charlie has half the contents of his mug downed before Wilde can even raise his cup to his lips.

"A boxer, you say? Are you *not* a detective?"

"No." He drinks deep from the mug again and then inspects it from top to bottom like he thought it'd be larger.

"Were you hired to follow me?"

"No, sir. I was asked."

"By whom?"

Charlie puts down the empty cup and laughs. "His Lordship told me you'd figure it out if I said anything about boxing. But then he said you're a good talker, too, one who sometimes only cares to listen to his own voice. You do talk nice. I'd talk to myself all the time if I had a voice like yours."

Wilde delight sours with realization. "Queensberry sent you."

Bosie's father is famous for his love of boxing. Even its rules bear his name, a fitting tribute for such a brute of a man.

Charlie raises his empty cup to acknowledge the truth, then shakes it to get the barmaid's attention. Wilde observes the girl's wicked little smile as she answers the summons. She doesn't find his broken nose so out of place, either.

"Thank you," he says once he has a full mug again. "Spying is thirsty work."

"How long have you been at it?"

"Today was the fifth time, sir."

"So often? We're better acquainted than I realized. I therefore insist you call me Oscar. It will make following me less tedious in the future."

"That's a funny way of looking at it, but you might be right. After the third time chasing you around London, I did start thinking of you as a kind of companion. You'd stop and I'd say to myself, 'Oh, what's he looking at now?' I wonder if it's shoes."

He laughs. They both do.

"Tell me about the fourth time."

"Last week," Charlie says, draining the glass again. "You made several stops before going to a pub called—"

"The Red Tiger," Wilde says, stiffening.

"You were there a bloody long time—or so I thought."

"What do you mean by that?"

"I waited across the street for more than an hour. Then I went inside and you weren't there. I figured you must have seen me and ducked out a back exit."

"In a manner of speaking," Wilde whispers, more to himself. "Did you talk to anyone in the tavern? Make inquiries?"

"No."

"Do you remember a short man behind the bar? Except he wouldn't have appeared short to any customer because he was walking on crates."

"Crates?"

"Never mind. Charlie, did Queensberry say *why* you were to follow me?"

The young man shakes his head. "His Lordship just told me to watch and if anyone tried to hurt you, I was supposed to—"

"*Hurt* me?" Wilde leans forward, touching Charlie's forearm. There's a lot of firm muscle under the coat sleeve.

"That's right. And if someone tried, I was to do my best to make sure it didn't happen."

"Queensberry sent you to *protect* me? The man's threatened to kill me more times than I can recall."

"That's not anything I know about."

Wilde stares at this earnest, improbable guardian angel in wonder. "Protect me with what, Charlie?"

Charlie smiles, bunches his hands into fists, and says, "Why with these, Oscar."

# CHAPTER TWENTY-TWO

They return to Tite Street, sitting across from each other in the cab of a carriage. Wilde says nothing, preoccupied with questions and confusion. Why would Queensberry, who only months ago threatened to thrash Wilde in public with his cane, be lending him a secret protector?

And what is Charlie protecting him against?

The lad could be lying, but Wilde senses honor and conviction in him. A thousand years ago, he would be decked in armor and riding out to save a village. The ethics of a warrior's code show in his eyes, and truthfulness is part of the creed. He'd rather die than be found false. He speaks with his knuckles, a brutal language that has no word for *lie*.

Wilde catches himself in a flight of fancy, Icarus on wings of desire soaring toward a sun with a crooked nose. He knows his heart is more like a barnacle attached to any pretty, passing hull. He imagines resting besides Charlie in some hotel room, kissing his bruised knuckles before kissing his crooked nose and then, at last, his lips.

He notices Charlie staring at him and they make awkward eye contact. His silence sets him apart from the class of youth who sell their bodies to lonely men. Wilde's never known a renter who didn't talk for hours on end. Maybe it's because they're too afraid of their own thoughts.

"What do you think of me, Charlie?"

Wilde touches his lips like they've betrayed him.

"His Lordship said you'd be this way."

"What way is that?"

"Wanting to fall in love."

The carriage's pace is miserably slow compared to the speed of Wilde's heart. "That's a pretty way of phrasing matters, Charlie."

"Well, it won't do, Oscar. I've been warned. His Lordship says you're a disgusting man."

Charlie laughs like he's just heard the best joke and Wilde blushes.

"I thought you were supposed to protect me from harm."

"I am."

"What you just said wounded me."

Charlie's laugh and smile fades. "I didn't mean to."

"No, I'm sure you didn't."

"Disgusting. What did his Lordship mean by that?"

"What do *you* think he means?"

"Well, you aren't dirty. And you don't smell bad."

Wilde sets his jaw. "For the first time since I've met you, you're coming across as false."

Charlie's cheeks go red almost as fast as the time he takes to make a fist and strike the carriage wall.

"I think," Wilde says, leaning forward, "that you know exactly what Queensberry meant. And you should know I care as much about his opinions as I do about manure in the road."

Charlie leans forward too, their heads almost butting. "The Marquess is a good man. My parents died when I was young, and his Lordship showed me kindness. No one believes me when I say that, but it's true."

"His *Lordship* can't even be kind to his own sons."

"Maybe it's easier to be kind to someone who's not family. There's less at stake."

"You still haven't answered my question. What do you think Queensberry means about my being disgusting?"

"I respect his Lordship's experience, but I think and judge for myself. I'll let you know what I think about you when I've got something to say."

Charlie settles back and looks out the window, drumming his fingers on his kneecaps.

"I apologize," Wilde says, his voice low. "For any offense I've given, and for any I'll no doubt give in the future."

"You sure are a funny one."

"Don't forget *disgusting.*"

Charlie smiles. "I'll make sure to remember, Oscar."

The carriage slows. The driver announces Wilde's Tite Street address.

"Will you come inside with me?"

"No, Oscar, I best not. I don't reckon you'll need much protection in the safety of your house."

"In my experience as a married man, my house is where I'm least safe."

"You're married?"

"Does that surprise you?"

"I guess it does now that I think about it. His Lordship didn't mention it, and I've never seen you out with a woman."

"Constance is away at the moment, but I shall have to invite you over for tea when she returns. She will enjoy your company very much."

"I'd like that," Charlie says, the youthful earnestness returning to his tone.

They exchange glances before Wilde gets out and addresses the coachman, handing him money. "Deliver this young man to wherever he wishes to go. Bill me if this amount doesn't cover it."

He watches the carriage depart. Charlie sticks his head out the window and waves. How Wilde wishes he could be inside the lad's head just now, eavesdropping on his thoughts.

Never in his life has he wanted to be held so highly in anyone's esteem.

# CHAPTER TWENTY-THREE

A noise from upstairs draws Wilde's attention just as he closes the front door.

"Oscar, is that you?"

He steps forward, gaze already climbing the staircase. "Bosie? Where have you been?"

"I'll explain everything! Come see what I have to show you."

Oscar reaches the fourth step when he notices the glow of his scarab ring. The gemstone hasn't shown any unusual properties since the first time when he was speaking with Arthur. Just now it has the brightness of emerald facets in sunlight.

"Well, come on, Oscar. What are you waiting for?"

Bosie's voice comes from Wilde's bedroom.

The ring's glow begins to dim. The effect is like water draining out of a basin.

Then it goes dull.

"Oscar!"

He taps the ring, shaking his head at the mystery of the light's meaning. Then he looks up the staircase and grins, anticipating Bosie's kiss. "Coming!"

Bosie appears at the top when Wilde arrives. He wears only an unbuttoned, crisp white shirt. Its hem falls around the top of his creamy thighs, framing his torso and his aroused state in the most inviting way.

"Dear boy," Wilde says, pulling Bosie's face to his chest. "How long have you been here?"

"Too long."

"I'm sorry I've been out."

"Had you stayed out any longer, I might have seduced your butler. He's quite interesting."

"Arthur?" Wilde pivots, looking toward the landing. "Is he here?"

"You needn't worry, Oscar. He knows. Everyone does."

Wilde pushes Bosie away, finding a smug expression on his face. "What are you talking about?"

"An end to secrets."

"That would be the ruin of us both, and you know it."

"But what if there were a world where our love wasn't scorned and we didn't have to hide it? Wouldn't that be better?"

"Of course it would."

"Wouldn't it be something worth embracing?"

Before Wilde can answer, Bosie kisses him on the mouth, with a passion not felt since the early days of their romance. But even those first kisses weren't as frenzied as those they exchange now. Their lust carries them away from the staircase to the bedroom door.

"I haven't seen you since the tavern," Bosie says, pulling on Wilde's shirt. "I take it you forgot about me?"

"Dear boy . . . I could never . . . you *are* my delight in this world."

Bosie pulls back. "Call for the butler."

"*What?*"

"Arthur. Call for him. You've got a big enough bed. Why waste space?"

"Bosie, have you lost your mind?"

"He's in love with you, Oscar."

"You *have* lost your mind."

"I saw the way he pouted when I dismissed him. Servants don't behave like that."

Bosie goes to the railing and shouts Arthur's name. Wilde seizes him and begs him to be quiet.

"You know the best way to shut me up."

Wilde wraps his arms around Bosie and pulls him into the bedroom, kicking the door shut behind him and throwing his petulant lover onto the bed.

"What in hell has come over you? I've never seen you like this even in your most childish moods!"

Bosie crouches on all fours, his hands clawing into the bedclothes. A lascivious, cunning expression moves across his beautiful face like a sharp knife, and he rubs his lips.

"I'm your delight in this world. Is that what you just said, Oscar?"

"Yes."

"But weren't you just in love with another pretty face?"

"What are you talking about?"

"In the *carriage,* Oscar. Your handsome little warrior."

Wilde gapes at him. "Did your father tell you about Charlie? Did you know he's been following me?"

Bosie's blue eyes have a hard sparkle about them. He leaves the bed and grabs Wilde by his right wrist, squeezing hard enough to make him wince.

"You're hurting me!"

"Yes, Oscar," he says, standing so close now their lips almost touch. "I *am* hurting you."

His grip tightens. Wilde tries to jerk himself free, but the force only increases. His fingers are turning purple.

"*Hurting* you, Oscar. So to the point. Real pain doesn't have any time for fancy words. Where are your pretty phrases now? How about: 'Oh Bosie, how you *wound* me!'"

Wilde cries out at a new flash of pain. His knees buckle. He shouts for Arthur, shouts for anyone. Bosie responds with a growl—a hiss. Looking up at his distorted face, Wilde sees sharp, inhuman teeth in Bosie's mouth. A broad, flat tongue lashes Wilde's face, its rough texture reviving terrifying memories of the panther in the labyrinth.

"Don't worry. I'm not going to kill you," Bosie says, though all pretense of an imitation ends. Wilde hears Stephen talking, the Stephen who prepared his opium. "We have unfinished business, Mr. Wilde. The Great Goddess would like a word with you."

Wilde calls for help a final time and green light explodes from his scarab ring. It submerges the room like a tsunami wave that crashes in the center of Bosie's chest. The impersonator is flung to the floor kicking and howling as tendrils of light lash his body.

"Goddess, protect me!"

Wilde stares at the ring in awe as green energy pulses from it with a fury he feels in his chest. It rips away all traces of Bosie, incinerating his clothes and false flesh, burning away the golden hair like a cheap wig. Beneath it all is a creature with ashen skin, hairless, its eyes yellow even under the ring's blazing light. Its slit black pupils fix him with a stare of unmitigated hate as it hisses again from its open mouth. Wilde steps forward, the ring stretched out in front of him, and the crawls and squeezes itself under the dark recess of the bed frame.

"Who are you? What do you want from me?"

A bitter laugh answers, followed by another hiss. This one is less strong, however, and more like an asthmatic wheeze.

Might the creature be wounded?

Swallowing, desperate for help, Wilde pivots toward the open door and hollers for Arthur.

The laugh under the bed changes and becomes a recognizable, nervous chuckle. Wilde looks back to the bed as Arthur's voice comes from beneath it.

*"I had your coat mended, sir. Not a bad tear. Could have been so much worse."*

"This cannot be."

Now Bosie's voice says, "Come join us, Oscar. There's room under here for another. The three of us will have a splendid time."

A frantic voice calls Wilde's name from outside the room. Charlie appears in the doorway, holding Wilde's cane. The boxer squints at Wilde's ring.

They exchange no words. Wilde nods toward the bed and Charlie comes to stand beside him, dropping the cane in favor of making fists. Together they watch a shape emerges from underneath the frame. Wilde sees Arthur's head snaking out on a hideously long and pliant neck. Only its eyes, squeezed shut against the green light of the ring, belie the strength of the creature's defiance.

"Who are you?" Wilde says.

*"One of many."*

"Are you Bosie or Arthur?"

*"Both and neither."*

The creature's hands appear, clawed with yellow nails filed to points.

"Get behind me, Oscar," Charlie says, jumping in front of him, fists raised.

Laughter mocks his bravery.

*"Little warrior, do you wish to spar with me?"*

Without waiting for an answer, the creature lunges, seething, claws swiping. Charlie dives, grabbing Wilde and pulling him down and out of the way just as those jaundiced nails slice through the place where they stood. Wilde rolls onto his back and sees Charlie already on his feet, circling his opponent with taunting footwork, offering his chin. The creature has the lightning reflexes of a cat. But Charlie's just as quick. He moves his head, dodging another swipe that could have ripped his face open. The creature's momentum carries it past him, and Charlie delivers a hail of blows into the base of its spine..

"All muscle," he says, grinning. "You're like pounding a slab of meat. That's all you'll be when I'm done with you."

Despite Charlie's inspiring bravado, Wilde sees his champion's true advantage is the scarab ring's green light. It keeps the creature's eyelids shut, forcing it to fight blind. How long can this advantage last? Might the ring choose to go dark at any moment? These thoughts go through Wilde's head in an instant as gets up, retrieving his sturdy cane along the way.

Charlie continues to weave and punch. But he's slowed just a bit. Wilde wonders if he even realizes. Charlie still shows a manic smile, reflecting a dominant, predatory mindset. Youth never realizes when it's getting fatigued.

Then it happens. Charlie ducks another swipe from the creature's left hand, but as he turns the claws of the right hand slash across his back. He shrieks and crumples, trying to kick himself along the floor as the creature gloats over him.

*"You have made me very hungry, little warrior. Your blood smells far more delicious than your sweat."*

Wilde takes the cane in both hands and bashes it against the creature's neck. The thick wood snaps, leaving Wilde holding a sharp splinter the length of a stiletto. The light from the ring begins to recede—or so it seems for one horrific moment. Not waning, the light instead pulls back to envelope the fragment, concentrating its strength into a green suffusion that seems to have its own intent and purpose. Wilde feels the shard vibrating, urging him forward like metal responding to a magnet. Surrendering, he lunges just as the creature opens its eyes at last and drives the sharp tip deep into the beast's side.

Stricken, it howls and bashes Wilde to the floor as purple fluid seeps from the wound. Wilde drapes himself over Charlie, determined to protect him. But the creature's in no mood for immediate revenge. It staggers to the door and then into the hallway. Moments later Wilde hears a heavy thud and guesses the beast chose to jump to the floor rather than take the stairs.

The front door opens with a sharp bang—

And the light from his scarab ring goes out.

# CHAPTER TWENTY-FOUR

Wilde helps Charlie down the steps, charmed by his breathless enthusiasm and determination to chase the creature. When that proves impossible, he insists on going room to room to ensure the home's safety.

They reach the kitchen when Charlie's legs buckle. Wilde helps him all the way to his study, where he puts the lad in his favorite armchair.

"I should get a doctor," he says, easing Charlie's shirt up. There's a four-inch cut across his pale, muscular back.

"To hell with that. I don't even feel pain."

"Forgive me, but you don't sound convincing."

Charlie laughs. "I know myself and I know cuts, Oscar. This one won't kill me. It'll leave a scar, though. I collect those like autographs."

Frowning, Wilde fetches a towel and a basin of water. Soaking the fabric, he eases it against the boxer's skin, working around the cut, dabbing at the blood. He wrings the towel, wets it again, and reapplies, pained whenever Charlie winces, scolding himself for doing anything to increase his discomfort. Charlie stares straight ahead in rigid silence.

"I can only say your skin should be autographed with kisses—not cuts."

"Is that what you say to his Lordship's son?"

Wilde pauses with the towel over the wound. He looks at the floor, considering. "I say different things to different people. Sometimes I am too flippant. I'm sure you think so."

"Why?"

"Because you're very serious. And nothing annoys the very serious like the very glib."

"Aren't you ever serious, Oscar?"

"I'm being serious now. Flippancy in humor is a fine thing; flippancy in love is hurtful. I fear I've been hurtful without realizing it far too many times. But I promise you right now I speak the truth, even if it won't win me your approbation."

"My what?"

"Your approval."

Charlie snorts laughter. "You could have just said so in the first place."

"You're right, now that I think of it. They mean the same thing, and the first five letters of both words are identical. One should be as economical as possible with letters. There are only twenty-six of them, after all."

Charlie giggles, a sound as delightful and unexpected to Wilde as hearing a mute bird sing. Wilde rinses the towel again. The blood has staunched a fair amount, and despite himself he lets his gaze roam over the young man's back. He counts several *autographs* of various lengths and severity. Before he's aware of it, he's traced one with his index finger, provoking a squirm in Charlie.

"Enough of that, Mr. Wilde."

"Are we back to formality?"

"We are if you start getting *that* informal."

"I apologize," Wilde says. "I forgot myself in . . . admiration."

Charlie turns his face to him, and the blush in his cheeks proves another genuine surprise. "There's nothing to admire about me, Oscar."

"Dear boy, I'd have trouble finding anything about you *not* to admire. There's more courage in your little finger than I have in my whole body."

"Well, it seems to me like there's more to the ring on your little finger than anything I ever saw. When I realized you'd left the cane behind, I made the driver stop and I got out and ran back to your house with it. Then I heard the sounds coming from upstairs and knew I had to rush to your defense. But I didn't do much except get myself sliced."

"You saved my life, Charlie, and I shall never forget that."

"The ring did more good than me. What *is* it, Oscar? Something to do with electricity?"

"I'm afraid I can't explain," Wilde says. "Any more than I can explain the creature that attacked me."

"There's plenty I need to tell his Lordship, but I don't think he'll believe me. Monsters and glowing rings . . . it sounds like something out of church, and his Lordship doesn't believe in God."

Charlie gets up despite Wilde's urging.

"You're bleeding hasn't stopped."

"Oh, I've bled longer from a bout with tougher blokes than whatever-it-was. Try going ten rounds against a bruiser from Northampton who weighs 20 stone! Never you worry, Oscar. I heal fast. But I'm worried about you, ring or no. I can't report to his Lordship and leave you here alone. If the whatever-it-was comes back and that ring *doesn't* drive it off for some reason, you'll be defenseless. So, I'm asking you to come with me."

"Charlie, regardless of the reasons he sent you to protect me, I can't conceive of Queensberry having any warm feelings for me. He'd not want me showing up on his doorstep. If he wants me safe, it's because it benefits him somehow—nothing more."

"Then trust me to protect you from his Lordship as well."

He extends his right hand and Wilde stares at it.

"How remarkable."

"What?"

"That your hand, so ferocious when it's closed in a fist, should open up into the most wonderful—"

"Please don't say anything about flowers or petals, Oscar."

Wilde smiles. "I'll restrain myself with the deepest of regrets."

He takes Charlie's hand.

# CHAPTER TWENTY-FIVE

It's many hours from London to Queensberry's seat at Kinmount House in Dumfries, and Wilde falls asleep despite the frantic pace of the carriage. He soon dreams, though the quality of the dream feels like being awake. He finds himself sitting on a simple wooden chair in a room whose walls are lost to darkness. The chair hurts his back and he starts to stand up just as Constance says his name.

She steps out of the dark periphery, radiant in a green evening dress dotted with red clovers. She holds out a gloved hand to him, which he seizes and kisses like some ardent lover, some better husband. He even presses her fingers against his right cheek and fights back a burst of tears.

"If only you weren't a dream. I have so much to tell you, and even more questions."

"I'm not a dream, Oscar, and neither are you. Nor is this wholly reality."

"I don't understand."

"We're communicating through the space of a dream."

"Like the message you sent telling Mr. Mathers to find me at Robbie's?"

"Yes. Think of it as a bubble where our minds converge. Such bubbles can exist between anyone, even strangers."

"Are they always so undetailed?"

"Details depend up the intimacy and familiarity of the two minds."

Wilde frowns, ashamed of the barren environment. "We really don't know each other very well, do we? I'm sorry, Constance. I may have given you the children you desired, but you must be so unsatisfied with me as a husband."

"Satisfaction wears many guises."

"That sounds like something I might say."

"Rest assured it is something you *will* say."

"What?"

Constance crouches down beside him. "There are too many difficulties to explain. All I can say is that here, right now, we're in a mutual present. But that present has nothing to do with state of our physical bodies. I've come to you from a place in the future. Your physical present, wherever that may be—"

"I'm in a carriage. Constance, the most extraordinary thing has happened. I—"

She holds up a hand to make him stop. "I know."

"You've seen it in some crystal ball, I suppose?"

"No, I've heard it all from you."

"But how? Where are you right now, Constance? What's happening?"

"My poor Oscar," she says, touching his shoulder. "You'll have to wait to discover the answer to your questions."

"But how will I know when I reach it? Is it days ahead? Weeks?"

"You'll know by this dress. And you mustn't say anything to me about our dream encounter when that time comes. Do nothing that might change my course of action."

"Constance, what's wrong? Are you okay?"

"Only time will tell."

He nods, feeling unsatisfied. It seems like Constance is about to drift back into the dark and he grabs her arm. "My scarab ring. Tell me what you've done to it."

"I only attempted to unlock a power I suspected might be there. I can say no more."

"It's already saved my life. I must know how it works."

"*No.* I can only ask you to believe me. What some call *magic* has its own logic and laws, alien to everything, defiant of reason. *Discovery* is its essence. There can be no shortcuts, no quick knowledge. Its ways are experiential and revelatory."

"But the need is great!"

"The rules don't change according to need or context."

She steps back, beginning to fade. Wilde jumps out of the chair as his fingers pass through her like they would a trickle of water.

"What's happening? Is one of us waking?"

Her expression becomes sorrowful. This provokes him to reach for her again. Her body has even less substance than before.

"Constance, when will I see you in person? Can't you at least tell me that? Give me some crumb from the future so I'll have hope."

Her body shimmers, seeping into the encompassing dark.

"*Oscar . . .*"

"Yes!"

He strains to hear her voice.

"*Should I fall—should I die—*"

"Should you *die?* Wait. Constance, stay with me!"

# CHAPTER TWENTY-SIX

He jolts awake to find Charlie bent down and staring at the scarab ring. Wilde jerks his left hand away by reflex.

"Sorry, Oscar," Charlie says, sounding sheepish and guilty. "I wasn't trying to pinch it or anything."

Wilde looks at the ring as if it might be damaged. It takes him a moment to come to his senses. "Of course, dear boy. Such a notion never entered my mind."

"You must have sensed me staring at it. Or maybe the ring did."

"I don't think it's alive, Charlie."

"After what I saw I wouldn't put anything past it. That's why I was taking a closer peep. I was hoping to see if there was anything else about the ring that might interest his Lordship."

Wilde nods, and Charlie's sudden huff surprises him.

"You're mad at me."

"Dear boy, what on Earth gives you such a notion?"

"The way you took your hand away."

"I was having a dream and I was startled. Nothing more."

"Still, a gentleman would have waited until you were awake to ask, and that's what I want to be."

"A gentleman? Who says you're not?"

"Rough like I am?"

Charlie punctuates his question with a bitter laugh that makes

Wilde sit forward.

"Don't think I judge you based on accent or dress or grammar. These are unimportant."

"Compared to what? A pretty face? You like mine, I reckon. But that doesn't make me a gentleman."

"You've got a quick mind, almost as fast as the punches you threw in my defense. You're honest and forthright and brave. I'd rather have you at my side than the Queen or the Prince of Wales. There are plenty in this world who call themselves nobility; but you outclass them all in nobleness."

The carriage's dim interior makes it hard to confirm, but Wilde detects a blush on Charlie's cheeks. He's right, of course, Wilde tells himself. He touches the scarab ring, thinking of all the jewelry and trinkets he's given to so many young men just because their faces entranced him. And how many renters have received engraved silver cigarette cases from him? A hundred? Wilde purses his lips as he considers and stares into the darkness.

"Oscar."

He looks back to Charlie. "Yes?"

"I wanted you to know that no one has ever said what you just said to me. About being noble."

"I meant every word."

"I—I know. His Lordship says I might become a gentleman if I try hard enough."

"Queensberry hasn't a clue what a gentleman is."

Wilde knows the quip is a mistake even as he says it. Charlie sounds pained when he speaks. "I wish you wouldn't say such things about his Lordship. I can't help it if the two of you don't see eye to eye. But to me he's a *good* man, the best of all men. And whether you believe it or not, he *did* send me along to keep you safe. He's the only reason we're even having this conversation. I just think you should be more respectful to . . . both of us."

Wilde swallows, allowing the silence to linger a moment.

"You're right, Charlie," he says in a soft voice. "I was rude in my prejudice toward a man you respect so much. There's no doubt I've experienced only a small part of what I know to be a *remarkable* personality. I'll offer my apologies again and again until you accept it."

"Of course I accept it, Oscar!"

"But I must reiterate one disagreement with him. You already *are* a gentleman in every way that should count. Your past keeps you from thinking otherwise. You've been bitten too many times and at too young an age by the viper of this world's ugly realities."

"If you mean I've always been fighting, then you're right. I've always had to scrap to keep what's mine. That's what I was doing when his Lordship first saw me. I wasn't but ten and going up against a boy five years older than me. I must have looked like a dog snarling at a bunch of wolves. I saw his coach stop and his head peer out, a grin on his face as he watched us brawl."

Wilde knows the grin well. Queensberry flashes it whenever some nascent human misery amuses him.

"I'd stolen half a loaf of bread and meant to keep it for myself. The other boys decided to make it theirs. You can't blame me for fighting back."

"Of course, dear boy. Ten years old, you say? How old are you now?"

"Twenty-two."

Wilde looks out at the darkness of the window, frowning.

"I'll turn forty this year. Ten years ago, perhaps on the very day you were fighting for bread, I was preparing for marriage. I thought I was a man with keen insight into everything, who observed every detail. How blind I was. Perhaps I too rode by you in a carriage while you were fighting to survive, and unlike Queensberry I did not stop. If I had, you might have been rescued and mentored by me rather than him."

"Probably better that you didn't, then, Oscar," Charlie says with a laugh. "I don't think I'd have become much of a boxer under your watch."

"You'd be a fighter no matter what. But perhaps I could have taught you the power of the pen and made a writer out of you."

Charlie laughs even harder. "Me, writing poems and plays? Do you think I could have?"

"Oh yes," Wilde says, patting him on the leg. "But the world of the theater is a much rougher arena than the boxing ring."

The young man's eyebrows lift in amusement. "Is that so, Oscar?"

"I assure you it's true. Drama critics, you see, prefer to use knives."

# CHAPTER TWENTY-SEVEN

They arrive at Kinmount House just after dawn, finding Queensberry's estate shrouded in dissipating fog and the landscape glazed with chilly morning dew. The sunrise is just for show at this early hour and Wilde shivers, stretching his right hand toward the sky as if to pull the warmth closer. Charlie moves past him, going under the porte-cochere to the imposing, ancient front door. He calls for Wilde to follow and turns in expectation. Wilde doesn't move.

"Why are you standing there?"

"I think discretion is best, Charlie."

"You'd rather stay outside in the cold?"

"It is getting warmer all the time. I will tour the grounds while you and Queensberry speak."

Charlie shrugs but makes no further pleading. He pounds on the door four times and it opens half a minute later.

Wilde walks east, his mood souring now that he lacks the young man's company. His thoughts turn back to his dream meeting with Constance and her final words to him. *Should I fall—should I die.* The memory is kerosene for the flame of his worry. Without realizing it, he balls his left hand into a fist and raises the scarab ring to his lips. "Constance, are you okay? I'm here for you no matter the cost." He does not know what compels him to speak to the gemstone as if she can hear through it. The ring itself gives no reaction.

Turning in misery, Wilde gazes on the sheer scope of Kinmount House. It resembles a castle ready for a siege. The heavy stone façade looks like it could withstand all manner of artillery, and Wilde can imagine hundreds of people manning its windows and battlements. Queensberry is just the sort of man to enjoy a desperate last stand against—anything.

Wilde walks faster, past sentinel shrubbery three times his height, some still barren but most rediscovering their leaves with the promise of spring. A tawny cat springs out from one of the bushes, giving him a start. The cat darts around his feet twice and then springs back into a low crouch, its gaze fixed on him, meowing. Wilde checks a stab of dread by looking at his ring. The green stone does not glow. Wouldn't it, he thinks, in the face of a threat?

He resumes his walk, looking over his shoulder after a few steps.

The cat follows him.

Wilde laughs despite himself, refusing to believe the sight of a housecat can quicken his pulse. But as the cat breaks into a pursuing trot, Wilde turns to run. His shoes slip on the wet grass, and he tumbles into the cold, prickly branches of a shrub. The shock of the wet chill on his skin makes him wallow and flail, almost crawling his way free. He gasps, looking everywhere for the cat, expecting its claws on his face at any moment. He stands there, the noise of his panting the only sound he hears. Even the morning birds withhold their songs, perhaps in equal wariness of stalking felines.

"What the hell is wrong with you, man?"

The gruff, condescending tone makes him pivot. A living thunderstorm approaches and seems ready to bowl Wilde over before stopping short. The Marquess of Queensberry crosses his arm at the chest.

"Wilde."

He's never associated his own name with ugliness, but Queensberry has a voice suited for reading obituaries aloud on winter nights. There's harsh bramble in his sentences, each syllable a barren branch rasping against windowpanes. It's Bosie's voice when he's at his meanest, minus the charming pout and insolence of a beautiful face. Queensberry's single expression is a scowl, a nasty curve of his lips and narrowing of his eyes, all happening between thick, sandwiching mutton chop sideburns streaked black and gray.

"Well speak up, man," Queensberry says. "What's the matter with you?"

"I slipped and fell."

"Clumsy."

"There was a cat."

"A cat?"

"It—chased me."

Queensberry laughs. "Of course a man with your affliction is terrified of pussies."

Straightening, his pulse no less rapid, Wilde squares his back. "I've had more than my fair share of cats as of late. If you knew what I knew then—"

"Charles has blabbered his fantastic tale to me. So disappointing."

"Why disappointing?"

Queensberry circles Wilde without making eye contact. As he talks, he looks like he's arguing with himself.

"I should have sent an older man, someone not inclined to submit to your flights of fancy."

"I've known Charlie for only a short time, but I can tell you the young man *submits* to nothing."

"*Charlie*, is it?" The muscles along Queensberry's jaws flex. "So, you've gotten to him as well. Seduced him."

"I did not—"

"Maybe not like you did to my son, with your putrid hands and mouth. But Charles is still young enough to fall under the spell of all the rot you talk."

"I do not know what Charlie has told you. Whatever it was, he must have spoken very fast, for a lot has happened. No doubt you cut him off on every sentence. But I vouch every word he said is true. I'll also vouch for his integrity, his honesty, and above all his bravery. He saved my life from something almost as monstrous as you."

Queensberry steps right up to Wilde's face. Wilde stares down at him. This is as close as they've ever been to each other, and for all the man's vulgar cruelty, Wilde has to admit his eyes show decisiveness.

As the silence of their encounter lengthens, Wilde knows he should not speak first. The silence is a test of mettle. But he finds he cannot help himself.

"Where is Charlie now?"

"I put him by the fire. He was cold."

"*You* put him there?"

"Why wouldn't I?"

"It just seems almost kind of you."

"I'm kind to those who merit it."

"What about your own sons?"

"I have but one."

Wilde's eyes narrow. "Charlie?"

Queensberry moves back, his savage grin engraved on his wooden face. "Not biological, perhaps, but in *spirit*. My own seed blights me. Francis forsakes his allegiance to me to serve that snob queer Roseberry. Percy follows his older brother's lead. Then there's Bosie. I wash my hands of all three. I can never forgive them! I'm their father! Their father and—"

Queensberry makes his right hand into a fist and appears to swing it at Wilde. As Wilde starts to dodge, however, Queensberry's legs tremble and he slumps. Wilde finds himself catching the Marquess and holding him as this raging bulldog of a man dissolves into a prolonged, anguished wail. "Damn you, Wilde," he says, coughing and choking out the words as his body shakes and his failing legs gives even more of himself into Wilde's arms.

"You filthy bastard. You're the nightmare every father has when he realizes the devil needs only seconds to undo years of trying to raise a son right."

Queensberry's body convulses. He begins battering Wilde's back with erratic, ineffectual blows. Wilde shoves him away and the Marquess drops to all fours, head bowed.

"My sons . . . all damn three of them . . ."

Wilde tries to wipe any scent of Queensberry off his clothes. "You have *fine* boys who've grown into fine men. It's your fault alone if you can't accept that reality."

"I'll kill you before this is done, Wilde. You're a monster."

"Oscar?"

Both men look to their left and see Charlie approaching, walking at first and now running. Wilde can only imagine how strange this scene must look. Wouldn't Charlie interpret it as combat, and wouldn't appearances make it seem like Wilde has beaten *his Lordship* into submission?

Queensberry is fast in getting to his feet before Charlie arrives.

"Your Lordship—"

"Wilde was just confirming your story. I have questions."

Queensberry heads for the house. Wilde notices how he keeps his face averted, his posture bent forward, charging ahead as Charlie tries to keep pace. Such a proud, hard man. But as he stops to brush a last few beads of dew from his coat, Wilde realizes the droplets are warm. These are Queensberry's tears, the hot desperation of a father's worry.

You were right, Constance, he tells himself as he rubs his fingertips together. The essence of magic is discovery, and I have discovered what I thought to be impossible. It seems water can come to *every* desert.

# CHAPTER TWENTY-EIGHT

Charlie repeats his tale by the hearth as Queensberry jabs at the logs with a poker. Wilde observes he makes more aggressive stabs whenever some detail strikes him as too ridiculous to believe. Perhaps this is why Charlie makes one glaring omission in his retelling. There's no mention of the scarab ring or its peculiar power. Wilde notes the absence even as he twists the ring on his finger and suppresses a conspiratorial smile, glad he and Charlie have a secret between them.

"And then this monstrosity ran away?"

"It did, your Lordship. We gave chase but it was too fast. We returned and Mr. Wilde saw to my wounds."

Queensberry throws the poker down on the stone hearth and orders Charlie to lift his shirt. He stands there inspecting the bandage and the gouge beneath.

"This does look like it was made by an animal. A large one."

"Every word of our valiant friend is accurate," Wilde says. "I have no explanation for what happened, and nothing else to add except I should be dead without Charlie's courageous defense. You have trained a most remarkable warrior."

Wilde senses such compliments would give the Marquess immense pleasure if spoken by any other man.

"He did his duty," Queensberry says, pulling Charlie's shirt down.

He turns back to stare into the fire while Wilde and Charlie watch him, exchanging cautious glances.

"If I may ask, why did you send Charlie to watch over me? Our history suggests little good will."

The Marquess snorts laughter. "*Good will.*"

"Is there a more appropriate description?"

"A lot of rumors have reached me here, Wilde. Some are about you and Bosie. Some are about Rosebery and Francis. Rumors that you and our new Prime Minister are birds of the same filthy feather, both making nests with my sons. But there's another rumor that bests them all. Whispers of conspiracy."

Wilde leans forward. "What sort of conspiracy?"

"To have that answer at this point I'd need to be one of the conspirators. But the whispers say the four of you are a threat to the entire government. No doubt because of your proclivities."

"So now my *proclivities* are a threat to the entire British empire?"

"Strong walls are meaningless if there's decay from the center. Moral decay is no different."

"My dear Marquess, my only power is in my pen. When it comes to toppling governments, I'm afraid sonnets and plays have little influence."

"Flippant to the end—is that your motto?"

"I have no motto. I don't even have a goal other than to be in love every minute of the day. A revolutionary aim, perhaps, but not the aim of a revolutionist."

He glances at Charlie, who seems more youthful and boyish than ever before. It's in the way that he listens without speaking, like a child absorbing the words of adults talking about a world he doesn't comprehend. And it's in his posture, how he sits with his magnificent hands tucked under his thighs, pensive, eager.

"Last month, a Frenchmen named Bourdin tried to bomb the Royal Observatory. He had well-known ties to Club Autonomie—a bunch of anarchists."

Wilde stirs with realization. "You would link Bosie and myself to such a group?"

"You belong to the Fabian Society, don't you? Never mind the answer—I know you do."

"Very well," Wilde says.

"Do you deny the Fabians are in league with the world's anarchists?"

"I most certainly do. We are a peaceful group that seeks gradual social change."

"What peaceful group selects a wolf in sheep's clothing for its coat of arms?"

Wilde shakes his head. "It is a tongue-in-cheek jest, sir."

Queensberry waves away this explanation. "There's also the matter of what you wrote in *The Soul of Man Under Socialism*."

"I am surprised if you've read it—or understood it."

"Keep underestimating me, Wilde. As Charles will tell you, a boxer watches his opponent's footwork even if his attention seems elsewhere. I know the ways you shift. Everything about you is a façade and fakery. Look at this deceiver closely, Charles. Oscar Wilde: posing anarchist and posing Sodomite."

"I'll hear no more of this!" Wilde shouts, coming to his feet. Charlie, perhaps surprised by the sudden burst of energy and anger, stands too.

Queensberry appears unfazed. "You're good at drama, Wilde, I'll give you that. You and Bosie share the trait. That's my greatest fear."

"Then your greatest fear is that an impromptu dress rehearsal may break out in any minute."

"My fear is that the likes of Bourdin are the dress rehearsal for a play that needs a much larger stage."

Wilde narrows his eyes. "Nothing you've said so far suggests a fierce desire to protect me. Since I believe Charlie incapable of lying, I must conclude you've lied to *him*."

Frown lines grow deep on Queensberry's face. Wilde sees him and Charlie exchange a glance, and for once Queensberry seems unable to hold a stare. The Marquess offers a sarcastic laugh and turns back to the fire.

"You didn't send Charlie to protect me. You wanted him to be a spy, except he didn't know he was spying. His sense of honor wouldn't permit such a thing, I imagine, despite his loyalty to you."

Charlie's voice quavers when he speaks. "Your Lordship?"

"Oh, it's as I told you, Charles. Wilde speaks a lot of rot."

Wilde laughs at him. "Queensberry, you have no idea what's going on. How confused you must be. You hear rumors of a conspiracy and connect it to mundane political movements. You send Charlie to spy on me because you trust him more than any of your hounding detectives. As paranoid as you are, you no doubt consider any hired detective or policeman to be potential conspirators as well. Anarchists are everywhere, is that it? But you trust Charlie. You just had to deceive him into being your eyes. The appalling thing is you may be more right than you realize."

Queensberry straightens but refuses to turn from the fireplace. "What do you mean by that?"

"I wish I could say. But your son Francis and Prime Minister Rosebery may be involved."

"If Francis is involved in anything it is only because Rosebery has

130

corrupted him the way you corrupted Bosie."

"I have corrupted no one, sir. If anything, my company ameliorates the horrible consequences of a childhood dominated by—"

Queensberry pivots on him, ugly and seething. "Leave! Your voice has grated on my last nerve. But know that I and others will be watching. We'll counter every scheme of yours until the nation's eyes are open to the snakes in its midst."

"I should be happy to leave. I had no wish to come in the first place. I'll leave you to this cold, expansive mausoleum. I only ask that Charlie be allowed to come with me."

He looks at Charlie, who seems to be holding his breath.

"Take him. You've already won his heart."

"But your Lordship—"

"Another son of mine under your spell."

"I'm not under his spell, your Lordship. I saw what I saw. I fought what I fought, and I've got the wound to show for it. Begging your pardon, but I don't understand how you can dismiss it. There's *something* at work, sir, and it has to be challenged."

Queensberry waves him away and stalks out of the room. Charlie calls after him to no avail and stands there, hands hanging at his side, head bowed. A tremble shakes his shoulders.

"I know this is a difficult moment, dear boy," Wilde says, whispering. "You and I know the truth. The threat we face is not a mob of bomb-throwing anarchists. We have done combat with the true enemy, a foe we know to have *many* faces."

"Yes."

"If you'll continue to protect me and stand by my side, I should be most grateful."

After a moment, Charlie nods and holds out his hand. Wilde takes it. Fellowship was never more charming.

# CHAPTER TWENTY-NINE

"I want you to know that I understand how difficult your decision must be."

Charlie, downcast in the carriage, shrugs. "He thinks I've forsaken him for you."

"Queensberry can be a stubborn and suspicious man, but he will not long deny the depth of your devotion to him. It is often the case that just as we summit the peak of loyalty, others believe we've fallen into traitorous depths. But we know where we stand in our hearts. I am glad to have you with me, Charlie. I should be petrified without your company."

The boxer looks up, offering a shy smile. "Petrified?"

"Is the word unfamiliar to you?"

"Like half of what you say."

"It means terror. It means many other things, too, depending upon who you ask."

"I think a word should mean one thing all the time, no matter who does the speaking. That way no one gets confused."

Wilde smiles at this. "But that would be stripping the magic out of language, Charlie. To the poet, petrification is an emotional state; a predicament of mind and soul that may last minutes—or a lifetime. Ask a scientist, and you'll get a less cryptic notion with a focus on geology and chemistry and unimaginable lengths of time. It—"

Wilde sits back, considering.

"What, Oscar?"

"Maybe it's time we *did* ask a scientist."

Charlie shakes his head and laughs.

"You disagree with me?"

"It's not that, Oscar. I just wonder what it's like to know people like you do. You want to ask a scientist, something; well, you just happen to know a scientist, don't you?"

"Meeting people is easier than you think."

"For you, maybe. People see me coming and they turn around go the other direction."

"That is their loss. Before this is over, Charlie, you may become the toast of London. Everyone will want to know you, and it won't be because of me or Queensberry or anyone else. It will be due to who you are."

Charlie laughs as if he's being tickled. How delightful to see this serious young man overcome with mirth, Wilde thinks, even if the laughter comes from scorn and skepticism. He takes a deep breath and looks out the window. The cold egg of early morning has hatched a bright and warm day. In that moment, Wilde finds it difficult to believe there could be darkness lurking behind every pretty white cloud.

He shuts the window blind and settles back.

"The creature who attacked us bled when I stabbed it with the cane. London is the scientific capital of the world. We have zoologists, chemists, and biologists who might consult with us. A study of the blood might provide crucial insight into our enemy."

"Okay," Charlie says. "Where do we find them?"

"There is one genius we should approach first—and you, Charlie, would be crucial into winning his confidence."

"Me?"

"The man's name is Francis Galton. A brilliant polymath—learned in statistics, eugenics, and psychology, among many other disciplines. An adventurer as well, though he must be at least seventy now. He has well-publicized beliefs about the ideal traits of men and women. I, unfortunately, do not measure up. But you are the embodiment of his perfect man: good health, ability, and courteousness. Manliness above all."

"He told you he doesn't like you?"

Wilde laughs. "British society operates by a peculiar type of telepathy called the rumor mill. Though not instantaneous, the rumor mill allows people who've never spoken to each other to know their exact thoughts nevertheless. Let us say that Mr. Galton has made plain his dislike of me for much the same reasons as Queensberry."

"Sounds like we should leave him alone then. Isn't there anyone else?"

"None as brilliant and incisive as Galton. For our purposes, finding the second-best intellect won't do. We need him on our side."

"I'll help any way I can."

Wilde nods with a surge of fresh enthusiasm for his new plan, certain the microscope will reveal something the crystal ball has overlooked.

# PART THREE

# CHAPTER THIRTY

*Wandsworth Prison, July 15, 1895*

Stephen kicks Wilde onto his back and crouches down, shaking his head in mock sadness as he smirks. He touches Wilde's wet right cheek and then puts his fingertips to his lips.

"I can't tell the difference between your sweat and your tears. Both are equally delicious."

Stephen's laughter is joined by a chorus of guards just out of Wilde's blurry vision. Past experience allows his imagination to paint a clear enough picture of them. They're watching him and twirling black batons. The canvas of his body already bears deep purple and red splotches from their cruel paintbrushes.

No doubt these enthusiastic artists still see him as a work in progress.

"You're . . . a true gourmand," Wilde says.

"Still defiant? Well, then, I think the break we've allowed you has lasted too long. Up, dog."

Knowing any delay in compliance will result in more thrashing, Wilde summons his waning strength and manages to get on his hands and knees. His peripheral vision catches the five-foot high stack of cannonballs to his right. His head feels like a cannonball too, a burden he must somehow balance between his shoulders.

*"On your feet."*

He staggers up, swaying on legs whose muscles convulse at the thought of taking another tortured step.

"Now pick up the cannonball again and add it to the pile."

Wilde coughs, looking at the thirty-two pound cannonball, one of at least two hundred he's had to carry across the prison yard. He dropped this one at the halfway point when his arms, legs and back broke under the strain. It waits for him now like a hideous baby of round metal demanding its father's arms.

Wilde stumbles to his right and only just manages to stay standing.

Stephen's voice is dark and menacing as whispers into Wilde's left ear. "Bend down and pick it up, or I'll whip you like the human mule you are."

"Won't . . . won't the Great Goddess object?"

"Not as long as I keep you alive."

"The Greeks thought they'd mastered pointless torments with their dreams of Sisyphus and Tantalus. But they were amateurs compared to Egyptians."

Stephen slaps Wilde across the face, knocking him back to the ground. Blood fills his mouth and he swallows it at once, the only moisture his throat's known in hours. He wallows there in the dirt as the guards jeer and an absurd loneliness comes over him. He is the only human here. Wandsworth Prison can incarcerate hundreds of inmates, and the courtyard can accommodate at least fifty men at a time. But he is its sole resident now.

"Bring the cannonballs," Stephen says. "Since the slave wants to leave his here, let's help him out by making the new pile where he lays."

Wilde cries a moment later when the first cannonball strikes his right thigh. He shouts, pleading, managing to roll out of the way of another aimed at his stomach. He holds one hand up, beseeching mercy. Stephen and his henchmen have no humanity, and Wilde finds it fitting they've dropped their human faces in this moment of zeal. Hairless gray faces, all identical to his sight, leer down at him, their yellow eyes glowing with cruelty, their short, catlike ears curled forward to capture every moan and shriek he's destined to make.

They come to stand around him in a ring, each with cannonballs they hoist in one hand as if they were balloons. One steps forward, raises the cannonball above his head, and stands over Wilde's right kneecap.

Wilde gasps for air, terror mounting as he anticipates the release. When it does, he wills his stiff and exhausted muscles to move and the cannonball misses by a fraction. It hits the ground with the direst thud, and gravity has never been more real in Wilde's mind.

"*Please—*"

Another holds a cannonball over his left foot and drops it. Wilde dodges with even less energy.

"There's still some life in you after all," Stephen says. "Looks to me like you're less tired than you let on."

He brings a cannonball and holds it above Wilde's stomach. He releases it—Wilde knows he can't scramble away and tries to tense his abdominals. Just before the cannonball hits, however, Stephen catches it and pulls it back, his alien features showing all the delight of a cat toying with a mouse. He looks to the other guards.

"I think the prisoner would enjoy his humiliation more if it came with a recognizable face. What do you say we pretty ourselves up for the occasion?"

One by one, their faces contort and change. Stephen's face becomes Charlie's. Wilde's chest hurts to see it. To see *them*. For within seconds all of these inhuman monsters wear the face of the best humanity has to offer. He stares up at a ring of smirking Charlies.

Stephen crouches down to him. "I should have thought of this sooner. The sight of your little warrior hurting you is worse than any physical pain we can inflict. From now on, this is the only face you'll see when we punish you. The day will come when you hate him in your heart."

"*Never.*"

How he wishes there wasn't a croak in his voice in this moment of vigorous defiance. But he is a tree branch breaking away, losing its sap, becoming brittle.

"It can all end with such ease," Stephen says. "Agree to the Great Goddess' demands. Be her priest. Do these things, submit, and nothing will be denied you. I can come to you every night wearing any face and body you like. This one—or another, if it pleases you?"

His face turns into Bosie's, blond and innocent.

"I'll never be her pawn."

Stephen stands up, still wearing Bosie's face, and holds the cannon-ball over Wilde's head.

"Very well."

Wilde grimaces, knowing he will not be able to escape. He squeezes his eyes shut and waits.

*Qui patitur vincit.*

"Who said that?"

Wilde opens his eyes to see Stephen pulling back and glaring at his companions. When none of them speak, he repeats his question.

"Which one of you spoke?"

Wilde cranes his neck to see their reaction. They all seem baffled, looking at each other, reduced in an instant from mysterious creatures to dumb thugs.

Wilde looks to the sky, the clouds distorted by the tears welling in his eyes.

I'll endure, Constance, he vows to himself.

*Even if it kills me.*

# CHAPTER THIRTY-ONE

*London, April 10, 1894*

As soon as they meet, Wilde knows he made an accurate assessment of Francis Galton. After an infuriating half hour wait, the door to the scientist's consulting room opens and a bald, wizened man in his early seventies enters. Wilde and Charlie rise to meet him. Galton offers Wilde such minimal courtesy he's amazed they were granted an audience in the first place. But as Galton extends Charlie a generous handshake, Wilde congratulates himself on his acumen.

"Remarkable."

"Sir?" Charlie says, tone hesitant as he glances sideways at Wilde.

"Just noting the excellence of your face and form, young man. Are you married?"

"No, sir."

Concern edges into Galton's tone. "But you wish to be?"

"Of course."

"And have children?"

"Lots, I hope."

"Good! Find a suitable woman—I will give you a list of her necessary attributes—and then set yourself to the most agreeable task given to men. To *most* men, at any rate."

"I have children too," Wilde says.

"Of course," Galton answers, turning his back to him.

He sits down at his desk and clasps his hands in front of him as Wilde and Charlie take seats on the other side.

"I must say this visit is unexpected."

"I hope it is not unwanted."

Galton grunts. "The most imminent playwright of the hour doesn't grace my presence every day. What do you want, Mr. Wilde?"

"Your assistance."

"I'm afraid I know little about the world of drama."

"It's to the world of science I must make an appeal."

Galton raises his thin, white eyebrows and waits for more information.

"My friend Charles and I have recently encountered an . . . animal."

The aging scientist's brows remain arched. Wilde notices his gaze remains fixed on Charlie, as if all the words comes from him like a ventriloquist and his dummy.

"It was a creature, sir," Charlie says.

"We're all creatures, young man. We're surrounded by *creatures*. Could you be more specific?"

"You're quite right, Mr. Galton. But this particular creature appears to be unlike any other known to science."

"*Indeed?* How do you conclude that, Mr. Wilde? Are you an expert in what is and isn't known to science?"

Charlie bristles at this, a reaction both pleasing and alarming to Wilde. "I know animals, sir, and this one—"

"This particular animal was unusual, even to someone as unlearned as myself," Wilde says.

Galton's eyebrows lower. "Tell me more," he says to Charlie. "Where did you encounter it?"

"It was in Mr. Wilde's bedroom."

"We should give that statement some context, Mr. Galton."

"Indeed? Perhaps not too *much* context."

Charlie frowns, fidgeting in his chair. "Mr. Wilde left his cane in the carriage, you see, and I returned to find him being attacked."

"*Attacked?*"

"Yes, by—"

"Some sort of ape," Wilde says.

Galton cocks his head. "The only primates in London would be at the Zoological Garden. I'm sure none have been reported missing."

"But it wasn't an ape," Charlie says. "We don't know what it was, but it could change its face and its shape and—"

Galton's laughter sparks Charlie into standing up and leaning at him over the desk before Wilde can stop him.

"I swear on my life I'm telling the truth!"

"The truth about what? An ape that's also a chameleon?"

Wilde sighs. "Since Charlie has put most of our cards upon the table, I'll add another. This creature can also imitate other people's voices."

"Ah, we add a mynah bird to the mix! Well, why not, since we're being creative?"

Charlie slams one fist onto the desk, rattling the heavy wood and silencing the scientist in an instant. But there's no fear on Galton's face. If anything, he seems awed, overjoyed, like a man beholding a god. How peculiar his lust seems, so parallel to Wilde's own. It's the scientist's delight in finding a man who conforms to and confirms his notions of racial perfection. Rugged, attractive, earnest and unpretentious; gallant. What crime could Charlie commit, Wilde wonders, that Galton wouldn't pardon?

"I'll show you proof," he says, working the buttons of his shirt.

"Since all my body's good for is offering evidence."

Stripping his shirt off, he turns to bare his back. Galton rises, lips parted, gaze fixed on the wound. He takes back the bandages and stares for several seconds.

"A large beast, no doubt about it. But not an ape, I should think. And not a bite—"

"I already said it wasn't an ape. It had claws like a cat."

"Yes," Galton says, voice becoming distant. "More like a lion. I've seen cuts like this before, when I was a much younger man. It was in Africa in the early 1850s, on a mapping expedition I led. Fierce beasts on that dark continent. But this is London."

Galton draws back, looking Wilde up and down. Wilde detects naked uncertainty and distrust. The man is trying to reconcile his opinions of Wilde's character and mannerism with the gospel truth coming from Charlie's wound.

"You may put your shirt back on."

Charlie does, wincing a bit. "Now do you believe us?"

"I'm not sure what to believe. Perhaps a specimen of large cat has escaped the zoological gardens. It may have found its way into Mr. Wilde's home."

"Didn't you hear a word of what we've been saying?" Charlie says, shouting. "About it taking different shapes? About it talking? It wasn't a lion."

"Even sound minds can hallucinate in the heat of the moment. I imagine that you—"

"We didn't hallucinate its blood, Mr. Galton."

"Blood?"

"That's right. Oscar here wounded it while saving me."

"*He* saved *you?*"

147

"Yes, he did. And made the thing bleed for it too."

"I should like to see this blood. Where is it?"

"Quite where we said the attack took place, sir," Wilde says. "On the floor of my bedroom."

# CHAPTER THIRTY-TWO

Charlie insists on entering the house first and by himself, leaving Wilde and Galton to ponder each other for a few awkward, silent minutes until he returns.

"The ground floor at least is clear, Oscar. I'll check the upstairs."

Wilde grabs his arm. "Thank you for your bravery once again, but I think the three of us should go up together."

"What the devil does all this caution mean?" Galton says. "You claimed the beast fled."

"You might understand better if you allowed yourself to believe the *entirety* of our story."

They step over the threshold. Wilde walks into the sitting room and examines the furniture, the side chairs and accent tables. He observes the paintings on the wall, works by Rossetti, Hunt and Millais, fantastic scenes of intense individuality. Why do they seem stale to him now? Why do they seem false? Wilde turns, noting everything in its right place, nothing unusual. Yet all feels wrong and strange. Is the ceiling somehow lower? He reaches up, expecting his fingers to touch it. They do not. He can only say he feels taller, larger—a sensation he only experiences on the stage, congratulating another applauding crowd on their good taste.

What stage does he inhabit now?

"Oscar?"

Charlie calls from the staircase and Wilde finds him already half-way up with Galton paused just behind him, both looking impatient. Wilde joins them with growing unease. He wishes the second story of his home did not exist and there were no steps to demand further exploration. What awaits them at the top? What force has usurped him as the master of his own home?

They ascend.

"There's a noise coming from the bedroom," Charlie says.

They go together and open the door. Wilde sees Arthur on his hands and knees, his face red and sweaty as he scrubs at the blood-stained floor.

"Mr. Wilde! I'm sorry, sir, I didn't hear—"

Charlie rushes forward, grabs the butler and hoists him to his feet. A moment later he has Arthur pinned to the wall.

"You won't get the jump on me this time. Don't move. Don't even breathe. If you start to change, I'll make you pay."

Arthur whimpers and shakes. Behind Wilde, Galton demands to know what is happening.

"Charlie," Wilde says, risking a touch on his shoulder. "Let's not be hasty."

"Mr. Wilde, I swear—I swear I—I was just—"

Arthur's eyes bulge as he squirms.

Wilde looks at his scarab ring. No glow, no reaction. Tension eases out of him with a long exhale.

"This is *Arthur*, Charlie. This is my devoted butler."

"We know looks don't mean anything. We can't trust our eyes."

"Yes," Wilde says, now squeezing Charlie's left shoulder, prying him back. "But in this case, I have no doubt. Release him."

"If you're sure, Oscar," Charlie says, letting go. Arthur throws himself into Wilde's arms and trembles like a child.

"Easy now. It is okay. I will explain everything to you in time."

"I just stepped into your room and saw the mess, Mr. Wilde. I couldn't figure out what it was but knew I had to get it cleaned and—"

"Of course, dear boy. You've done nothing wrong."

He helps Arthur to the bed and sits with him as Galton kneels on the half-scrubbed floor. Wilde watches him dip his fingers into the bucket. His hand comes out discolored.

"Most strange. What has your man used as a cleansing agent?"

"Just water, sir," Arthur says, looking between them.

"Then this substance, whatever it is, has a consistency I've never experienced before. Not quite oil. Almost like jelly. And this is presumably in a diluted state."

"Is it safe to touch without gloves?"

Galton laughs. "Oh, probably not, but scientists must sometime be adventurous. This water is very cold. Almost icy. Why were you not using hot water?"

"It was very hot when I started," Arthur says.

"How long ago was that?"

"Perhaps ten minutes."

"That seems impossible. You can even see the beginning of condensation on the surface of the bucket. Water doesn't lose heat that fast without cause. I might even hypothesize a chemical reaction between this so-called blood and the water. I should like to call in assistants and collect as many samples as I can for testing. I'm afraid that means some of these floorboards will need to be removed and taken away."

Wilde smiles. "Please do! And if you don't mind, feel free to take the drapes along with you. I have grown very tired of them."

151

# CHAPTER THIRTY-THREE

As Galton summons his aides and begins working, Wilde takes Arthur downstairs to his study and settles him into a chair. Charlie accompanies them, stationing himself against the wall, his eyes unblinking, their stare scrutinizing. Wilde realizes nothing will convince him Arthur's not a monster.

"Here, good fellow," Wilde says, pouring his butler tea.

"You shouldn't, sir. It's not proper."

"Call it a reversal of roles. One I'm very happy to play."

Arthur looks at the cup and then at Wilde.

"*Please*, Arthur. It will calm you."

"I can't be calm, Mr. Wilde. Not with him in the room."

"That's Charlie. He's a good friend. Rest assured his attack on you was not personal. Call it . . . a case of mistaken identity."

"But I don't have an identity to be mistaken. I'm just Arthur, your butler."

"Yes," Wilde says, smiling. "Yes, you *are*."

"Can we really be sure?" Charlie says, and it seems like he's making his voice gruffer and deeper.

Wilde holds up his left hand to show the scarab ring's dullness. "I am sure. Come and sit down, Charlie. You and Arthur should become acquainted."

"I've gotten to know him well enough," Arthur says.

"A truly abhorrent first impression. Come, Charlie and sit. Take tea with us."

The boxer sighs and relents. Wilde starts to play servant again, pouring a second cup. As he hands it to Charlie, however, he hears a cat's meowing. The sound sends both of them to their feet.

A blond tabby sits in the library entrance, just looking at them.

"Do you have a cat, Oscar?"

"No."

"Perhaps the front door was left open and it got in," Arthur says, rising. "I'll take care of it."

The cat meows again and Oscar holds out his hands to caution them all. "No one move. I have seen this cat before—at Queensberry's estate."

"What?"

"I'm sure I encountered it on the grounds while you were speaking to the Marquess."

"Why didn't you say anything?"

"There was nothing to say. It startled me, but I thought it must be a simple housecat. But nothing is simple anymore, is it?"

"Come on, Oscar," Charlie says, stepping forward. "It's a full day's travel to his Lordship's estate. How could any cat get back to London so fast?"

"It could have stowed away on the carriage. Hidden itself."

The cat meows again, and Wilde detects urgency in its frail voice. He stares into its eyes and finds something familiar to him, something the prior encounter cannot explain.

"It's almost as if it knows me," Wilde says.

"Maybe we should have Mr. Galton take a look at it when he—Os-

*car*, look out!"

Charlie lunges as the cat leaps, but even he isn't fast enough. The cat strikes Wilde on the chest and its claws pierce through to the skin. Wilde winces, turning, grabbing the cat by the scruff to yank it free. Then man and cat make eye contact, and Wilde's intuition seizes him again.

"It can't be."

Arthur stands up. "What can't be, Mr. Wilde?"

"Somehow," Wilde says, keeping his gaze fixed on the cat's eyes, "this is not a meeting of man and beast, but of man and man."

"What's gotten into you, Oscar?"

Wilde hears both young men moving toward him and tells them to stay put. "I'm quite fine," he says, bringing the cat nearer to his face. Their stares remain locked and Wilde finds humanity on the other side, lurking in the cat's brain. He strokes the cat, now certain it is the same one from Queensberry's estate. He's never seen fur so blond, like satin gilt. The color reminds him of one person in the world. He remembers the first time he brushed the hair back along the lad's temple before plunging all of his hand into those golden curls. His fingers stove their way to the back of Bosie's head and drew his face forward into an open-mouthed kiss. When the kiss ended and both men pulled back, Wilde said—

"*I love you like no other. I love you like a blind man given the gift of sight.*"

Looking at the cat with even greater scrutiny, he speaks those words again. The cat meows.

"What do you mean you *love* it, Oscar?"

"Nothing," he says, tears threatening his eyes. "Nothing and everything."

He moves past them, leaving the library with Charlie and Arthur chasing him.

"Oscar, where are you taking it? We can't be sure it's not one of *them.*"

"Oh, I think we can. This cat is not a changeling like the monster that entered my house disguised as Bosie. Rather, this delicate creature that clings to me now is—*somehow*—Lord Alfred Douglas himself."

# CHAPTER THIRTY-FOUR

Arthur puts a saucer of milk on the ground where Wilde kneels, stroking Bosie's hair with ardent devotion.

"Mr. Wilde, sir, I know it's not proper for me to offer an opinion on your affairs. But perhaps I should go fetch a physician. Do you feel feverish?"

"I feel cool as can be. As for your opinions, I have always found them to be invaluable. Please know I'm aware of how this appears, and that my judgment is sound."

"Yes, sir."

"Arthur, I believe you'd feel better if you went back to your duties. Mr. Galton's assistants will be here any minute. Would you conduct them upstairs when they arrive?"

"Yes, Mr. Wilde."

Arthur bows and leaves, closing the door behind him. Wilde finds Charlie staring at the shut door.

"I still don't trust him, Oscar."

"Based on past performance, I think my ring would alert us to danger. It has not reacted at all to either Arthur or Bosie."

Charlie nods and also crouches down beside the cat. "You really think this kitten is . . . his Lordship's *son?*"

"Is it so impossible to believe considering what else we've seen?"

"But how did it come about?"

"It could only have happened after I left Bosie alone with Stephen. I have not seen the *real* Alfred Douglas since then. As to *how*—who can say?"

Charlie reaches his hand to scratch the cat's ears as it laps the milk and receives a hiss and a claw swipe for his efforts. Wilde laughs.

"I see Bosie remains temperamental."

"If this *is* his Lordship's son then I have a duty to protect him. And a duty to tell the Marquess what's happened, though I'd like to know how to go about it."

Wilde imagines Charlie standing outside Queensberry door and thrusting Bosie toward him when the Marquess appears. The bitter man would go and drown the cat the first chance he got, assuming he didn't want to waste a bullet.

Bosie nuzzles Wilde's hand and looks up at him. Again, Wilde experiences the uncanny sense of the humanity in those eyes.

"I wonder, Charlie. How much of his human mind remains intact? Do you think he can communicate if we could somehow contrive a system?"

Bosie meows and paws at Wilde's arm.

Grinning, Charlie says, "I'd take that as a *yes*, Oscar. Too bad he can't just talk to us."

Wilde raises his eyebrows.

"Charlie, on my desk you'll find paper and pen. Please bring both to me."

He fetches them. Wilde takes seven sheets and places them on the floor, drawing quadrants on six of them. He labels the quadrants of the first page *A, B, C, D*. He continues along these lines until reaching the final page, which hosts *Y* and *Z*. Looking at the alphabet, he thinks

Constance would be very proud of him for his makeshift planchette.

"If Bosie's intelligence exists inside the cat, perhaps he can spell out a message to us."

The cat has already gone to the array of papers, circling the alphabet.

"I'm not sure it understands, Oscar. It could be there's just not enough of Lord Alfred's mind crammed into the cat's tiny brain to—"

The cat hisses at him and strides forward to put its right hand on the letter O. It slaps at it twice for emphasis.

The men look at each other and then back to the cat. It's now tapping at the letter S.

"Good God," Wilde says, hands trembling as he records the letters. The cat moves to the letter C.

"I can't believe this," Charlie says. "It's spelling your name."

Wilde strokes the cat's flanks as he wipes the tears from his eyes. "Bosie, we hear you! We stand ready to listen!"

Bosie, Wilde soon finds, stands ready to speak.

# CHAPTER THIRTY-FIVE

*i do not know how long i have been like this i do not know if it is real or*
*not i do not know if you are real here is what i do know*

   *you left and s followed but s came back those eyes i wanted those eyes i*
*was drunk and his eyes made me sober he touched my arm his index fingers*
*were bold i told him i was his*

   *very well his eyes said this and he stood i followed my heart fast and he*
*led me to the bookcase the bible was like you said*

   *the door he took me in so dim his eyes so bright breath great goddess and*
*s kissed me blew air into my mouth i fell he took me floor pain thrust*

   *s in me each thrust turning me world smaller s laughing each thrust*
*more his pet*

Bosie's labored spelling goes on for more than an hour and when he
finishes Wilde looks over the transcription and tries to parse the words
into sentences as Charlie looks over his shoulder.

Arthur knocks and enters. "Mr. Wilde, I thought I should tell you
that the men upstairs are now ripping up the floorboards like they said
they would."

Wilde nods, aware the butler lingers in the doorway staring at the
alphabet on the floor.

"As long as they leave the stairs in place, they can have as much as
they want. You may go now, Arthur."

"Yes, sir," he says, closing the door with obvious reluctance. As soon as he's gone, Wilde and Charlie go over the notes. Bosie jumps into Wilde's lap and throws a hiss at Charlie.

"Now, Lord Alfred, there's no reason to be like that," Charlie says.

"He must recognize you."

"I wouldn't think so."

"No? As close as your relationship with Queensberry is, I would think you've met each other several times."

"I've never meant Lord Alfred in person. His Lordship kept me at a distance except when his sons were away. He put me up at a place in the village and we'd meet at a gymnasium most of the time. He spent many hours teaching me to spar."

"Perhaps Bosie's senses are heightened, and he detects his father's scent on your clothes. He never liked his father before we met, and the disdain worsened after we became friends."

"We all choose our loyalties."

The comment lingers like a physical thing in the room, far heavier than an off-hand remark should be. Wilde studies Charlie, wondering if he meant to imply something.

Charlie takes the paper out of his hands, looks it up and down and shakes his head. "I can't make out any of this."

"That's because you lack context."

"Who is S?"

"S is short for Stephen, the man—or creature—at the heart of this mystery. I believe it was Stephen who attacked me in my bedroom, though I cannot be sure. I have reason to believe there are many more like him. If that is correct, he might be their leader."

"It almost reads like he and Lord Alfred had—"

Charlie pales and his eyes widen before he sits back, fingers digging into his kneecaps. Wilde knows has no right to be hurt by the young man's reaction. Nevertheless, he feels an acute sting.

"Your observation is quite correct."

"I wish it weren't."

Wilde sits back. "Do you know what a renter is, Charlie?"

Charlie stares hard at the ground and gives his head a brief shake.

"They are men—young men like yourself, usually—who are paid by other men for the pleasure of their company."

"People pay other people to talk to them?"

"Yes, among other things."

Charlie raises his head. "You pay too?"

"Sometimes."

"For other things?"

"Yes."

Charlie grunts.

"The day you followed me around London and lost me at The Red Tiger, I was hunting for a renter named Stephen. He'd been described in terms approaching the mythological, and I wondered if he even existed. Part of me didn't care. The chase itself alleviated boredom. I played detective and learned about a supposed opium den inside the Red Tiger. That is where I met Stephen, and that is where Bosie suffered his transformation."

"This Stephen sounds like a dangerous chap."

"Lethal, I should think. I have reasons to believe he is also the creature you fought in my bedroom."

Charlie jumps to his feet. "Then I want to go to The Red Tiger. I'm ready for a rematch."

"Not yet."

"We're like a carriage stuck in mud if all we do is stay here!"

161

"Patience, Charlie. We're not simply staying put. We're uncovering clues even now, between our interview with Bosie and Mr. Galton's efforts upstairs."

"But I'm feeling bloody worthless."

Wilde smiles. "Now is a good time to rest yourself and let your wound continue to heal. When the moment of action comes, I know you'll be in the thick of it, protecting me."

Bosie's claws dig into Wilde's thigh, provoking a wince.

"What is it, Oscar?"

"Jealousy, I do believe," Wilde says, extracting himself from Bosie's clutches. He places the cat on the ground, where it returns to the alphabet and starts to spell out a rather petulant demand that Charlie leave.

"I'm afraid that can't happen, Bosie. Though if you continue to misbehave, I can have you put in a box and crated back to Kinmount House with an explanatory letter. Your father will consider it some ridiculous joke on our parts."

Bosie answers with plaintive mewling that stops at the loud report of approaching footsteps. Galton and three men appear in the doorway. Intellectual excitement must be Galton's elixir of youth, for Wilde swears the man looks spry.

He notices his ring beginning to glow. He shoves his hands into his pockets by instinct, posture stiffening. What has signaled the alarm? Galton, or one of his assistants?

"We've accomplished what we needed to do," Galton says. The first assistant carries a large burlap sack overflowing with floorboards. The second carries Arthur's pail of water and the third two glass beakers filled with liquid of a royal purple color.

The ring could be reacting to the creature's blood, Wilde tells himself, feeling unconvinced.

He swallows. "What happens next, Mr. Galton?"

"Examination! Our chemical inquisition will coax out every secret, I assure you. I predict it will take time, of course. I say, what's this you've got on the floor?"

"Oh, that . . . I was just reacquainting myself with the alphabet."

"The arrangement looks nearly like a periodic table," Galton says with a hearty laugh. He motions for his assistants to depart. As soon as they're gone, Wilde eases his left hand out of his pocket.

The ring's glow is gone as well.

# CHAPTER THIRTY-SIX

"You must be daft, Oscar!" Charlie says when Wilde announces he is going to take a nap. He stands in front of Wilde with his arms at his side but both hands curled into fists and his jaw clenched.

"I know the idea of such passivity offends you. It must seem very unserious."

"Yes."

"I can only ask you to go on trusting me as you have been. Whenever I'm struggling over a decision, such as where a story should go next, I find sleep—"

"But *I'm* not struggling, Oscar. I know exactly what our next step is. I've already told you."

"I'm not convinced going to The Red Tiger is the right course of action just yet. Please, Charlie. Let me sleep on the idea."

Charlie throws his hands into the air, spinning away and stalking over to an armchair. He sits down and glares at the wall.

"Perhaps you could do with some sleep too," Wilde says.

"I'm not tired. How can I get tired from sitting around doing nothing?"

Wilde nods, pained but also charmed by Charlie's sulking. He says nothing else, realizing any more words will aggravate Charlie further. With Bosie cupped in his right arm, Wilde leaves his library and goes upstairs. He finds his bedroom floor upturned, full of treacherous gaps.

Navigating these, he rests himself on the mattress without undressing and closes his eyes even as Bosie presses against his face.

"Constance," he says, whispering. "Constance, if you can hear me, I need your advice."

Drowsiness steals over him, petting his eyelids down, abetted by the warm, pleasing sound of Bosie's purring. Soon enough he opens his eyes to a dark room lit only by the low flame of an oil lamp. He sees his face reflected in the lamp's disfiguring bronze.

He turns and probes the surrounding darkness.

"Constance?"

Why doesn't she answer? The void presses in, swallowing more of the visible space. The lamp's fire flickers. What would happen if the darkness fell upon him? Would he wake? Die?

Something in-between?

His pulse sews a rapid stitch in his chest as he repeats his wife's name, shouting it this time.

A person luges at him from out of the dark. Startled, it takes Wilde a moment to realize it is Yeats. He grabs Wilde by the shoulders and shakes him, his eyes frantic and tired.

"Remember your Shakespeare, Mr. Wilde! Remember *the play's the thing!*"

"The play? What play?"

"Remember your Shakespeare, Mr. Wilde! Remember *the play's the thing!*"

"I heard you before, Will. Can't you hear me?"

Yeats repeats the same lines. Wilde extricates himself from the man's grip and steps back. Yeats continues his pantomime, hands out grasping nothing.

"Remember your Shakespeare, Mr. Wilde! Remember *the play's the thing!"*

"Where is Constance? Where are you? I have so much to tell the Order and I don't know how to proceed. Should I go back to the house where the labyrinth is? Where can I find any of you?"

"Remember your Shakespeare, Mr. Wilde!"

"I do remember my damn Shakespeare, plays and sonnets alike."

"Remember *the play's the thing!*"

"Yes, from Hamlet—Act 2, Scene 2. But what does it have to do with anything? What are you trying to tell me, Will?"

But there's no arguing or pleading with this messenger. He can only listen to the same words over and over, fretting over something obvious he must be missing. His mind feels like an urn of ash flooded with sudden water, making mud. A terrible certainty overwhelms him that he will not wake up until he has guessed the nature of Yeats's warning. The only change that happens is the intensity and strength of the vision's words. Yeats is screaming now, shouting beyond the strength of any human voice. Wilde puts his hands over his ears and falls back, dropping to his knees beside the lamp. As Yeats's shrieking threatens to break his eardrums, Wilde takes a desperate risk and blows at the lamplight with all his might.

The light dies and the darkness rolls over him.

Yeats' words cease.

Wilde opens his eyes to find himself in his bedroom, with Bosie still curled beside him. The cat wakes as soon as he moves and meows. Wilde gets up, leaves the bedroom, and moves through the quiet house with Bosie following. He finds Charlie in the library, sprawled asleep on the corner divan. A light snore comes from his parted lips and Wilde takes a moment to admire the openness of his face in this unguarded moment.

Bosie bounds upon his chest, sending Charlie springing up in a fighting stance, head swiveling back and forth. Wilde scolds the cat as Charlie begins to relax.

"I was having a dream."

"About what?"

"Can't remember," Charlie says, rubbing his chest. "That's funny. How could I know I was dreaming if I can't even recall what it was? Reckon I was more tired than I knew. What time is it?"

"Around one in the afternoon."

"Then at least we didn't sleep the day away."

"Do you still feel like venturing to The Red Tiger?"

Charlie grins. "More than ever."

"Then let's go and make an investigation. Perhaps we'll find something promising. If not, at least the tavern serves cheap pints."

Charlie gestures to the cat. "What do we do with Lord Alfred?"

Wilde scoops Bosie into his hands and peers into his eyes. "I don't think you should come with us."

The cat hisses and swipes at him with its right paw.

"Yes," Wilde says. "I know you're upset."

"Maybe we should bring him with us. If he was changed there, maybe going there can get him put right again."

The cat meows over and over again.

"It seems Bosie agrees with you. But how can we make him inconspicuous?"

"That coat you've been wearing looks like it has big, deep pockets. Maybe Lord Alfred can fit inside one."

The cat darts to the closet door and scratches at it.

"Once again, it seems Bosie agrees with you."

Wilde retrieves the coat, puts it on and then puts Bosie into it. The cat fits, and as he settles Bosie inside, Wilde pauses to reflect on the fact he's about to go to an opium den with his transformed lover tucked away in his coat pocket.

"What is it, Oscar?" Charlie says when Wilde laughs.

"I was just thinking how I've always endeavored to be stranger than the time I'm living in. But it seems the present has raced far ahead of me in oddness."

They head out.

# CHAPTER THIRTY-SEVEN

In the brief time Wilde's known Charlie, he cannot think of anything that's ever distracted his stalwart guardian from either purpose or sense of duty. This makes Charlie's sudden absence all the more jarring when Wilde turns around and finds himself alone. He scans through the crowds and discovers him half a block back, stopped before the long front window of the J. Sainsbury shop.

Curious, he thinks. London's shops have so many enticements, displays of immaculate suits and glittering jewels and shoes of exquisite craftsmanship, but Charlie stands so mesmerized by the offerings of a grocery store that he doesn't seem to notice Wilde sidling up beside him.

The glass shows hanging ham hocks and rows of salted pork wrapped in wax paper. Wilde steals a peripheral glance at Charlie's face and discerns a distant, haunted expression. This compels him to touch Charlie's arm and turn his attention.

"What is it, dear boy?"

A sudden, sour look ages Charlie's appearance in an instant and lends him a touch of Queensberry's features in the downcast turn of his lips. This is too much to bear and Wilde moves his body between Charlie and the window.

"Please," Wilde continues. "Tell me what's upsetting you."

"Passing by this food reminded me of my starving days and fighting for my meals. If I had money, if I was his Lordship, I'd go inside right now and buy as much as I could and then find boys like me and feed them."

"Charlie, if Queensberry or any so-called gentlemen in this city had your sensibilities, the world would be a better place."

"Aren't you a gentleman?"

"I'm supposed to be. Maybe being a gentleman isn't something to aspire to, Charlie."

"I wasn't trying to be mean."

"You're not being mean at all. The simple truth is that I have never fed any child other than my own. I find altruism and charity a terrible thing."

"What's wrong with charity?"

"It perpetuates the inherent unfairness of the established order and blinds people to the need for change. While there are many forward-thinking individuals, humanity as a whole is reactive. Only crisis sparks action. Charities offer just enough relief to keep the crisis point at bay. This is monstrous. The altruist is like a kind slave owner whose very kindness makes slavery seem less abominable than it is."

Charlie frowns and tugs his arm away, but Wilde holds fast to it.

"Challenge me."

"What?"

"Dispute what I've said, Charlie. Call me wrong—and prove it."

Charlie looks everywhere but at Wilde's eyes. "I—I can't. I'm not smart the way you are."

"Debate is just another kind of boxing."

"I don't want to debate. We're wasting time."

"Queensberry criticized my membership in the Fabian Society, a group whose goals include the feeding of all children. But have any of its members ever walked into a butcher's shop and purchased meat for the poor? Does not doing so this make us hypocrites?"

"I couldn't say."

"What if I insisted the best way to effect change is for everyone with money to go into every butcher's store, buy up all the meat, and throw it *en mass* into the Thames?"

"You're making fun of me," Charlie says, pulling his arm free. He cheeks flush crimson and the darkness enters his eyes, lending them a black glower. His hands clench into fists.

Wilde retreats two steps when he sees the tremble in Charlie's bottom lip.

"I'm sorry."

"I just don't want to see children go hungry."

Charlie walks away.

Wilde does not move. He stares at the ground, almost panting as he works at slowing his pulse. After several seconds, he offers a shy, almost apologetic glance at the food in the window. All he sees on the other side is Charlie as a boy, his nose broken for the first time, one eye black, a swollen upper lip. He stares at this phantasm, puts one hand against the glass and says, "I'll never write a sentence of political philosophy again."

"Mr. Wilde?"

He turns and sees a man and woman approaching him. The man says, "Sir, if I may, I just wish to tell you how much my wife and I loved *A Woman of No Importance*. Such brilliant humor!"

"Bastards," Wilde says.

The woman gasps, both hands covering her mouth. Her husband's brow furrows. "I'm sorry, Mr. Wilde?"

"You, her, myself—all bastards."

"Mr. Wilde, if we've given offense, then—"

He puts his hands on the man's shoulders. "I must ask you both for a favor. It's an easy enough thing. I want to give you money."

"Money, sir?"

"Yes. I want you to take it into this butcher's shop and buy that entire shelf of meat. Do you understand?"

The woman says, "But what in the world should we do with it all?"

"Give them away to any child who looks hungry."

The man looks baffled. "Why would we do that, Mr. Wilde?"

"Because stomachs that rumble for too long quit caring who or what fills them. And that, perhaps, is how new religions get started."

# CHAPTER THIRTY-EIGHT

Wilde stands under the pub's sign, shaking his head at discovering yet another change. It seems the establishment is now called Spotted Leopard.

"The leopard may not change its spots, but *you* are as flexible as a chameleon, aren't you?"

Pivoting, he scans the area for Charlie as Bosie pokes his head out from the deep coat pocket. Wilde puts a reassuring hand on him and pushes the cat out of sight. "I can't begin to know what you're trying to tell me, Bosie, but I urge you to be still. Now is the time for utmost secrecy."

The cat quiets and Wilde resumes his search for Charlie, whom he never caught up to after their argument. He walks to the alleyway and finds it empty. No one stands waiting across the street. Both foot and carriage traffic are so light Wilde's left feeling like he's slipped into a pocket of his own.

He faces the tavern again, half-surprised the sign didn't change again in the minutes since he last observed it.

Charlie must already be inside, he tells himself.

Wilde would consider going in alone a foolish risk but just the sort of action for Charlie to take in his brash, agitated state. He looks at his scarab ring and finds a faint but steady glow coming from the green stone.

"Trouble," he says, looking at the door. There's quite a crowd inside to judge from the laughter filtering through the dirty windows. Scowling, he looks up and down the street again, urging his eyes to conjure Charlie everywhere. A fantastic paranoia enters his thoughts. What if Charlie became so mad that he hailed a carriage and is even now on his way back to Queensberry?

He strokes Bosie's fur and scolds himself for his behavior in front of the store window. His philosophical flippancy insulted Charlie's sincerity. It would serve him right if Charlie abandoned him.

But no amount of despair will let him believe Charlie would do such a thing. The young man's honor would not permit it, and this leads Wilde to consider another possibility. What if Charlie saw the sign and concluded The Red Tiger must be further up the road?

He starts walking in a hopeful pursuit when Bosie claws him, striking flesh even through multiple layers of fabric. The pain forced Wilde to stop and Bosie once more rises out of the pocket and stares at the tavern door, meowing.

"We will go inside, Bosie. I promise. But first we *must* find Charlie."

Bosie reacts with a prolonged hiss. Even without language, Wilde understands the pummeling way his lover argues. And as usual, he submits to it, but only after securing a promise that Bosie be quiet and still.

The noise coming from inside the Spotted Leopard suggests the warmest, most inviting gathering of all time. He stops with his right hand on the door. The scarab ring shows a steady, almost angry light. If he is stepping into danger, as seems likely, should he have his only defense on display?

He puts his left hand into his pocket, opens the door and steps through.

174

The pub is empty.

"This cannot be possible," he says, moving forward. His footsteps echo on the floorboards. The tables stand vacant, their chairs tucked in prim and proper.

"What can't be possible, Mr. Wilde?"

He turns to the bar and finds a familiar sight.

"Chyron."

The little barman waves at him with his right hand. His left presses a towel over his mouth. Wilde sees the towel used to be white. Much of it is now red.

"Is it *me* you find impossible, Mr. Wilde?"

He approaches the bar. "Where are the people who were here?"

"That is a very philosophical question, isn't it? Here *when*?"

"Here *now*. I heard them just before I came in only moments ago."

"Moments ago?" Chyron laughs, adjusting the towel over his mouth.

"Yes."

"Well, things are never the same, moment to moment, are they?"

"This does appear to be a Heraclitian tavern, sir. It seems one never steps into the same establishment twice."

Chyron slaps at the counter, lowering the towel and throws back his head in silent merriment. The man's bloody mouth and missing front teeth prove a shocking sight. He's been punched, Wilde thinks. He's been—

"Charlie."

"Oh, is the little brawler who did this to me a friend of yours?"

"Yes. Where is he now?"

"He wanted to see Stephen. I asked him to pay the fee. He said he had no money. So, I smiled at him and said no money, no Stephen. Smiling was my mistake. You don't show your teeth to a brawler. He held up his fist and said, 'Here's your payment.' I reckon he overpaid."

Wilde shakes his head, unable to believe Charlie would assault the man as Chyron describes. He inspects the towel again. Most of the blood has a crusty, dried appearance. "He wasn't that far ahead of me. Did this only just happen?"

"Just? It must have been two hours ago."

"Chyron, that *cannot* be. He was no more than ten minutes ahead of me at the most."

"Ah, well, Mr. Wilde. The only real pleasure when it comes to time is losing track of it. Came up with that aphorism myself. You feel free to use it in a play if you like it as much as I do."

Wilde waves off the offer. "So, you maintain that Charlie beat you into submission?"

"That's the long and short of it, sir."

"You took him to the bookcase?"

"Aye, I did, and showed him the trick. You know, at that point I thought he might be a young inspector with Scotland Yard, out to make a name for himself by revealing the existence of our little side business. Do you know what the problems with investigations are, Mr. Wilde?"

"I haven't a clue."

"They always turn up something!"

Chyron breaks into a bloody laugh so violent that he falls off his crate and disappears behind the bar. Startled, Wilde waits for the man to get up. Chyron's laughter echoes like he's fallen down a chasm.

"Chyron?"

Wilde races around the bar, kicking away the crates. He stomps the floorboards and can't discover even the slightest hint of give. He crouches to inspect beneath the bar. Chyron is such a little man he could have a hiding spot here, like a magician's trick box. But the wood seems to be thick and all of one piece.

Laughter sounds above his head.

He bolts up, almost striking his head against the lip of the bar, and finds Chyron seated, hands clasped in front of him, mouth and chin stained with blood.

"It seems the roles are reversed, Mr. Wilde. Fetch me a pint and be quick about it."

Wilde stares at him and Chyron laughs as he slaps the countertop again.

"Have I rendered the illustrious *wit* speechless? Does a *cat* have that eloquent tongue of yours?"

Bosie moves in his pocket. Wilde thrusts his right hand into it to remind Bosie of their agreement. Meanwhile his pocketed left hand curls into a fist as Wilde fights the urge to reveal the ring and shine its light straight into the strange barman's eyes.

Chryen motions for Wilde to lean in and rises off the stool, pitching himself forward. In a lowered voice, he says, "I hear tell this pub has a secret chamber that *you* might be able to show me."

If these aren't Wilde's exact words to Chyron on their first meeting, they are as close to identical as his memory allows.

"Secret chamber," Chyron continues, laughing. "Makes this pub sound like an ancient pyramid. But I don't see the sands of Egypt swirling about our feet, do you?"

The front door blows open, and Wilde glimpses a desert landscape where London used to be. He just stares at it, lips parted.

Chyron joins him in looking. "Who is to say the real secret chamber isn't the world on the other side of the front door?"

The door shuts just as mysteriously as it opened, and Chyron swivels back to Wilde, his stare manic, better suited for an asylum than a pub.

"I just wish to find Charlie. Then the two of us will leave."

"Just like that, eh? You won't stay for a cup of tea with Stephen? Or perhaps another taste of the breath of the Great Goddess?"

"I fear we've both already overstayed our welcome."

Chyron smiles at this and then points to the doorway leading to the bookcase. "Help yourself, Mr. Wilde. You know the way."

"You won't stop me?"

"Do I look like I'm in any condition to stop anyone?"

Wilde sidesteps away from the bar, his gaze on Chryon the entire time. Just as he reaches the doorway and pivots to leave, however, Chyron calls out to him.

"Thank you, Mr. Wilde."

"Thank me? For what?"

"For keeping your left hand and that ring of yours hidden away in your pocket. I've had already had a bad day. Having to kill you would have made it so much worse."

# CHAPTER THIRTY-NINE

Shaken and almost breathless, Wilde hurries to the bookcase with his left hand free. The ring's violent emerald glow reveals the spines and seems to sneak around the edges like tendrils that would grip and tear the false door from its place. Before that can happen, however, Wilde pulls on the King James Bible, hears the familiar click, and the bookcase swivels.

He enters the opium den and the ring's light flares even brighter, forcing Wilde to turn his head a moment. The ring outshines the wall lamps and reveals the floor with its myriad pillows and cushions. He sees one body there, and the shock of recognition jolts him.

"Charlie!"

Wilde bends down and shakes him by the shoulders. Charlie's lolls to the left. Wilde pulls back both lids and finds the eyes unfocused.

"Can you hear me? We must get out of here right away. I will try to carry you."

As he works his hands under Charlie's body, a voice calls out to him.

"So good to encounter you again, Mr. Wilde. I believe we have unfinished business."

"Stephen," Wilde says, rising. Left arm extended, he aims the ring in the direction of the voice. Its light reveals the opium bar but there's no one standing behind it.

"That's an interesting trinket you possess, Mr. Wilde."

"Indeed it is. I seem to remember it causing you great harm."

"The wound has healed."

Wilde turns, looking everywhere as he tries to keep his pulse controlled. Moving a few paces away from Charlie, he smiles and gambles on bravado. "I wonder if that's true."

An edge enters Stephen's voice, like a man offended by insult. "You'd accuse me of lying?"

"You're the one in hiding just now. Skittishness speaks volumes. Show yourself. I grow tired of speaking to a shadow."

A figure emerges from behind the bar. Stephen reveals himself in what Wilde now presumes to be his natural state, hairless and ashen, his head something like a shaven cat's skull, the ears like tiny triangles, the nose broad and flattened. He stands there with his eyes shut, though Wilde detects movement under the lids. Wilde thrusts the ring a fraction closer and sees a flicker of discomfort enter Stephen's expression.

"I see you're still afraid of the light."

"You *are* a goading little man."

"I've seldom been called little."

"But that's what you are, like all of your kind, good for one of three things."

Wilde swallows against a hardness in his throat. "Oh?"

"Slaves, pets, or my personal favorite—food."

This answer chills Wilde as he struggles to keep his wits. "How do you make the determination?"

"Who says I am the determiner?"

"If not you, then who?"

Stephen's mouth opens in a broad, mirthless grin. "The Great Goddess."

"Does this goddess have a name? Surely not Athena. I've seen no wisdom from her as yet."

Stephen's expression becomes a hateful rictus as a warning hiss comes from his mouth. "Do *not* mock the Great Goddess, Wilde."

"In my experience only the very brittle disdain mockery."

Stephen moves around the bar showing little problem with his blindness. Wilde steps back. His left arm has become heavy enough that he must brace it with his right hand. He stares at the ring and urges greater light from it, pouring all of his hope into the glow. The light expands, provoking a muffled shriek from Stephen as it forces him to turn away.

"I'll just be collecting my friend and then I'll trouble you no more."

"The little brawler? No, the Great Goddess has taken a liking to that one. He is to become a pet."

Bosie stirs in Wilde's pocket and leaps free before Wilde can stop him. Stephen's ears twitch at the small thud of the cat's landing. He sniffs the air and smiles.

"*Another* pet! I remember the blond-haired lord very well."

"Change him back," Wilde says, swallowing against a tightening throat. "Change him back and I'll spare your life."

Stephen laughs even as another burst from the ring makes him shield his closed eyes with his right forearm. "It cannot be undone. But I think you will appreciate watching the same process done on the little brawler. Put the ring away and let me show you. I'll even let you help me break him in first."

Wilde drives forward with the ring, sending a bolt of energy that strikes Stephen in the chest and hurtles him to the bar. Still Stephen laughs despite his obvious pain.

"Your thoughts are easy to discern, Mr. Wilde. Look at your Charlie lying there, waiting for you. Supple, warm, defenseless. Just as you've desired him."

"You're misreading my thoughts."

"This from the man who says he can resist everything except temptation!"

"You seem to know more about me and my work than I would think useful, considering my unimportance."

"Mr. Wilde," Stephen says, grinning, "I assure you that your *importance* will be revealed to you in good time."

Bosie rubs against Wilde's leg, drawing his attention to the floor. Then Bosie hisses toward the surrounding darkness. Wilde comprehends the warning just as begin to gather and emerge.

"Very good, boys," Stephen says. "Looks like the trap's been sprung."

One by one, panthers slink into view. Wilde counts seven in all. Their eyes are also closed against the ring's light, but Wilde has no doubts about their ability to navigate by scent and sound. Their razor-sharp fangs look white even against the green glow. He shuffles his feet, breathless to the point of lightheadedness.

"Was that a step back I heard? Really, Mr. Wilde, your courage doesn't inspire."

Stephen comes forward.

"Slaves and pets are made in much the same way. Do you want to know the key difference? It's not just a matter of size. *Function* matters a great deal as well. Pets of course have little purpose beyond amusement. The little blond lord escaped before we could give him all the petting he deserved. We're glad to have him back. Slaves, however, are another story. They build. They fight and kill upon command. They do any task assigned to them, no matter how odious they might find it. Take this lot, for instance. You know all of them."

"I'm afraid we have no acquaintanceship."

"Slaves," Stephen says. "Show Mr. Wilde your more recognizable faces."

Wilde cannot restrain a sharp intake of breath as the panthers begin to transform. The panthers shed their fur and their bodies break apart like shells, revealing naked, youthful flesh. Men rise in place of the beasts, and Wilde doesn't need to see their eyes to recognize their faces. Paul, Brandon, Carl, Sebastian, and Alexander. His favorite renters. But the last man to stand troubles him the most.

Alfred Wood.

"You," Wilde says. "But why the long subterfuge to bring me here the first time?"

"The Great Goddess wanted to judge your qualities."

"For what? Enslavement?"

"The greatest slave of all," Stephen says, and bellows laughter to the point Wilde can stand no more of it. In that moment, he draws his left hand back, imagining himself like Charlie about to throw a punch. When his arm releases, the ring sends out a blast of energy that strikes Stephen in the chest and turns his merriment into a howl. He falls back, striking his head against the bar. Wilde turns, expecting Wood and the rest to charge at him. But they all go to form a protective circle around Stephen.

They begin to chant, a collective singsong in a language that sounds ancient and archaic, something from a civilization long dead. The chant grows in pitch and intensity, hurting Wilde's ears. Bosie hisses and leaps at Wood, only to be swatted into the darkness. Wilde sees him disappear, calls out to him, but can do nothing to help. The chant rises like it would shake all of London. Wilde cringes, stabs one finger into his right ear, and retreats to Charlie.

Alfred Wood leaves the circle and leaps at Wilde. Light leaps off the ring's gemstone like the lash of a whip, strikes Wood in the chest and thrashes him back into the cluster of his companions, bowling them over and breaking the chant. Wilde seizes the moment to scoop Charlie into a sitting position.

"Wilde!"

He looks and sees Stephen standing alone, his arms raised. He shouts toward the ceiling, no doubt an invocation for his Great Goddess. Alfred Wood and the others get to their feet and gather at Stephen's back, adding their voices to the new prayer.

The scarab ring's light begins to dim. The metal band becomes so hot it feels like it's melting into his flesh.

Wilde shrieks and starts to pull the ring from his finger. He stops himself in the last moment. What if the light hasn't faded? What if the ring isn't burning him? What if the chanting is making him hallucinate?

Forcing himself to endure the pain, he keeps his left hand out and tries to ignore the ring's waning energy. He works his right hand under Charlie's body and tries to hoist the uncooperative weight. "Charlie, please. Please, if you can hear me at all, if you can find your way back to me, I need your help."

Charlie's head falls forward. He coughs and his body spasms.

"That's it," Wilde says, exerting all his strength to lift Charlie to his feet while keeping the ring out for protection. The screams of Stephen and his changeling army continue at a furious rate. Wilde can't even hear his own thoughts now. The one thing he knows is that none of his adversaries have moved. If the ring's powers are ebbing, wouldn't they be pressing their advantage? He clings to his hopes as he drags Charlie to the bookcase. It won't open. All the prying and pulling he can muster won't budge it an inch.

"Mr. Wilde!" Stephen calls. "There is no escaping destiny."

Destiny, Wilde tells himself. The word's been on his mind his whole life. The belief he was meant to be better, greater than his fellow man. The sense of being able to achieve things others could not, to take risks and know only rewards. But there was always a shadow over these bright notions, a certainty that his life will burn like a matchbook all at once rather than as a series of matches, more magnificent as a burst but also short on chances. Guilt and failure can be the most perverse carriage horses, especially in the reins of terror.

He sways on his feet, almost dropping Charlie. The ring, flickering and dying before his eyes, seems to compel his left hand into making an actual punch. He strikes the bookcase and the barrier swings open. Wilde pulls himself and Charlie through, stumbling onto the floor on the other side. He kicks the bookcase shut again and just lays there, pulse too rapid to allow him anything except the shallowest of breaths.

Bosie, he thinks, knowing it's impossible to go back. He squeezes his eyes shut against grief, telling himself his lover will somehow be okay.

"Here, what's this?"

A man appears in the doorway. It is not Chyron. Wilde has no idea who it is, but he wears the clothes of a barman, and he has a white towel draped over his right shoulder.

"What are the two of you doing in the back of my pub?"

Wilde laughs despite himself, envious of anyone with so mundane a question to trouble the mind.

# PART FOUR

# CHAPTER FORTY

*Wandsworth Prison, August 12, 1895*

Wilde wakes when he falls out of bed and strikes his head on the floor. He makes an unintelligible sound and reaches up a flailing hand to take a weak grip on the mattress frame. He attempts to pull himself up, managing less than an inch before collapsing with his right cheek against the cold, dusty floor.

What day is it? What month? He can only organize time according to the last time he was fed . . . three days ago.

With supreme effort, he rolls onto his back and rests there in silence for several minutes, making little swallows in his parched throat. He imagines himself as Christ on the cross, surrounded by an applauding audience at this, his last performance. His lips manage a rueful smile and a ragged, exhausted laugh. Opening his eyes a fraction to look at the ceiling, he says, "Gallows humor. Forgive the impudence, Lord. I don't need new enemies."

He loses consciousness, but for how long? A few minutes? Hours? A metallic rasp jars him back to the waking world.

Someone has opened the food slot.

He rocks his body back and forth until momentum gathers and carries him onto his left shoulder. The cell door looms large before him, but less threatening because of the tray there. A tray—a plate—and something on the plate.

An illusion, he tells himself. But starved as he is, he'll eat a fantasy.

A voice whispers from the other side of the door. "Wilde?"

He can't find the strength or the oxygen to answer loud enough to be heard, but he kicks and inches himself along the floor, reduced to a pathetic, humiliating wallow toward something that might be nothing more than a cruel prank. He would not put it past Stephen to offer food and remove it just as it's within his grasp.

He remembers being able to reach the door in three strides. Now it takes him three minutes. The tray is not retracted, however, and he reaches a trembling hand to touch the food. His fingers sink into the soft luxury of hot, buttery bread.

Wilde pulls the small loaf into his lap, slumps against the door and crams the bread into his mouth, breathless in his chewing and swallowing. He devours half of it in two minutes.

"*Wilde.*"

He looks toward the food slot above his head. "Who are you?"

"Amicus profundo."

Wilde responds with a bitter laugh at the Latin. How quaint such repartee seems, and how worthless.

"A friend from the depths? Robbie?"

"Anonymity for now."

Wilde chews another piece of bread, but slower, enjoying the taste. "I know your voice, but . . . knowing a voice means nothing anymore. Is it you after all, Stephen? Is the bread tainted? Will it only make me sick?"

"Don't insult me, Wilde. I've risked *everything* to bring it to you."

Wilde pushes himself away from the door, strengthened both by the bread and a growing certainty.

"Open the larger slot. Let me see your face."

"No."

"You're the man who came to me before. Who whispered my wife's Latin motto when I needed strength. But how could you know it?"

No response comes from the other side. After a moment he detects the faint, light noise of footsteps sneaking away, almost as stealthy as the tread of a panther. Wilde takes another bite, but what he struggles to swallow most is his utter disbelief.

The Marquess of Queensberry has saved his life.

# CHAPTER FORTY-ONE

*London, April 15, 1894*

Wilde stumbles out of the pub with Charlie half-slung over his shoulder. He has no notion of the hour other than its nighttime. He turns right, with no plan in mind other than putting as much distance between this place and themselves as possible. A coach slows to a halt in front of him and Robbie leans his head out, shouting, "Oscar!" Wilde stares in disbelief as Robbie opens the door and beckons to them.

"How on Earth did you know we'd be here?" he says as they get Charlie inside.

"It was Constance. I was in my room, about to drowse off, when she just appeared to me with instructions. Well, after what I've already seen, I wasn't about to doubt or disappoint her."

Wilde squeezes his forearm. "No doubt the reason she chose you in the first place."

They shut the door and Robbie tells the coachman to get the carriage moving. As it lurches forward, his gaze lingers on the unconscious Charlie.

"Who is *this*, Oscar?"

"A friend, and the only man I've ever met as courageous, noble and loyal as yourself."

"He looks to be in a bad way."

"He's been drugged with opium. Or perhaps with something that is only being *called* opium. We just escaped with our lives when you arrived."

He looks at his scarab ring. The green stone shows no light, and the band is cool to the touch. His skin is not burned. So, it *was* an illusion, he tells himself. If so, then perhaps the changing tavern sign, the differences in appearances—all facades of the mind.

"Constance must have known just when you'd need me."

"It heartens me if she's alive and well. My last contact with her was . . . unsettling, as if she stood on the edge of an abyss."

"She seemed fine when I saw her."

"That makes me very—"

Charlie mutters something and his right arm twitches. He makes a fist and throws a hook, only just missing Robbie, who crams himself into the corner of his seat.

"Easy now," Wilde says, grabbing the flailing arm.

"Not safe," Charlie says, his voice a slur.

"I assure you we are. We're in a carriage, heading for—where *are* we going, Robbie?"

Wilde listens to the street address, recognizing it straight away. "The residence of Francis Galton. Are you sure?"

"I don't know who lives there, Oscar. Constance didn't say. She just made me repeat what I told her so that I had it down. But why would she or anyone in the Golden Dawn send us to him?"

"Perhaps because I'm already in consultation with him."

"Why?"

"Scientia vincere tenebras," Wilde says, smiling. "I thought it best to ally myself with experts in *both* realms of knowledge."

"Danger," Charlie says, head lolling. Wilde and Robbie both look at him.

"No, Charlie. See here," he says, holding up his left hand. "The ring would tell us."

"Him."

Charlie's right hand raises, pointing at Robbie before dropping back to the carriage seat, all energy spent.

"*Me?* Oscar, I swear I don't know why he'd point at me. Am I not here because Constance sent me?"

"Yes," he says, hating the edge of doubt in his tone.

"Oscar, the man's hardly conscious! He's fighting something in his imagination and conflating it with me."

Wilde looks at his ring again, drawing Robbie's curiosity. Wilde tries to explain its new abilities as best he can.

"Well," Robbie says, "if it warns you of trouble, and if it's *not* glowing in my presence, doesn't that confirm I'm safe?"

Wilde wants to agree with this assessment, but questions plague him. Could the ring's powers be exhausted? Was its waning light *not* a hallucination after all? Or could its present dull state be the hallucination? Perhaps the ring is blazing in the cramped confines of the carriage, and he sits here insensate to it, like a deaf man with his back to a screaming herald.

"I think it best if neither of us moves until the carriage comes to a stop, Robbie."

Robbie crosses his arms at the chest. "If it satisfies you, Oscar, I'll sit here still as the grave."

"Let us hope *its* stillness lies many decades in wait for us."

The carriage speeds them through the dark.

# CHAPTER FORTY-TWO

When they arrive at Galton's home, Wilde finds a blaze of activity happening in the windows. Men smoking, drinking and laughing register in every pane, their boisterousness loud enough to be heard in muted tones from the carriage.

"It seems Constance brought us to a party," Robbie says. "This looks like we're outside the Albermarle Club. Who knew men of science were so jovial?"

"Perhaps the celebration indicates Galton's made a breakthrough related to our problem. It may be why Constance sent us here."

They look at each other.

"Very well," Robbie says. "Should I get out first? Assuming you're still afraid I'm going to stab you in the back."

"That's unfair of you."

Robbie's expression softens. He apologizes, opens the door and gets out. "I'll pay the coachman."

Wilde works Charlie toward the door. Robbie returns to help him.

"Constance seems to have even taken care of the payment in advance, Oscar," he says, grinning. "The coachman refused my money."

Wilde turns to look up at the driver on his perch. An elderly fellow smiles down at him and waves.

"Very well. Help me get Charlie to the doorstep. If nothing else, we can get a bed for him."

Robbie puts Charlie's right arm around his neck and they advance. "Since we're friends again, Oscar, I'll admit I wouldn't mind sharing that particular bed. Go ahead and call me incorrigible."

"The only thing the incorrigibility of youth has on the incorrigibility of age is stamina and speed. Fortunately, age has learned of the pleasure inherent in taking one's time."

They reach the door and Wilde knocks.

"I cannot imagine how we must look," Robbie says.

"We'll be a true test of the unflappability of Mr. Galton's butler."

But Galton himself answers the door and stares at them.

"Mr. Galton," Wilde says. "I can only apologize now and hope to explain later. We're in urgent need."

Galton shakes his head in confusion even as he lifts Charlie's face for inspection. "What's happened? Where the devil have the two of you been?"

"Searching for answers," Wilde says, the only words that come to mind. The old scientists motions them inside and leads them down a hallway. Several men of various ages cast critical stares at them. Standing in clouds of cigar and pipe smoke, they seem like Olympians who've happened to notice three mere mortals.

Galton opens the door to a little room with a divan and urges them to rest Charlie there.

"Searching for answers, eh?" he says as he thumbs back Charlie's eyelids. "You've been searching for some time. I was beginning to think I'd never speak to you again."

"How long have you been trying to contact me?"

"Five days."

"I would swear you were at my house only this morning, removing my floorboards. But no matter—I believe you."

"All my messengers returned telling me no one would answer at your address. Finally, I came around myself and met your butler. The lad looked frantic, saying he had no idea where you were."

"Poor Arthur. I will have to send word. I—I didn't intend to be away as long as I apparently was."

Galton grunts at this and sits back. "Our young friend appears to be drugged with opiates."

"Yes."

"It's disgraceful such a fine specimen as this would fall into that gutter."

"Rest assured, Mr. Galton, that it was done against his will."

"Monstrous," the old scientist says with genuine contempt. "The only thing we can do is keep him safe until the effects wear off. How long would you say he's been in his present condition?"

"Hours, perhaps. I can't be sure."

"Very well. We'll leave him to rest here. I assure you he couldn't be in a better place tonight, scientifically speaking."

"What do you mean?"

"I mean to say that the leading men of every scientific discipline in the country have convened under my roof tonight."

# CHAPTER FORTY-THREE

Galton leads Wilde and Robbie into another room occupied by six men. "I am pleased to introduce the man who is perhaps the genesis of tonight's wonderful symposium. Gentlemen, I give you Mr. Oscar Wilde."

Wilde exchanges glances with Robbie as the scientists applaud. He then looks to Galton.

"If I am tonight's genesis, I shall endeavor to be as biblical as possible."

This wins a laugh from everyone and Wilde bows.

"Yes, indeed," Galton says. "Thanks to your consultation, I have made a discovery whose conclusions will outstrip even the profundity of Darwin and Davy. Of course, I tried to tell you about it first, but as you could not be reached, I brought in all these great men now exchanging ideas in my home."

"I see."

Galton points to one man, perhaps forty years of age, and says, "For example, here we have Leonard Dobbin of Edinburgh University, quite the expert on all matters of chemistry. And here we have the preeminent physiologist, Walter Gaskell."

"I am humbled to be in the company of such esteemed scholars. May I inquire as to what your discovery is, Mr. Galton, if it requires such a diversity of expertise?"

Galton claps his hand on Wilde's forearm, his friendliness disconcerting considering the man's prior reaction to him. An imposter? Wilde glances at his scarab ring for reassurance. Finding it dark, he can only chalk up the change to the exultation of the moment.

"Of course! Gentlemen, please excuse us. I will show Mr. Wilde my astonishing findings. We will return soon."

He leads them from the room and down another hallway, pontificating along the way.

"I've often thought myself blessed to live in the 19th century, a time ushered in by the Age of Reason. Ours is in an age of perpetual breakthroughs in all of the sciences. The map of the world is being colored in by bold colonizers with dispassionate, analytical minds. But other maps are expanding too. What is the periodic table, after all, if not a map that grows as each new element is rooted out of darkness."

"That is very well put," Wilde says.

"Of course, my personal passion—my scientific country—is biology. I have been across the globe pursuing biological mysteries, and as I've aged and become more aware of lurking infirmities, I thought my time in the light over. All one can hope to do when the sun is setting is cast a long shadow. Who knew I could make a discovery so close to home, and so bright as to be its own sun?"

Galton opens a door to an isolated room that makes Wilde think of Victor Frankenstein. On the nearest table, tongues of flame from a row of six small burners lap the bases of beakers suspended above them. The glass containers hold liquids of different colors. A single brass microscope sits on another table in the room's center.

Wilde turns his head at a sharp inhale from Robbie and follows his frantic gesturing.

The scarab ring blazes like a beacon.

He jams his left hand into his pocket just as Galton turns to smile at them.

"The wood from your bedroom floor, as well as the water from your butler's wash pail, have been subjected to every conceivable test. The results are hard enough for the scientific mind to comprehend. They may be inconceivable to you. I would therefore like to preface their revelation with an anecdote."

Wilde swallows, his gaze shifting around the room. The ring must be reacting to the blood, he tells himself.

"If you feel that's best," he says. "Robbie and I are an eager audience."

"Very good. On my first expedition to Africa, I encountered what seemed at a distance to be a great, moving carpet. Coming closer, I found this carpet to be the greatest mass of ants I ever witnessed. The general organization of ant colonies is well known, of course."

"Even to laymen," Wilde says.

"Quite so. But like everything on that dark continent, even the ants were stranger than what we're accustomed to in the civilized world. I stood watching thousands upon thousands of ants working together, linking themselves for a single-minded purpose, and—are you familiar with *the uncanny*, Mr. Wilde?"

"Sir," Wilde says, "I feel of late rather overly familiar with the concept."

Galton nods and grunts his approval. "Then you'll understand how I, as a much younger man, felt when this swarm of conjoined ants rose and took on the full outline of a man. This outline was my height. They even formed two separate legs. It was as if these hundreds of thousands of ants had recognized me and chose to confront me as a mirror image. It lasted only a few seconds. In the blink of an eye their structure collapsed and that carpet of ants flowed away from me. I told myself I had hallucinated the experience out of illness. But as you can see, I never doubted what I saw, and that certainty has prepared me for the infinitely more astonishment I found in the blood samples from your home."

"Please tell us."

Galton points to the microscope. "Perhaps your young friend would like to take a look through the eyepiece."

Wilde nods to Robbie, who goes to the table and listens as Galton instructs him about fine-tuning the view. With their backs to him, Wilde risks a glance at his ring. Its glow continues unabated.

"Good Lord."

Wilde hides his left hand again. "What is it, Robbie?"

"Drawings, I think."

This observation draws a pleased laugh from Galton. "Your characterization is as good as any. Have either of you looked at blood under great magnification?"

They both say no.

"Comparative hematology has fascinated me for many years. It is too difficult to describe in brief, but suffice it to say that all blood, mammalian or reptilian, avian or aquatic, have similarities—none of which exist in the blood sample on the microscope."

"May I see, Robbie?"

He squints into the eyepiece and stands there for half a minute, unable to organize his thoughts about what confronts him.

"Hieroglyphics?"

Galton claps his hands. "Very good, Mr. Wilde!"

He pulls back to look at the slide itself, finding only a blotch of red on the thin glass strip.

"What could explain this?"

"Nothing so far known to science. But the reach of our microscopes improves every day. I've already been in touch with Dr. Altmann in Germany, whose recent developments in staining techniques have improved our view of the unseen world greatly. It may be possible that all cells have these images embedded in them *somewhere*."

"Incredible."

Galton slaps Wilde's back. "It is gratifying to see you of all people at a loss for words, Mr. Wilde!"

The old scientist inclines toward the eyepiece and hums to himself.

"Sir," Wilde says. "You said that the Empire's top scientists are gathered here tonight to exchange their thoughts."

"Yes, quite correct."

"Considering the apparent nature of the symbols, I wondered if you have also brought in—"

"An Egyptologist?" Galton says, looking up and smiling. "Yes, naturally, and also the very best expert available to us. No less than the director of the National Museum, Mr. Edward—"

"Thompson," Wilde whispers.

Galton's eyebrows lift. "Do you know him?"

"Only a little. We spoke . . . some time ago."

"Then you should take this opportunity to renew your acquaintance."

"He's here *now*?"

"Indeed—somewhere. Probably holding court on the sketches he made while looking through the lens. He studied almost a hundred samples. You and your friend wait here. I'll go and find him."

# CHAPTER FORTY-FOUR

As soon as Galton leaves, Wilde checks the scarab ring again and finds it blazing with green fire.

"We should get Charlie and go," Robbie says.

"But it could be reacting to the presence of the blood."

"Or it could be that any or all of the other people in this house aren't people at all."

Wilde starts to reply when Galton reenters with Edward Thompson following. He once again conceals the ring.

"Mr. Wilde!" Mr. Thompson says, stepping forward. "It's most extraordinary to see you again at this occasion. Your social circle really must be quite expansive to know so many dignitaries in both art *and* science."

Wilde shakes his hand. "In truth, sir, the fact is quite the opposite. I've always believed one can never have too few friends. One aspires to none at all, but alas, it's almost impossible to go through life without picking up some along the way."

The museum director shakes his head and laughs. "There's perhaps much to be recommended in your inverted proverb, Mr. Wilde."

"Proverbs are first cousins to riddles. It seems we find ourselves confront a riddle worthy of the Sphinx. What do you make of the hieroglyphs revealed under Mr. Galton's microscope?"

"I am perplexed as everyone else by the seeming impossibility of their existence."

"Am I given to understand you undertook a prolonged sketch of many slides? If so, I'd like to know more. For instance, are they always the same hieroglyphs?"

"Not at all," Mr. Thompson says. "Which only makes their existence more amazing."

"Then they're definitely Egyptian?"

"I'm reluctant to affirm such a thing yet, considering the outlandishness of the assertion. Mr. Galton's enthusiasm aside, I think you'll find the rest of us quite cautious. But I will say the symbols I copied are remarkably similar. Not all, of course. There were glyphs that I've never seen before."

"Interesting," Wilde says. "One thing I'm very curious about is whether you were able to deduce actual meaning from the arrangement of the symbols. If so, it might give a whole new meaning to the phrase *blood lore!*"

Wilde sees Mr. Thompson steal a glance at Galton, perhaps wondering if he's at liberty to divulge all he knows.

Or perhaps thinking something else altogether, Wilde tells himself. The light from his scarab ring has never had accompanying warmth, but just now a steady heat builds within his left pocket, as if the light would burn through the fabric.

Mr. Thompson walks over to the microscope and peers into the eyepiece.

"It is amazing what science has achieved, isn't it? We're so concerned about the stories we tell ourselves and the facts we know. But this little device shows us there are other stories and facts surrounding us. Being otherwise invisible, perhaps they are truer. No doubt God lurks somewhere unseen in all of this. If not God, then a goddess."

Galton laughs. "Go on and tell Mr. Wilde your belief about the hieroglyphs, Mr. Thompson. The cat will be quite out of the bag soon enough, no need to keep it a secret."

"A pertinent analogy," Mr. Thompson says, still looking through the scope.

Wilde stiffens. "Well then? Robbie and I are both eager to hear about your findings."

"The hieroglyphics seem to describe the rise of a cult, one centered on a goddess old even by the standards of ancient Egypt. Bast—or Bastet. She was quite prominent in Egypt during the Second Dynasty, some four thousand years ago."

"Interesting," Wilde says. "What was she the goddess of, exactly?"

Mr. Thompson lifts his face from the microscope and smiles at Wilde. "Surely you've guessed."

"I'm afraid I don't know what you mean."

"Cats!" he says, taking a step forward. "My apologies, I was only thinking of your 'Sphynx' poem again. Cats were revered in Egypt for many reasons. Unfortunately for poor Bast, Egyptian society was in great turmoil during the time of her ascendancy, with rival priests all promoting their favorite deities, as well as their personal agendas. With the eroding influence of centuries, she eventually met the fate of most gods."

"Irrelevance," Wilde says.

Galton laughs. "Let me riff on Mr. Wilde's earlier sentiment about friends and say when it comes to gods, one can never have too few."

"But surely only one god is sufficient as long as that god is true," Mr. Thompson says. "What we find in the microscope gives evidence that more than two thousand years of Christian tyranny are wrong."

"Did you say *tyranny*, Mr. Thompson?"

"What else can a false religion be called, Mr. Wilde?"

"I am not sure that *any* religion is completely false," Wilde says.

Galton chuckles, touching Wilde's arm. "Just the opposite, I should say. *No* religion is true. Thankfully science has helped man forsake the basilisk for bacillus."

"Nothing is false if it captures some whiff of human desire, some shadow of human need. The loupe of science may reveal cracks in the gemstones of history and religion, but it will never stop most of us from preferring those flaws," Wilde says, wishing the conversation was as philosophical and frivolous as this sparring might suggest. Mr. Thompson remains standing in place, but a heavy sweat now bathes his face, even beading on his heavy black beard. There's a noise from somewhere else in the house and Wilde sees his gaze go to the room's only exit.

"What was that?" Robbie says.

Mr. Galton puts his hand on the door. "The hour is growing late. I suspect it is the sound of champagne corks popping."

Then why, Wilde wonders, are people toasting with screams?

# CHAPTER FORTY-FIVE

Wilde loses sight of Mr. Thompson when the door bursts open and several scientists rush in, knocking Galton down in the process. He yanks his left hand from his pocket, revealing and reveling in the blazing green light.

But no one else seems to notice it in their panic.

"No windows," one says, hand over a bleeding cut in his forehead. "We've doomed ourselves."

Wilde helps Galton to his feet. The old man trembles. "What on Earth is happening?"

More gunshots ring out, followed by cries and pleading.

The chemist Leonard Dobbin clutches his left arm. Wilde sees more blood. "They're shooting us! They've come to kill us!"

"*Who?*"

"The anarchists—the same ones who tried to blow up the Observatory. It has to be them."

"They hate science."

"They hate order!"

So many voices begin talking at once Wilde has trouble hearing the gunfire.

"I was by the front door when they came in," Dobbin says. "Five or six of them. Two went upstairs. All of us together . . . too tempting a target . . ."

More shots, more screams. Galton stands witless next to Wilde as they watch the men begin barricading the door with anything they can find. Robbie pulls Wilde back and they retreat to the furthest wall to watch these cool, educated men descend into mindless survival tactics. They push the nearest table against the door, jarring loose one of the beakers. It breaks on the floor and black smoke rises from the floorboards.

"Cover your nose and mouth," Wilde says at the first whiff of a foul, acrid odor. Robbie obeys.

The harsh scent seems to bring Galton to his senses. He stumbles back to the center table, his hands out to ward off the scientists as they look to strengthen the barricade. They knock him to the ground and haul the table to the door. The brass microscope breaks apart on the floor and Galton crawls to it, hunching over the pieces. As smoke builds inside the room, Wilde sees the old man weeping and holding a fragment of his prized slide before his eyes.

Someone barges against the other side of the door. The scientists push back against the table, all their weight thrown into the defense.

Wilde makes his left hand into a fist and holds it out in front of him.

"Will the ring protect us against anarchists?" Robbie says.

"I suspect not. But I don't think that's what we're up against."

"Why? The way Constance described it, creatures from the spirit world don't have much use for guns."

"They might if the object is to conceal who they are. Galton's discovered a secret about them they'd like to keep unknown. And it seems clear to me that Mr. Thompson had already chosen his allegiances, either by coercion or free will."

Another blow against the door sends the scientists falling back and casts the tables asunder, shattering the remaining beakers and over-turning the burners. Their flames spread quick, skating across the fluid to take hold of the table legs and floor. The door meanwhile explodes open and four men storm the room, firing pistols. The light from Wilde's ring lances into their eyes like radiant pokers, driving them to their knees in a shrieking frenzy. The light batters them without mercy and their flesh begins to smoke like kindling under the concentrated sun-light of a magnifying glass.

"They're burning up, Oscar!"

"Not quite," Wilde says, advancing, bracing his left wrist with his right hand. The light floods over his foes, obliterating their masks, shat-tering their false shells, revealing the hairless, ashen creatures beneath. They writhe and fall upon their sides, guns dropped, hands clawing at their faces.

"Now's our chance!" Robbie says, running to Galton. But the old man sits weeping over his broken microscope and shattered dream, in-sensate to any urgency. Wilde and Robbie abandon him and escape the room just before the fire makes the doorway collapse.

Led by Wilde, they trace a tortured, suffocating route back to Char-lie. Each hallway and room reveals carnage and butchery. Shot men lay bleeding and calling for help. They pause in one doorway where two enormous panthers gorge themselves on a fallen man. Wilde's outrage explodes and he strikes them with the ring's light, gnashing his teeth to their agonized hissing. He steps toward them, determined to shove his hand down their throats and burn them from the inside out. Only Robbie's pulling embrace prevents him from this vengeance. He shouts at Wilde, telling him what his senses already recognize.

Mr. Galton's house will collapse in minutes.

He relents and they race down a hallway. The smoke thickens and the green light becomes a sudden enemy, aiding the smoke in obscuring their vision. Wilde bends forward to clear his lungs in a series of ragged coughs.

"Charlie!" Robbie shouts. "Charlie, can you hear us?"

Another panther leaps at them from the haze. Wilde's mind flashes back to his encounter with the beast in the labyrinth's mist. He brandishes the ring and sends a lance of energy straight into its yellow eyes. The powerful cat drops crippled and whimpering, ramming its head into a wall in frustrated rage.

Wilde and Robbie run.

"Where is Charlie's room?"

"It wasn't far from the front door."

"Well, where the hell is *that?*"

Wilde can't answer. Glowing, angry eyes float at him in the smoke. There must be twenty panthers surrounding them, crouching in their viciousness and eager to spring. But no attacks come. The panthers will not challenge the ring's power.

"There, Oscar! The front door!"

"Then Charlie's room must be—"

A horrible crash comes from behind them. Robbie grabs Wilde by his coat and throws him forward just as the ceiling collapses. Wilde turns to look at the remains at his back. There is only ruin and fire.

"*Charlie.*"

He just stands there, hands at his sides, face wet with sweat and tears.

I've lost Bosie and now I've lost Charlie, he tells himself, turning his gaze down to the ring. How worthless it seems now. How impotent.

"Oscar, we've got to leave!"

"I can't continue, Robbie. I'm sorry."

210

The ring dims. Wilde's stands there inhaling the nasty, scorching smoke and with a cold detachment watches the light die. Part of him wants to take the ring off his pinkie and fling it into the rubble.

Robbie spins him around and shakes him.

"We've *got* to go on."

Wilde lets Robbie lead him from the burning house. They stagger away with no direction in mind until a voice calls out to them.

"Oscar, the carriage we arrived in—it's still here."

"Aye," the driver says, staring at the burning house like it's an ordinary sight. "The woman who hired me paid me a king's ransom to bring you here and wait no matter what happened."

"*Constance.*"

"She never gave me her name."

"You're very courageous to wait here for us, payment or not," Wilde says.

The man nods and then glances to the house. The sounds coming from the engulfing flames belong to the imagination of Dante.

"Best be getting in, I think, and I'll take you to the next place you're to go."

"Which is?"

He scratches his head and laughs. "Funny thing is, she wouldn't tell me. But she said my horses would know the way."

# CHAPTER FORTY-SIX

Neither of them speak in the darkness of the cab. Wilde hangs his head and lets silent tears fall for Charlie. Bosie's ambiguous fate made it easier to subdue grief, but Wilde can find no hope in his heart for Charlie. His one wish now is the opium kept him insensate to the pain.

He twists the scarab ring off his finger and places it in the palm of his hand.

"Meaningless," he says.

"What, Oscar?"

"What good is this ring if I couldn't use it to save someone I care about as much as Charlie? I'd rather have given him the ring and swapped places in the rubble."

"That's selfish."

Wilde winces at the rebuke. "You've no right to judge me like that."

"I've got every right. You remember what Constance and the others said. We're in a fight we don't even understand. The stakes are higher than your life or mine or anyone else's. If the ring can help us win in the end then nothing else matters."

"I assure you other things matter, Robbie. I don't even want the ring any more. It's yours if you'd like it."

When Robbie stays silent, Wilde pulls back the window blind, intending to pitch the ring into the night. But what he sees paralyzes him.

"Good God."

Robbie leans toward the window. "Where are we, Oscar? I've never seen fog like this."

"I have—in the labyrinth."

He puts his head through the window and yells for the driver to stop.

No one answers but the carriage comes to a halt.

Robbie opens the door.

"Wait," Wilde says, pushing the ring back onto his pinkie.

"If you wanted us to stay in the carriage you shouldn't have asked the driver to stop. Come on, Oscar."

"Not until we have some notion that it's safe."

Robbie scowls and gets out over Wilde's further objections. The mist swallows him in moments. Wilde reaches one arm out the door, groping for his friend, finding nothing.

"Robbie?"

The answering voice isn't male. Wilde strains to hear a woman singing—

*Come forth my lovely languorous Sphinx, and*
*Put your head upon my knee.*

He recognizes the words at once, for he is their author. But they never sounded lovelier or more alluring. As the singing continues, Wilde finds himself standing outside the carriage. He has no memory of stepping out of it and understands as never before the concept of the siren's song.

He holds on to the carriage door even as the song pulls his imagination into the mist. He doesn't remember letting go. He doesn't remember taking a step. There's no crunch of gravel to give evidence of his footfalls. There's only movement as gentle and fluid as the voice.

*"You have kept me waiting, Oscar."*

Wilde sways. "I was unaware we had an appointment."

*"I have been waiting for you to discover my name."*

He turns. The mist is everywhere, lovely and white.

Bast, he thinks. The word conjures the taste of honey in his mouth. "If time was of the essence, why not give it to me sooner?"

*"Much potential is lost when discovery is denied."*

"Constance?" he starts to say, then bites it back. He may or may not be in the labyrinth, but the woman with him is not his wife.

*"Speak my name, Oscar."*

"Who says I know it?"

*"If you did not, this introduction would not be happening."*

Wilde pivots again, unable to pinpoint the speaker. The source changes from sentence to sentence and even from word to word.

"Your name is Bast."

*"Your queen."*

A shape emerges in front of him. At first it seems like a naked woman approaching, but the figure that emerges is an enormous panther, far larger than any he encountered during the attack on Galton's home. Its coat gleams black and its yellow eyes glisten.

"This land already has a queen," Wilde says, raising his left hand. "Stay back."

The ring shows no light, no power.

*"What so astounds you, child?"*

The voice coming from the panther's mouth has notes of seduction and sarcasm. Surely this is the voice of Sacher-Masoch's Wanda.

"My ring."

*"You're surprised your troublesome jewelry finds no threat in me?"*

"Yes."

*"Because I am no threat. Mothers harbor no harm for their children."*

214

"You call yourself a mother, Bast?"

The panther offers a silken laugh. "Do children call their mothers by their first name?"

"Mine was an unconventional childhood."

The panther and Wilde circle one another.

"*You're afraid.*"

"Yes."

"*I do not wish this. Think of the place where you feel the most safe and secure.*"

Wilde imagines his home library. The panther opens its terrifying mouth and a gust of hot wind shoots forth. The mist swirls and dissipates. As it goes, new details emerge. He sees floorboards and then familiar furniture. He finds himself staring at a wall lined with bookcases.

"Is this better?"

Wilde turns to discover one of the most stunning women he's ever seen sitting in his favorite armchair. Long black hair flows in a simple braid that falls over the front of her right shoulder. Dark eyes, sultry red lips, pale skin—he recognizes her as so many men's ideal of alluring femininity, which he tried to capture when he wrote "The Sphinx," his long poem so admired by Mr. Thompson.

"Cozy," she says, and no voice could better match her face.

"*Safe.*"

"No place is really safe for a man like you, Oscar."

"What do you mean?"

"You already know. Stray a little from the narrow path you walk, and the world will brand you a criminal because their hearts are chained to the morality of a false god."

"Your code is different?"

"My morality is not based on nonsense rules that chain the heart and the mind to cold stone tablets. I also don't require faith without evidence. My favors are not bestowed through cryptic means, and I am not hypocritical in my wrath."

"I take it you see yourself as a liberator of mankind?"

She smiles. "With your help."

"I don't see what use I could be to you."

She rises, noiseless, delicate, and walks around him, trailing the fingers of her right hand along his shoulders. Once more she sings—

*Come forth my lovely languorous Sphinx, and*
*Put your head upon my knee.*
*And let me stroke your throat and see your*
*Body spotted like the lynx.*

"Beautiful," she says, pleasure purring in her voice. "I know all of your words, from the sanguine to the decadent to the flippant."

"I'm honored."

"Your *honor* is yet to come. I think of the public prayers you'll write in the future. I see you on your knees, arms raised before the obelisk of my temple, chanting those prayers as thousands upon thousands of men and women join you in chorus."

"This sounds like you want me to be some kind of priest."

She reaches up and kisses his lips. Wilde tries to pull away from her, but she puts one hand over his eyes. In the darkness her palm brings he finds a vision of St. Paul's Cathedral crumbling, throwing dust into the air like ash from a volcanic eruption. He sees all of London, men, women and children, laboring from sunrise to sunset, clearing the debris so a new structure can rise, a different temple dedicated to a different deity.

It takes the form of a pyramid.

# CHAPTER FORTY-SEVEN

Wilde stumbles back, rubbing his eyes as if to scrub the vision from his mind. His back strikes one of the bookshelves just as the door opens and Constance rushes through, accompanied by Yeats and Robbie.

"Oscar, are you okay?" she says before he can speak. She touches him all over, patting his arms, shoulders and chest.

"I believe I'm solid," he says, looking at all of them in a daze. Robbie comes forward and embraces him.

"Looks like we had a repeat of our last go in the labyrinth. The Order managed to whisk me safely to the center, but something happened to you."

"You were intercepted," Yeats says.

"Am I really at home?"

"Yes," Constance says. "This is your library. We've been trying to break into it for two days."

Wilde turns, contemplating this information. "It felt like twenty minutes."

"Tell us everything, Mr. Wilde."

He does to the best of his ability. Wilde notices Constance and Yeats exchange several glances over the course of his telling. When he finishes, Constance moves around the room, inspecting every corner and cranny—except her eyes are closed. This goes on for several minutes before she opens her eyes again.

"Something very powerful was in the room, and it tried to conceal its presence upon leaving."

"Is this Bast really a—a goddess?" Robbie says.

"To the minds of ancient humanity," Constance answers.

"What is she to *you?*" Wilde says.

"An entity from another realm, possessed of powers that hold dire consequences for our own. But we have power, too. Will, go and tell the Order what we have discovered. Spread the news to all adepts across the world."

"At once," Yeats says.

"Robbie, I'd like you to go with him. I need to speak with my husband alone."

Robbie nods and leaves the room with Yeats. As soon as they do, Constance sits down on the very armchair Bast last occupied. Wilde kneels down and takes her hands.

"There's something else I must tell you."

"Oh?" she says.

"Bast showed me a vision of London transformed. There was a pyramid where St. Paul's cathedral stands. I stood atop it dressed like an actor from a play, and maybe that is a fair analogy. It seems she wants me to be her high priest."

Constance stares off into the distance. Wilde snaps his fingers in front of her face. Her gaze shifts to meet his eyes and they stare at each other for a long moment. He's surprised when her fingers lift his left hand up. She touches the scarab ring and a look of inexplicable sorrow enters her expression.

"You've lost hope."

"What?"

She closes her eyes, seeming to meditate, and a tear runs down her cheek. This shocks Wilde into standing up.

"You feel you failed your friends," she says.

"Yes."

"Let your grief and anger come out, Oscar."

"No."

"It will poison you otherwise."

"Then let me be poisoned!"

Constace takes a deep, calm breath and looks at him with unblinking eyes. "I always knew you used flippancy to distance yourself from people and situations. Serious things can be hurtful, so you work your own magic and turn the serious into the ridiculous. But now you're face to face with something that thwarts your abilities."

"I'd never cheapen his memory by doing that."

Constance touches his forearm. "You're not speaking of Bosie, are you? There's another, someone you've come to care for more than Lord Alfred."

Wilde rubs his eyes before they have a chance to water. "His name was Charlie."

"His absence has cleft your soul."

"Constance, I know I've always been prone to falling in love with ease. This time was different. Perhaps the strongest love is always unrequited, though I should hate to think so. I couldn't save him. I had this ring and it overmastered all of Bast's disciples, yet none of that mattered. I could only stand in defeat as his body burned."

"You saw this?"

"No."

"Then—"

"Don't say there's hope that he survived, Constance. It would be impossible."

"If fate has taken him from you, Oscar, then concentrate on pleasant memories of your friend."

"We had so little time! I find myself imagining a thousand pleasant might-have-beens instead of a handful of things that *were*."

"My poor, suffering husband," she ways. "The innate power within your ring is hope, which is in large part our ability to love. I sense nothing from the gemstone now. But that is not a reflection of the ring, Oscar. It's a reflection of a change in you."

"Then maybe you should give the ring to someone else. Robbie, perhaps."

"It's your ring, Oscar. It always has been."

"Then find more rings and do the same *procedure* on them. It seems sensible that everyone should have such a weapon."

"If only everyone could. Your ring is very, very old. It may have been crafted when Bast enjoyed her first reign. The gemstone is a scarab beetle."

"Yes."

"Do you know what that symbol meant to ancient Egyptians?"

Wilde shakes his head.

"It is the symbol of Khepri, god of the morning sun. God of renewal, god of fresh starts."

"God of hope," Wilde says, his voice low.

"This ring was fashioned as a symbol of these things, Oscar. Perhaps it was always intended to be worn in defiance. It has an innate magic that has defied the perils of thousands of years to find its way to your finger. I take strength from the notion that your ownership of it isn't mere chance. But it's worthless if you can't find hope within yourself."

Wilde sighs. "I can only feel what I feel."

She rises, puts her hands on his shoulders, and kisses his cheek. "That's for the hurt in your heart, Oscar. Maybe it will heal and find hope again."

"Because you need me in the fight?"

"Because I care about my husband."

She pulls away, leaving him hanging his head. Thoughts blaze through his mind, burning up before he can even take note of them. He stands there battling an internal chaos as his gaze lights upon a glossy red envelope upon the table.

He takes it up and what he finds clears his mind and lets him focus. "Constance," he says, handing it to her. "I don't remember seeing this."

She opens it and reads the brief card. "From Edward Thompson, director of the National Museum. An invitation to a gallery opening— a new Egyptian exhibit. The reception is tonight."

They look at each other.

"Bast left it here, Constance. I'm sure of it."

"I also have no doubts."

"Surely she knows we won't go."

"But we must!"

"Why?"

"We've skirted the edges of Bast's game. She wants us to come forward and become players."

"That sounds like she's making a taunt."

"In a way."

"How can it be wise to submit to it?"

"It's not necessarily wise, Oscar. But there comes a point when the challenge must be meant. We've made our study. Delaying the encounter further won't give us an advantage."

A keen excitement radiates in his wife's face, astonishing Wilde. "You *want* this fight, don't you?"

"I try to keep my hubris in check."

"But admit the idea of combating Bast excites you."

She laughs. "It's the Irish in me."

"We Irish are also in love with noble, futile efforts."

"No," she says. "This goes far beyond mere concepts of nationality. To stand as a member of humanity and go toe-to-toe against a goddess ... to strive against such power ..."

She heads for the door.

"Constance, where are you going?"

She pivots, flashing a devilish smile that disconcerts him. "It's a lavish social event, Oscar. I want to make sure that I've selected my wardrobe with care."

# CHAPTER FORTY-EIGHT

Wilde doesn't see his wife again for five hours, but the alarming sounds coming from her bedroom keep him close to her door. Sometimes he hears a blacksmith's hammering, followed by the hiss of hot steel meeting water. At other times Constance sings in a language unfamiliar to him, and other voices—ethereal, haunting—join her.

But when he sees her at last, she appears wearing a bright green dress accented with red clovers.

"Do you like my armor, Oscar?" she says, turning.

His throat goes dry from immediate recognition and he struggles with a simple word. "Armor?"

"When it comes to magic, the seamstress is just as wily as the blacksmith. I do wish it could be more comfortable."

He forces himself to smile. "A fascinating essay topic to write about for the Rational Dress Society."

Constance stares at him. "Something's wrong."

"Yes."

"Tell me."

"You made me promise not to do so."

He watches her reaction as she processes this response, and a hint of worry enters her expression.

"We've communicated in a dream."

"Yes. In my past and your future—from a time I fear is fast approaching."

"I see," she says, smoothing out a wrinkle in the fabric.

"Constance, maybe I *should* tell you."

"No! Say nothing else!"

"But whatever knowledge I possess might be able to help you."

"It will only bring harm. There are rules to follow in this contest; laws as fundamental as anything found in physics. The consequences for breaking one is so dire even Bast abides by them."

"What about dream communications from someone else? Yeats has also appeared to me from some point even further in time."

Her warning look gives him the answer and they stand together in awkward silence.

"We should go," she says.

"You're still determined?"

"More than ever."

He gazes into the face of this woman, this warrior, unable to guess how her life with him has been satisfactory for even a moment.

"I'll do anything you tell me to do, Constance."

"Then I command you to be *you*," she says, and they leave holding hands.

PART FIVE

# CHAPTER FORTY-NINE

*Wandsworth Prison, August 30, 1895*

"Rise and shine," Stephen says, stomping the floor by Wilde's right ear. "It's a beautiful day for a coronation."

Wilde rolls onto his back, sensible to the presence of several people standing over him. He sees Stephen and his changeling henchmen. He also sees an older but sturdy man, stout and hardy for his age. The man's face would be unrecognizable to most beneath its various levels of disguise, but Wilde would know the Marquess of Queensberry anywhere. They make brief eye contact and Queensberry steps forward to kick him in the leg. Wilde gasps, cowering back as Stephen and the others laugh.

"That's for not acknowledging your queen fast enough," Queensberry says, with only a hair of affectation in his brutish tone.

"You're not bad for a human, Locke," Stephen says. "If the Great Goddess is determined to have one of you for her High Priest, I'd nominate you. This one is better fitted to be the first sacrifice. Look how plump! Even starvation hasn't made him shed his fat!"

They laugh at Wilde. He glares up at them with as much defiance as he can muster. If he could summon spit he'd soak their faces with it. But his mouth knows only sand.

"Victoria is the only queen I acknowledge."

Stephen bends down to him. "The Queen is dead," he says in a gloating whisper. "Long live the Queen."

Then it's done, Wilde thinks, another burden for his spirit.

"How different you'll find London when and if you ever leave this cell, Wilde. You should see the new obelisk in Trafalgar Square, right where Nelson's statue used to be."

"The British would never submit to such a thing."

"Nationalities don't make your kind any different, as much as you'd like to think so. Thousands of years haven't changed mankind at heart. Most go about their lives not noticing anything. Most are glad to have others do their thinking for them. Others spend their time judging the wind and aim to make sure their sails are always full. Isn't that right, Locke?"

"Smart men do," Queensberry says, staring at Wilde.

"That's right—smart men. If you were as clever as people make you out to be, Wilde, you'd quit being stubborn and lift yourself up. You'd be more precious to the Great Goddess than anyone in this room. You'd like that, wouldn't you? Give you a thrill I suspect, bossing me around, having me at your beck and call as the High Priest. Maybe even forcing me to change my appearance so you could enjoy yourself a little?"

His face riffles through a series of handsome transformations, stopping at Bosie. He presents this face back to Queensberry and Wilde sees a flash of rage in the man's eyes. But only a flash. Queensberry has mastery over himself.

"Get him cleaned up, Locke. The Great Goddess wants to have a private party for a few honored devotees who'll watch her put on the crown. Ritual has always amused her."

# CHAPTER FIFTY

*London, April 17, 1894*

"Here we go into the lion's den," Constance says as their carriage arrives at the National Museum.

"Panther would be more accurate."

They step out and a young man in black formal wear meets them with his right hand out. Wilde places the invitation into it and their greeter turns to lead them inside. Wilde notes many changes to the edifice since his last visit, including the absence of Grecian columns. The building has taken on a sandstone pigment, and twin engravings of a jackal-headed figure guard the main entrance.

Once inside, he sees no trace of the statues of Shakespeare, Damer and Banks. Steles with elaborate ornamentation now possess those places without explanation. One contains row after row of tiny hieroglyphics. Another has a single, dominant image of a woman with a cat's head. Constance nudges him and whispers, "That is a temple stele, Oscar. And that one there is a promulgation stele."

"Can you interpret the symbols from here? What does it promulgate?"

"The overthrow of old orders and the embrace of the new."

Their guide leads them into a vast, elegant banquet hall. Here he bows and parts ways with them, leaving them to stare. There must be two hundred revelers, all dressed in exquisite fashion. The men constitute a sea of black luxury in their evening suits, and the women are like colorful boats afloat on it. Laughter and cheer seem to be the room's dominant sounds. How nice the occasion would be, Wilde thinks, were it *just* an occasion. His gaze sweeps the room, wondering who is and isn't human. He looks to his scarab ring and finds it lifeless.

They enter the room, smiling and nodding at anyone who makes eye contact. Some people exclaim his name, though whether they do so in excitement or effrontery, he cannot know. An elderly man approaches and Wilde makes a stiff bow of acknowledgement only to be snubbed when the man brushes past him.

"If most of these are changelings, they've become *very* good an imitating the manners of rich Londoners."

Constance makes a fanciful grunt at the observation. "Do you see anyone you know?"

Wilde gives the room another scan. This time he finds someone he missed before. About fifty yards to their right, a man with receding hair stands next to a short obelisk, delivering some sort of lecture to a handful of listeners.

"That is Edward Thompson, the museum's director. He took part in the attack on Galton's home where Charlie died. I have a strong suspicion he's one of *them*."

"Be cautious with your assumptions, Oscar."

Constance walks toward the obelisk, pulling Wilde behind her. He catches snippets of different conversations along the way.

*"The National Museum is the jewel of the Empire—"*

*"Never seen so many relics, a true marvel—"*

*"Of course, I'm concerned about security. With so much of the government here, if the anarchists were to strike—"*

*"No, I don't know anything at all about Lady Gwendoline—"*

*"I feel as if all of ancient Egypt is in this room—"*

*"A female Egyptologist? I hope she's more attractive than Mary Bro-drick!"*

Mr. Thompson ends his lecture as soon as he sees them, to the clear gratefulness of his listeners. Wilde notes their hurried departure before turning his anxious attention to the director.

"Oscar! I'm so delighted you could be here. Is this your charming wife?"

"I am," Constance says, extending her hand. Mr. Thompson bends to kiss the top of it and Wilde detects nothing from the man other than supreme happiness.

"You're a ravishing sight, Mrs. Wilde. Such a radiant dress! I count myself so lucky to have you here. See, it's just as I told you it would be, Oscar. I'm surrounded by Parliamentarians."

Wilde smiles. "Yes, you can distinguish them from ordinary men by how they all look alike."

Mr. Thompson grips Wilde's forearm and leans in as if to whisper something conferential. But all he says is, "They act alike too. It must take a profoundly uncurious mind to have a successful political career. I see them reacting to our most spectacular acquisitions with all the interest of someone noting new carpet. Even Lord Rosebery clearly feigned any genuine interest in—"

"The Prime Minister?" Constance says. "Where is he?"

Mr. Thompson turns, looking about the room. He points to the back corner. "Right where I last left him, in fact. Over there with his assistant."

Wilde recognizes Bosie's brother first. Their resemblance is so strong that from a distance Wilde could believe Lord Drumlanrig to be Bosie himself.

"Stay here and enjoy yourself, Oscar. I need to see about something."

Before Wilde can answer, Mr. Thompson puts a hand on his shoulder and starts leading him away. When they reach a somewhat private spot, the museum director's grip tightens, and he speaks in an urgent whisper. "Why are you here?"

"Sir, I am here because you invited me."

"I made sure no such invitation was sent."

The men stare at each other. "You can always tell when a man is unaccustomed to sweating," Wilde says. "The shininess of his brow looks like condensation on a marble statue. I have noted the effect in the mirror from time to time."

Mr. Thompson wipes his forehead and scowls. "You and your wife must leave now."

"Why?"

"Don't pretend you don't know."

Wilde squares his shoulders. "Then I take it that was really you at Mr. Galton's house."

"Yes."

"Your treachery damns you, sir."

"It's *not* by choice," Thompson says, looking around. He takes Wilde's arm again and leads him still further away. "When Lady Gwendolyn came to me with her promises, I dismissed her at once. Then she showed me examples of the artifacts she boasted about being able to obtain. I was astonished."

"You were greedy."

"Greedy—*yes*—on behalf of the museum. On the behalf of science! I didn't realize I was committing myself to a Faustian bargain."

"Faust dealt with the devil, Mr. Thompson. Your compact is with an entity far worse."

He grimaces. "I fear you're right. I beg you to take your wife and leave here. Leave the *country*."

"You know Bast's—"

"Don't speak her name," Mr. Thompson says, cringing.

"The Great Goddess then, if it brings you less distress. But you must have an inkling of her interest in me. I doubt your first invitation to me was your idea."

"I'm very sorry to have brought you into this chaos."

"So why do you think I can escape it now?"

He just shakes his head. "All you can do is try."

"You understand why I should distrust you."

"I'm trying to help you, Wilde!"

"Perhaps. But this concern might also be a mask for your true intentions. I wonder if your fear of the Great Goddess is as great as you claim?"

"Look at my eyes and tell me if you don't see the fear."

They lock gazes.

"What if I were to tell you I saw jealousy instead?"

Mr. Thompson's mouth opens. "I have no such feelings."

"One of the Great Goddess' lieutenants told me she sees the world in terms of slaves and pets. Which one are you, sir? Or is there any real difference? The Great Goddess has chosen me to be her High Priest. Is that a fancy title for highest slave, or highest pet? Is that where your aspirations lay, Mr. Thompson? A dedicated Egyptologist like you must feel slighted. Perhaps you scheme to eliminate me as competition?"

The director grits his teeth like a man whose been slapped in the face. "I swear I'd kill myself on the spot if it could undo the harm I've already caused. I want nothing else to do with her. She terrifies me."

Wilde purses his lips, contemplating. Mr. Thompson is either a great actor or a man possessed by violent guilt. The man's lack of tears convinces Wilde it is the latter. Guilt, in Wilde's experience, tends to be a dry emotion in sincere men. Many false young men—Bosie most of all—have cried on his shoulder out of some expressed remorse, and he has cherished their theatricality and performance. Wilde studies Mr. Thompson's tearless eyes a moment longer and makes his decision.

He reaches out to the man, who almost collapses into his arms. They sit down at an empty table in the farthest corner of the room. "I do wish you and your wife would leave," Mr. Thompson says. "The two of you must be the most blameless people in the room."

"Let me find Constance. Tell her everything you've told me."

"In the name of God, why? She wouldn't understand anything I have to say."

"Mr. Thompson," Wilde says with a sympathetic smile, "Constance will have understood your words before you even speak them."

# CHAPTER FIFTY-ONE

When Wilde approaches his wife, he finds she has Prime Minister Rosebery entranced in conversation. Bosie's brother is not with them.

"Ah, Oscar," Constance says, all smiles. "Prime Minister, do you know my husband?"

Rosebery bows, the essence of courtesy. "By your words, of course, Mr. Wilde."

"Then you know me completely," Wilde says, and all three share a laugh. He makes the subtlest gesture with his eyes to urge Constance away, but she touches his forearm and remains in place.

"The Prime Minister was just telling me of a new reformation plan. Is that the right word for it?"

"Right enough, I suppose. We're looking into some architectural improvements throughout the empire, but we'll start in London."

"My husband would be very interested in what you were saying about the need of an empire to reflect its broader—*constituents*."

Wilde waits for an explanation.

"I believe the Empire should strengthen itself to the maximum extent," the Prime Minister says. "In that regard, yes, I feel certain changes are needed. Cultural adaptations reflective of both our territorial holdings and the military victories that secured them. Such things have been happening already, of course. Take Cleopatra's Needle in Westminster. Such a beautiful obelisk. My understanding is your own father played an important role in bringing it to England, Mr. Wilde."

"That is true," Wilde says, almost to himself.

"Seeing it must be a source of great satisfaction for you. A virtual testament to your father's foresight."

"Satisfaction wears many masks," Wilde says, and catches himself. He stares at Constance, who looks puzzled.

"So many people in England have an interest—an obsession, even—in Egyptology."

Constance laughs. "This museum is proof of that."

"Indeed," Rosebery says. "I suppose it has to do with the romance of ancient worlds, the intense mystery of it. How did Shelley put it in that poem of his? 'I met a traveler from an antique land'?"

Wilde bites back the desire to quote the entirety of "Ozymandias" from memory. "Having of late met some travelers from an antique land myself, I can tell you the experience left much to be desired."

Rosebery cocks his head and waits for an explanation.

"Will you excuse us, Prime Minister? There's something I must ask my husband."

"By all means. I need to find my private secretary. You know him, don't you, Mr. Wilde? His brother is your close friend, I believe."

"He is indeed," Wilde says, grateful when Constance pulls him away.

They start walking.

"Our troubles seem to be increasing by the minute, Oscar. Unless I'm very much mistaken, the man we've been talking to just now was not a man at all, and certainly not Lord Rosebery."

"I have no doubt. Mr. Thompson, however, is human—all too human—and just admitted his complicity in Bast's scheme. I believe you should hear what he has to say."

"I think that's—"

Constance stumbles, groaning as she puts her right hand on her forehead. Wilde catches her as her knees buckle.

"Is the lady ill?" a man says, rushing over. Others join him as Wilde settles her to the ground. They form a circle, tight with curiosity, and Wilde urges them back. He fans his wife's face, telling himself this is some trick on her part, some deception. Constance's eyes move back and forth beneath her lids. Her lips mutter words and he inclines his ear to listen.

*"Should I fall—should I die—"*

My God, he thinks, a chill shooting through him as his stomach turns leaden. The moment has arrived. Her present and my past are meeting—

And the future?

A secondary tumult turns the surrounding crowd to look at something more interesting than an unconscious woman. A very recognizable, belligerent voice bellows above all others, his voice gaining power as it brings all other to silence.

"Where's my son, Rosebery? I'll thrash you into the Thames, you bugger!"

Shocked, appalled gasps answer the question. Holding Constance's hands, Wilde cranes his neck, unable to see Queensberry but imagining the situation well enough. He doubts Mr. Thompson extended an invitation to the Marquess. No doubt Queensberry found this gala event the perfect occasion to bully his way past the doormen and make a scene. As Queensberry's ranting increases, Wilde pictures him brandishing his cane in the air.

"Oscar."

He bends down at once as Constance's eyelids flutter and open.

Strength enters her hands, squeezing against Wilde's grip.

"Now I know what you wanted to tell me earlier."

"What happened, Constance? Why did you faint?"

"It was a reaction to Bast. Her presence is very strong here now, readily felt. She has entered the museum."

"Then let us go."

"Absolutely not. Help me stand."

As they rise, the surrounding crowd breaks into prolonged jeering to counter Queensberry's ranting. The Marquess' voice betrays distance. He's being pushed back, thrown out.

*"Buggers! You're all buggers! Where's my son, Rosebery?"*

"What's happening?" Constance says.

"A mad dog wandered into a room of hungry panthers, and no one is better off for it."

"If only his perspective could be enlarged and his temperament refined," Constance says. "He has traits that could make him a valuable ally."

Wilde laughs until he sees the sharpness of his wife's stare.

The jeers turn into applause, too loud and sustained to celebrate Queensberry final removal. Wilde and Constance pivot as Mr. Thompson, looking quite recovered from his earlier breakdown, announces the arrival of the museum's *greatest patron*, Lady Gwendolyn.

# CHAPTER FIFTY-TWO

"It's Bast," Wilde says, watching Lady Gwendolyn and Mr. Thompson move through the crowd. Her bright white dress makes her long black hair even more striking and accents the tan features of her face. No one would doubt Mr. Thompson's assertion that she just returned from an excavation in Egypt.

When Constance doesn't respond, he turns and finds her studying the procession.

"Tell me about her, Oscar."

He raises his eyebrows. "I've already told you everything I know."

"Watch her. *See* her as only you can see her."

Wilde looks back to Lady Gwendolyn. He watches her hold out her slim, elegant right arm, the hand covered in a delicate white glove. Man after man bends to kiss her fingertips.

"She enjoys attention. No—more than that."

"Explain."

"She wrings adoration from people like a sponge. Even the women are obsessed. See how everyone pivots to watch her back after she's passed? Regality surrounds here, but this is someone who would consider any queen or empress below her station. This is a person used to being worshipped with full-throated prayers. Perhaps she has even seen sacrifices committed on her behalf."

"Then what does she remind you of?"

"Several actresses," he says, trying to smile. But his lips refuse him. Wilde's brows furrow as he concentrates.

"*Oscar?*"

"She reminds me of myself." His gaze slips to the floor.

"I doubt you require full-throated prayers."

"But we both love praise and adoration. That's the point you wanted to make, isn't it? You didn't want my observations about Bast at all."

"*Nosce te ipsum*, Oscar. Now more than ever, it's important you have a complete inventory of your desires, thoughts and feelings."

"And my vanities."

She nods. "Such knowledge may be your only nourishment if starving days come."

Wilde stiffens. *If starving days come.* What does Constance know or suspect? Has she already foreseen his fate?

Lady Gwendolyn makes an unexpected turn toward them. Her posture now carries an almost vulgar voluptuousness, her strides long and sensuous, shoulders back, her long dark hair falling over the front of both shoulders like a glossy mink stole. No woman in England would carry herself with such open seduction and for just a moment it seems to Wilde she wears nothing at all. He must admit even he feels the heat of her influence.

Constance never moves even when Lady Gwendolyn stops right in front of them with Mr. Thompson at her side. The museum director's face has no color below the black and gray whiskers of his beard. Even his eyes appear lusterless. His clasped hands hang near his waist, pinching and worrying each other as if each blames the other for the predicament of the whole.

"Lady Gwendolyn, I have the honor of introducing you to London's most esteemed playwright, Mr. Oscar Wilde. And this is—"

"Mrs. Wilde," Lady Gwendolyn says, smiling at Constance. "It's very nice to meet you in person."

Constance inclines her head to the right in a slight nod. "You sound as if you've heard of me."

"You have a small reputation," she says, and casts a dismissive nod to Mr. Thompson, who leaves with evident eagerness. Wilde tracks him through the gathering, heading for the exit. But he's stopped at the last moment when a tall, lean figure steps in to block the doorway. Wilde's lips part from the shock of recognition.

William Butler Yeats is here.

"What reputation would that be, Lady Gwendolyn?"

"It's not for being as obtuse as you're trying to make yourself sound."

Wilde looks between them, wets his lips and tries to summon wit. "We're never as dumb as we sound, or as smart as we look."

To his astonishment, Lady Gwendolyn laughs, put one hand on his forearm and pulls him along with her as she starts working. Wilde looks back at Constance, who remains rooted in place, her expression neutral.

"Toying with my prey is such a small pleasure," she says, leaning in whisper.

"Is my wife prey to you?"

"Her and those other amateur magicians she hosts in that child's tea party she calls an Order. I sense their presence here."

"But you're not sure how many there are. That's of interest."

"Why?"

"It shows you're not omniscient."

She flashes a coquettish smile. "Or perhaps I'm imitating your wife and pretending to stupidity."

"I don't think so. My recent experiences with this game we're calling *magic* suggests the essentiality of discovery as an ingredient to success. That presupposes the impossibility of any player's omniscience."

"That's the cleverness I want in my priest."

"I'm afraid I've considered your offer and must decline."

Her smile fades. "You'll discover only misery if you do."

"Then I am a fortunate masochist. Misery is my greatest happiness."

Lady Gwendolyn places her right palm flat against his chest. "Then I will bring you wave after wave of joy. Shall we begin by making you a widower?"

She steps around him and starts toward Constance, who continues to watch them with such impassiveness Wilde fears she's been bewitched.

"Not her," he says, seizing Lady Gwendolyn's wrist.

"You always do the unexpected, Oscar. You stand here, a fraudulent husband protecting your wife as if you felt ardent love for her."

"A creature with your vast knowledge must know there are many kinds of love besides the romantic. The love I bear Constance is the understanding that all the times I've failed her may be redeemed by a single moment of courage. If that moment has arrived, even if it requires my death, I am content."

"Gallant words. But I promise you a different fate than—"

She stops, alert like a cat to the subtlest change in the room. Wilde watches her turn in a slow circle. When he sees her face again, he finds a tremendous smile and the dark sparkle of predation in her eyes.

Constance steps forward. The long hem of her dress rustles as it would in a breeze. The fabric crackles with energy and glows as if sewn by threads of green light. Wilde holds his breath as the illumination builds around her like a bubble.

"I call upon the warriors of our ancient land," she says, her voice booming. "I beseech Danu and her children, the mighty Tuatha de Danann to stand with me now. I invoke the charms of fairy music to sing the song of your destruction."

Constance rises into the air.

# CHAPTER FIFTY-THREE

Wilde falls back, caught up in the surge of panicked people pushing for the exits as a burst of energy swirls around Constance's floating body. Bast remains on the ground looking up at her, arms crossed at the chest. The energy gathers strength around Constance and then lances out in a bolt that strikes Lady Gwendolyn, throwing her off her feet with a gratifying scream. Wilde shouts his wife's name, striving in vain toward her.

A few feet away, a man convulses, tearing away his clothing and his flesh with it, revealing the hideous figure of a changeling. In an instant, Wilde discerns several more men and women going through identical transformations even as the crowd threatens to stampede them. Across the room, a couple standing on a table and clutching each other as if the room were flooding reach out to Prime Minister Rosebery, who smirks at them and tears his face off with all the ease of a mask.

Above all this chaos, like a beacon, Constance hovers, suffused in light, her powers turning the air hot. Wilde's heart pounds to behold her gloriousness. One of the changelings becomes a panther that bounds across the floor, leaping between tables, gathering steam until it springs up at her with its jaws gaping—only to burst into flame when it touches her dress.

"Mr. Wilde, employ your ring with haste."

He turns to find Yeats standing at his side. In his right hand, the

244

lanky poet carries a leather-bound book smaller than his palm, opened to a page of microscopic text. A glass ball with a bright red flame somehow burning in the center of it occupies his left.

Wilde lifts his left hand to show the scarab ring's lifelessness. Yeats' eyes widen and he starts to speak when a panther springs in front of them, swiping with its left claw. Yeats pushes Wilde aside and then faces off with the beast. They circle each other. The panther issues a challenge in the form of a low rumble in the throat. Yeats answers in language Wilde can only guess at, though there seems to be a singsong quality to the words, a sneering rhyme like something a Nordic bard might write from the fjords of his ragged imagination.

The panther leaps. Yeats dodges and spins, throwing the ball down behind the panther as it lands. The glass shatters, spraying the panther's black coat with gleaming shards. The cat shakes its sleek flanks, but the pieces hold fast. Then Yeats reads from the book, though to Wilde this seems for show. Yeats speaks with the quick assuredness of someone quoting from memory. The shards respond to his speech, glowing and gathering themselves together. The panther howls, thrown onto its back, four paws flailing. The cat gets smaller by the moment. As the pieces of glass on the ground reconstitute and summon the fragments lodged in the cat's fur and flesh, the cat is pulled backward, diminishing with each centimeter. The panther reduces to the size of a kitten and then smaller. In a last ditch effort to escape, the little panther transforms into its hairless, changeling form. Its substance is less than a child's doll, shrinking and shrinking, until Wilde cannot even see it when the red flame within the crystal ball sucks the creature into it and leaves the ball whole again. Yeats stoops to retrieve the weapon with a smile of immense satisfaction. He holds it up to Wilde to show the inner flame burning even brighter from new fuel.

More members of the Golden Dawn have joined the fight. Wilde sees duels everywhere. Radiant beams shine down from Constance, striking her comrades and seeming to enliven them even further. Her voice echoes across the room, coordinating, inspiring. More panthers try their luck with her and meet the same fiery fate. Her dress now appears to be a robe of pure power, a blinding light that somehow doesn't blind Wilde at all. He sees fantastic silhouettes within the light, thousands of riders on horseback with swords and banners uplifted, all charging forward within Constance's being.

His spirits rise. Wilde looks to the ring again, urging it to life, desperate to join the fight. But the ring stays dead. "Work damn you," he says just as a panther slams him to the floor, leaving him on his back in a stupor. The beast gloats over him, polluting his lungs with its acrid breath. It bares its yellow teeth and moves in for the kill.

A heavy blow from the left diverts the panther's attention. It scatters aside and turns to face the new attacker. Wilde sits up as his defender steps over him. Can this be the Marquess of Queensberry standing between him and the panther, his heavy cane clutched up in both hands like a cricket back?

"If you're a dumb beast, you'll have a go at me," Queensberry says, his harsh voice never more menacing. "You'll find my meat tougher than Wilde's."

He strikes the floor with the cane to complete his goading. The panther hisses but doesn't move.

Wilde gets to his feet.

"This is a surprise, sir. A most welcome one." he says.

"I didn't come here to defend you, Wilde. I was after Rosebery. But as I was leaving, I heard a woman speaking into my head, calling me back, telling me I was needed. Must have been *her*," he says, with a nod of acknowledgement toward Constance. "So, everything Charlie spoke of is true. I saw Rosebery transform but I lost sight of him. It's my great hope this one here might be him."

The panther hisses again.

"Mealy-mouthed bugger," Queensberry says, lunging forward with the cane swinging. He beats down on the panther's neck. The cat scampers to the left, then stops and lunges forward in such a fluid motion Wilde has trouble seeing where one action ends and the other starts. Queensberry proves almost as quick. Wilde guesses a younger version of Bosie's father might have dodged the counterattack without a nick. Nearing fifty, he's lost just enough agility to let the panther capitalize. One hooked claw drives into his calf, toppling him with a cry. Queensberry falls, losing the cane, which rolls out of his grasp. He pulls himself forward half a foot before the panther attacks again.

Wilde curses at his useless ring and stoops to pick up the cane. He swings at the panther's head, delivering a hail of blows. The cat's muscular body makes him feel like he's striking the side of a brick wall. But the monster yields, surrendering its prize, and Wilde stops to help Queensberry to his feet. The Marquess leans on him for support and the men stare into each other's eyes.

"This is a strange day," Queensberry says, panting but grinning, his face flushed with the obvious thrill of battle.

"It will take many hours to sort out which part is the strangest."

The panther stalks back to try them. This time Yeats intercedes, smiting the crystal ball into the ground between them as he orders their retreat. Neither Wilde nor Queensberry protest and together they limp to a remote corner and survey the battle as the panther is diminished to nothing and sucked into reconstituted glass.

"Where is Bast?" Wilde says.

"Who the devil is Bast?"

"An entity disguising itself as an aristocrat named Lady Gwendolyn. It is the thing responsible for this carnage."

And for the deaths of Bosie and Charlie, he thinks, though there's no way to explain that to Queensberry now. Needing hope, Wilde lifts his gaze to Constance. With her arms outstretched and her head thrown back, she seems like an enchantress from one of Rossetti's paintings. Wilde gazes at this avenging angel with the belief that victory is at hand as the Golden Dawn fight beneath her. Some have fallen. The bodies of friend and foe alike lay on the floor, but there seem to be more members of the Order still on their feet.

Time slows for him. At first, Wilde thinks the spectacle has overwhelmed his senses. Then he realizes another force is at hand. Queensberry's ragged respiration becomes a drawn-out action, as does the blinking of his eyes. The beads of sweat streaming down his cheeks slow to a syrupy stillness.

As everyone in the room freezes in place, Wilde hears a voice to his left.

"You ask where I am, Oscar. The answer is simple. I am always with you."

Bast walks toward him, stepping around scenes of suspended combat with all the casualness of someone navigating the trash of a picnic. Wilde holds up his right hand.

"No further."

"If I relent, it's of my choosing, not your ability to compel."

She does halt, though, and turns to inspect the carnage with an approving nod.

"Your wife and her allies aren't without skill, but their powers are nothing compared to the human sorcerers of ancient times. Do you know why that might be so?"

Wilde shakes his head.

"You've already spoken the answer when you were taunting me."

"You mean discovery? Constance said it was the essence of magic."

"A crude but accurate formulation. The ancient magicians were the first discoverers. Everything was new to them, and this made them all the more powerful. But they didn't understand the nature of their power. They wrote their knowledge down, and in doing so they made all future magicians weaker."

Wilde points to Constance. "Does that seem like diluted force to you?"

Bast responds with a curt smile. "I will kill your wife now if you wish. I didn't want to deny her a few more minutes of imagined glory."

Wilde trembles. Constance, he thinks, tell me what to do? But no voice answers this plea. She hangs in the air, magnificent—but motion-less.

"Or you can ransom her life—all of their lives—with a promise."

"I will not be your priest, Bast."

Bast raises her right hand, index finger extended and pointed at Constance. Wilde seizes her wrist and tries to jerk her arm down, an act as impossible as trying to move a rusted lever with words alone. Unable to do anything else, he places himself in front of her finger.

"You still insist upon self-sacrifice, Oscar?"

"I'd rather die in her place a thousand times over."

"Excessive martyrdom is a poor trait even in a priest. Very well. I will indulge your wishes to the fullest and see how long it takes to purge the foolishness out of your head. Be as stubborn as you like. You'll find my patience will outlast you, and you'll provide my faithful children with some amusement in the meanwhile. When you break at last, you will embrace the position I offer you with an eager and thankful heart."

She casts Wilde aside with the mere flick of her wrist and disappears. From the floor, he watches time accelerate again. Constance convulses. She seems to be choking, gasping. Her light flickers and her body lands with a sharp, violent thud.

Wilde gets up and runs to her even as the tide of the fight turns around him. Yeats starts toward them, his expression stricken, his eyes watering. He stops after a few steps. He and Wilde trade stares. Wilde begs for his help, but a sudden and inexplicable neutrality comes overs the young poet's face. Turning, Yeats calls for a retreat.

But are there any members of the Order alive to hear him?

In the space of an eyeblink, as he cradles his wife, Wilde finds the world changed around him. There are no panthers. There are no corpses or broken tables or burning rubble. The men and women who fled the gala in terror are returned, and all stare at him. Mr. Thompson stands over him with Lady Gwendolyn to his right, her hands clasped over her mouth.

"Help," Wilde says. "Someone."

Constance's body spasms. Her hands lay limp over his at her abdomen, and for the first time he senses his fingers squeezing something solid. Looking down, his eyes and mouth both open wide from the shock of discovery.

He grips the haft of a knife buried in his wife's stomach.

# CHAPTER FIFTY-FOUR

Someone screams and Mr. Thompson begins to hasten the nearest guests away as Wilde stands, his hands bloodied. Lady Gwendolyn points an accusing finger at him. He stares at it, remembering moment ago when he stood between it and his wife.

"Oscar Wilde has murdered his wife!"

"That's a lie," he says, but what can he do to explain the blood on his hand and clothing? Confusion courses through him like fever chills. Where is Yeats? Where is anyone who can help him?

"I saw him do it," Lady Gwendolyn continues to the man nearest her, who places himself between her and Wilde with proper gallantry.

"Constance, I—what's happening?" He kneels beside his wife's body, still unable to comprehend the knife. "We were fighting and—Lady Gwendolyn is Bast—the Golden Dawn—Yeats—"

Hands detain him. He gives no struggle as police lead him away with his head bowed.

When he lifts it again, he finds himself in a new place and with a change of clothes. Solemn faces surround him. He stands in the Old Baily on the dock in front of a judge. How did he get here? How much time has passed?

A grim barrister confronts him.

"Then you admit you had been fighting. Do you deny you were angry enough to kill her?"

Wilde squints and tries to summon words. He pivots to the right, aware of the crowded room's immense silence. Not even the random cough disrupts its heaviness.

"I'll repeat myself, Mr. Wilde. You admit you were fighting. Do you deny you were angry enough to kill her?"

He now recognizes his interrogator. It is Frank Lockwood, the government's Solicitor-General and England's greatest prosecutor.

"I . . . Constance and I were not fighting with each other. We—"

"Your Honor, the prosecution is prepared to show evidence from multiple parties testifying to the abusive nature of Mr. Wilde's behavior on the evening of the museum exhibit."

"*Abusive?* We were—"

He looks at his hands, remembering the blood. Now they're white and clean. His jewelry is gone, including the scarab ring.

"Where is it?" he says in a whisper.

"Where is what, Mr. Wilde? The knife you plunged into your wife's stomach?"

A ripple of nervous laughter spreads through the room, drawing a sharp rebuke from the judge.

"My ring," Wilde says. "Where is it? I must have it."

Lockwood scoffs and leans in at him from the other side of the dock. "You stand accused of uxoricide and you worry about *jewelry?* Your flippancy damns you."

Another man whom Wilde recognizes at once rises. He is Edward Clarke, also a very skilled and notable attorney. "My client is suffering from clear disorientation. May it please the court to adjourn and give Mr. Wilde time to recover himself?"

The judge growls an agreement and the audience dissolves into a general commotion as two guards seize Wilde. Their touch stirs a defiance in him. He shouts that he's not guilty and demands his ring. He fights against the guards' restraining arms, certain they must be changelings. "Can you not see them for what they are?" he shouts. "Do you not recognize them as panthers?"

This produces derisive laughter from the audience. Wilde sees multiple people mouthing the same sentence: *"He's mad."*

The guards drag him into a prison cell shut the door. Wilde glares at them from the other side.

"Give me my ring."

"Prisoners don't have possessions," one guard says. Wilde watches both men leave. He pulls at his hair, closes his eyes and rests his forehead against the bars.

"Constance, if you can hear me, tell me I'm not losing my faculties."

He rubs the strip of pale flesh on his pinkie and holds his left hand close to his heart. Then he sits down on the edge of a cot, the room's only furniture, and lets his head hang forward. Why should he seek the ring now, when either it failed him or he it? He couldn't use it to help Bosie or Charlie or Constance. Might as well sink it in the Thames, he tells himself.

Footsteps approach. He looks up to see Mr. Clarke. His lawyer is a harried man in his early fifties with busy eyebrows and mutton chop sideburns reminiscent of Queensberry. Unappealing beads of sweat nest in the hairs.

The lawyer stands on the other side of the cell door, squares his shoulders and clears his throat.

"Let me be frank, Mr. Wilde. I'm at a loss as to how to defend you."

"As am I."

"The presumption of madness may be your one hope."

"The disorientation you saw from me is genuine, Mr. Clarke. I find myself in a growing confusion."

"You're under tremendous stress."

They regard each other a moment without speaking. Wilde ponders certain curiosities of fate. The threat of lawsuits have surrounded him of late, though those concerns all seem like they belong from another life and lifetime. It nevertheless occurs to him that Edward Clarke is just the man he would have sought to defend him in any civil matter. If Bast concocted this fantasy to torture him, she might at least be thanked for not skimping on his legal representation.

Wilde gets to his feet. "I take it I am being tried for murder?"

Mr. Clarke's eyebrows lift. "Are you implying you were not aware of this?"

"I only wish to review the facts for the sake of clarity."

"Very well," Mr. Clarke says, supreme patience in his tone. "The Crown's facts are these: you and your wife attended a gala event at the National Museum. You were described as having a very tense relationship that night, as if you were boiling with rage. There is much speculation as to why. What isn't speculation is you assaulted your wife with a large knife, killing her with a stab wound to the stomach."

"I was seen doing it?"

"The primary eyewitness is Lady Gwendolyn."

"Whose reputation is no doubt unimpeachable?"

"Mr. Wilde, I wouldn't make light of the matter. Even if no one saw you, the fact you were found holding her with the knife still in your hand is difficult to overcome. Your erratic behavior isn't helping your case."

"I see."

"The trial will resume tomorrow."

"Am I to be questioned further?"

"No. The prosecution is already content with the performance you've given so far. They will be calling Lady Gwendolyn and the Marquess of Queensberry."

Wilde steps up to the cell door. "Queensberry? Do you know what he will say?"

"I know Mr. Lockwood very well. He enjoys sharing details of his strategy with the opposition when he considers his position to be unassailable. I must say in this case he's being exceedingly free."

"And?"

"Lockwood intends to use the Marquess to link you to several recent incidents of political violence from the anarchist movement. The Marquess also blames you for the disappearance of his youngest son and the murder of Lord Drumlanrig, which he believes you staged to make it appear to be a suicide."

Wilde blinks. "Lord Drumlanrig is dead?"

"It's only the most vivid scandal in London—after your own situation. Considering Queensberry's erratic nature, I would never bring him forward as a reliable witness. But the death of one son and the disappearance of another have generated tremendous sympathy for him even among those predisposed to despise him."

Wilde takes a deep breath, remembering the brief moment when he and his arch nemesis fought together against the panther.

"I feel like a man thrown out of my own reality. The only thing I can compare it to is experiencing a grief that concerns no one else."

"What do you mean by that?"

"I mean that a grieving man and a happy man may walk side-by-side down the street while inhabiting two very different worlds. Happiness is an experience that gathers and unites. But all mourners, even in a community of shared grief, cries alone. I do not have a community of shared grief, Mr. Clarke. Do you know why?"

The lawyer shakes his head.

"Because I alone know what's been lost."

"Oh, I should think plenty of people know what's been lost," Mr. Clarke says, an icy edge entering his tone. "Your children must feel the absence of their mother, for example."

The mention of his sons gives Wilde a jolt.

"In all this madness, I hadn't stopped to think about . . . Where are they?"

"They are wards of your wife's family."

"They're safe?"

"I have every reason to believe so."

Wilde nods. "That gives me hope, Mr. Clarke."

"I am glad for it. Hope is an important thing."

"So I've been told," Wilde says.

PART SIX

# CHAPTER FIFTY-FIVE

*Wandsworth Prison, August 30, 1895*

Stephen shoves a washed, shaved and dapper Wilde out of the prison cell and pushes him into the courtyard. Ten panthers lounge in the sun, their black fur shining and shimmering in the sunlight. Stephen halts a moment, pointing them out.

"You're wearing so much fragrance right now they can't recognize your human stink."

Wilde brushes a bit of dust from his sleeves. "It's good of Bast to let me attend her *momentous* occasion in proper attire and hygiene."

"Still flippant," Stephen says, circling him. "When we return, I'll take more aggressive action to drive that obnoxious quality out of you."

"You're assuming I won't give in. Perhaps I'll agree to be her High Priest just to turn the tables on you. I assume what you said during our torture session with the cannonballs is true and even you—and all of them—will become subordinate to me."

Stephen opens his mouth to show many sharp teeth. "You won't amuse the Great Goddess much longer. She'll get tired of you and her protection will be lifted. Then I'll gorge on your bowels."

He forces Wilde to the prison gate, which opens to reveal a waiting carriage. The driver sits in rigid profile from his elevated perch.

"Off to the coronation," Stephen says.

"May I presume we're going to Buckingham Palace? Or does Bast insist on Westminster Abbey for her charade?"

"It's the Abbey," the driver says, turning to look down at him. Wilde recognizes Queensberry, still in his heavy disguise as Locke. "I imagine it'll be called the Great Pyramid of London after the Goddess is through with it. Good riddance to an old false god."

Queensberry spits on the ground for emphasis, and his blasphemy draws a hearty chuckle from Stephen, who pushes Wilde into the carriage. He then climbs in himself and closes the door. Wilde hears the crack of a whip and the coach jolts forward. He rocks back and forth, touching his left pinkie. Even after so many months of the ring's absence, sometimes he still feels its phantom weight against the skin.

"You liked the intimacy of carriages," Stephen says, drawing Wilde out of his thoughts.

"What?"

"The lads you thought were renters told me you liked to take them into carriages and close the windows."

"The grave's a fine and private place, Stephen. But carriages are where lovers embrace."

"I hear there was a lot more than embracing happening when you'd pay the driver to steer in a circle around London for two hours."

"It's meaningless to taunt a man about things that seem like they happened in another lifetime."

"The Great Goddess will be glad to hear your past is becoming a distant memory."

"And how are your desires fulfilled? Do you turn into a panther and rub up against some statue of Bast like any rutting alley cat?"

Stephen lunges at him in the cabin's tight confines, dropping his human mask in an instant. Wilde finds himself choking, throttled by implacable hands. He coughs and sputters, unable to even plead for his life. There's a dim awareness that the coach has stopped. Stephen seems unaware of anything as he bears down.

"I've waited so long for this. I hated you the moment I saw you. You're everything foolish and pointless. Why the Great Goddess ever chose you, I'll—"

The door opens. Fighting the encroaching darkness of asphyxiation, Wilde wonders if he's hallucinating. Queensberry, Robbie and Yeats stand in the open doorway. Yeats carries his little book and his glowing crystal ball.

"Stephen," Queensberry says, dropping the disguise in his voice. His fierce grin distorts the layers of makeup around his mouth.

Stephen releases Wilde and turns all of his attention to the three men. "Locke, what is the meaning of this? The Great Goddess—"

"I'm an atheist," Queensberry says, and steps back as Yeats shatters the crystal ball on the floor of the carriage, sending a grapeshot of shards into Stephen's face.

# CHAPTER FIFTY-SIX

Stephen fights as Yeats's chanting increases in speed and volume. He shrieks and claws, gouging the carriage's interior and then his own flesh trying to rip the glass shards from his body. The pieces stick tight despite his mutilating force and Wilde sees his body shrinking.

Over his protests, Robbie and Queensberry all but carry him about one hundred yards from the coach, toward the edge of a wood. "It's safer to be out the way," Robbie says as they set him down. "Even Will wasn't sure if his weapon would work on the likes of Stephen."

"It seems to be," Wilde says, rubbing his throat.

"Yes," Queensberry answers with a hearty sneer. "Yes, it does."

The three of them stand by as Stephen's cries become tiny and pathetic. Wilde's spirits grow in direct proportion to Stephen's diminishment, but he still cannot believe victory will be theirs. Memories of being tormented and abused at Stephen's hand go through Wilde's mind and turn his torturer into an invincible evil. He hugs himself, looking at the ground until Stephen's cries go silent. The silent persists for half a minute, until Yeats turns around with the crystal ball in hand.

Robbie and Queensberry celebrate their victory with a shout. Wilde remains quiet even as Yeats brings the ball to him. The red fire inside it casts a bright light even against the power of sunlight.

"Is it finished?"

"Yes," Yeats says. "Stephen is defeated."

"Show some pleasure, Will," Queensberry says, slapping Yeats on the back with enough force to send the lean poet forward a step.

Yeats slips the crystal ball and the little book into his pockets. "I can assure you I have my fill of joy right now. Joy and relief."

"Useful bit of glassware that thing keeps proving itself to be," Queensberry says. "But a gun would be faster."

Yeats ignores the quip and asks Wilde if he's okay.

"I'm no worse for wear," Wilde says, still rubbing his throat. "I confess my delight is only surpassed by my confusion."

Robbie pats his back. "We couldn't let you languish behind bars any further, Oscar. We needed to show you that you still have friends."

"Dear boy," he says, wiping his eyes. "I never doubted it."

"We've been biding our time, waiting for the right moment to contact you," Yeats said. "Thanks to Queensberry's bravery, we knew now was the time to strike."

Queensberry allows himself the slightest smile as Wilde bows in gratitude. "Whatever Bast did to everyone at the museum, it didn't affect me. The world changed and the fighting was done. Everything was normal except you weren't standing beside me anymore. You were in the middle of the room with a knife in your wife's stomach."

"It seems knowledge of Bast's existence offers one some immunity to her ability to alter reality. Think of the knowledge as an anchor or a mooring," Yeats says.

"We're boats in very treacherous seas," Wilde says. "I'm glad at least to be out of the tempest of Wandsworth Prison."

He notices Robbie looking downcast and demands to know what's wrong.

"I'm afraid this freedom is only a temporary reprieve, Mr. Wilde. We need you to go back to Wandsworth. But you must return to it a changed man, devoted to Bast and eager to become her high priest."

"When I've suffered so much by refusing that offer? It would betray everything I've fought for."

"Quit being prideful, Wilde," Queensberry says. "We've all done things of late we never imagined or wanted. So, swallow your gall for the greater good."

"We need you to put your trust in us, Mr. Wilde," Yeats says. "If not in us, then in your wife."

"You may have forgotten that I'm a widower."

"Death is not so final as you might believe. Even now she offers her guidance in hints and signs."

Queensberry scoffs, drawing Robbie's ire. "Why is the afterlife so hard to believe in after everything else you've seen?"

Wilde holds up a placating hand to prevent them from arguing. "Let's say I agree to your course of action. How can I continue on to Bast's coronation ceremony without Stephen? Won't she demand to know where he is? What answer could I give?"

*"That's where I come in, Oscar."*

Wilde spins around at the sound of Bosie's voice coming from the woods behind him. But it's not Bosie who steps into view. Wilde sees a changeling, hairless and gray.

"Who are you?" he says, and when the changeling makes no response he addresses the question to Yeats, Queensberry and Robbie.

"This is Bosie," Queensberry says, with evident feeling in his voice. "This is my son."

# CHAPTER FIFTY-SEVEN

Seated across from each other in the carriage, Wilde watches the changeling assume the fair-haired visage that sparked his desire from the moment they met. There are, however, differences between memory and the face he finds now. Bosie's lips show no trace of the imperious little smirk that used to frequent his expression. His eyes, though untouched with crow's feet or any obvious sign of age, nevertheless seem set in the sockets of a much older man.

"I know you must have questions, Oscar."

"But no idea how to ask them."

"Do your best."

Wilde shakes his head. "How is this not a trick? Can you really be *my* Bosie?"

"I assure you I am. Ask me anything about our past, and I will answer."

"You were a changeling the entire time?"

"No."

"Then how did this happen?"

"Do you remember the last time you saw me? I had been transformed."

"Into a cat. Of course I remember. We were attacked at The Red Tiger. You jumped into the dark and I thought you must be dead. It feels like only a matter of weeks to me."

Bosie's eyes shift to the left as his lips press into a tight, thin line. "For me, it's been thousands of years."

"*What?*"

"That darkness was—somehow—the ether of time itself. I fell without direction, as if in an endless void. Then a light appeared in the distance, and the light suctioned everything toward it. I passed through into another world. No, not another world but another time and place. My paws sank into burning sand. I stood in a desert, and as I crested a dune, I saw a pyramid under construction."

"Are you telling me you were transported to ancient Egypt?"

"I heard voices from across the desert. They were joined in song. What choice did I have except to find the singers? I stumbled from dune to dune, following my hearing. The sands petered out and became a rockier plain. I saw workmen, Oscar. Many hundreds of them, cutting and carving a massive obelisk. And despite the oppressive heat and the heavy sweat on their backs, their labor seemed a joy to them."

Wilde tries to imagine the scene. "To see those marvels as they were being constructed . . . except for the terror you must have felt, I envy you the experience."

"The worse terrors were yet to come. I was spotted by one of the masons, who smiled and dropped his tools. He motioned for me to come to him. When I didn't, he came to me. I tried to run but he was faster. He scooped me into his arms and stroked my ears. Then he brought me among the laborers, who stopped and showed me the great-est reverence. I could not understand what they were saying, but it was obvious I excited them."

Wilde smiles. "And I thought my own adoration of you to be exces-sive."

"The mason left the group and took me to the pyramid, passing through a throng of thousands. There were guards at the door, changelings in their natural state. They moved to stop the mason, but then he held me aloft. They stepped aside as soon as they saw me, and the mason entered the pyramid.

"The next chamber was as beautiful and vibrant as any room I've ever entered. Fresh artwork on the walls repeated the same hieroglyphic over and over, a woman with a cat's head, seated on a chair. I did not understand the meaning then, but in time I learned to translate it as *Bast enthroned*. The mason took me into another room where the hieroglyph was realized in flesh. Bast sat on a seat of gold, naked, a woman from the neck down. Her head was a panther, and her gleaming yellow eyes gave the impression of noticing every detail. A man stood beside her, his hands crossed at the chest, looking very somber. I took him to be a priest.

"There were others waiting to have an audience with her. I saw three women with newborn infants, but they were holding them like offerings, pushing them out at arms' length toward the goddess. Bast urged each mother to her in turn and took the babies and brought their mouths to her right breast. The first child suckled, and as it did a transformation occurred. The baby's skin turned gray. The wisp of hair on its head fell away, and then the skull itself changed."

"It became a changeling," Wilde says in a whisper.

"The process was quick. Once finished, Bast handed the child to her priest, who took it away. Then she repeated the process on every child offered her, until at last only the mason stood waiting. He thrust me out toward her. You might not think cats have facial expressions, Oscar, but they do. I'd been locked in my feline body long enough to recognize them, and Bast smiled at me and took me into her hands.

267

She brought my head to her mouth. I was terrified, thinking she would consume me. Instead, she bathed me with her tongue, grooming my fur with all the affection a mother cat shows for her kittens. Every lick brought a new understanding. Bast and the mason exchanged words, and after the baptism of her tongue, I found I could understand the language. She thanked him for bringing such a beautiful child to her. The mason bowed and said he knew I would make a fitting sacrifice. This was an unfortunate thing for him to say. Bast became wrathful, asking him how he would dare think of me as a sacrifice? Then she declared that for his callousness, *he* would be shown the slab.

"The mason cried and begged forgiveness, but Bast showed no mercy. The priest summoned guards who dragged him to an altar on the other side of the room. Bast held me as she watched the mason flail, and a gloating purr came from her throat. The priest was quick with the knife. It was the most horrific thing I have ever seen, and my fear came out in the form of involuntary meowing. Bast cradled me, smiled, and brought my mouth to her nipple.

"'You will grow strong, little one,' she said. 'You will become great in my service.'" I took her milk. It was like ingesting acid, Oscar. I felt it eating my body from the inside out. But as my old parts fell away, new parts took their place. My skin shed its fur. My arms and legs expanded. My paws became hands and feet. I had only the vaguest sense of how I looked, but I knew what Bast had done to me. When the change was finished, she surrendered me to the priest, whose hands were still wet with blood. He took me away and I learned the fate of the three babies that preceded me. Within the pyramid was another space, filled with crude boxes not much larger than cradles, stacked one on top of the other. Several hundred of them at least. Before I was placed inside one, the priest and an assistant covered my body in salve and began to bind me tight in strips of linen. I could not breathe, yet I lived. I could not speak no matter how I tried to shout. And as the bandages covered my mouth and then my eyes, I knew my fate was living mummification.

"Wrapped away, I was placed inside the box. I knew only darkness and every second felt like a grain of sand building into a dune on top of me. Was I asleep? Was I awake? There was only quiet and darkness for century upon century."

"Dear boy," Wilde says, leaning forward to squeeze Bosie's right kneecap. "I cannot begin to imagine the torment you've endured."

"The torment was being alone with the thoughts of the worst person in the world. That's how I came to see myself upon reflection. Century upon century of reliving temper tantrums, childishness, and moments of pure petulance. I thought of how poorly I'd treated those I loved. You above all."

"You never—"

"I was vile to you. I showed you no appreciation. I used you."

Wilde tries to swallow against the dryness in his throat. "It's how youth behaves."

"Youth," Bosie says, adding a sardonic chuckle. "Now I'm more than three thousand years old."

"How did you escape your confinement?"

"I heard voices. English voices. How strange it was to hear my own language after thousands of years. There came a crack of light in the darkness. It was like having the black universe break open to reveal a blazing sun. Our chamber had been discovered by excavators. Archaeologists. I heard a man say, 'The museum won't like this at all. More damn cats. Lady Gwendolyn sure knows how to find mummified kittens.'

"Our boxes were taken from the pyramid and transported away.

We were loaded into the cargo hold of a ship."

Wilde sits back in wonder. "You went back thousands of years in time only to return to London in the present day as an ancient Egyptian artifact."

"No one's fate ever came around in a fuller circle than my own. Our mummies were stacked in a room in the basement of the museum. I feared I might languish there for another thousand years. But a man came, accompanied by Bast."

"The man must have been the museum director, Edward Thompson."

"She told him her children had been away from their mother far too long, and now it was time for us to wake. Then she chanted, and my body responded to the words. My bindings broke apart. Our boxes splintered and we stood, grown, her loyal soldiers. One of them was Stephen, and it was clear Bast favored him above all others."

"A favorite son?"

"Yes."

Wilde nods. "It sounds like you must have returned to London before I even learned about the Red Tiger."

"Many months before, in fact. I was forced to take the disguise of a renter. Stephen used us to infiltrate and learn the secrets of British society. This amused me to some extent. I was hoping to encounter you, but we never met. I did, however, meet and service myself. I'd like to think I gave him a good time. I certainly charged him enough for the experience."

A mischievous gleam enlivens Bosie's eyes.

"I suppose it is a good thing you've always preferred younger men," Wilde says.

# CHAPTER FIFTY-EIGHT

Bosie transforms himself into Stephen as the carriage comes to a stop, and Wilde experiences a surge of anxiousness.

"Forgive me," he says when Bosie touches his shoulder. "I should like to never see Stephen's face again."

"I understand. I wish there could be a different way."

Oscar smiles. "How strange it is to see compassion and concern in the face of my most terrible tormentor. It is balm enough for me. But perhaps you should lose that kindness before our audience with Bast."

"Rest assured I know all of his mannerisms. I can imitate him to perfection."

"I had no idea the Douglas family possessed such acting talent. You and your father both."

"I wouldn't applaud my father's performance too much, Oscar. Locke's main motivation is he despises most of humanity."

Wilde smiles. "A role he was born to play."

Queensberry calls to them from the driver's seat, announcing their arrival at Westminster Abbey. Bosie opens the door and pulls Wilde out with a brusque tug that almost sends Wilde falling to the pavement.

"Keep on your feet," he says, and Wilde must agree with Bosie's prior assertion. He imitates Stephen to a tee.

Wilde looks at the towering Gothic architecture before him. The abbey's great rose window with its dark glass seems like an eclipsed moon lurking overhead. Statues and engravings decorate the tan spires. Here, he thinks, is all of England in one building. Its religion, its monarchy, its chaos and the peculiar British sensibility that always seems to keep disorder at bay. Layer upon layer of conflict reside within its masonry. Here is a reminder of the country's great age and resilience. How meaningless it must all seem to a creature such as Bast. Will she raze it and put a pyramid in its place? Will she occupy it just to smirk at the icons of Christianity and its defeated saints? As Bosie pushes him forward, his gaze drops to the sturdy entrance doors, their wood the color of ancient wine caskets, and he notices the living gargoyles flanking the entrance. Panthers larger than any he's seen except for Bast herself sit hunched there as if their presence would be accepted—even expected—by any onlooker. Wilde can only wonder if some enchantment prevents everyone else from noticing them, or if most human eyes are so unobservant they require no special magic at all.

If not for Bosie's guiding hand, Wilde doubts he'd be able to pass between the monstrous cats. He does so trembling, and they enter a transformed world. The interior's splendor of art, history and literature—all gone, replaced with a blank sandstone surface. He sees a crew of workers painting hieroglyphics with one dominant image repeated over and over. Wilde knows its meaning.

*Bast enthroned.*

Bosie pushes him onward.

"Where are we going?"

"You'll find out soon enough, Wilde."

Bosie shoves him so hard he pitches forward and lands on his hands and knees. When Wilde starts to stand, Bosie places a foot on his back and forces him down.

"That's better," Bosie continues, standing over him, hands on his hips. If Wilde didn't know better, he would swear Stephen himself torments him. "You're going to see royalty. Do you think a beast like you should walk into the presence of Her Majesty? No. On all fours. You crawl the rest of the way."

Wilde closes his eyes. If Stephen actually were here, Wilde would expect a sharp kick in the ribs.

"Which way should I crawl?"

"Where in the Abbey would you go if you're looking for royalty?"

Wilde waits a moment before answering. "The coronation chair."

"With intelligence like that, it's no wonder the Great Goddess chose you for her priest. Everyone else is an idiot by comparison. Now move and be quick about it, unless you want me to kick you all the way from here to St. George's chapel."

Wilde scrambles forward, gaze on the floor, cheeks burning hot as they move past coterie's of mocking men and women. Are they changelings or are they opportunist humans who've detected a change in the weather? He hears his name whispered between them and for the first time in his life feels ashamed to be recognized.

"Make way, fools," Bosie says, almost but not quite shouting. "You look upon the high priest of the Great Goddess."

Before anyone reacts, a roar comes from within the chapel. It sounds to Wilde like several buglers sounding an army's triumph. Bast's voice rings forth—

"*Bring him before me now!*"

All others clear a path and Bosie leads him through a final door and closes it behind them. Wilde stops, not daring to lift his head and face the power he senses in the room. He can well imagine this being the force that made Constance swoon.

"Why is he on his hands and knees?"

273

"Great Goddess," Bosie says. "Wilde has not yet repented of his stubbornness. He—"

"He is my High Priest whether he acknowledges it yet or not. I have raised him up and set him above you. Never forget this."

Wilde risks a look askance as Bosie drops to his knees and beseeches forgiveness. His sidewards glance discovers Bast in her hieroglyphic form, a panther's head resting upon a woman's naked body. For all the magnificence radiating from her, both alluring and dangerous, he cannot help noticing how small she looks. The coronation chair is almost seven feet tall. The legs of the chair have ornamental golden lions for an adornment. As Wilde stares them, each one seems more and more like a Sphynx.

"Rise, both of you."

They do, and Bast motions them forward. Wilde steels himself against a tremor as Bast's yellow eyes size him up without any detectable emotion other than cold victory.

"Does my cherished son speak the truth, Oscar? Are you still stubborn?"

"I was—until this moment."

Bast shifts to the right, eyes gleaming.

"Seeing you now, my heart finds the rightness of the destiny you've chosen for me. I know it is pointless to resist further. I am broken. The fragmentation is due to my own arrogance, and I beg you to put me back together again, better and finer than what I was before."

"My priest at last," Bast says, almost jumping from the chair. She holds her arms out to Bosie, who drops to one knees and raises his hands out in supplication. "You have done well, my favored son. Was there ever a task given that you did not accomplish? What shall your reward be?"

"My most desired reward would be another task I can perform in your service, Mother."

Bast's eyes glow bright. Her feline lips stretch back in a smile of immense satisfaction.

"My esteem for you shall be boundless. But leave us now, child. Let me speak with my High Priest alone."

Bosie rises and turns. As he does, he makes the briefest eye contact with Wilde, who senses an edge of concern. But what can either of them do now except continuing to play their parts to the hilt?

Bast places Wilde's face between her hands. Despite the appearance of slender human fingers and skin as smooth as silk, he feels himself in the grip of two rough, massive paws.

"Tell me of your new desires, my priest."

"You are my epiphany."

Her panther's head melts away, replaced with the more alluring visage of Lady Gwendolyn. Wilde cannot imagine a more seductive smile.

"Through the prayers you will write to me, I will become the world's epiphany."

"Yes, Great Goddess."

She caresses his chin. "As a generous mother, I am glad to know it only took mild punishment to correct your course. Would it surprise you to learn that death is distasteful to me?"

"No, Mother. Of course not."

Bast cocks her head to the left, and it seems her golden eyes search for any sign of deceit in him. Wilde counters with a shield of sincerity honed by long years of practiced deception.

"There have been times when I dealt out death by the thousands. No doubt such times will come again, and soon. But it is not to my liking. I would be a goddess of life. While humanity cannot be immortal,

I could grant all of you such longevity as to make death seem like an unpleasant rumor. Who but I taught the Egyptians their mummification rituals and the care and respect for the dead? I can name every man who has ever served as my priest. And when they died, blind and deaf from extreme age, I came to their beds in my most ferocious form to honor the fierceness of their devotion. I cleansed their bodies with my own tongue, and then I took my human form and set my delicate hands to the task of wrapping their anointed bodies in linen for all eternity."

"That is very beautiful," Wilde says, and not without genuine surprise at the compassion in Bast's voice.

She walks back to the coronation chair. Halfway there, however, she turns back to him and shows an almost coquettish smile. "Which part of yourself will you sacrifice, my Priest?"

"Sacrifice?" Wilde glances back in search of Bosie. "I wasn't told there'd be a sacrifice."

"It's not a matter of telling. It's a matter of spontaneous offering."

"I have no money."

Bast laughs at this. "One seldom meets a man such as you—fool and philosopher in one spirit. Do you think I could cherish any earthly possession? What piece of yourself do you offer?"

"Piece of myself?" Wilde says as sweat breaks out on his forehead from the terror of comprehension. He looks down at his feet and his gaze travels up his body. What part of himself can he do without? It's an unfathomable question for one who likes the entire ensemble so much. What would appease him by seeming a greater sacrifice than it is? He thinks of dress rehearsals for his plays when he's had to convince some offended actor or actress that their part, though small, is in fact the crux of the drama's success.

He holds up his left hand and extends his pinkie.

"I offer you the finger that bore my instrument of defiance."

Bast's lips purse and then smile.

"Through this offering," Wilde continues, "I pledge to never defy you again. I make this sacrifice with a thankful heart."

Bast comes forward. "Eloquent words, my priest. I do sense your gratitude. A small sacrifice need not be offensive if it is backed by great symbolism."

She takes Wilde's hand and brings the pinkie to her mouth, sucking it in and out twice before holding it there. He feels the faintest pressure of her human teeth and it sends his pulse into a chaos of dread and anticipation. Is this a ritual, a teasing game? They make eye contact and hold it. Her yellow eyes widen. Bast's head transforms with the speed of an eyeblink. Wilde sees his pinkie in the panther's mouth and the incisors bear down, rending the flesh and shearing through the bone in an instant.

He screams and falls back with nothing to hold but a stump at the base of his pinkie. He hears Bast call for Stephen and in a moment Bosie's arms wrap around Wilde's crumbled body. Wilde babbles, staring at the spurting blood as a fever of agony overwhelms his wits. He loses consciousness a moment, coming to when Bosie slaps his face even harder than Stephen would have done.

"My priest, you must learn the mysteries of blood. You will see much of it from now on."

Wilde tucks his left hand under his armpit and rocks back and forth on his knees.

"Tomorrow," she says, bending down to look Wilde in the eyes, "you will begin your new studies. You will learn my language and rituals. You will comprehend the art of linen wrapping by bandaging your own hand. Return him to his cell now, my son, and treat him with the kindness that is his due."

"Yes, Great Goddess," Bosie says, and helps Wilde to his feet before they stagger away.

# CHAPTER FIFTY-NINE

When he returns to his cell, left hand wrapped in cotton but nothing given for the pain, Wilde notes a single distinct change. The thin, torturous prison mattress has been replaced with a thicker pad, something almost worthy of being called a bed. Bosie guides him to it, helps him sit, and says a few harsh words loud enough for any lurking changeling to hear. Then he places his hand atop Wilde's head, caresses his hair, and kisses his temple before whispering words of hope.

"Can you stay?"

"No, Oscar. But my heart will be with you."

He shuts the door and Wilde slumps across the bed, weak from blood loss. He falls asleep despite the pain and wakes hours later to find moonlight falling on him through the window, lending his bloody bandage an appearance like black flesh. After staring at it a moment, Wilde grits his teeth, the agony rekindling like a fire surging up his left arm. He leaves the bed, falls to his knees, and takes a deep breath with his eyes closed against the dizziness. Bit by bit, he makes his way to the window, where he manages to stand and look up at the moon. For a crazed, beautiful moment, he finds Constance's face there.

"My dearest wife," he says. "Is it true what Yeats said? Is death not final? Do you even now watch over me?"

He does not want to blink his eyes, but he cannot help himself. When he sees the moon again, Constance is gone and no amount of calling will bring her back. He turns from the window and slides down to the floor to sob. He clutches his left hand and the blood, if it was ever staunched at all, seeps fresh into the soggy bandage. The sight of it makes him think of his surgeon father, dead for almost twenty years. If he were here, would he apply a tourniquet? What comment would he make on the wound? Wilde closes his eyes and remembers himself as a boy in his father's study, staring at that damned mummified dwarf he brought back from Egypt. The vision of it now feels like a foreshadowing of fate.

There's a rattle at the door. Wilde watches the steel plate for the food slot slide back, but no tray passes through. It's almost half a minute before anything else happens.

"Oscar? You there?"

The voice brings a fresh stab of pain. This time it's in Wilde's heart.

"Oscar, it's Charlie. I'm here."

Wilde shifts his body, staring at the door as his lower lip trembles. He brings his knees up against his chest and buries his face against his legs. The last time he heard this voice, it came from Stephen taunting him in the prison yard. Paranoia dominates his mind. Has he been victimized by some elaborate trap? What if Stephen isn't dead at all? What if the men he took to be Queensberry, Yeats and Robbie were all changelings playing an elaborate game to break his will?

Is this the final twist of the knife?

"Go away," Wilde says. "I don't believe you."

"It's your own Charlie. I swear it. His Lordship said he saw you today. He said you're doing the bravest thing imaginable. He's come to respect you the way I do."

Wilde peers at the open slot and cannot find a hint of the person speaking from the other side.

"If what you say is true, why didn't Queensberry tell me you were alive?"

The ensuing silence threatens to snuff out any spark of hope. Then—

"I begged him not to."

"Why in the name of God would you do that?"

More silence follows, silence with a tangible heaviness.

"Remember the store, Oscar?"

"Store?"

"We were on our way to The Red Tiger and I saw all that food in the butcher's window. And I stopped and stared at it. When you asked me what was wrong, I said—"

"You remembered being hungry as a child," Wilde says, coming to his knees. The pain in his hand dwindles. He inches closer to the door. "You wanted to buy everything you saw and give it away."

"Then you made fun of me."

"The most idiotic moment of my life." Wilde stretches forward with his right hand and strokes the door with his fingertips. "I'm sorry—so very sorry, Charlie."

"You made me so mad I stalked off. I felt betrayed. I'd told you something I didn't mean to share, and you treated it like you did everything else."

"But I was changed in the process. I saw myself for the fool I was."

He hears a low laugh. If Wilde had any lasting doubts about the authenticity of the man on the other side of the door, they're gone now. Even the most skilled changeling couldn't capture the magic in Charlie's rueful chuckle.

"I was determined to go on to that pub without you. I went in and demanded to see the hidden room. The strange little barman tried to make trouble for me, so I bashed his teeth in and helped myself."

"I saw your handiwork, dear boy. I wasn't too far behind and yet I was hours late according to The Red Tiger's strange timekeeping. I found you unconscious."

"They overpowered me."

"What do you remember after they drugged you?"

"Nothing until the fire."

Wilde shoulders up to the door and places his head by the open slot. "I had no hope for your survival. The roof collapsed and kept me from you. Forgive me for saying this, dear boy, but once I thought you were dead, a part of me died too."

Charlie doesn't answer. But Wilde feels his presence, so warm, so near. He peers through the slot but the space is too narrow and the outside too dark.

"Charlie, can you open the door?"

"No, Oscar. I haven't a key."

"Then would you slide back the larger plate? Let us not play Pyramus and Thisbe when the wall between us has a window."

"I—should go. I was only able to come with the help of Lord Alfred."

"*Please*, Charlie."

"Oscar—"

"Let me see your face. Let me touch it so I know all of this isn't a hallucination."

He hears nothing from the other side, not even a hint of breath. Wilde puts his right hand flat against the door and makes another plea.

The sound of the panel bolt shooting back obliterates his last trace of pain. He wipes the tears from his eyes and thrusts his right hand through the opening.

"Where are you, my boy?"

"Here," he says, and Wilde feels his hand clasped between Charlie's. The warmth of Charlie's skin has all the effect of bringing water to the desert.

"Place my palm against your cheek. I can't think of anything I've wanted more in life."

"It's better if you don't."

"But why?"

Another silence, and then—

"I'm different now."

"Different in what way? Nothing changes you in my mind."

"I wish I lived in your mind, then."

Wilde hears the slightest whimper, the most alien of noises he might associate with Charlie. Then his hand is moved up and his palm pressed against a surface both waxy and rough.

"What am I feeling?"

"Don't act like you don't know."

Wilde's brow furrows, and then his eyes open very wide. "Dear boy . . . how thoughtless of me not to realize your escape was not without cost."

He sighs, desperate for some power that might course through his fingertips and heal Charlie's burn scars. He pulls back his hand.

"Don't want to touch me now that I'm all rough and ugly?"

"I would keep my hand on your face for hours on end. Have you heard of Braille?"

"The bumps for the blind?"

"That's right. Your scars are Braille to me, and I read there the story of your heroism and the nobility of your soul. I only withdraw my right hand so I can show you my left. You see, I too am changed and altered.

Look."

He shifts his body to push his left hand through the opening. Charlie gasps. "His Lordship didn't say you'd been hurt."

"The pain is nothing compared to what you've endured. But if the loss of a finger bring us closer together through the camaraderie of sacrifice, I shall consider it a tremendous gain."

Wilde clamps his teeth against a fire of pain when Charlie grasps his left hand and presses it to his chest. The agony of the pressure is nothing compared to the pleasure of feeling his wild, strong heartbeat. Wilde feels the young man's pulse strumming through his arm, overriding the pain and encouraging the rhythm of his own pulse.

"I suppose it's a good thing I'm not a boxer. I might have trouble throwing a punch."

Charlie eases Wilde's hand away.

"Dear boy—did I offend you? If so, I'm sorry."

"You didn't offend me. I want to show you my face now, Oscar. I didn't think I could. I'm so ashamed. But it's only right since you showed me your hand."

"Don't do anything that makes you feel uncomfortable."

"I don't feel uncomfortable anymore. Not with you."

Wilde moves back from the portal and waits, his left hand tucked under his right arm. As the seconds become minutes, it seems Charlie has lost his nerve. He considers what words might revive his courage before concluding the time for words has passed. Silence must have its soliloquy while the actors on this terrible stage stumble through private monologues of thought.

Charlie brings his face to the opening.

The dim light is still enough to reveal heartbreaking details. Wilde keeps his lips pressed tight, determined to maintain a neutral expression. But how can neutrality be maintained when his chest hurts? The left side of Charlie's face has the complexion and appearance of a melted candle. The eye is narrowed by scar tissue and the brow burned away forever. He has only half a mouth. Wilde thinks of John Merrick. Then he thinks of something far more personal—Dorian Gray after the picture's destruction and the immediate, startling changes to a beautiful face.

He curses himself in his mind for even making such a comparison. Dorian got his just desserts. Charlie is the only man he's ever known besides Robbie who deserves a youthful immortalization. This disfigurement cries out as evidence of cosmic injustice, an affliction akin to Job's; and if the God they've all worshipped allows such cruelties with only a shrug of acknowledgement, then maybe Bast deserves her second coming.

Wilde finds his breath ragged from surging anger. He works to calm himself, realizing several minutes have passed without either of them speaking. Only one question comes to him—

"Are you in pain?"

"Not any more. I had a devil of a time for several weeks after it happened. I wanted to die, but his Lordship refused. One time I begged him to kill me and he put a knife in my hand and said, 'If you've got enough courage, you'll put it in your heart. If you have even greater courage, you'll drop it on the floor.' And I did. After that he devoted himself to nursing me day and night. He spared no expense with doctors, who did what they could. Sometimes I'd be in a fever, rambling away, and I'd have a moment of sanity when I could see his Lordship looking down on me. He had tears. Can you imagine it, a great man like that crying over the likes of me?"

"Charlie, you more than anyone else I know are worthy of tears.

Look at my face now. Can you see them?"

"Yes," Charlie says. "Do you see mine? No—don't see them. Feel them. Give me your hand again."

"Only my left is worthy to touch them," he says, extending it. "Pain to pain."

Wilde puts his forehead against the door and pledges better days ahead for both of them.

# CHAPTER SIXTY

Their encounter lasts less than an hour, and Wilde cannot sleep after Charlie leaves. His body is too enlivened by pain, his mind by hope. He stands at the window watching the sky brighten and remains there until the lock on the cell door clanks. Wilde pivots to find Bosie, disguised as Stephen, bringing a familiar man into the room. Mr. Thompson carries a bundle of books, chalk and a slate board.

"Here's your new pupil," Bosie says, giving the museum director one final, harsh shove. The force of it sends Mr. Thompson tripping forward as he drops his books, spilling them across the floor. For a moment he looks offended and prepared to protest, but then Bosie glowers at him and Wilde sees his bravery wilt. He has sympathy. Bosie really does a quite perfect imitation of Bast's favorite son.

They make eye contact and share the briefest smile as Mr. Thompson bends to gather his belongings. Then Bosie leaves and locks the door behind him.

"May I help?"

"No. I have it all now."

"I take it you're here to teach me Bast's *rituals*?"

Mr. Thompson turns up a face red and sweating. "I wouldn't know what those are. I'm sure I don't care to know."

Wilde holds out his left hand, the bandage crusted and in need of changing. Mr. Thompson shudders and drops the few books in his

287

grasp.

"I'm very sorry, Oscar. Your predicament only makes me feel worse and worse."

"I take it that you have an accurate memory of what happened at the museum gala? You know I did not kill my wife."

"Of course I know it."

"Then I am in need of your insight about something I have pondered since the first day of my incarceration. If Bast can alter reality with such ease, why does she insist on process? Why use her changelings to infiltrate our society? Why bother with subterfuge of any kind?"

"I have no knowledge about the extent of her powers."

"It seems to me there can be only be a few possible reasons. One may have to do with her feline nature. Who hasn't watched a cat toy with its prey, a ruthless torturer? I trust we both find the road this leads us down chilling."

Mr. Thompson nods.

"The second, more hopeful interpretation is that her powers have a limit. She did not, after all, change the reality of the world. She changed the perceptions of a few people in a room, making me appear to be a murderer in their eyes. It is like an illusionist convincing a small audience that a trick is real. That audience then goes forth and tells their family and friends, spreading the power and permanence of the illusions. Belief and certainty are contagious things. She can achieve her broader, more visible transformations to London and beyond, but it requires incrementalism and patience, much like any social change. I'm a member of the Fabian Society, and we've had many discussions along these lines—the uses of cultural institutions to affect attitudes over a few generations, and so on."

"I would not admit to associating with such people."

Wilde laughs. "So, the man who sells out his country—his *race*—has the gall to criticize my associates? My political interests are benign to any sensible man who wants to rectify social wrongs."

Mr. Thompson's blush deepens. "I know what I've done is indefensible."

The food slot opens in the door and a tray slides through. Both men stare at it.

"Well, come and fetch it, Mr. Thompson," Bosie says. "Mr. Wilde must be hungry."

The museum director's shame turns to rage in an instant. "I'll not be treated like a waiter!"

"You're whatever the Great Goddess says you are. Tutor, waiter, court jester. Now bring this tray over to your student. There's gauze for his finger. Show our High Priest the ancient ways of wrapping bodies. He'll be doing that a lot in the near future."

"But I don't know anything about mummification!"

"Then I suggest you find the answer in one of your books very fast."

Mr. Thompson seizes the tray as the slot is slammed shut. Wilde sees both fresh bandages as well as bread and butter. He takes up a piece and stands there chewing it and studying Mr. Thompson's face. He finds a blank expression and distant, averted eyes.

"Should we consider this our second luncheon?"

Mr. Thompson makes no comment and Wilde, not feline, stops toying with the man. He finishes eating and sits on the edge of the cot with the fresh compress.

"I'm preparing myself for intense pain when I remove the old dressing. I hope there will not be too much blood."

"Good Lord," Mr. Thompson whispers, turning away.

Wilde moves the bandage a fraction and at once it feels like he's ripping his skin away. His breath hitches and he sits forward gasping, eyes watering.

"You should have a medical doctor," Mr. Thompson says, still facing away. "This is monstrous."

Panting, Wilde says, "Is there in fact anything about mummification in your books?"

"Not that I'm aware."

"Perhaps you should occupy yourself making sure while I go about the grim work of tearing myself open."

Mr. Thompson mutters a curse and kneels around his scattered books. Wilde goes on listening to the museum director talk to himself as he leafs through a variety of pages, sometimes stopping to read. Wilde closes his eyes, telling himself if changelings can rip away the entirety of their bodies then he can manage the brevity of a missing little finger. He grips the bandage, take several deep breaths, and jerks once.

His scream sends Mr. Thompson spinning around and falling over, kicking himself against the cell door. Wilde staggers, crying, clutching his left hand against his shirt. There's fresh blood, but not much. It seeps from the ruined place where the black skin makes the protruding piece of bone extra white. He wonders if there'll ever be a time when he can look at the wound with clinical detachment. Then he thinks of Charlie, confronting so much more every day, unable to hide his disfigurement in a pocket. Anger with himself overmasters his pain. Wilde lowers his left hand and asks Mr. Thompson for the fresh gauze.

"But I still don't know what to tell you," he says, handing over the clean dressing. "Even if the information is buried inside one of these books, none of them have an index. It might take days—"

"It is of no importance," Wilde says, beginning to wrap the wound in the only logical way he can see, moving over the decapitated pinkie once, then circling the wrist, then across the lower knuckles of the remaining fingers. He repeats the process until the length of the bandage is spent and the lower half of his left hand is almost immobilized. No blood spots emerge. The pressure of the wrapping is perfect.

"It looks to be very well-done," Mr. Thompson says.

Wilde nods. "Perhaps I will prove to have a natural knack for mummifying bodies. I enjoyed wrapping gifts when I was a boy. Maybe that was a foreshadowing of where my true talents lay."

Mr. Thompson just stares at him and Wilde moves back to perch on the edge of the mattress.

"I've rendered you speechless?"

"Yes," Mr. Thompson says.

"Then I am already recovering my strength. Let us proceed to our second lesson of the day, assuming bandaging myself was the first."

"Learning hieroglyphics," the director says, his tone uncertain.

"Good! I will need your help there, as I doubt I will prove to be so talented an autodidact with Egyptian writing as I was with the wrapping. But teach me at a slow pace, Mr. Thompson. My pain will no doubt prevent my mind from retaining new information, and I intend to buy as much time as I can."

"For yourself?"

"For the world."

# CHAPTER SIXTY-ONE

"I thought I told you to go slow," Wilde says, rubbing his eyes hours later as Mr. Thompson wipes away a series of images from his slate and begins to draw new ones. "I don't believe I can memorize another image."

Mr. Thompson stands before him holding a slate with three hieroglyphs on it. "This *is* slow. But we don't have to dally, regardless of your intent. Now look at these new drawings, which were found on the walls of Bast's earliest temple at Bubastis. This rattle in her hand is known as a sistrum. As her priest, you must learn to play this rattle in a certain way. Indeed, these particular hieroglyphs promise her worshippers an age of divine music for their devotion."

Wilde sighs. "With a chorus of human screams?"

He rises and goes to the window.

"At least I'll be priest to a goddess who enjoys the arts."

"Actually, most of them did. Ancient Egyptians and their religious practices put great emphasis on dramatic works. Their plays were not at all in the Greco-Roman tradition."

"That is not necessarily a *bad* thing."

Mr. Thompson dismisses the comment with an annoyed wave of his hand. "Most were religious in nature, often satirical to the point of heresy. It seems when it came to the dramatic arts, the pharaohs and even the gods themselves did not mind self-deprecation."

"Then they intuited an important lesson some of our British politicians have yet to learn," Wilde says. "Those in authority—and despots most of all—do not like to be mocked, but the most cunning of them will invite it in order to disarm. Tell me more about these Egyptian plays. Who wrote them? The priests?"

"It seems likely."

Wilde grunts and stares out at the courtyard. Dust swirls there in energetic eddies, reminding him of sand. His thoughts shift to memories of the carriage ride to Westminster Abbey and what he saw inside. He recalls the things Stephen said in the courtyard, the transformation of Trafalgar Square. *We don't have time to dally, regardless of your intent.* Mr. Thompson, he thinks, how right you may be—and that terrifies me.

"Tell me about London," he says.

Mr. Thompson's silence compels Wilde to turn around and make eye contact. He finds the museum director setting down his slate.

"I'm sorry. I thought we were still talking about Egyptian drama."

"I apologize for the abrupt change of topic. But I must know."

"What can I tell you? London is as it's always been, overflowing with too many people who have too little time for much of anything beyond the tip of their nose."

"You're telling me nothing is changed?"

"You talk like a man who already suspects the answer to his question."

"And you speak like someone who'd rather not confirm my suspicions."

"There's a subdued mood in the city," Mr. Thompson says. "In some ways it's as if everyone has an innate sense of the coming darkness."

"What about London itself? Bast is transforming it, isn't she? The sweep of Egyptian relics that were overtaking every gallery in your precious museum is now spreading out to the streets. Is that not so?"

"Yes." Mr. Thompson's voice sounds husky and dry.

"The past colonizes the present block by block. Do the people not realize it?"

"People see what they want, Mr. Wilde. They always have."

"That's still not an answer."

"Why would the presence of Egyptian artifacts spark alarm? Your own father helped bring Cleopatra's Needle to Westminster almost twenty years ago. Is Bast responsible for the Egyptian Hall in Piccadilly? The only difference in the recent transformations is the quality of the artifacts."

"What do you mean?"

"The crates that came to the museum carried objects that were thousands of years old and looked it. Some of the overflow you saw during our luncheon took months of restoration. The latest edifices, stela and statues being erected around London are so fresh you would believe our own architects fashioned them as period pieces."

"Or perhaps the artisans of the period are now having their work brought here after completion."

Mr. Thompson look to his books as if they have answers. "I don't understand."

Wilde steps back from the window. "There are many peculiar pubs in London, but one rises above them all in . . . singularity. Sometimes it is called The Red Tiger. Sometimes it is not."

"Is that meant to be a riddle?"

"Only in the sense that facts themselves are riddles now. You must trust me when I say time dances to a different tune at the pub I'm talking about. It contains a secret room not unlike a hidden chamber in

294

a pyramid or tomb. I have indisputable proof that this chamber can take someone into the distant past. What I cannot prove is whether the reverse is true. Regardless, discovering the secrets of that pub may be critical to any plans we draw against Bast."

Mr. Thompson's eyebrows arch. "*Are* there plans being drawn against her?"

"I hope so," Wilde says. "Otherwise, my capitulation is pointless. There is just one thing I know for certain. I *must* get my scarab ring back. Do you remember it?"

"Such beautiful jewelry would be hard to forget."

"It was taken from me when I was put on trial. I can only assume Bast possesses it or destroyed it, though my heart tells me neither is the case. It is a strange certainty, a powerful hope that's reawakened in me. I *will* get it back, and when I do, I will wield it with greater strength than ever before. I ponder just one thing."

"Which is?" Mr. Thompson says with a laugh.

Wilde raises his bandaged hand grins. "Whether or not the ring will look as good on my right hand as it did on the left."

# CHAPTER SIXTY-TWO

Charlie comes again that night. He puts his face in the open panel and asks for Wilde's right hand, which he places against his ruined cheek and holds it there for a long moment. Wilde has never been more content with silence.

"Your skin is as smooth as a woman's, Oscar," he says at last.

"I'm afraid prison has roughened it at least a little."

"You're the only man I know who doesn't have bruises and scabs on his knuckles. Even his Lordship, gentleman that he is, has scrapes."

"All of you are fighters."

"I don't want you to be a fighter, Oscar. I want you to stay just like you are."

Charlie's grip on his hand becomes fierce to the point of discomfort, but Wilde refuses to withdraw.

"I once wrote a book about a man who wishes to stay just the way he is. It was a foolish wish."

"A lot of men like me can't read. I could just a little before I met his Lordship, but he's the one who had me taught all the way. I can't say I've had much use for reading in my life."

"Quite right. Most books are useless, including mine."

"Don't say what you don't believe. I know there's a different world besides the one I've lived. There's the world of books and each book is its own world, or at least that's how it seems to me."

Wilde smiles. "Worlds—windows—doors—it has all the same consequences of escape."

"While I was getting better, I asked his Lordship about your books. He told me what he thought of them, but I wanted to see for myself. I told his Lordship they would be good practice for my right eye."

"You mean you've read them?"

"The one you just mentioned, about Dorian. And a book of essays. I can't say I understood any of those. But the story . . . it was the ending that got me."

"I see."

"When you wrote about how his beauty ruined him, it made me sad. I never even got the chance to be beautiful, and now . . ."

"You were beautiful when I met you, and you're more beautiful now."

"How can you say that and mean it, Oscar? Look at me."

Wilde pulls back his hand and then puts his face to the portal so they can see each other. Charlie starts to withdraw into the shadows until Wilde calls him forward with the gentlest of urging. They lock gazes, unblinking.

"Let me explain what beauty is, Charlie. This quiet moment between us is beautiful. Here we stand, two wounded men stranded on a shrinking island. But we deny victory to the sea of chaos by turning our faces to each other, by finding understanding and sympathy. The larger concern remains, but our subtle defiance of it is beautiful. We say our lives, our friendship, our ability to love will not be dominated. We will not surrender our hopes to any tyranny. The man who created Dorian Gray may have thought beauty was in the flesh. The man you look upon now has the hard-won wisdom to know better."

"I don't know what to say."

"Say they were good words."

He laughs. "They were good words, Oscar. And I'm still glad your hands are smooth."

"I would be happy to make them bleed in your defense."

"I'd rather bleed in yours."

"Then it's settled. Let's try to avoid bleeding all together."

"That's a fantasy even prettier than your words. I'm going to fight. His Lordship says the time is coming. I spend all day in my room training."

"Do you know what the plan might be?"

"No. I was just told to be ready."

Wilde frowns. "Then we have almost identical information. I was led to believe I have a role to play, but no actor can embody his performance without having some knowledge of the plot. Maybe there's a reason to be kept in the dark."

"*There is.*"

Bosie's voice surprises both of them. Charlie pivots and says, "Lord Alfred!" in the same deferential tone he reserves for Bosie's father. A moment later Bosie's face, so blond, fair and youthful for a man of his years, appears in the portal.

# CHAPTER SIXTY-THREE

Bosie opens the cell door and steps through, followed by Charlie. Even as he embraces his old lover, Wilde notices Charlie's sheepishness and how he turns his face to the wall. Bosie breaks the embrace and squeezes Wilde's forearm before asking Charlie to come to them. Wilde remembers how a transformed Bosie used to hiss his displeasure at Charlie's presence. The difference in the man now goes far beyond any change in appearance. Wilde senses no jealousy or anger in Bosie and wonders about his own feelings. Does he desire Bosie any more? Was the youthful petulance a crucial part of the attraction? He cannot fathom it being so, not now. As they exchange glances, Wilde senses a new understanding between them, something akin to former lovers who've moved on from each other but found a profound friendship in the aftermath. In that moment, Wilde realizes they will support each other. They will be allies.

But they will never be together again.

Bosie puts one hand on Charlie's shoulder. "The path out is clear for you, and there's a coach waiting. I need you to go now. Oscar needs his rest."

"I assure you I've never been more awake."

"I know," Bosie says. "That's a problem."

Charlie starts to leave. Wilde goes to him and turns his scarred face to the moonlight. He caresses it with his left hand.

"Visit again soon, dear boy."

"The bandage is rougher than your skin," he says, and brings Wilde's right hand to his other cheek.

There's a moment of silence in the cell after he leaves, as if both Wilde and Bosie contemplate Charlie's fading footsteps. At last Bosie says, "Be careful with your heart when it comes to him, Oscar. He has tender feelings toward you now, but he's not like us. He won't be able to give you what you want."

"I know. There was a time when I believed otherwise, but . . ."

"But what?"

"That belief, like all others, is gone." He sits down on the edge of the mattress and holds up his left hand. "As my injury goes, so goes mankind. People are always losing parts of themselves. Some have the pieces ripped away, others through the natural shedding that comes with age and experience. Arguments end friendships, death ends families, some new science upends the priest's faith . . . or an old, forgotten god shows up to disprove the scientist's empiricism. Cherished old buildings fall into dust and leave a space very much like the place where my pinkie used to be."

"Lay down, Oscar."

"I told you I'm wide awake."

"I have something to counter that," Bosie says, pulling a small vial from his pocket. "Put your trust in me and drink it down. It will put you into the sleep you need. There are people waiting to meet you in a dream."

"Who?"

"That's for you to discover."

Wilde takes the vial and removes the little cork stopper. The liquid inside has an orange tint and a foul odor. He turns his nose away on the first whiff.

"What's in this?"

"I don't know the ingredients."

"Who gave it to you?"

"Yeats. Drink it now, Oscar."

Wilde sighs. "Very well," he says, holding his nose. He tilts his head back and empties the nasty liquid down his throat. The effect proves instantaneous, like swallowing death itself. His vision clouds and he swoons, falling forward with a vague awareness of being caught in Bosie's arms. Then he's settled onto his back.

He wakes with a gasp in a low-lit room, dingy by almost any standard except that of a man used to imprisonment.

"Will, he's awake!"

Wilde stirs, groaning, squinting. "Robbie?"

"It's me, Oscar. Don't try to move. Your body's very weak."

As soon as Robbie says this, Wilde feels it for himself. He seems like a wilting flower, his petals crumbling away on the slightest breeze. Corpulent flesh sags around brittle bones. His lungs rattle on every strained breath. He works to lift his head and look at his body. His hands clasp each other above his stomach. There's no bandage on his left hand. He has his pinkie, but the scarab ring remains missing.

"What's happened to me? Is it the drink?"

"No, Mr. Wilde, it is not the drink," says Yeats, coming to stand over him. "The potion only put your body into sleep."

"But this isn't my body. And it doesn't feel like a dream."

"You are occupying an alternate version of your body, just we are occupying alternate versions of ourselves."

Wilde stares up at Yeats, noting the emerging streaks of gray in all that luxurious dark hair. And Robbie, though still youthful, has the start of wrinkles around his eyes, and his hairline is a little receded.

"You're both older."

"These bodies are older, Mr. Wilde. The minds temporarily controlling them are our own."

"I don't understand. Where is this? *When* is this?"

"We are in Paris, Oscar. It is November in the year 1900."

"I've been pushed forward in time the way Bosie was thrown back to ancient Egypt?"

"No, Mr. Wilde. Lord Alfred went back bodily. The three of us have done something quite a bit more complex and temporary. We have projected our minds not only to future versions of ourselves, but versions that exist in one of the many potential realities of existence."

"Potential realities," Wilde says, his voice a whisper. "Which one is this?"

"One where Bast never returned, and our lives continued without her disruption."

"There are a lot of alternate versions of us, Oscar," Robbie says. "Isn't that amazing to think about?"

Wilde works to swallow back a growing hardness in his dry, faulty throat. "How many of them are free of Bast?"

"All others, in fact," Yeats said. "It is difficult to calculate an exact number of alternative realities, but ours is the only one to suffer her threat."

"That would imply that our world, our reality, is some kind of aberration." Wilde manages to raise the bedclothes and inspect his body, finding it both recognizable and foreign. "What has happened to me? This body feels thirty years older than it should."

"You go to prison, Mr. Wilde. Incarceration appears to be a fixed part of your destiny across almost every reality."

"You mean this pathetic creature I'm inhabiting really did murder Constance?"

"Your imprisonment is due to a rash lawsuit against Queensberry," Yeats says. "Lord Alfred goads you into it after a series of follies. The Oscar Wilde you inhabit now endured two years of hard labor, the loss of his fame and fortune, the loss of his family. Upon his release, he goes into exile, a broken man with little interest in anything except satisfying his basest pleasures. Robbie here, and a few other dedicated friends, do their best to support him even as he lies to their face. At this moment, Mr. Wilde, he—you— are near death."

Wilde touches his left pinkie. "Where is my ring?"

"It appears he pawned it, perhaps for a drink."

"I cannot conceive of that. Did you bring me here to show me the life I've experienced, for all its misery, is not the worse fate after all?"

"We brought you here because it guarantees the privacy of our conversation. Bast's powers have grown. Her consciousness probes everywhere, threatening even the safety of dream communication. But even she cannot reach us in another reality."

Wilde summons the strength to lift his hand and grip Robbie's forearm. "Where is Constance? I should like to see her again."

Robbie looks away.

"She's dead, Oscar. Two years ago."

"How?"

"Complications from surgery."

Wilde shakes his head. "Her powers couldn't save her?"

"She had no powers, Mr. Wilde. She never became the leader of the Golden Dawn. Indeed, it seems the Golden Dawn itself is nothing more in these other realities than an esoteric club of pretenders and fools. These are realms where only the material world has meaning."

"Then even Bast would just be a figment of the imagination here."

"Yes."

"I cannot decide if our reality is the best—or the worst. My poor Constance . . . my poor children . . . what has become of all of you?"

"We did not bring you here to dwell on the decisions of our doppel-gangers, Mr. Wilde. In the world we know, the Golden Dawn remains strong. Our alliances stretch across the globe. All adepts are rallying to the cause of humanity, men and women of genius and subtlety. Constance's courageous stand against Bast has become a rallying cry."

"I wish to be in the fight. I should be honored to make the same sacrifice she made. You came and asked me to submit to Bast and become her priest. I have done this disdainful thing without question, but now I must know what you intend for me to do."

"Patience, Mr. Wilde. Remember your Milton: 'They also serve who only stand and wait.'"

"Not good enough," Wilde says, trying to rouse his ponderous body to show the fire he feels. His efforts only produce a louder rattle from his lungs.

"You're our mask, Oscar."

"Mr. Ross has it correct," Yeats says. "Because of you, Bast feels like her agenda proceeds according to her wishes. This distracts and disarms her while we refine our plans. The best thing you can do is to embrace your role with as much seal as possible."

"*Zeal?* How long will it be before she tests my commitment further? Do you ask me to be zealous about sacrificing an animal—or a child—to keep convincing her?"

Even Yeats appears chastened and stared long and hard at the floor. "I know we cannot even begin to stand in your shoes."

304

"Might I at least know the location of my scarab ring? It would fortify me."

"It appears to be as gone in our reality as it is in this one," Yeats says.

"How can that be? Was it destroyed?"

"All trace of it has been lost. That's all we know."

Wilde scowls. "I was a fool when I had it last. Constance told me my hopefulness fueled it, and I squandered that power in a fit of despair. I was useless when it came to the battle at the museum. You can't know how often I've relived that night in my head, imagining a better version of myself fighting alongside my wife. Perhaps with my assistance she would not have died."

"There's no need to feel guilt, Mr. Wilde."

"*Need* has nothing to do with it. Robbie, I beg you, help me sit up. There must be something else I can do."

Robbie assists him, though Wilde finds he has so little strength he starts to fall over as soon as he's not supported. Robbie braces him.

"The Red Tiger," Wilde continues. "Have you investigated it to the extent it requires? Maybe, somehow, I could help there. I have insights into its strange powers."

Yeats puts up a placating hand. "Mr. Wilde—*Oscar*—I assure you it is not gone without scrutiny. Indeed, we regard this pub as the lynchpin to our plans. But at the moment, it remains too difficult a target."

"Tell me more."

He sees Yeats and Robbie exchange quick glances.

"No."

"Why are you keeping me ignorant?"

"It's for the best, Oscar," says Robbie.

"That we've told you even this much shows the regard we have for you. Bast's connection to you will grow as your service to her advances.

305

I fear she might even be able to read your unconscious thoughts in time. We plan to carry out our plans well before then, but if there should be any delay . . ."

Wilde sees Yeats' lips moving, but the words become a buzz. Then his pulse hammers in his ears and he falls back, gasping, clutching his chest. He sees Robbie's face hovering over him, his mouth forming *Oscar* over and over. Yeats joins him, and the mute contortions of his mouth remind Wilde of the dream where the poet repeated the same words over and over—"Remember your Shakespeare, Mr. Wilde! Remember *the play's the thing*."

He says it back to Yeats now, feeling like he's babbling.

Robbie settles his head onto the pillows and strokes his hair. After a moment the roar of his pulse subsides, leaving Wilde gasping and sweating. "This is death," he says, not above a whisper. What a curious, dark gift it is to experience death but not be dying, to sense the dwindling powers of this body that both is and is not his own. Robbie's face fades in and out.

"What's happens to Oscar's mind if his body dies here, Will?"

"He will not be harmed."

Robbie grips Wilde's forearm. "You're absolutely sure of that?"

"Very sure, Mr. Ross."

Wilde swallows, forcing air into his aching lungs. "I'm not going yet. I must endeavor to outlast that hideous wallpaper."

Yeats bends down to him. "What did you mean when you told us to remember our Shakespeare?"

"It's something you told me."

"I have no recollection of that."

"It was in a dream."

Yeats goes rigid and holds up his hands. "It is imperative you tell

306

me nothing more."

"I understand your fears," Wilde says. "Constance taught me the rules. It's just that for a moment, as I almost lost consciousness, the movement of your lips refreshed my memory."

"Let us speak no more of it," Yeats says, his tone stern. "Fate must always be fate, a discovery earned by the hard labor of time."

"Then would it be okay if Oscar tells me?" Robbie says.

"No. Whatever I said has a meaning reserved for Mr. Wilde and myself. We must discover it alone, and all other curiosity in the matter must be denied at all costs."

Wilde's body spasm and he finds it hard to breathe again. His pulse becomes a jeering in his ears as he tries to reach for Robbie's arm.

"I am just . . ."

"Oscar?"

Yeats and Robbie fade out.

"Just going . . ."

Wilde closes his eyes and opens them to find himself alone in his prison cell in Wandsworth. Then he shivers because, for a moment, this terrible room has all the warmth and familiarity of *home*.

# CHAPTER SIXTY-FOUR

In the morning, Wilde hears brisk footsteps approaching his cell. He rises, prepared to greet Mr. Thompson for another round of lessons. When the door opens, however, he finds Bosie and Queensberry confronting him, in their disguise as Stephen and Locke. The look in their eyes tells him they are all to stay in character.

"Come along, Wilde," Bosie says. "The Great Goddess wants to see how you've progressed."

"But I've only just begun my lessons!"

"Better hope you're a quick learner," Queensberry says, moving forward to seize Wilde's right wrist and jerk him forward.

There's a part of Queensberry who enjoys this, Wilde tells himself as he's prodded into the hallway. He then accompanies them out to the courtyard. Wilde notices none of the panthers lounging there as they were before. Indeed, it feels like Wandsworth might be deserted except for the three of them. But if that's so, why would Bosie and Queensberry insist on maintaining appearances?

Unless *other* eyes are watching, too.

They pass through the gates and approach a waiting carriage. Bosie and Wilde get inside. Queensberry assumes his role as driver. Wilde hears him give a vulgar shout, followed by the brisk flick of a whip.

The carriage bolts forward.

Within the cabin, Wilde stares at Bosie, noticing the slightest shake of his head. He interprets this as a warning to keep up the act.

"I should hope I don't disappoint the Great Goddess. I've been working very hard, but it is difficult. Hieroglyphics are a challenge."

"The Great Goddess will let me motivate you if she's dissatisfied with your performance."

"What would she have me do? I still know nothing of her rituals."

"Sounds to me like you need a better teacher."

"Mr. Thompson has done just fine, I assure you."

"The Great Goddess will judge that. You can still lose her favoritism, and if her favor turns against you there'll be no protection. I wonder how delicious your heart must taste."

Wilde shudders, unable to quench a fear this might not be Bosie after all. The malice in his tone is too genuine.

"I—I shall endeavor to keep your curiosity unsated."

Bosie crosses his arms at the chest, his expression flashing clear contempt. It's as if he's determined to impress someone invisible to Wilde's eyes.

After thirty minutes, the carriage begins to slow.

"Almost there now," Bosie says. "I'm going to enjoy watching you fail, Wilde. The Great Goddess might be so disappointed she abandons you on the spot. Then you're mine."

Wilde chooses to ignore the taunt and looks out the window to see Buckingham Palace. Its magnificence only inspires darkness in his thoughts. He thinks of Queen Victoria. How was she murdered? And what has become of the rest of the royal family?

The carriage stops. Queensberry wastes no time getting the door open. He reaches into the carriage and drags Wilde out, all but throwing him to the ground. Wilde now senses tremendous tension in both Queensberry and Bosie. Looking up, he sees why. The grounds of Buckingham Palace look like the plains of another land. Panthers lounge everywhere, hundreds of them enjoying casual dominion over everything they see. Their yellow, scrutinizing eyes have all turned toward the carriage. Some rise and stalk toward it, as noiseless as shadows. Only their easy loping pace keeps Wilde's urge to shout locked away in his throat. Were they to charge at him, he knows he'd scream and dive into the coach for protection.

More panthers approach. Bosie and Queensberry move to flank Wilde. Is this an ambush? Has their deception been discovered? He casts a peripheral glance at Bosie and finds him calm, even imperious in his expression. As the panthers reach a distance of fifty yards, Bosie speaks unfamiliar words in the unmistakable tone of a command. The huge cats stop and rise up on their hind legs. One by one they begin their transformation, assuming the familiar form of the changeling, hairless and gray, their heads rounded like ashen moons.

Bosie takes Wilde by his right arm and pulls him forward with Queensberry flanking him on the left. The changelings fall in line behind them and they come like a might host to the palace doors. Two men in red coats guard the entrance. Sweat makes their upper lips and brows shiny and marks them as human. Their Adam's apples bob from pronounced swallowing. Wilde can only wonder about these men. Are they willing traitors to humanity? Have they capitulated to save their lives?

They open the doors and as they do, Wilde hears the faintest rumble of disgust in Queensberry's throat. It's the subtlest communication of the contempt he has for the guards, but in that instant it has all the eloquence of a speech in the House of Lords. How hateful his charade must be to him, Wilde thinks, marveling at a restraint and discipline he'd never thought possible from Bosie's father.

Passing into the palace, Wilde twists his head back from a sudden scorch against his skin. The air is hot like standing next to a fireplace. Blinking, with no choice but to endure it, Wilde tries looking forward even as the temperature dries out his eyes. The royal palace contains no trace of the British character. Without knowing better, he might assume he's gone to The Red Tiger's secret room and followed Bosie back to ancient Egypt. The interior feels hollowed-out, transformed into a single vast space of sandstone-colored walls. A ramp rises in the distance, leading to a platform high above them. Wilde can make out no details regarding what awaits him there. They progress toward it on a pathway lined with obelisks covered in hieroglyphics. Somewhat to his surprise, Wilde finds at least a few of his lessons with Mr. Thompson have stuck. He interprets several of the images, discovering a monotonous theme—Praise to Bast the queen, praise to Bast the Eternal Mother, praise to Bast the Unvanquished Goddess. Wilde looks from right to left, becoming more certain the obelisks contain an ongoing narrative like an engraved Bayeaux tapestry: *Bast rises from her chair and boards a boat. Thousands mourn her departure. Bast travels across a treacherous ocean, facing and subduing many dangers. Bast reaches a new shore where thousands cheer her arrival.*

They reach the ramp. There's one obelisk here, with a single, familiar image engraved on it to finish the tale.

*Bast enthroned.*

Bosie stops and turns, speaking at length to the throng behind them. Whatever he says excites them. They make purring sounds in their throats and they drop to their knees. Their eyes look toward Wilde and it seems like they now find him worthy of rapturous adoration.

From high above them, somewhere at the top of the ramp, Bast roars. The deafening sound causes Wilde's shoulders to bunch. The changelings bow their heads.

Bosie grazes Wilde's right hand. "The Great Goddess calls her priest for a long overdue audience.

"I—am ready."

The three of them ascend the ramp, which rises at an ever-steepening inclination, surely exceeding the height of the palace's ceiling. Wilde's steps grow heavier, and the thud of his pulse rings out under the bandage, forcing him to cradle his left hand. If only Bosie could risk telling him what he knows, the importance of *discovery* be damned. He must have some insight, some foreknowledge of what is about to transpire. The most striking thing Wilde notices is Queensberry no longer flanks him. He's moved to walk shoulder to shoulder with his son, leaving Wilde alone to their left. Halfway up the ramp, he risks a direct look at both of them and finds grim determination in their expressions.

"What is it?" he whispers. "Please tell—"

Bosie grabs Wilde's left wrist and squeezes until it hurts. Flushing, chastened, Wilde hangs his head and trudges on, his chest tightening. He tries to imagine what task Bast has in store for him, and then he considers how she'll punish him for failing it. Will Bast claim another finger? Or perhaps his entire left hand?

They reach the top of the ramp. Wilde looks back and almost swoons. The obelisks look like tiny needles from here, the kneeling changelings an assembly of figurines from a doll's house.

Bosie prods him to face forward.

There is a throne in front of them and Queen Victoria sits upon it, comfortable and plump, her lips pouty and downturned above a receding chin. She wears her thinning gray hair pulled back from her broad forehead and her eyelids droop, making her seems half-asleep and bored. No finery, no raiments, no clothing at all covers her fleshy body, but Wilde refuses to avert his eyes. Victoria grins to reveal a mouth of sharp teeth.

"Do you like this form, my priest?"

Working to keep his nerve from breaking, Wilde bows. "You have captured our former queen's tedious expressions quite well, Your Highness."

Bast laughs at this, joined by Bosie and Queensberry. She stands and seems to step out of Victoria's form with all the ease of someone stepping out of shadow, the disguise melting away to reveal a voluptuous body with a panther's head.

"You have described her well, my priest. She was a woman with many vain titles and countless sorrows. Ending her unhappy life was a kindness on m part."

Queensberry steps forward and drops to one knee. "Praise be to the true queen of our minds and hearts."

Bast extends her right hand and places it atop Queensberry's head. It lingers there, thumb stroking his hair. Her head tilts to the right as if considering something.

"If every man and woman had your heart and mind, there might be no need for a priest at all. Your early and profound devotion should be rewarded."

"My faith in you is its own reward," Queensberry says, his voice filled with such conviction Wilde has trouble believing it could be false.

Bast turns and walks toward the throne. She goes past it, and Wilde realizes there's considerable space on the other side. Bosie directs Wilde forward and the two of them make a few steps forward before pausing when Bast looks over their shoulder.

"Come as well, my faithful child," she says, motioning toward Queensberry.

He hesitates only a moment before joining them.

There is a slab behind the throne, a stone table about seven feet long and five feet wide. A series of ceramic jars rest on the floor beside the table. The jars have hieroglyphics on them Wilde cannot read.

Bast stands at the head of the table and faces him.

"Have you studied well, my priest?"

"I—I have tried."

"Do you feel ready for your first test?"

"My Queen—Great Goddess—it has been only a few days. I would not be adequate. I know nothing of language or rituals yet. This is not the fault of my teacher but—"

Bast laughs again.

"This is not a test of your knowledge, my priest."

"Then I do not understand."

"I wish to know your conviction, your ardor. Look at this exemplary human," she says, pointing to Queensberry. "A mere man like yourself, yet he has all the fire and fidelity I could require. Watch and learn from him."

Wilde and Queensberry stare at each other. The Marquess remains motionless, as does Bosie.

"What is your name, child?"

"Locke."

"Do you know hieroglyphics, Locke?"

"No, my Queen."

"Do you know anything about my rituals?"

"I . . . know only what my beating heart tells me."

A smile draws back the mouth on Bast's panther head. "Come to the altar, child."

Wilde steps between the Marquess and the table. "I'm sure I need no education from this man."

"Some lessons cannot be learned from books, my priest, just as some teachers serve their students best by setting the perfect example."

Queensberry touches Wilde's shoulder. Wilde turns to stare into his old adversary's eyes. He finds them wet but clear. He pushes Wilde aside and gets upon the table without a word and rests himself flat on his back.

"Most beautiful," Bast says, bending down to caress Queensberry's cheek. "Your reward is well-earned and bestowed with the same generosity of spirit you have shown to me."

"What reward?" Wilde says. He turns, looking to Bosie, who remains standing rigid, his gaze distant.

"Come and have your question answered, my priest, if you are truly so innocent as to have to ask it."

Seeing no alternative, Wilde goes to Bast's side. They look down upon Queensberry, who stares past them.

"In days of old—days that shall find renewal in this green land—it was a mark of honor for servants to follow their masters into death. As I cannot die and as this mortal has found great favor with me, I have decided to grant him the sacrificial gift. I shall claim him now, while he enjoys a robust health, and spare him later indignities. His soul will be freed, and every part of him preserved. Here, my priest."

Bast holds out a golden dagger, encrusted with green jewels, its point so tapered Wilde thinks he could pick his teeth with it.

"No," he says, voice quavering.

Bast continues to hold out the blade. "How is it the man on the slab has more courage than the man who is offered the knife? Why should I countenance your cowardice? Why should he sully his sacrifice with your faithlessness?" Her voice gets louder, angrier. "Have I made so poor a choice in my High Priest?"

"He only needs a little more motivation, Great Goddess," Bosie says, coming forward to deliver a swift kick to Wilde's thigh. The force of it knocks him over, writhing, and Bosie kicks him again. "Get up, Wilde! I promised our queen I'd break you and you'll stay broken!"

"Bring him to his feet and take him to the altar," Bast says.

Wilde struggles against being hoisted up. How can Bosie and his father stay in character now? Don't they have some plan? Where are Yeats and the Golden Dawn? Will no one stop this madness? Wilde cries out as he's shoved toward the altar and almost falls across Queensberry's legs. Bosie jerks him back at the last moment and forces his right hand up. The sacrificial blade is placed against his palm and Bosie forces Wilde's fingers tight around it.

"You can't expect me to do this," Wilde says, almost talking to the knife. His gaze drops to Queensberry in search of answer. The Marquess remains still and impassive. There *must* be some escape plan, some imminent rescue. It is the one plausible explanation for his tranquility.

He turns his teary eyes to Bast. "What kind of god requires human sacrifice?"

Queensberry answers the question. "Name a god that didn't?"

His words draw all attention to him. The Marquess reaches up and wraps both hands around Wilde's wrist. He draws the blade down over his heart.

"Such faith," Bast says, her voice almost a whisper, almost awed. "He diminishes you more and more in my eyes, Priest."

"Do your duty, Wilde!" Bosie shouts.

"Are there—are there words to speak? Prayers to say? How can I sacrifice this noble man when I can't give him due honors?"

Bast begins speaking in an unknown language, her tone gentle—even soothing. Wilde swallows. The haft of the knife grows warm against his palm, and the blade itself begins to gleam. He shakes his head and meets Queensberry's eyes again, finding neither sympathy nor remorse there. Such a hard man, Wilde tells himself. Harder and stronger than I could ever hope to be.

The knife slips closer to Queensberry's chest. It feels to Wilde like it has its own consciousness, its own will. How he wishes this were so.

I cannot do this, Wilde thinks. I won't be responsible for this travesty. This cannot be part of Yeats' great plan.

The tip of the knife touches Queensberry's shirt.

Wilde gasps. The blade passes through the fiber and indents the flesh. He tries to bring the knife back. Why is the blade so heavy? He grits his teeth and makes one last attempt to avoid this evil.

For a moment, the knife seems to relent. But then Queensberry's hands move. He grips Wilde's right hand and drives the blade down. Wilde loses his balance and falls forward as the knife sinks into the man's chest. A cough and a gurgle come from Queensberry's parted lips, followed by a frothy spit as his head lolls to the left. The Marquess blinks, eyes shifting everywhere, surely a reflection of the chaos in his head. He lifts his head a few inches to lock gazes with Wilde a final time. They hold the stare several long seconds and then the energy drains out of his body and Queensberry's head falls back against the slab.

Bast ceases her foreign whispers. She moves Wilde aside, removes the knife and begins cleaning the blade with her tongue.

"It is well done, my priest. I am disappointed but not insensible to your struggle. The next time will be easier, and you will know the words to the sacrificial prayer. Now you will learn the far happier ritual of preservation. Take back the blade. I will show you how to remove the organs and ready them for mummification. Together, we have given this man eternal life."

Wilde takes the knife, knowing he has little choice.

"He wanted to be cremated."

Bast's cocks her head. "And how would you know *that*, my priest?"

"I . . . overheard him say it."

"A strange thing to overhear."

Wilde swallows. "One doesn't eavesdrop to hear the ordinary, my queen."

Bast's laughter rings through Buckingham Palace.

# CHAPTER SIXTY-FIVE

Several hours later, with his clothes and skin covered in Queensberry's dried blood, Wilde leaves the palace. Bosie places him inside the coach, shuts the door and then mounts the driver's seat himself. Wilde stares at the floor, not blinking, unable to close his mouth. Horrific images flash through his thoughts. What have his hands done? What else will they do in the future that awaits him?

The carriage goes at breakneck speed. Wilde hears the horses complaining over the continuous cracking of a whip. The cabin shakes from a violence that threatens to make the coach's wheels fall off.

He opens the window and shouts a plea to stop.

Bosie slows the carriage, but only after several more minutes at the same reckless pace. When the sudden halt comes, Wilde pitches forward, crashing against the other side of the cabin and crumpling to the floor. Bosie throws open the door and stands there *as* Bosie, his youthful face stamped with grief. He reaches in and pulls Wilde out.

The carriage has stopped in a village on the outskirts of Wandsworth Prison. Wilde imagines many of the jailers and their families once lived here. Perhaps they still do, but the street seems deserted, and the houses look abandoned, their windows dark. Wilde and Bosie embrace, rocking each other, weeping.

"Dear boy, how truly sorry I am."

Bosie spasms in Wilde's arms, his body trembling from the force of his sobs.

"All those years of hating him . . . only to find love in the end . . ."

"He was courageous, defiant and true—and you are your father's son."

"He more than any other knew the dangers. There are men and women who have pledged their loyalty to Bast out of fear or opportunity, but my father knew someone had to pose as full-throated convert. He was a better actor than I ever imagined. When we were told to bring you to Buckingham Palace, he suspected what Bast's reasons might be. He wanted to use the moment to strike, but the Golden Dawn has a different plan."

"I hope it warrants the profundity of his sacrifice."

"I've lost faith in them, Oscar. That's why I'm not taking you back to Wandsworth. My father used to rage that you had to languish there while *the mystics* twiddled their thumbs. Well, no longer. Follow me."

"To where?"

"A safe place."

They go down the empty street to the smallest of the houses. From its dusty, closed windows, Wilde hears the sound of a struggle in the form of gasps, curses, and rapid footfalls.

"His practice never stops," Bosie says.

"Whose practice?"

Bosie answers by taking a key from his pocket to unlock the front door. Bosie leads him through the dark foyer to another room lit low by oil lamps. There they stop and Wilde watches Charlie, stripped to the waist, shadow boxing. His hands go through a battery of assaults, upper and undercuts, sudden short punches, blazing hooks. His feet shift him everywhere, springing, pivoting, dodging. A sheen of sweat on his back reflects the yellow glow of the flames, mesmerizing Wilde with the magnificence of the young boxer's physique. Charlie swears, makes vows, mutters promises of destruction. He is ballet dancer and avenging knight. Wilde touches the base of his throat, his chest aching to behold such valor. It would content him to stand here for hours watching unseen. But Bosie knocks on the wall and Charlie spins about, fists raised, looking like two halves of different creatures fused together. The scars on the left side of his face continue down his torso, sparking a helpless anguish in Wilde's heart.

They stare at each other. In other circumstances, based on their previous interactions, Charlie might turn away or blow out the lamps to hide himself. Wilde sees a look of confusion on the young man's face. "Oscar," he says, coming forward as if in a trance. "Is that blood?"

"It is," Bosie says. "Charlie, fill a tub with water. We need to get Oscar out of these clothes."

"Yes, Lord Alfred," he says, backing away without taking his gaze off Wilde. Then he turns to do as he was bidden.

"This is where Charlie's been staying, along with my father."

"How do we tell him what's happened?"

"He would take the news best from you."

"You can't make that request of me! The depth of feeling he had for your father is—"

"I know. I also know the regard my father had for Charlie. Believe me when I say it is better that he does not hear the news of my father's death from . . . a rival."

"Better from you than from the man who killed him."

"You can't blame yourself. My father was committed to his role. He all but plunged the dagger into his own heart and this sacrifice has eliminated Bast's doubts about you. I felt the level of her satisfaction and assurance like a purring in her throat. Her guard is lower than it has ever been because she feels she has you under her thumb."

"Why am I so crucial to her plans?"

"It's worship she craves, Oscar. It's like milk and honey for her, and her high priest is the funnel. She chose you—"

"I know why she chose me. She thinks we're the same, creatures who need a mutual feast of adoration at all times."

They turn at the sound of Charlie's return. He's put on a shirt and steps forward, his shoulders squared, expression grave.

"That blood is his Lordship's—isn't it?"

"Dear boy—"

"*Isn't it?*"

"Yes," Bosie says.

Wilde detects the slightest quiver in Charlie's lips, but it lasts less than a few seconds.

"His Lordship spoke to me early this morning. He told me there was a good chance he was saying goodbye. I've never seen his Lordship be gentle before. Even when he nursed me back to health it wasn't with a woman's tenderness. I wouldn't have wanted that, I don't think. But what he said today had me boxing every minute until you stopped me. It was all I could do, pretending to be by his Lordship's side, protecting him and him protecting me."

Wilde wipes his eyes. "I am ashamed of many things I said about the Marquess, Charlie. I've never been more wrong about a man in my life. I cannot say that we were friends, but I never counted myself more fortunate or proud to call him an ally. Your judgment was better than mine."

"He made two requests of me. Oscar, Lord Alfred, he wanted the three of us to avenge him."

"We will," Bosie says.

Charlie nods, tight-lipped, and reaches into his right pocket. "Then you'll need this. His Lordship put it in my keeping before he left. His second request was I give it to you, Oscar."

He places a small jeweler's box into Wilde's right palm.

PART SEVEN

# CHAPTER SIXTY-SIX

When Yeats arrives with three additional members of the Golden Dawn, the four of them ignore Wilde's greeting and launch into rituals of chants and gestures. Wilde watches Yeats blow handfuls of blue-tinted dust against every windowpane while another draws a chalk labyrinth on the floor of the empty dining room. Bosie and Charlie stand beside him until the ceremonies are complete. Yeats approaches them, his expression stern.

"The steps we've taken may grant this meeting some level of secrecy, but I urge you to reconsider this conference, Mr. Wilde. We can arrange to meet—"

"I have no wish for us all to meet in alternate versions of ourselves in a happier reality."

"Even though it would guarantee we would not be compromised?"

Wilde raises his right hand and shows the scarab ring on his pinkie. "We will *not* be afraid of our own voices in our own world. Now come and join with us."

They gather in a circle, the members of the Golden Dawn, Wilde, Bosie and Charlie, and Mr. Thompson. Wilde steps into the middle of it and turns, meeting every gaze.

"You are now all aware of the sacrifice made by John Douglas, Marquess of Queensberry. He embraced the risk to help the cause of humanity, and because of his courage I am positioned as Bast's High

Priest—according to the wishes of the Golden Dawn. I demand to know the next step."

"We've already discussed this, Mr. Wilde."

"Actually, we haven't discussed anything. We have talked much about the power of *discovery*." He raises his right hand, curling the fingers to make a fist. The scarab ring shows with all the prominence he intends for it. "I submit to you the time of discovery has arrived. But it is not me discovering your plans. Rather, it is you discovering *mine*."

A murmur goes through the assembly. Everyone looks to Yeats, who squares his shoulders and says, "Very well."

"The play's the thing, William—as you've told me. We will not ponder when you tell me, or under what circumstances. The matter is settled. What remains for me is to discover what you meant, or will mean, by your communication. I believe that discovery is unfolding at this very moment."

"What do you mean, Oscar?" Robbie says.

"Very simply, I intend to write a play."

"An unusual form of combat," says a man from the Order.

"Do you mean to destroy Bast with acerbic witticisms?" says another.

Wilde purses his lips a moment. "Under my tutelage with Mr. Thompson, I have learned the ancient Egyptians had a taste for theater. Is that not so?"

"It is," says Mr. Thompson.

"And these plays were of a religious nature, perhaps even written by the priestly caste?"

"Yes."

"Well then," Wilde says, turning to look each person in the eye. "I was a playwright, and now I am a priest. It seems fate has determined to merge these qualities together."

"You intend to write a play *for* Bast?" Yeats says. "To what end?"

"Indeed—to what end?" Wilde says, turning to Bosie, who steps forward.

"The Order needs to distract Bast's attention. You've said so yourself, Yeats."

"That is true."

"Oscar's play would be a greater distraction than anything you can conceive. If he writes a play in celebration of her, she will make it a grand event. All of her loyalists will be drawn to the performance."

"You said the Order considers The Red Tiger the lynchpin of your plans, but that it remains too guarded by changelings."

"Yes."

"Could you attack it if my play drew almost every changeling away?"

Yeats rubs his chin. "Your way with words is considerable, Mr. Wilde, but I doubt any drama is capable of distracting Bast from detecting our threat. She and her forces would descend upon us before we could complete the assault."

"I have thought of that," Wilde says. "I'll just have to make sure she finds my play so mesmerizing that she stays in her seat."

Yeats shakes his head. "Mr. Wilde, as much as it pains me to say it, the pen isn't really mightier than the sword. And in our case, the swords required must all be Excalibur."

Wilde grins. "Oh, the pen itself may not be. But I think you're shortchanging the *ink*."

The scarab ring's green stone begins to glow.

# CHAPTER SIXTY-SEVEN

Wilde walks back into his prison cell, accompanied by Bosie and Charlie. He stops at the threshold and stares at the window and the cot.

"It is strange, the things one can get used to. Or rather, the things I *thought* I'd become accustomed. This room has been my world for many months. Now that I'm a priest, I should call it my sacristy. But how hateful and unfamiliar this space seems to me after just a little bit of freedom."

"Don't stay here, Oscar," Charlie says. "There's no need. Lord Alfred is the only jailer."

"I'm afraid I must. We must maintain appearances."

"Then may I come and visit you?"

"Often. Your visits are an inspiration."

Charlie smiles at this, and for a moment his face seems restored. They embrace, and Wilde cherishes the fierceness of Charlie's hug. He wonders about all those alternate versions of himself existing *elsewhere*. Could there be some universe, some world, where he and this wonderful young man share an uncompromising love?

Or is that world this one?

He breaks the embrace to wipe his eyes.

"Is there something wrong, Oscar?"

"No, dear boy. I was only contemplating the wonders of magic."

Bosie asks Charlie to step out of the room, which he does with the same obedience he always showed Queensberry. Wilde sits down on the edge of the mattress.

"Are you okay?"

"I'm not sure," Wilde says. "I begin to feel the weight of what I must do, and it makes me question my abilities. If you were to put a blank sheet of paper in front of me now, I fear you'd find it still blank in the morning. What if the fate of our world hinges on one man's writer's block?"

"I'll wager my life on the power of your creativity every time. If you end up writing the world's obituary, we'll at least go out laughing."

Wilde smiles but finds his cheer fleeting. He touches the scarab ring, feeling the cold stone against his fingertips. "Constance tied the power of this ring to my ability to hope. I know that I'm never more hopeful than when I'm writing. My horizons are never broader, and I see so many possibilities. When a play is unfolding for me, when the characters seem to be speaking through me like spirits; that is its own kind of magic. And that is what I must connect to the power inherent in the ring, so that the words are imbued and drip with its influence."

"Tomorrow Mr. Thompson will come with a new title in his collection of text books. You must be careful with it, for it is very old. Almost as old as I am," Bosie says with a wry laugh.

Wilde raises his eyebrows. "What is this book?"

"It has no title. Think of it as any one of the many illuminated, esoteric manuscripts buried in the moldy libraries of ancient monasteries. It is in some sense a handbook, its contents containing Egyptian spells and rituals. I discovered it among Stephen's possessions after I assumed his identity."

"Does the Golden Dawn know about this book?"

"No."

"Wouldn't it be wise to have Yeats look at it?"

"Why? So they can sit on it and fret while brave men like my father sacrifice themselves?"

"I've been as frustrated by them as you are, but we must be fair in our criticisms."

"Come off it, Oscar. They're the least urgent people I've ever met."

"Mystics no doubt reckon time differently than you and I."

Bosie laughs. "Please don't talk to me about time."

Wilde bows his head and apologizes.

"The Golden Dawn is not the same without Constance's leadership," Bosie continues. "She had the right amount of caution and courage. Yeats is too scholarly to be decisive. No, it is better you receive the book without their influence. Likewise, it is better I do not keep the book with me, as it could draw unwanted attention. It is safest tucked away with your unsuspecting—and unsuspected—milquetoast tutor."

"You say the book belonged to Stephen? What manner of spells are inside it?"

"Ones that could do us a lot of good. Bast may consider Stephen a faithful son, but it seems Stephen was less loyal to his Great Goddess than his ardor let on. I was present at his transformation. He was one of the infants offered up to Bast while I was held in the mason's hands. He went through century after century in solitude just like I did. But in his case, it was like a second gestation, the sarcophagus a second womb. By the time he was rediscovered and freed, he knew only hatred of Bast—and profound fear of her. Had he lived, he would have attempted to overthrow her at last."

"He thirsted for vengeance but drank from the cup of obedience. You almost make me pity him, Bosie."

"I wouldn't waste the tears. Had he succeeded, we might find ourselves dealing with an even worse tyranny. We have gotten the better of the situation, inheriting Stephen's knowledge with Stephen himself out of the way."

"Then the spells inside the book can harm Bast?"

"Harm? I don't know. But they might hinder her."

"We must pray that is enough."

"Very well," Bosie says. "I suppose we should wish each other a good night."

They embrace, and when Bosie breaks it Wilde realizes he's transformed into Stephen.

"It is late, Wilde. Past time for you to be in bed. After all, I run an orderly prison."

"I wonder if I might make one request of my warden."

"One—since you've been a model inmate."

Wilde grins. "I should like a pen and supply of paper, if I may. It seems I have some writing to do."

# CHAPTER SIXTY-EIGHT

As soon as Mr. Thompson sets his books and slates down, he presents the special text to Wilde with trembling hands. "Lord Alfred said you'd know what this is."

The book isn't much larger than his palm. Wilde takes pains at opening the first page and says, "What is it with mystics and wizards that compels them toward chapbooks?"

"I should have realized you'd find even this situation humorous."

"What's wrong, Mr. Thompson? It is only a collection of ancient curiosities."

"You don't believe that any more than I do. I *would* have before I fell into Bast's trap. I yearn for the days when I'd have thought there's no more magic in these spells than there are in a trick by Maskelyne."

Wilde purses his lips. "I take it you've reviewed the contents of this book?"

"I would ask that you don't tell Lord Alfred."

"It will be our secret," Wilde says, going to sit on the mattress. He looks through a few pages and shakes his head. "I know I've had few lessons with you, but none of these symbols are recognizable to me."

"They are very rare—in some cases, almost compound."

"Compound? Do you mean the equivalent of a neologism?"

"The analogy will suffice."

"Can *you* interpret this book, Mr. Thompson?"

"With difficulty."

"Then I should appreciate any summary you can give me."

The museum director sits down beside Wilde and they both look at a page. "When Lord Alfred told me about it, I expected something similar to a *Book of the Dead*. Is that familiar to you?"

"I can't say that it is."

"The Egyptians had complex beliefs about the afterlife. The very wealthy had spellbooks designed for them that were meant to assist their souls in overcoming a variety of obstacles and tests. It was therefore called a *Book of the Dead*. No one version was quite identical to the other."

"But this is a different kind of work all together?"

"I don't pretend to be an expert on Egyptian occult practices, but I have made some study in them, and I can say I've never seen incantations like this. I will show you an example."

He directs Wilde to turn the brittle pages until he finds a picture of a woman upon a slab. The woman has the head of a cat.

"I take it this is Bast?" Wilde says.

"It must be, but I do not think this particular image is to be found anywhere else on Earth."

The image is surrounded by the same hieroglyph repeated over and over. Dark lines extend from each glyph and connect to the table. Wilde stares at the symbol, haunted by the familiarity of it.

"Recognize it, Mr. Wilde?"

"I do, as odd as it seems. But I don't know why."

"Perhaps you'll remember more if I mention the name Francis Galton."

Wilde's lips part and stay open a moment. "The image in the microscope—from the blood of a changeling. Stephen's own blood, I believe."

"That's right. I didn't recognize the hieroglyph when I saw it. I didn't understand what it could mean."

"But you've come to a conclusion?"

"I believe it is almost like a stamp or a brand, as on livestock."

"The brand of Bast?"

"Yes. But it is more than a mark of ownership. It is a conduit for her influence, perhaps. A tether tying the changelings to her."

"Hence these lines?"

"Yes."

"Then what does this page show? A spell of binding?"

"Yes, but turn the page."

Wilde does. He finds close to an identical scene, except for one significant change.

"The connecting lines are gone."

"And the next page?"

Wilde makes eye contact with Mr. Thompson before returning his attention to the book. He turns the page and stares.

"What am I seeing? This looks like the first image. The lines are back."

"They are, but do you not detect the subtle distinction?"

Wilde shakes his head. "What am I missing?"

"Go back two pages and look at the image of Bast. Notices the small points that begin each line."

Wilde follows Mr. Thompson's directions. "I do see it. Like when you put a pen against paper and hold it a moment. The ink begins to pool and seep."

"Exactly. You'll see the connecting lines all begin with Bast. Now go back to the final image and look."

Wilde flips with such excitement the upper right corner of the page breaks. Both men wince, exchange cautious glances, and Wilde moves with more deliberation. He sees the difference between the images at once.

The lines now begin at each repeating hieroglyph.

"The bound have become the binders?"

"Yes, Mr. Wilde! This is nothing less than a spell of overthrow, a chant of rebellion."

"Bosie told me Stephen had such designs."

"The book's content certainly bears it out. The incantation that follows takes up the next several pages, and after that you'll find other spells with similar revolutionary designs—all aimed at Bast."

Wilde closes the book, places it upon the mattress and rises. He feels so light and free he can't help but stand. His mind entertains so many possibilities, so many hopes. His right hand trembles. The scarab ring blazes with a burst of uninterrupted green light. He shows it off in Mr. Thompson's transfixed gaze.

"Everyone says *discovery* is the essence of magic. Writing and storytelling have always been my primary means of discovering all manners of truth. Plots and thoughts reveal themselves, insight into the human condition arises; a witticism comes forth wholly formed like Athena. This is *my* magic, Mr. Thompson. I know that at some point in our future, a play will be important—even vital. As I've ruminated on this, I felt this mysterious play must be my own creation and related to my role as Bast's priest."

"Do you no longer feel that way?"

"In fact, I still very much feel that way. But now I see greater possibilities and potential, a blending of the power in words both ancient and new. New? Not even born! But I will midwife them from my mind. And the power in this ring will be a bridge between them. With luck, the play will be the thing to catch more than just the conscience of our new queen."

# CHAPTER SIXTY-NINE

Wilde is sitting on the floor with Charlie beside him, both laughing, their backs to the wall with the window overhead, when the cell door opens. Bosie enters, shedding Stephen's visage as he does.

"Ah," Wilde says, adjusting the papers in his lap. "Here's my charming warden in this, the merriest prison in England."

Charlie gets to his feet. "Oscar has been trying out some lines from his play to get my reaction, Lord Alfred. I think they are very funny. What was the one?"

"I have no idea."

"Oh, go on, Oscar. It's on that other sheet."

Wilde smiles, not bothering to find it. "'The good ended happily, and the bad unhappily. That is what Fiction means.'"

"No! The *other* one. The one you said I inspired."

"'The simplicity of your character makes you exquisitely incomprehensible to me.'"

Charlie all but slaps his thigh at this. It occurs to Wilde that until the young man came to visit him last night, he's never heard Charlie laugh in such a way, so free and helpless, as if being tickled—an adorable giggle that always ends in a breathless wheezing.

"I am writing this play for an audience of one, dear boy. But if I had my wishes, that one person would be you."

Bosie takes another step toward them. "Charlie, I should like to talk to Oscar alone for a bit."

"Yes, Lord Alfred."

Charlie nods at Wilde, all laughter, all joy gone. When he doesn't smile, the scarring seems to creep toward the unblemished side of his face like evil weeds threatening the best of gardens. Wilde starts to protest there's no reason for him to be sent away, but Bosie quiets him and touches Charlie's arm in passing.

"Go only out of earshot. This won't take long."

"Yes, your Lordship."

When Charlie leaves, Bosie helps Wilde to his feet and they sit together on the edge of the mattress.

"It seems you're making progress."

"I have some good lines. Charlie's been a good muse."

"I'm glad," Bosie says, patting Wilde's thigh.

"Something's wrong. Tell me."

"Bast is becoming impatient."

"Does she think a play can be written in a week?"

"A goddess' notion of time isn't the same as ours, I imagine."

Wilde runs his right hand through his hair. "How far along does she expect me to be?"

"She is ready for dress rehearsals to start. But I have managed to assure her that you are working on the third draft and need more time."

"Third draft! I have no *draft* at all." Wilde stands up and walks to the window. "Bosie, even with Charlie for a muse, I find it difficult to write in this cell. I'll always be a creature of comforts."

"You were meant to write a play by the seaside at Worthing, with Constance and your children nearby."

"I suspect you would have been there, too."

"No doubt disrupting your life and your writing."

340

"That's not true."

"It is more than true, Oscar. I know that in hindsight."

"We both have the advantage of hindsight, Bosie."

"But mine is several thousand years vaster. I wrote a letter to you about it, did you know that?"

Wilde turns. "When did you give it to me? I have no recollection."

"It's not something I could have given you. I composed it on the paper of my mind as I endured the tedious passing of centuries. It was filled with resentment and bitterness toward you."

"I take it this was a very long letter."

"Yes, once I quit focusing on you and started noting my own stupidity, arrogance, and childishness. It became a letter to myself, to my ever distant and petulant younger self. It came from depths I never knew I had. Perhaps I did not have them at all before Bast locked me away for eternity."

"Forgive me if I sometimes seem to forget how much you've suffered and continue to suffer. I would not wish that upon you. In the period since our reunion, there have been moments with you when I seemed to feel the great chasm of time in you, and the change it is wrought. Sometimes I feel like I'm talking to a stranger, and then I realize I too am changed. We're different men now."

"Yes," Bosie says. "But just now we need all the genius of the old, flippant Oscar Wilde."

He moves his body like a dog shaking away water, and he transforms into a duplicate of Wilde himself, right down to the missing pinkie.

"I'm going to summon Yeats here. It's time you left Wandsworth, Oscar. Go to where you were meant to write this play with all the speed and brilliance of the man you *were*."

341

Wilde stares at his mirror image, speechless a moment. "But how can you play me as well as Stephen?"

"Stephen's importance has declined in Bast's court of late. Having sold her on your undying loyalty, I have made myself far less substantial in her mind."

"But what if she comes here looking for both of us?"

"She is a *queen*, Oscar. Queens do not come, they summon. And she summons through Stephen. She will not even think about him when I enter alone, pretending to be the exact thing she wants—an obedient, devoted priest. All I require from you are manuscript pages as proof of your progress. Their existence will appease Bast and buy us time."

On the cusp of crying in gratitude, Wilde kisses Bosie on the mouth. Bosie does not transform himself, however, and breaks the kiss with a laugh.

"We put Narcissus to shame."

Wilde laughs too. "Very true, dear boy. But you'll remember my old adage—to love oneself is the beginning of a lifelong romance."

# CHAPTER SEVENTY

Two days later, Wilde and Yeats sit together on deck chairs just off the beach at the resort town of Worthing. Yeats maintains an impassive expression, more schoolmaster than mystic. He clears his throat every time Wilde looks up from his writing to glance at the sea, until at last Wilde puts down his pen and turns to the man.

"Don't you ever find inspiration in the sea, William?"

"Is your play a nautical adventure, Mr. Wilde?"

"No. Oceans and dry wit do not mix well."

"Then I suggest you keep your eyes on the paper. Time is critical."

"Perhaps the writing would go better if I could be alone with my thoughts, William."

Yeats frowns. "I am only trying to protect you against distraction."

"I've always found nothing makes me more productive than when my attention is called away from the task at hand. Just look at the pages I've completed today."

"I agree you've made remarkable progress, Mr. Wilde."

"Thank you for the concession."

"But we're still behind schedule."

Wilde gets out of the chair, stretches, and starts toward the beach over Yeats' loud objections. Only a sudden realization halts his steps. Even after all I've endured, even after all the profound changes I've professed for himself, how easy it is to return to my old ways, he thinks.

Wilde turns back, chastened, expecting a harsh glare from Yeats. But the young poet stands there reading the manuscript pages Wilde left behind.

"What do you think so far?"

"There are some amusements."

"I am overwhelmed by your approval, William."

"Do you have a title for it yet?"

"I was thinking *The Importance of Being Earnest*."

Yeats visibly stiffens, as if experiencing a brief, shooting pain.

"What's wrong? Don't you like it?"

Yeats sits down with the pages and stares out at the water. "Maybe I should have been considering the waves with the same interest you've shown them, Mr. Wilde."

"What do you mean?"

"The sense of tides and patterns. Place an unmanned British warship or a glass bottle on the sea, and the same forces may drive them to the same island time after time. My experience occupying an alternative version of myself has made me more sensible to the probability of predestination. My poems, for example, had no differences in titles, no dissimilarity in wording. A distinction of punctuation here and there, perhaps, but—"

"You are a rock in the ocean of time and space, consistent in all realities," Wilde says.

"Consistency is not just a rock, Mr. Wilde. It is *bedrock*. For the most part, we are always ourselves in temperament and judgment and habit, down to the words we always misspell, the food we choose from menus, and the impulses we either follow or struggle to defy. It seems even the creative spark burns the same in every version of our minds. This sentence you wrote, for example. 'To be natural is such a very difficult pose to keep up.'"

"What's wrong with it?"

"Nothing at all. It's just that I have read it before."

"Where?"

"From the play other iterations of yourself create and call *The Importance of Being Earnest*."

Wilde sits down, pondering this revelation. "Are you saying you have already read the entire play I am only beginning to write?"

"Yes."

"If I am indeed writing the identical play all other versions of me write, even under such extraordinary circumstances as this, then you might as well dictate the words to me. Time is a critical factor, after all."

"I cannot do that, Mr. Wilde."

"Then why tell me anything about the play? You must have a reason."

"I'm worried," Yeats says. "My fears may be unfounded, but they plague me all the same. These other realities, these other occurrences of *us* are not taking place in isolated bubbles of existence. There is a connective tissue to them."

"Now you sound more like Francis Galton than a mystic, William."

"Science where science is due, Mr. Wilde. I'll go further. If all these realities constitute a sort of body, the whole of which is incomprehensible to us, then Bast herself becomes a cancerous tumor. If she succeeds here, her dominion may spread to other realities where her existence is otherwise mythological."

"How could she? You said yourself that magic is only parlor tricks in other realities."

"Yet the powers we used here did allow us to succeed in occupying those alternate versions of ourselves. Our reality can exert influence over the others in a peculiar way, while there appears to be nothing they can do to reciprocate. This opens the door to unimaginable malevolence should a being such as Bast turn her attention to it."

"Perhaps she has no interest in doing so," Wilde says. "Or perhaps we are overvaluing the extent of her power."

"Do you believe it wise to leave so much up to the whims of *perhaps*?"

Wilde stares out at the sea again, his gaze following its undulations, his skin sensitive to the salty pinpricks of the breeze. He imagines the wind as the breath of the Great Goddess blowing across the world.

Across every version of it.

"Our fin de siècle threatens to become everyone else's fin du monde. Give me my manuscript, William."

He accepts the pages, presses his lips into a tight line, and then tears it all in half as Yeats grabs his wrist.

"What are you doing, Mr. Wilde?"

"It is time to separate ourselves from these other realms. I am *not* the same man as the other Oscars, for good or ill. I will not produce the same play as them. I have decided on a new course, one I'll call *Lady Gwendolyn's Pride*. Bast will no doubt find much pleasure in the title."

"But to start over now—"

"I will work faster than ever. Listen, William: do you hear that burst of applause?"

Yeats turns, showing a genuine, startled look that makes Wilde laugh.

"It is the clapping of my other selves, from across whatever boundaries that contain them. They approve my decision. If there's one thing we comprehend, it is that every Oscar Wilde is determined to stand out, even in a theater packed with a thousand of us. Waves of fate may send us all to the same shores of desolation, but we swim against the current to the last. It is the cause of our souls, we plead it for ourselves, and we are our own accusers and our own redeemers. Reality means little to us even as it comes crashing down on our heads. Bring me fresh paper, William. Let me start afresh on the task of working a very literal magic!"

# CHAPTER SEVENTY-ONE

*Literal magic.*

Wilde ruminates on the phrase as he sits, ten days later, at a desk in the middle of a circle formed by Yeats and other members of the Golden Dawn. He has never written at such a frenetic pace, each sentence like an unburdening. No, more than that: an untethering. The manuscript for *Lady Gwendolyn's Pride* rests in a stack before him and Wilde knows the work has separated him from whatever strings the grand puppeteer Fate has secured to his alternate selves.

The plot is unlike anything he's ever conceived. A conniving woman passing herself off as an aristocrat named Lady Gwendolyn comes to the home of a very rich but senile man who believes her to be the Queen of England. The old man lives with two dozen cats he believes to be his ungrateful human children, though he cannot remember ever having a wife. Always adaptable, Lady Gwendolyn encourages his delusion and promises to marry him and make him the King of England and make the cats heirs to the throne. The arrival of the rich man's adopted son, Charles, a boxing enthusiast, complicates the scheme. Unknown to both of them, Charles is Lady Gwendolyn's child, abandoned at birth twenty years earlier.

Yeats has confirmed the play bears no resemblance to *The Importance of Being Earnest.*

"This new work is very barbed, indeed, Mr. Wilde," he said upon reading the second act. "I cannot imagine Bast will be pleased to see herself rendered as a confidence woman."

Before Wilde could answer, he found his story championed by Mr. Thompson. "You needn't fear, Yeats. In many ways, this is just the sort of play the ancient Egyptians enjoyed most. Social, political and religious satire was popular in plays, and it was acceptable to make fun of the pharaohs, priests and even the gods. We're not dealing with the Judeo-Christian god who will not be mocked."

Yeats' eyebrows rose. "I'm afraid I cannot find the sense of humor in Bast."

"I'm not calling her light-hearted or mirthful. I'm only talking about the cultural traditions she must have had a hand in creating."

"As I've already noted, a wise despot knows how to wield self-deprecating humor," Wilde said. "Tyrants may gain great leeway by allowing a little public scorn and making sure they laugh louder than anyone."

Yeats looked between them and gave a grudging nod.

"I suppose if she sits still long enough for our spell to take effect, it will not matter one way or the other."

Literal magic, he tells himself, watching the ink glow green on the page as he writes the final act, the confrontation between Lady Gwendolyn, the senile rich man, and Charles. The ink's illumination stems from his scarab ring, its power enveloping the pen and the entirety of his hand as he composes to the pleasing, enigmatic sound of Yeats leading the Golden Dawn through chants and rituals taken from Stephen's ancient book. Wilde finds their collective noise enlivening, generating a hum throughout his body. Magic coalesces with magic, the power within the spells fusing with the power in the ring and turning every word he writes into part of a grander incantation, a subtle enchantment woven over the course of the plot.

Wilde bends toward the page as his hand races across it. His cursive blazes like green flame, and he swears he hears a voice whispering from the screech and scrawl of the pen tip. For a moment, the voice sounds like it belongs to Constance.

He stops writing and picks up the paper, bringing the Golden Dawn to a baffled halt. Wilde sees them staring at him as he brings the paper to his lips for a kiss.

"My dearest wife," he says. "No one ever had a better ghost writer."

# CHAPTER SEVENTY-TWO

Wilde dozes on the divan, his light sleep broken by the sound of the cottage door opening. A cool ocean breeze refreshes the dark room. He shifts, keeping his eyes shut, pleased by the compensation of heightened hearing. The gentle creak of the floorboards seems like a song, and he smiles because he knows it means Charlie has returned from his long night's journey. He discerns the length and subtlety of the steps, imagining each floorboard like a piano key. All at once, he can see the room, the entirety of the house through sound, and when the creaking stops so very near to him, Wilde knows Charlie is staring at him from the doorway.

"Was the ride to Wandsworth uneventful?"

"Oscar," Charlie says, his voice hesitant, edged with embarrassment. "I didn't mean to wake you."

"Sleeping is only a useful way to wile away the hours when you're not here. To sleep while you're around is a monstrous notion."

More creaking, the sound of Charlie entering the room. Then the soft complaint of a cushion compressing as Charlie sits down on the only chair. His breathing is fast. Wilde's eyes shift from left to right under their lids, trying to interpret the meaning of Charlie's quick respiration. Might he be physically hurt from the ride?

Startled by the idea, Wilde starts to open his eyes just as Charlie thanks him for keeping them shut.

"Whatever for, dear boy?"

"I just imagine you're thinking of me the way I used to be, not the way I am. It makes me feel better knowing there's a place in your head where I'm normal."

Wilde's eyes grow damp under their lids.

"You were normal before. Now you are beautiful, worthy of every painter's attention."

Charlie laughs.

"It's true," Wilde continues. "I see you with perfect clarity as you *are* right now, and the canvas of my mind has never welcomed a better portrait. I paint you true and you are all the more beautiful for it."

Wilde hears the slightest groan from the chair and sense Charlie is now sitting hunched forward, maybe with his elbows on his knees. Could he be crying? Isn't there the slightest indication of a hushed sob? Wilde's fingernails dig at the divan's fabric and curls it against his palms.

"May I describe what I'm seeing, Charlie?"

Half a minute passes before Charlie says yes.

"I see you without a shirt."

"But I'm wearing one."

"My internal painter has a distinct dislike of clothing on his models," Wilde says, making Charlie laugh. "So, you are shirtless. The scars on your face also touch your neck and torso."

Charlie's voice is small and pleading when he responds. "Please don't see me as a monster."

"Yours is a beauty unlike any ever encountered. My painter weeps at the hopelessness of capturing it with his feeble skills. Monstrous? You are a jewel. Your skin has the gloss of a pearl in moonlight."

"Me—a pearl?"

The chair groans again, this time accompanied by the slight whisper from the floor. Wilde's eyes move again, reading the sounds. Charlie has left the chair. He is standing beside the divan. If I reach my hand out, I would touch his hip, Wilde thinks.

"Do you know the gospels, Charlie? Do you know the parable of the pearl of great price?"

Charlie's embarrassed silence gives him the answer.

"Queensberry would not have valued a religious education for you," Wilde says. "The pearl is the kingdom of Heaven and what one must give up to obtain it. To me you are that pearl in every way."

"Pearls come from oysters, don't they?"

"Yes, Charlie. They do."

He does not hear Charlie move. But in the next moment he feels the weight of the young man's head resting upon his stomach, and he must open his eyes. Charlie is on his knees before the divan. Wilde sees the back of his head and places his palm atop it, his fingers lost in Charlie's black hair.

"There are times when . . ."

Charlie's voice hitches.

"When what, dear boy?"

"When I wish I could give you more. Give you what you want. I guess you wouldn't now anyway, the way I look."

"You are more beautiful to me now than you ever were before. But we're all capable of giving only so much of ourselves to others. Some parts cannot be surrendered no matter how hard we try. If two people love each other, if they have faith and fidelity, they accept what parts their friends have to offer with gratitude and make no demands for the whole."

"His Lordship always said you were a greedy man. You wanted everything you saw. He was wrong."

"We were wrong about each other. We have all gone through such suffering that it's impossible to not be transformed. I will blaspheme now and say we bear wounds Christ himself never endured, and though none of us were born sinless, we surely stand just a worthy to save the world."

Charlie's arms move over Wilde in an embrace, and Wilde places his hands atop Charlie's.

"I would like to make one request of you now, Charlie."

"Name it."

"You must only say yes if you're comfortable. I wish to lay in bed with you and drape my arm across you. We need not be undressed."

"But why?"

"I want, for a little while, to feel like I am the one protecting you."

Charlie lifts his head, meets Wilde's gaze, smiles and says, "Yes."

They go to the bedroom together, in silence, and lay beside each other without pulling back the bedclothes. Both men rest upon their right shoulders, and Wilde feels the initial tension in Charlie's body dissipate. He goes from laying rigidly on his side to rolling a little bit into Wilde's chest. Wilde cups his left arm across the lad's waist and holds him as Charlie begins a faint, charming snore.

Wilde smiles, listening. His thoughts turn to Bosie. He would not at this moment exchange bedmates, but he wishes his arm could stretch far enough somehow to make both men feel protected. He closes his eyes and imagines Bosie at Wandsworth. Wilde sees himself as a voice encouraging Bosie to turn himself into a bird and fly away, anything to gain a reprieve from the tedium of self-imposed incarceration.

Charlie stirs, making a slight whimper. Then he wakes with a gasp.

"Dear boy," Wilde soothes, stroking his hair. Charlie surprises him by rolling over to face him.

"I dreamed about your wife."

"What?"

"That's who she said she was. Her name was Constance."

Wilde strokes the hair back along Charlie's right temple. "Yes, Charlie. My wife's name was—is—Constance."

"She thanked me for looking after you. She seemed so kind. She touched my face and I was healed."

He touches his face now, fingers lingering on the scars. Wilde watches them curl away into a fist.

"I can't really remember my mother, but if I did, I'd want her to look like that," Charlie says. "She wore a pretty dress."

"What color was the dress?"

"Green."

Wilde rolls onto his back and smiles at the ceiling.

"The mind is an oyster, and each dream within is a pearl," he says.

"Do you want me to go, Oscar?"

"No, dear boy," he says. "Sleep and have more strange dreams. But make sure to remember them. I want to hear about every one when you wake up."

# CHAPTER SEVENTY-THREE

With his hair powdered gray and walking with an exaggerated stoop, Wilde hobbles along the Thames, sometimes glancing up at the looming London Bridge. The usual congestion of thousands of pedestrians and carriages is gone, replaced by steady streams of heavy carts freighting stones and artifacts. The horses pull their loads with their heads hanging down and panthers strut among them like overseers. One panther perches on the edge of the bridge and looks down upon the water like a black gargoyle. Further down, a processional throng that includes several teams of horses and dozens upon dozens of men labor to move an obelisk that must be three hundred feet long. The sight of this particular structure chills him more than all the others, though he cannot explain why it should evoke such particular loathing. He nevertheless feels a queer and hateful association with it, a certitude his own name appears somewhere on the stone. Mr. Thompson has told him many obelisks functioned as coronation monuments for the pharaohs, and the sheer size of this one suggests nothing less than the celebration of a new reign. In his mind's eye, he sees Big Ben crumbling and this obelisk rising in its place.

A familiar voice calls from his back. "Do you need help, sir? Perhaps you'd like to take the arm of a nice younger man who enjoys the company of older gentlemen?"

Wilde almost forgets his disguise as he turns to grin at Robbie, who takes his arm. They resume a slow walk.

"I almost didn't recognize you, Oscar. I was waiting and looking and you still passed under my notice."

"I would have seen you if I wasn't keeping myself stooped. Now I half-wish for blindness. Between my time in Wandsworth and Worthing, I haven't had more than a glimpse of London in over a year. Everywhere I look I find Bast's revolution advancing fast."

"Yes, Oscar," Robbie says, sighing. "She builds on both the city block and on the minds of men. You can see how many she's enslaved to her will."

"How did it happen? Is it fear? Coercion?"

"There's something more sinister than that. I'll show you."

After another quarter of a mile, they leave the river walk and enter London proper. Robbie stops on the other side of the street from an apothecary. Wilde sees hundreds of people waiting in line.

"I've never seen such patience," he says. "Milton said they also serve who only stand and wait, but I've seldom observed anyone who could wait more than a few minutes without complaint. What's being administered to them?"

"The Breath of the Great Goddess."

"More than opium, I should think."

"I can tell you nothing about it," Robbie says. "But the Golden Dawn has found a way to create a mask that makes us look like we've been dosed. I've seen the changelings go door to door across the city and into the countryside making sure no one escapes the Breath. Those who have become Bast's slaves."

Wilde grimaces. "'Milton! Thou shouldst be living at this hour.'"

Robbie grips his arm with gentle firmness. "We don't need Milton.

We have Wilde."

"Your faith in me has never flagged," Wilde says. "I cannot express the fullness of my appreciation for your confidence."

They resume their walk and at times they seem to be the only foot traffic. Parts of London feel depopulated, the facades of buildings shorn away and replaced with Egyptian structures. They pass a storefront whose windows are covered in the same repeating hieroglyph, done in red paint. *Bast enthroned.* The vision Bast once showed him of St. Paul's falling into rubble feels on the cusp of reification. Wilde straightens a bit and looks around, in expectation of discovering a pyramid on the horizon. He blinks and rubs his eyes against a sudden sting and discovers granules of sand on his fingertips.

A panther crosses their path and stops to look at them. Wilde catches a glimpse of its suspicious yellow eyes and stoops lower. The great cat moves on.

"Perhaps it is best we get you off the streets as soon as possible, Oscar."

"I must visit The Red Tiger first."

"But that's in the wrong direction from the rehearsal hall."

"Nevertheless, I have to see it."

"Oscar—"

"I'll go alone if I must. But I *will* go."

"You know I wouldn't let you go by yourself."

Wilde pats his arm. "Faithful, faithful Robbie."

They make the trek to the pub with neither speaking much. Wilde keeps his gaze at the ground, noting the accumulating sand. The nearer they get to The Red Tiger, the more drastic the changes in environment and architecture. Within a quarter of a mile of their destination, no trace of the street remains. The rows of shops remain, jutting out of small dunes in a way that makes them seem like relics of a forgotten civilization.

Not forgotten *yet*, Wilde vows.

They reach the pub and Wilde finds it unrecognizable. The old façade has fallen away, replaced with tan sandstone. The dusty windows are gone, the single door replaced with a large open portal in the shape of a trapezoid. If he were to be given a photo of this structure, surrounded by sand, Wilde would think it the uncovered remains of a tomb from the Valley of the Kings.

"No guards," Robbie says. "That shouldn't be, not if this place is as important we suppose."

"No *visible* guards."

A voice comes from within the portal. "Oh, I'm visible enough, I think."

Wilde and Robbie fall back as a figure steps into view.

"Chyron."

"You know his person, Oscar?"

"He's not a person. I don't know what he is."

Chyron flashes a perfect smile. "Like my teeth, Mr. Wilde? It took awhile to get them fixed. I must say you've aged a great deal since I last saw you."

"Courtesy of the Great Goddess?"

"Bless your sense of humor, Mr. Wilde."

"Why do you say that?"

Chyron comes closer to them and Wilde holds up his right hand, the scarab ring green energy flaring.

"You can put that down. I have no allegiance to Bast."

"No allegiance? You've been guarding this place from the start."

"Aye," Chyron says, "but not on her behalf."

"Then whose?"

Robbie leans into Wilde's right ear and says, "Don't speak with any more with him, Oscar. We should leave."

"Use your wits, Mr. Wilde. Don't they tell you the answer?"

Wilde stands up to his full height. "Stephen."

"Oh, good guess, and right on target. He's the one I'm loyal to. After all, he summoned me."

"Summoned?"

"Or created. Truth be told, I can't necessarily tell you just how I came to be. I cannot even tell you what I am. A spirit? The personification of spell? I don't suppose it matters. I linger here doing very little ever since he died."

"*Oscar*," Robbie says in an urgent whisper.

But Wilde takes a stride closer to Chyron. "How do you know this?"

"I'm tied to him. I would have gone to his aid if I could, but he also made sure I was rooted to this place. Didn't want me leaving my post unprotected, you might say. I heard his anguish and his terror. I felt it in whatever bones I have. Devious device your friend Yeats has. I tell you, the poets around these parts are not to be trifled with."

Wilde glances at Robbie, who looks ready to flee at a moment's notice.

"What did Stephen hope to gain from this place?"

Chyron shrugs. "Some people will do anything to see their mommies."

"This is ridiculous, Oscar. Why believe anything he says?"

"Mr. Wilde knows the answer to that, my young friend."

Wilde meets Robbie's questioning gaze. "Because if his loyalties lay with Bast, then he would have told her everything he knows."

Chryon claps.

"But you haven't told her," Wilde says, turning back to Chyron. "Why?"

"Self-preservation, for one. It'd be awkward explaining my existence since my existence represents betrayal. I don't believe Bast would treat me with kindness."

"Then are you on my side?"

Cyren laughs. "I have but one side, Mr. Wilde."

"But you acknowledge Stephen is dead."

"The mission he gave me continues, though. I will defend this place to the utmost of my being. I will confuse and confound. I will kill all attackers. I know they're coming. I suspect that's why you're here."

"It doesn't have to be this way, Chyron. You're a creature of free will."

"Am I?"

"I have to believe it. Join us! There were no cookbooks on that trick shelf, but you might be the key ingredient in the stew we're making for Bast."

"That's a nifty image, Mr. Wilde. But have you heard the one about too many cooks?"

Chyron starts laughing and walking back into what used to be The Red Tiger. Wilde watches him until he disappears and then he stands staring at the dark opening and shaking his head.

"Poor Ariel," he says, whispering. "Lingering here with your Prospero dead. Stand ready. This time the tempest is coming for you."

PART EIGHT

# CHAPTER SEVENTY-FOUR

Wilde and Robbie sit with Yeats toward the back of an otherwise St. James Theater. On stage, a select group of men and women rehearse *Lady Gwendolyn's Pride*. Of them, only Florence Farr has ever acted. The rest are members of the Golden Dawn and allied occultists, trained in the subtleties of incantation but not elocution.

But Wilde knows well, just now they are practicing weaving. For the first time in his life as a playwright, however, his thoughts are not on the rehearsal.

"What do you make of this creature Chyron?"

"An unfortunate variable in the equation," Yeats says, gaze fixed forward on the actors. He has a copy of the play on his lap and makes annotations in pencil, circling certain words and adding stage directions.

"But how will you deal with him when the time comes? Will your crystal weapon work on—whatever he is?"

"It would not be effective against the non-corporeal, if he is in fact a spirit."

"Then what *would* be effective?"

Yeats turns, and Wilde sees the first trace of true annoyance he's ever noticed in the man. "The play's the thing just now, Mr. Wilde. The Order will consider what Chyron told you later. We may never know the exact truth of The Red Tiger and the time portal there. Was it created by Bast? Was it created by Stephen as part of his plot against Bast? Any number of possibilities exist and none or all of them may be true."

"But if Bast has no knowledge of its existence, we may raid The Red Tiger whenever we choose, independent of what happens in the theater. We could go after it before we even perform the play."

Yeats shakes his head. "She *will* sense the power of the assault, Mr. Wilde. It will draw her as surely as the sudden sound of artillery fire would pull us all from theater right now. For the moment, we'll stay with the plans we have drawn and make our attacks concomitant."

Yeats turns back to the rehearsal, allowing Wilde to consider the man's fine profile, intelligent and dignified.

*I tell you, the poets around these parts are not to be trifled with.*

No, Wilde thinks. Indeed, they are not.

Yeats surprises him by standing up and waving his arms as he approaches the stage. "It's not working," he says, as the members of the Golden Dawn gather toward him.

"What does he mean it's not working?" Robbie says, leaning into Wilde's ear. Together, they hurry to hear Yeats' instructions.

"The magic we've fused into the ordinary words requires the greatest subtlety to come together," Yeats says. "I have been listening and making notes. Certain words must be emphasized, even though the emphasis has no bearing on the scene and might perplex an ordinary audience."

"This won't be an ordinary audience, Will, so I don't see how that matters," Florence Farr says, and the other actors give a warm, supportive laugh.

"No, indeed. But it's more than that. There are precise points where certain actions *must* be taken. They will seem quite ordinary—a hand gesture, a step, sitting down on a chair. But miss even one of these queues, and the spell is threatened, and the incantation we are trying to weave over Bast like a net will fall apart. I venture to say there has never been a bolder, more intricate work in the entire history of sorcery. But it will be pointless if we fail."

"But how can you know it's failing, Will?" Robbie says.

"Because I have been through three rehearsals now without being affected. This piece of magic will not discriminate. Everyone in the audience will fall under its paralyzing force—if it works."

Yeats shows his notes to the actors, who make studious copies on their own pages. After half an hour, they regroup to start again.

Yeats, Wilde and Robbie sit down and watch the rehearsal resume. This time none of them speak as the actors commence with fresh intensity. Florence Farr plays Lady Gwendolyn with a delightful devilry. Soon enough, however, Wilde notices the occasional odd lilt or over-emphasis in certain words, the unexpected gestures and motions that threaten to be too distracting at first. Then the combination of cadences and movement begin to work on his mind. He feels his limbs getting heavier and unmovable, as if his wrists are bound to the armrests. No panic accompanies the sensation of being restrained. A happy comfort pervades him, making every word he hears pleasant and desired. It occurs to him the experience is not unlike taking the breath of the Great Goddess into his lungs. This realization shocks just a bit of wakefulness into him. He lifts his head and looks at Robbie and Yeats. Both have their eyes closed, their chins resting on their chests. He laughs as warmth spreads through his torso. They both look so comfortable. He should like to be as comfortable as they.

His eyelids shut.

# CHAPTER SEVENTY-FIVE

He passes through a garden of lush and vibrant colors, where even the meanest of flowers possess a beauty surpassing any on Earth. He pivots, enraptured by the strong limbs of trees unbowed despite overflowing with fruits tinted silver and gold. Fragrances enliven his senses. He bends to touch the grass and delights in the tickle of the delicate blades against his palm. He sees his left hand restored, the scarab ring at home on his left pinkie. He flexes his fingers, overcome with emotion and touching his eyes to wipe away the expected tears. But his eyes are dry, and sometime tells him it is impossible to cry in this place.

"Oscar?"

He looks toward the sound of his wife's voice. "*Constance?* Where are you?"

"Follow the trail of flower petals."

"But I see no trail. I—"

A daisy petal floats down and drops at his feet. Other petals follow, from many different flowers, like the most beautiful rain ever conceived. He walks on their gentle carpet, winding through the garden, moving among terraces and brooks. Songs sung in whispers come from the water, arresting his progress a moment. He bends to cup his hand into a pool but stops when Constance's voice rebukes him.

"You mustn't, Oscar. The waters are sacred."

He looks over his shoulder and sees Constance walking toward him. She wears her dress, her warrior's armor, and her loveliness surpasses even the flowers.

"Is this heaven, Constance? Or have you brought me to Eden?"

Constance smiles and takes a silver apple from the nearest bough. She presents it to him.

"I trust of late you've not been listening to any serpents."

She laughs. "You're always at your most flippant when you're also at your weariest. Eat the apple, Oscar. It will restore your soul."

He takes a bite and finds a cold, delicious sweetness on his tongue. Constance's promise proves true. Even before swallowing the fruit, a remarkable energy enervates his spirit. He feels a decade younger.

"If there was ever fruit from the Tree of Life . . ."

"Here all fruit is equal, and none forbidden. We meet in one of the gardens of the Otherworld, tended by the wise hands of the Tuatha De Danann."

"The fairy folk?"

"Yes, Oscar."

"What am I seeing, Constance? Do I converse with your soul? Are you dead?"

"I was spared the void through the grace of the Tuatha De Danann. But Bast destroyed my body. I linger here now."

"This does not seem like a bad fate."

"No," she says. "It isn't. Come and sit with me. I'll call the boys."

Wilde grips her right arm. "Cyril and Vyvyan are here?"

"Protected and safe. Look there."

He follows her pointing finger to a hill in the distance. He sees several children there, boys and girls of exquisite beauty. His sons play among them, perfect, radiating happiness.

"Wonderful," he says.

"They will be able to leave when the world is safe."

"They've grown. God, it's been so long since I've seen my sons."

"I'll summon them."

"No—not yet. Let them be happy."

Her lips hint at a frown. "Seeing their father will not make them unhappy."

"I suppose part of me has doubts."

Constance takes his hands and squeezes them. "Let's talk alone for a while. But I will not let you leave until those doubts are gone."

She leads him to stone bench and they sit, still holding each other's hands like youthful lovers.

"Have I come to you in a dream?"

"Yes."

"I wish I might have come to you earlier."

"There is a right time for everything, Oscar, that seldom strikes according to the clock of our desires."

"But you have been watching over me."

Constance smiles. "To the extent that I can."

"And you visited Charlie?"

"I could ask of no better friend for you."

"He has so much courage—and so much hurt."

"I know," she says. "I hope in some small way I was able to strengthen him."

"Can anything be done for his scars? Is there some spell, some force to restore him to how he wishes he could look?"

"No, Oscar. Only the magic of self-acceptance can help him. He must discover that power for himself. Once he does, every mirror will become an ally."

Wilde shakes his head and leaves the bench, walking over to the nearest stream. He sees his reflection in the water. "The magic of self-acceptance," he says. "For some of us Bast is the easier foe."

"For most of us, I think. It's one reason gods get fashioned in the first place. They're a totem for our imperfections and insecurities."

"But Bast wasn't fashioned by us."

"No. She is an Elemental, like the Tuatha De Danann themselves, beings of a different realm that sometimes intersects with our own."

"How many of these Elementals are there?"

"I couldn't say. *Many*."

"Can we not ask them for help?"

Constance shakes her head. "Why would they care? Most Elementals aren't even aware of us."

"But the ones who are?"

"The same answer applies, Oscar. Do you concern yourself with two factions of ant colonies competing in the back yard? Do you care which one wins? Could you possibly bother yourself with scrutinizing such a battle, pondering which side to choose before interfering in their war? Likewise, if you came upon a man who seemed obsessed with lording over an ant hill, sometimes destroying it, sometimes feeding it for his own pleasure—would you bother to intercede on the ant hill's behalf?"

Wilde scowls. "If our world is so unworthy, why does Bast want to rule it?"

"Because there *are* people who content themselves with ruling over an ant hill and thinking of themselves as a deity."

"Then might we find another Elemental with similar aspirations, who would help us?"

"Would that leave us in a better position, Oscar? Who is to say

Bast is the worst of all options when it comes to subjugation? I'm afraid the ants must fight back on their own."

Wilde returns to the bench and hunches forward, hands clasped in the space between his knees. "I've been telling myself that we're left to our own resources in this fight, but some part of me refused to believe it. I find myself haunted now."

"I will help you ease these troubles."

She stands and calls for their children.

When the boys arrive, ruddy from running, they swarm their father with kisses and hugs. Wilde embraces them, crying in joy, the three of them collapsing onto the grass and rolling together with all the sweetness any reunion could allow. He sees Constance watching over them and his heart fills with the helium of hope. He rises, picking his boys up in each arm, and joins with her as a family.

"What shall we do now, Oscar?"

Wilde takes a deep breath, kisses Cyril and Vyvyan on the top of their heads, and nods toward the path ahead of them. "A stroll among the flowers is the most trivial of things, isn't it?"

Constance smiles. "Very trivial indeed."

"Then let us spend this important time doing the least important thing possible. Come along, my boys. I will tell you a fairy tale."

# CHAPTER SEVENTY-SIX

He wakes with Florence Farr and the other performers gathered around. Wilde sees Yeats still unconscious but Robbie appears to be wide-awake.

"I wouldn't normally be happy about putting the audience to sleep," Farr says. "But in this case I'd call our performance *spellbinding*."

Wilde tries to nod but finds his muscles sluggish, almost frozen. "It worked," he says, sounding like he's speaking through a yawn. "Now we just have to come up with some antidote to protect ourselves."

"Willie would have the answer to that," Farr says. "My guess is there isn't."

"Oh, I think there is," Robbie says, and springs out of his seat like a man waking from the most refreshing nap. Wilde, still unable to budge his arms or legs, stares in awe at this sprightliness.

"How?"

"I was with Constance, Oscar."

Florence makes an exclamation in a language Wilde doesn't know. He sees her with her fingertips pressed to her lips, her eyes radiant, gaze fixed on Robbie.

"We were in a garden so beautiful I don't know that I can describe it."

"I can picture it well enough," Wilde says, smiling.

"It was in a place she called the Otherworld, Oscar."

"The Garden of the Tuatha De Danann," Farr says, her eyes brimming with tears. "Our Lady Constance has been granted a favor only she could be worthy of."

"She was a queen of beauty," Robbie says. "She took me to a place where carnations grow. But carnations unlike any I've ever seen. Their petals felt as luxurious as satin and were green like her dress. She told me they had a special power, and of all the flowers in the garden they were favored most by the Tuatha De Danann. She said whoever took up the symbol of the green carnation would find there a shield of courage and guile. Constance took one of the petals, placed it into my palm, and closed my fingers around it. And when I woke, I was refreshed."

Robbie opens his right hand, revealing a pale pink petal. As Wilde forces his hand up to reach for it, his scarab ring flashes and the petal absorbs the light like a sponge soaking up green water. Wilde and Robbie exchange smiles. Suddenly, to their left, Yeats begins laughing, a chuckle that turns into a full-throated roar quite unlike anything Wilde's ever heard from him. Despite this, Yeats appears to be battling a lazy slumber, his eyes half-open, his hands planted on the armrests.

"What is it, William?"

"I was communicating with you in a dream, Mr. Wilde. I was telling you the same thing over and over again. 'Remember your Shakespeare. The play's the thing.'"

"Then we've come full circle," Wilde says.

The surrounding members of the Golden Dawn and its allies murmur with excitement. "Help me up, Florence. I feel as if I have a thousand-pound anchor weighing me down. The sensation is most gratifying."

"Let me see if I can unburden you," Wilde says, taking the green petal from Robbie's hand. He touches it to Yeats' arm and the effect is like watching the untethering of a hot air balloon. Yeats jumps up with the same energy Robbie displayed, patting his torso and legs.

"Remarkable. The spell's influence is undone."

"It is the power of the Tuatha De Danann," Farr says. "That petal came from a carnation in their garden."

"Indeed?"

Robbie recounts his meeting with Constance, waking with the flower petal, and the infusion of energy from the ring.

"Even now she watches over us," Yeats says. "But so many things from the Otherworld become ordinary in our realm. I do not believe what Mr. Ross had in his hand when he awoke to be anything other than a petal off a regular carnation until Mr. Wilde's ring endowed it with power. The carnation absorbed it just as it absorbs dye and holds the power just as it holds the color."

"It becomes a shield, just like Constance said."

"Robbie," Wilde says. "I feel in the days to come, we must visit every florist shop still available to us and buy whatever carnations they have in stock. On the night of the performance, certain members of the audience are going to be wearing exquisite green flowers in their button holes!"

# CHAPTER SEVENTY-SEVEN

On the morning of the performance, Wilde returns to Wandsworth prison in the company of Charlie and Robbie. Robbie wears the brown and beige uniform of a theater usher, with a vibrant green carnation pinned to his lapel. Wandsworth remains unpopulated, lonely and forgotten. Sand now fills the courtyard.

"I wonder if it was necessary for Bosie to maintain the pretense of being you, Oscar. It doesn't seem like anyone else has been here for a long while."

"He knows more about Bast's ways than we ever will. If he felt the façade must be maintained regardless of circumstance, then who are we to question him?"

They open the door and Wilde sees himself sitting on the cot, wearing a dress suit, complete with cummerbund, stiff white shirt and bowtie. He gets up to bow as they enter. When he straightens, Wilde finds himself looking at Stephen's face—but the lips show Bosie's mischievous smile.

"I congratulate you on an outstanding work of prayer, oh Priest of the Great Goddess."

"Prayer?"

"The play, of course. Bast is in such high spirits since I delivered the finished work to her. I believe she hasn't even killed anyone in a week."

376

"If this is so, her sense of humor is either non-existent, or far superior to any I imagined," Wilde says. "It is one thing to accept a satirical portrayal of oneself; quite another to *revel* in it."

"Oscar, your play is marvelous. But it is not quite the play I gave to Bast."

"What do you mean?"

"In my time spent impersonating Stephen and you, I have come to know her mind in terrific detail. She often summoned me to her throne room to show her my progress. Thank God for Charlie always delivering me your new pages in the nick of time. She got a good laugh over Lady Gwendolyn. She sees the old rich man as a symbol of the world before her coming, senile and befuddled."

Wilde shakes his head. "Thank God for audiences, otherwise no work should have much meaning at all!"

"As the play progressed, however, she began to excoriate me for not making Lady Gwendolyn more—shall we say—*correct*. I realized she would never accept the play you were composing, so I was obliged to write a play of my own more suited to her tastes."

Before Wilde can react, Charlie steps forward. His tone sounds wounded when he speaks. "Are you saying you wrote me out, Lord Alfred? Oscar said he based Charles on me and made me the hero. I—I liked the idea."

"You're still there, Charlie. But I'm afraid you now die in the end."

"*What?*"

"It was necessary that Lady Gwendolyn be triumphant. More than that, Oscar. In the play Bast read, Lady Gwendolyn is revealed to actually be the Queen of England, traveling her kingdom in disguise, looking to reward fidelity."

Wilde looks to the floor and sighs.

"Oscar, I assure you I only made the changes with an understanding of what would please Bast. That my alterations happen to be a genuine improve over the original is mere icing on the cake."

"*I die in the end?*"

Wilde puts a hand on Charlie's shoulder. "Dear boy, it is no great loss to die in fiction. They'll remember you in the same breath as Little Nell. Keep in mind we're also talking about the work of an inferior artist rather than my play. I close the curtain with you alive and happy, and therefore you remain that way forever."

Bosie laughs. "The majority of the changes I made occur in the last act. By the time Bast notices these differences, our spell will already be in place."

"I suppose we will know soon enough," Wilde says, looking between Bosie and Robbie. "With the two of you already in costume, I suppose I should get dressed. It has been a long time since I wore a formal suit."

"It will be longer still," Bosie says, turning to the cot. Wilde sees a bit of folded fabric there he mistook for a sheet. As Bosie unfurls it, he realizes it's a white linen tunic. He holds it up to show the stripes of blue and red along the neckline.

"What is that?"

"Your priestly garb, Oscar."

Wilde frowns, holding the cloth against his body. Its inadequacies become apparent at once.

"It seems the priests of ancient Egypt were rather less modest than the Catholics and Anglicans."

"I approve," Robbie says.

"But Oscar can't go on stage wearing this! It's—not dignified."

"Thank you for always championing me, Charlie. But in this case I must bow to the requirements of the role, no matter how heinous."

He begins to undress. As he does, Bosie's attention turns to the green carnation on Robbie's lapel.

"That is beautiful."

"Beautiful, yes," Robbie says. "But also essential."

"Only Oscar would ever consider a flower *essential*."

"Several more may be essential for me," Wilde says, grimacing as he confirms the tunic's perilous brevity. "I'll need to weave them into a shield for my modesty—"

Bosie shrieks, stumbling back holding his right hand. "Get it off—oh God, get it off!" Charlie rushes to him even as his form reverts to the natural state of a changeling.

"Your Lordship, what's wrong? How can I help?"

"Get it off," Bosie repeats as Wilde crouches by him too. He sees one of the carnation petals lodged in Bosie's palm like a shard of green glass.

"He was just touching the flower in my lapel," Robbie says. "Oscar, what's happening?"

Charlie works the petal free with a grunt, falling back from the effort. Blood seeps from the gash in Bosie's palm. Bosie holds his injured hand out at arm's length and breathes through clenched teeth.

"But how?" Robbie says. "It's a flower petal."

"Dear boy," Wilde says, putting a hand on Bosie's shoulder. "I assure you I had no idea it would hurt you. The flowers are meant to protect those who wear them—nothing more."

"I wish they were as discriminating as your ring. The pain is ebbing, at least. Help me stand."

Consternation enters Bosie's expression as soon as he's on his feet.

"Your Lordship?"

"I can't seem to make myself transform."

"Are you sure?" Wilde says.

Bosie closes his eyes. The muscles in his face strain, the sinews in his neck stand out from tension. He lets out a loud exhale. "The ability has all the ease and speed of thought. But now—*no*. It must be the power of the carnation. For the moment at least, I am locked in this form."

"We must consult Yeats."

"There's no time," Robbie says.

"But this is something we didn't expect!"

"Unexpected or not, Robbie's right. There is nothing to be done at this point. Maybe it's a blessing this happened. There will be many changelings in the audience tonight. Should any of them touch one of the carnations and have a similar reaction, Bast will know something is very wrong."

"I'll make sure the word goes forth right now," Robbie says. "We'll hide them away and only bring them out if our lives depend on it."

Robbie and Charlie leave. As soon as they're out of earshot, Bosie moans and slumps into Wilde's arms.

"I can't hold it back any longer. I'm sorry."

Wilde gasps as Bosie spasms in his arms. "You're in serious pain!"

He tries to settle Bosie onto the bed, but it's all he can do just to bring him to the floor with some gentleness. Bosie continues to flail and convulse, making horrific choking noises as he struggles to speak. "Don't know what's wrong. Like I've been poisoned."

The muscles in Bosie's arms and legs visibly cramp. A tic stretches the left side of his face into a rictus of torment. Wilde tries to steady his old lover but the power of his seizures throw him aside, leaving Wilde helpless as he watches Bosie jerk and cringe and writhe.

"I'm on fire. Oh God, I'm burning."

Wilde scrambles to the cell door to call for help. But who could bring assistance? Even if Robbie and Charlie came back, what help would they be?

"Oscar."

Bosie's voice now sounds weary rather than agonized. Wilde turns and finds Bosie curled into a fetal position, panting but otherwise still.

His scalp looks smudged with gold.

"Hair," Wilde says, whispering as he risks a step forward. He kneels down. "Bosie, are you regaining your ability to change?"

Bosie doesn't answer. More blond hair appears, pushing through skin turning pink and healthy. Wilde finds the same color claiming dominion across Bosie's body. The shape of his ears change. Bosie rolls over and they stare at each other. His eyes have turned blue. Seeing this encourages Wilde to cup his hands around Bosie's face.

Within moments, it is the true face of Lord Alfred Douglas.

The changes progress across his body, faster and faster. Bosie's moans subside. His breath becomes calm and steady.

"It's over," he says at last, pushing up to his hands and knees.

"Then you can transform again," Wilde says. "The flower's influence is gone."

Bosie begins laughing.

"Gone? I hope it lasts forever."

"What do you mean?"

"I mean I'm cured, Oscar. I've been purged of the milk Bast fed into my veins. Her grip on me did not want to loosen, but the power in the carnation throttled her wrist until her fingers let go. I'm *me* again."

# CHAPTER SEVENTY-EIGHT

Wilde caresses the green carnation, the implications of Bosie's cure occupying most of his thoughts as the hour of the performance nears. He stands backstage of the St. James Theater as urgent preparations occur around him. Actors approach Yeats, but not to consult with him any further on the play. They are wishing him luck before he leaves to lead the attack on Chyron and The Red Tiger. At last Yeats turn away from all of them and approaches Wilde, who offers him the flower.

"May it be your shield if you need one, William."

Yeats takes the flower, touching its petals and looking upon it with evident admiration. "These carnations of yours are curious and wonderful, Mr. Wilde. Just as hybrid flowers are made through cross-pollination of different types, it seems your creation is its own hybrid of magic. That they could overwhelm Bast's enchantment over Bosie is heartening indeed."

He pins the flower to his lapel. Wilde notes its crookedness.

"I wanted to ask your opinion about whether or not their power could help Charlie."

Yeats' gaze becomes piercing, his lips pressing into an even thinner line than usual. "There is nothing that will solve his disfigurement, Mr. Wilde."

"But if the flower could bring Bosie back to normal—"

"Lord Alfred's affliction was rooted in sorcery. Charles's scarring is not."

"Are you saying magic is only good against magic? I find that statement . . . narrow."

"Neither your opinion nor mine matter in this case. I trust you haven't suggested to him his face might be restored."

"I'd never do that without consulting you first."

"That was wise. False hope is a terrible thing."

Wilde grits his teeth. "I don't believe any hope is false."

Yeats surprises him by putting one hand on his shoulder. "I apologize for the bluntness of my words. It is easy to see your affection for one another, just as it's easy to see and feel Charles's discomfort with himself. But he has made great strides. Don't rob him of making even greater ones."

"Rob him? What the devil do you mean by that?"

"Queensberry introduced me to a man who hid in shadows and kept his tortured profile out of sight. That is not his behavior now. He will only become stronger with time, and he will discover that self-acceptance is—"

"Its own kind of magic."

"Precisely."

"But what if he cannot find it after all? Why should he even have to make such a terrible journey if there's any possibility it need not be made at all?"

Yeats shakes his head. "You feel the pain he suffers."

"Yes."

"Let me suggest that the pain makes him a better man."

Wilde scoffs at this. "Your suggestion is offensive to me."

"It is better to feel pain than nothing at all, Mr. Wilde."

"Now you sound like you're posing as Queensberry."

"I'm comparing his pain to the numb spectacle I witnessed on my way here. Across all of London, the people are abandoning their tasks and moving into the streets. There is a look of dumb serenity on every face. It is like watching a mass migration of sleepwalkers, and all I could think about was that line from Blake. Do you know which one I mean?"

"Considering the abundance of large cats plaguing us, I might guess 'The Tyger.'"

Yeats's eyes narrow a moment, his cheeks going red. He stretches out his right hand like a sorcerer preparing to cast a spell, but instead of an incantation, he speaks verse—

"In every cry of every man,
In every infant's cry of fear,
In every voice: in every ban
The mind-forg'd manacles I hear."

"'London,'" Wilde says.

"Yes. The entire population wears Bast's manacles now. They are insensible to the reality of their situation. Compared to them, I would rather have Charles's pain and a hundred worse torments. I'd rather see my scars than live in blindness."

"And where are all these blind people going?"

"They're coming to attend your play, Mr. Wilde."

"Here? The St. James can accommodate a thousand people at most."

"There are over three hundred theaters and concert halls in London. Bast has declared your play a matter of national public performance. Every theater in the land is hosting it, as well as every park and square. Every acting troupe except ours has rehearsed Lord Alfred's false play."

Wilde blinks. "Then you knew of the changes he was making?"

"Of course."

"You might have told me."

Yeats flashes of look of genuine puzzlement. "To what end? Would the knowledge assist you in any way?"

"I have always believed the less useful a piece of information is, the more vital it becomes."

This quip prods a smile from Yeats. "Lord Alfred's changes were judicious and prudent. Bast is won over. Her faith in you now borders on obsession. It might even be debated whether you're supposed to be under her thrall, or her under yours."

Wilde looks down at his ridiculous tunic. "Maybe I can capitalize on that and make a request for trousers."

"With luck and courage, you'll be free to wear what you wish when the sun rises tomorrow. Here."

He hands Wilde a scroll.

"What is this?"

"An invocation. It is to be delivered in Bast's ancient tongue."

"I couldn't begin to do that," he says. "My lessons with Mr. Thompson stopped well short of pronunciation."

"We've taken care of this problem for you."

Wilde unrolls the scroll and finds a series of meaningless phonetics. He attempts to sound out several of them before glancing up to see Yeats' reaction.

"Credible enough. Bast won't expect anything like perfection. She may even be charmed and touched by your attempt."

"Like a mother watching the struggles of an idiot child?"

Yeats lets the remark pass. "When the time comes, you must step out to the center of the stage and face that balcony seat. Bast will be there. You will bow and then read the entire contents of the scroll. It should take no more than five minutes."

"What will I be saying?"

"These words declare that you are her high priest, and through you the hearts of all humanity become hers. When you have finished, bow with deep reverence toward Bast. Hold this position of supplication for ten seconds, and then step backwards until you are off the stage. The play will begin at once."

"Then what do I do?"

"Nothing, Mr. Wilde. Your role in our efforts will be done. If the spell holds her, the Golden Dawn and its allies in the audience will attack and seek to destroy her while I lead the assault on The Red Tiger. It is quite possible none of us survive, but if our deaths thwart Bast and end the menace she represents, it will be worth the sacrifice."

Yeats extends his hand, but Wilde ignores it and straightens the carnation on Yeats lapel.

"May all the luck of the Irish be on our sides, William."

# CHAPTER SEVENTY-NINE

Wilde stands off-stage watching the seats fill. How odd the scene plays out before him compared to memories of other opening nights, when handsome ushers escorted couples to their seats and the gilt adornments of the theater did not outshine the notes of gold, the sheen of silk and the sparkle of diamonds in the audience. How often he stood where he stands now, listening to the murmur of building excitement. He felt the anticipation of their laughter and tasted *a priori* the triumph of his words and wit.

No one comes by escort now. The audience takes their seats like they know the exact place they're supposed to be. How many of them are human, and how many changelings? Wilde leans forward for a more complete view. All is silence except for footsteps. Church funerals have more mirth. No one wears jewelry or finery. Stripped of context, Wilde would think this some government-mandated performance for the indigent. One man wears rags like a peasant and looks haggard and sunburnt, which makes his bright smile so jarring. Mind-forg'd manacles, Wilde thinks, a chill spreading across his stomach.

As the crowd gathers, as the silence deepens, Wilde experiences a unique nervousness. He's faced hostile and mocking crowds, but he's never confronted such an intense quiet. He puts the scroll aside before the sweat of his palms soaks it to illegibility and dries his hands against his tunic. All seats are full now except for the grand balcony. Where is Bast? Why isn't she here? The questions spark his pulse. What if it's all a trap for them? What if Chyron told her their plans? What if Yeats is already dead?

One thing comes to relieve him from the bombarding questions. He sees Robbie seated toward the back, by the door. Bosie sits beside him. Even from a distance their expressions look resolute and assured. I am not alone, Wilde tells himself. I have never been alone.

In that instant, he feels the presence of his wife at his back, her hand squeezing his shoulder. Wilde turns, finding nothing. He touches his right pinkie as the crowd rises and turns toward the balcony. His scarab ring rests in a chest on the floor a few feet away. Wilde knows if he lifted the lid he'd be blinded by the green light of the stone. Unable to go onto the stage wearing it, he comforts himself by anticipating the moment the ring will be on his finger again.

The applause grows, all the more jolting for the silence it breaks. Wilde looks to the balcony and finds Bast there, soaking up the adulation. Her appearance gives him a small shock. She stands there in her hieroglyphic form, a woman with a cat's head. Is this what all the humans in the audience see? Or are their eyes clouded? He glances at the man in rags and finds him clapping with the same ardor as everyone else. But does he think he applauds Queen Victoria?

Wilde stirs out of his contemplation as the applause dwindles. Florence Farr moves up behind him and gives a nudge. "Oscar—it's time. Open the scroll."

He stumbles forward, almost to the stage. The sight of panthers arrests his attention. One sits beside Bast as docile as a pet, its yellow eyes gleaming. Two more block the upper entrances. A fourth lounges in the middle of the right aisle. Their collective purr vibrates in his chest.

*"Oscar!"* Farr whispers.

He forces himself to the stage. His presence there sparks no applause at all. He stops in the center, faces the balcony and bows. "Great Goddess," he says, his thoughts chaotic. He looks down to the scroll, squeezes it, and gets mastery of himself once again. Unrolling the scroll and holding it aloft, Wilde works at sounding out the strange phonetics. His voice rings through the auditorium, and as he listens to himself, he finds a growing confidence in pronouncing the foreign sounds. His sudden fluency startles him. It's as if knowledge of this language has been locked inside him all his life, freed now by his life's master key of standing before an audience.

He finishes the scroll, lowers it, and bows toward the balcony as Yeats instructed him. A single clap answers him. Bast rises, applauding, and her action brings the audience to a collective emulation. The thunder of it sends a thrill through Wilde's body. He pivots, unable to breathe as he bows to acknowledge their adulation. A moment later he feels the tears in his eyes. Wiping them away with his fingertips, he finds himself flushing. What a disgusting creature I am, he thinks. Bast chose her high priest well. This is my true food and I have starved a long time.

Stricken, sickened, he begins to leave, only just remembering Yeats' directive to walk backwards. He forces himself to embrace the etiquette of the ceremonial exeunt, glad to have the curtain rising behind him. As soon as he gets off-stage, Wilde collapses in a lonesome corner, rips the scroll in half and begins to sob over his vanity.

# CHAPTER EIGHTY

He's still in the corner, despondent, when a familiar and very welcome face appears in front of him. Wilde blinks, rubbing his eyes. "Charlie? I thought you were going to be with Yeats at The Red Tiger."

"I told him I'd never been to a play before and didn't want to miss the opportunity."

Wilde grips his right forearm. "Dear boy, I'd rather your first theater experience wasn't so poor."

"What's wrong, Oscar?"

"Nothing."

"Nothing?" Charlie throws a playful punch into his arm.

"I'm burdened by what might be called the *over-examined* life. It is a devilish thing to believe yourself a changed man, a better man, and then have those pretensions burned away in an instant."

"You're the best man I've ever met. Even His Lordship comes second, in my opinion."

"I have a terrible hubris, a vanity, a thirst for worship that Bast understands very well. It's part of me. It always will be. I could spend years locked away in prison, submitting to every torture imaginable, and it would still be with me. I wonder . . ."

"What do you wonder?"

"It doesn't matter. They are questions of fate."

Charlie takes Wilde's right hand and places it against his scarred face.

"Was this fate, Oscar?"

"Dear boy—I don't know."

"I think it is. I've been thinking a long time about it, because I'm not as quick as you when it comes to deciding."

"That's not true at all."

Charlie sits down beside him until they're shoulder to shoulder. "You know the one thing I like about my face now, Oscar?"

"What?"

"I don't blush. The scars don't change color like my cheeks used to. I always hated how red in the face I got when someone said a thing I didn't like for one reason or another. His Lordship said I gave everything away in the face, but no matter how hard I tried, I couldn't make myself not blush. Well, now I don't."

"Two people far wiser than I have told me self-acceptance is its own kind of magic."

Charlie smiles. "I think they're right."

"I don't know if I'll ever have self-acceptance," Wilde says. "But I must hope self-resignation will suffice."

Charlie stands up and pulls Wilde to his feet.

"His Lordship taught me to fight, but you're the one who taught me courage. You showed me bravery. Be resigned to that. If you need worship then you can get it from me. I'll never get tired of giving it."

Wilde cups his left hand behind Charlie's head, brings it against his chest and squeezes his eyes shut. "Dear boy," he says. They stand together in silence. Wilde listens to the actors on stage, alarmed by how much time he's spent brooding. The second act nears its conclusion and the spell should be well on its way to completion by now—if Farr and the others have performed it right.

He and Charlie move toward the curtain and peer out from the right side of the stage. Wilde finds many nodding heads, the way the aged get when they're fighting a fit of drowsiness in the middle of their afternoon tea. At least one man appears to be in a sound sleep.

"Is it working?"

Wilde steps away from the curtain and nods. "It seems to be."

"What about Bast?"

"I can't see the balcony without stepping onto the stage."

Charlie reaches into his pocket and takes out a green carnation. "Guess I better get myself ready," he says, working it into the buttonhole of his coat.

Wilde goes to the small chest and lets his fingers rest upon the lid as the second act ends and the actors hurry back to gather around him.

"We're doing it, Oscar," Florence says. "I can feel our ropes tightening around this *Great Goddess* with every word we speak. Surely our lady Constance is watching over us with a smile."

"I know she is," Wilde says. "And now to see our task through to the end."

He opens the chest and stares into the heart of a burning green light.

# CHAPTER EIGHTY-ONE

A roar shakes the chandelier midway through the third act. Wilde and Charlie move to the curtain and peak out. On stage, the play has stopped, the actors rattled by Bast's display of rage. Even Farr looks dumbstruck.

"Florence," Wilde says in an urgent whisper. "You must continue. The spell's not completed."

The actress looks back in the direction of his voice but doesn't move.

"For Constance," Wilde shouts. "For the world!"

Farr turns to the audience, trying to say the lines. Her voice comes out in a stammer, drowned out by another roar from Bast.

"*Priest! Show yourself, Priest!*"

Everyone on stage looks toward the curtain.

"The game's up, Oscar," Charlie says. "Bast knows what we're doing."

"But did she discover it too late?"

Making his right hand into a fist, Wilde rushes onto the stage. A collective hiss rises from the changelings throughout the audience. Wilde sees them writhing in their seats. They look like planks of wood trying to extricate themselves from an embedded nail. In the balcony, Bast's hands seem rooted to the armrests. She twists her shoulders back and forth, grunting, her body transforming with every gesture. Wilde watches her become Victoria, Lady Gwendolyn, and then several other women. Guises from centuries ago? Random changes? He cannot guess as he watches her cycle back to her hybrid cat and human shape.

*"What have you done, Priest?"*

Wilde turns to Farr and the others. He cries out to them and every ally in the audience. "We have our chance! Attack! Attack now!"

Across the vast dimension of the theater, blazing green lights appear like stars bursting into existence. Bosie and Robbie spring forward, their carnations aglow on their lapels. Members of the Golden Dawn rise, striking at every changeling they find. The flowers hurt them just as they hurt Bosie, forcing them out of their human disguises, bringing shrieks as they thrash in the chairs. New blasts of energy turn the air scorching hot, boiling away the sweat building on his brow. Farr and her company have formed a circle on the stage and direct spells at Bast, shrouding the balcony in harsh white light and smoke. There's a sound like a point-blank exchange of cannon volleys and the stage floor splinters, throwing everyone off their feet.

It takes Wilde more than a minute to recover. He gets to his knees and looks through the haze. At least three of the acts lie dead or unconscious. Florence Farr bleeds from a gash in her high, fine forehead. In the balcony, Bast almost gets to her feet before a force like a thousand pulling hands jerks her back into her seat. Wilde rises, raises his right fist and wills energy from the scarab ring. His mind overflows with scenes of Bast's destruction. He sees her burning in flame, drowning in water, disintegrating to dust amidst a gusting wind. Green energy lashes the balcony. Every part of himself, all of his hopes and desires, fuel the assault. He steps forward, urging his wrath and channeling it through the ring. "For Constance! For Queensberry!"

Only Charlie's cry distracts him. He risks a look to his right and sees panthers invading the theater from the top entrance. They bound toward the members of the Golden Dawn, scattering them and then pouncing.

Charlie moves to jump off what's left of the stage against all of Wilde's pleading. "The panthers are trying to get everyone into single combat, Oscar. It's the only way they stand a chance. I can help us regroup—"

A panther springs at Charlie out of the thickening smoke, its eyes a harsh and bitter gold. Charlie whips the carnation from his buttonhole, closes his fingers around it and swings. His entire fist glows green as it strikes a blow against the panther's right flank and crumples it at his feet. As Charlie stands gloating over it, Wilde sees another panther moving in from behind. He dives forward, thrusting his right hand forward to drive bolts of energy into the panther's eyes. The great cat shrieks as the force of the attack flings it off the stage and into the rubble.

"Oscar, look to the balcony!"

Bast half-stands, holding the position despite obvious strain. She howls, her roar shaking the theater, and rises another inch. She thrashes her body like a fish trying to shake off a net.

"The spell's weakening," Wilde says.

"If she gets free, we won't have a chance. You're the only one who can stop her Oscar."

"No. It's going to take all of us."

Two more panthers leap onto the stage, one at the back and the other taking a position between Wilde and Bast. The Great Goddess's voice booms over the tumult of attack and parry, and Wilde feels a summoning in his bones. She's calling her followers wherever they may be, urging them to her defense. How many changelings are there? Thousands? If they all converge now, what hope can their handful of survivors have except a valiant but futile last stand? I must strike now, he tells himself. There is no choice. Constance, if I die, I hope to see you in your garden soon.

The ring blazes with a light equal to the surge of fortitude in his heart. He aims its power at the panther and a concentrated force greater than he's witnessed so far decapitates the beast. The brutality of the act stuns him. Even Bast stops her struggle, stares at the dead panther, and then shrieks at Wilde in a mix of English and foreign tongues. Her tone translates across all languages. Wilde hears himself cursed, convicted and condemned. Rage strengthens her. She gains two more inches against the pull of the spell. She is almost on her feet.

Wilde raises his ring and stares down the rifle length of his arm as he aims at Bast's head. The power in the ring feels like a team of feral dogs desperate to be unleashed. Just before he does, however, Wilde sees a figure appear on the balcony, and everything fades—the shouting, the howling, the unnatural noises of metal twisting and glass shattering, the subtle tearing of flesh, the pleading from raw throats. His right hand goes to his chest, fingertips pressed over his heart. He loses sight in his peripheral vision and the darkness narrows further, closing out Farr and Charlie, the panthers, the changelings, the supreme destruction all around him.

All he sees, all he hears—is Bosie.

"Do you recognize me, Bast?"

The goddess turns to stare into his face. Wilde sees them lock gazes.

"Does this refresh your memory?"

Bosie opens his dining jacket and reveals the ceremonial dagger that took his father's life. Wilde drops his hands to his side. The ring's energy seeps into the floor around his feet.

Bast's eyes widen. *"Who are you?"*

"I am Stephen. I am Oscar. I am Lord Alfred Douglas. I am your priest."

He takes the knife back and drives it into Bast's heart. As the blade sheathes there, the binding power of the play's spell breaks and the goddess rises. She transforms as she moves, turning into her most primal form, a panther three times the size of any other in the theater. She swipes Bosie's off the balcony with the merest flick of her right paw and dives after him, the dagger still lodged in her chest, her fur slick with blood.

Bast hisses over Bosie, raking his body with her claws. "Your Lordship!" Charlie cries, throwing himself upon the panther's back. For a moment he straddles Bast like a child riding a pony, pummeling the top of her skull with his fists. Bast throws him aside with a single shake and brings her gaping mouth toward Bosie's head.

Wilde attacks, battering Bast's flanks with pulse after pulse of green fire. The same force that sheared away the last panther's head elicits only a flinch from the goddess. Nevertheless, Bast forsakes her immediate vengeance and rounds upon Wilde, her eyes bright as lighthouse beams in the darkest of nights. She prowls toward him, her right front leg betraying instability. Wilde backs away, turning his fire on the shaking leg, hoping it will buckle.

But it doesn't. Bast rears back and roars, a deafening sound that forces Wilde to put his hands over his ears. She springs as soon as the ring's power is redirected and knocks him flat on his back. Her enormous paws pin his arms to the floor. She grinds the scarab ring's gemstone into the floor with more and more pressure until he hears the subtlest crack.

"No," he says as the ring's light dies. Now the only illumination he sees comes from Bast's baleful eyes as she gloats over him, and her rough tongue swipes across his face as it did when she intercepted him in the labyrinth. He clenches his teeth against the raw, protracted scrape as she tastes and savors him. A blast of air as hot as a furnace and reeking like a charnel house draft comes from her flaring nostrils, sending him into a helpless, choking cough. Her mouth opens and descends upon him, and Wilde sees images of himself reflected in the sharp, white perfection of her teeth.

Her jaws start to close—and stop. Bast's head jerks up to evaluate a new situation. Wilde cranes his neck to see two men standing near him. One is Yeats, tall, lean and bloodied. The other, to his absolute shock, is Mr. Thompson. The museum director could not look more out of place here, yet he maintains a resolute expression. Yeats moves first, and Wilde sees he carries a collection of glowing green carnations. With a savage thrust, he drives this bouquet and the entire length of his arm into Bast's mouth. Now the panther chokes, scurrying back like any chastened house cat. Yeats moves with her. For a moment, with his arm lodged in her up to the throat, he seems to be pushing her along rather than following.

"Get up, if you can," Mr. Thompson says. Wilde manages it, staggering as Charlie comes to assist.

"Did you succeed at The Red Tiger?"

"Yes. But only Yeats and I survived."

"Then you've fared better than us," Wilde says, wincing and holding his side. He shows his scarab ring and the broken gemstone.

"You don't need the ring!"

Mr. Thompson waves a book at him. Wilde recognizes it at once, a volume he last saw in the director's office during their first meeting. It is his own work, a copy of "The Sphinx." Wilde looks at it without comprehension even as the director presses it into his hands.

"What's Oscar supposed to do with this?" Charlie says.

Mr. Thompson's eyes flash with a savageness Wilde has never seen before.

"*Read.*"

Fingers shaking, Wilde opens the book as Yeats falls away from Bast, his right arm shredded and mangled by the panther's jaws. Mr. Thompson steadies him as the four of them watch the enormous beast convulse. Bast stumbles to the left, hacking like any cat trying to rid itself of a hairball. But Yeats has lodged the carnations very far down its throat. They cannot be dislodged, and their magic works against her. Wilde sees her shrinking, shriveling. Her mighty panther becomes a human woman collapsed on the ground, trying in vain to pull the dagger out of her breast.

It is Lady Gwendolyn.

"Priest," she says, her voice so weak it seems no other effort is needed.

"Will she die?" Wilde asks the question to Yeats, who shakes his head and gestures to the book.

Bast begins to laugh. She pulls the dagger free and smiles at it. "I will be my own priest," she says, her voice stronger. But Wilde notices she still doesn't get to her feet. "I will sacrifice you all to me. Starting with him."

She gestures toward Bosie, who lays unmoving some fifteen feet away. Robbie kneels by him.

Bast makes a sweeping gesture with the tip of the blade. "Then all of you. But you last of all," she says to Wilde. "You will die atop the corpses of your comrades, and I will call it the the Pyramid of Bones."

"Read, Mr. Wilde!" Yeats says, shouting as he makes one brave lunge at Bast. They grapple for the dagger for just a moment, its fate unseen until the poet's body goes rigid. Bast pushes him aside, jerks the blade free from his chest and starts to rise.

"*In a dim corner of my room for longer than my fancy thinks*

*A beautiful and silent Sphinx has watched me through the shifting gloom.*"

Bast stops, her gaze fixed on Wilde in a hateful stare.

"*Inviolate and immobile she does not rise she does not stir*

*For silver moons are naught to her and naught to her the suns that reel.*"

He does not understand the power in his voice. Wilde has charmed men and women alike with his speech, but there is no precedent for her reaction. Bast stumbles back. Her grip on the dagger lessens. Wilde continues reading, forcing out the words despite the pain of his body, despite all the confusion plaguing him.

"*Upon the mat she lies and leers and on the tawny throat of her*

*Flutters the soft and silky fur or ripples to her pointed ears.*"

He hears the sound of the knife hitting the ground. "Look at that," Charlie says, drawing Wilde's eyesight from the paper. Bast is smaller. She's shrinking and changing. The sight of it fascinates and exhilarates him. The desire to discover what effect the rest of the poem will have on her makes him read even faster, until he's almost breathless from shouting the lines.

"*Away to Egypt! Have no fear. Only one God has ever died.*

*Only one God has let His side be wounded by a soldier's spear.*"

Here Wilde stops, swaying. He finds himself confronting a simple housecat, black and glossy, shivering, still bleeding, looking too scared to flee. He lowers the book, all his zeal to continue dissipated.

"Finish it, Mr. Wilde," Mr. Thompson says. "There's so little left."

"Of the poem—or of *her*?"

Mr. Thompson steps forward. "Of the spell."

"What spell? We weren't able to complete the play's performance."

"This book is a parting gift to us, Mr. Wilde, found on the book-shelf in The Red Tiger. When the battle ended, there was nothing left of the structure except a bookcase and a single book. Yeats assessed Chyron correctly. He was a spirit, something like a demon or a genie, summoned by Stephen in his quest to overthrow the Great Goddess. He was telling the truth when he told you he was sworn to defend The Red Tiger. But he was also dedicated to Stephen's desire to defeat Bast. When he failed in the first task, he all but got down on his knees in the rubble and pointed to the book. I recognized it, of course. Stephen knew of Bast's infatuation with your poem just as I did, and he reached the same conclusion we did. When the time came to challenge her, he intended to read your poem to her and weave a hidden spell over her. But Stephen's spell would contain Chyron himself."

"What do you mean?"

"His very being was meant to inhabit the words. This was his ul-timate purpose—and his gift to us. He begged us to allow him to flee into the book, to join with the text, and fulfill his role. You hold him in your hands. *Finish* the poem."

Wilde looks back to Bast, who now tries to scurry away. Charlie dives for her, his quick hands catching her mid-jump. The cat shakes and claws and hisses but Charlie holds it tight, lifting the little creature up toward Wilde, who reads—

*"Get hence, you loathsome mystery! Hideous animal, get hence!*

*You wake in me each bestial sense, you make me what I would not be.*

*You make my creed a barren sham, you wake foul dreams of sensual life,*

*And Atys with his blood-stained knife were better than the thing I am.*

*False Sphinx! False Sphinx! By reedy Styx old Charon, leaning on his* oar,

    *Waits for my coin.  Go thou before, and leave me to my crucifix,*

    *Whose pallid burden, sick with pain, watches the world with wearied*
eyes,

    *And weeps for every soul that dies, and weeps for every soul in vain."*

# EPILOGUE

*Bubastis, December 20, 1895*

The cat stirs in its wooden crate, showing an agitation it hasn't displayed since Wilde, Charlie, Robbie and Mr. Thompson departed England in one of the very cargo ships that once brought so many of Lady Gwendolyn's relics into the country. The journey proved uneventful, the days measured out in dreary silence and uncertain glances until the morning the ship's horn blared and drew its passengers to the deck. The one moment approaching happiness was seeing the Port of Said with its handsome mosque on the skyline and the harried work of fishermen preparing to depart for a day of toil, wrestling and folding nets onto the floor of their skiffs. It was not the sight of them that gave Wilde any happiness, but rather the sound of singing. It reached him on the deck and made him wish he knew the words, as he imagined it must be a song to make their work go better. He knew his own labor would have no music.

Nevertheless, just as the ruins of the ancient city comes into the view of their camel caravan, he begins whistling the tune of the fishermen as best he can recall it.

"I'm glad to find you cheerful," Robbie says, coming up alongside him to the right.

"When is Oscar not cheerful?" Charlie says, now flanking him on

403

the left.

Wilde smiles, lacking the heart to refute their interpretation of his whistling. The box, pressed to his lap with his left hand, shakes and the cat's sudden, plaintive meowing captures everyone's attention. Even Mr. Thompson halts his lead camel and turns around.

"That's the first sound I can recall her making since we embarked on this journey," he says.

"The first sound she's made at all," Robbie says.

Charlie stares at the box and then meets Wilde's eyes. "She must know where she is."

"Perhaps," Wilde says.

"How can she?" Robbie says. "Florence and the surviving members of the Golden Dawn all inspected her and found no sign of her former intelligence. This isn't a case like Bosie's, where his mind remained intact."

Charlie grimaces. "Maybe we shouldn't go through with this plan after all, Oscar."

Wilde now finds all gazes falling upon him. He understands their hesitation, their fear. He looks past them to the ruins only a few hundred yards away, a smattering of rocks and broken statues. His imagination yearns to see the city as it must have been in its glory, though he feels no sympathy or remorse for the rubble.

"Gentlemen," he says. "It's been kind of you to come this far with me. Perhaps I should make the last portion of our trip alone. If you'd like to wait here—"

"I'll be at your side to the last step," Charlie says.

"I will too," Robbie says with somewhat less enthusiasm.

Wilde nods, coaxing his camel to resume its trot. He rides past Mr. Thompson, who falls into place just behind them, and they enter the desolate plain five minutes later. Here the dismount and Wilde carries the box with him as he surveys the debris.

"Bubastis—the city of Bast," Mr. Thompson says. "In its zenith, some three thousand years ago, this place would have rivaled London in magnificence."

Robbie shakes his head. "Thanks to Bast, London almost rivals its ruins."

"Here her worship began, here her cult grew," Mr. Thompson continues. "There would have been magnificent stelas proclaiming her ascendancy. This was once a vibrant, happy place. Herodotus tells of Bast's followers—"

"Forgive me," Wilde says, "but I'm sure I speak for us all when I say none of us wish to hear another word about Bast's *followers*."

He dismounts from the camel and carries the box toward a solitary, broken obelisk. Weather has blasted most of the hieroglyphics into illegible trace markings, but Wilde sees the remnants of one familiar image. Of all the things he's beheld since the day he first set off to The Red Tiger, of all the marvels and horrors, this simple drawing overshadow them all.

*Bast enthroned.*

Wilde sets down the box, opens it and removes the cat. He holds it close to his chest and points at the image. The cat meows, and he cocks his head to speak into its right ear.

"You've cost me so much, yet I cannot even begin to weigh my losses against the greater toll you've inflicted on the world. A murdered queen, a shattered government, an empire left in chaos. London in shambles, a world in doubt. Who am I to compare such momentous things to the loss of a finger—or even the loss of my wife? Not to mention the deaths of Bosie and Yeats . . . But all have suffered an unimaginable cruelty.

Were Queensberry alive, he'd have you secured inside a pillowcase and drowned in the Thames. Your actions warrant such brutality, but my sense of vengeance has more poetry."

He places the cat on the ground and crouches before it.

"Here is where I leave you. Here where you were worshipped, in this place you sought to recreate at the expense of so much blood—how long will you survive? Do you comprehend my words? Do you realize the savageness of your fate?"

The cat stares at him with a dumb innocence that would make him feel sadistic and cruel if maintained much longer. But then it hisses and swipes its right paw at him, only just missing. Wilde grins and stands up straight.

"In your time, cats were venerated. You'll find no such worship in the mind of the modern Egyptian, though out here I doubt you'll survive long enough to meet one. The desert has many predators, but perhaps you will prove wily enough to avoid being a quick and easy meal. I take my leave of you now, dear Lady Gwendolyn, dear Bast, dear Great Goddess. I'll gift you with the words of a woman far wiser than either of us. Maybe you too will take them as a personal motto—*Qui patitur vincit.*"

Wilde walks away, stopping only once to look back. The cat sits at the base of a shattered obelisk, pawing at a broken hieroglyph and making the most piteous noises in its throat. Then he meets the eyes of Charlie, Robbie and Mr. Thompson, welcomes their collective nod of agreement, and resumes his whistling, gazing off at the horizon, glad to know the lone and level sands do indeed stretch far away.